*A*lice
I Have Been

**Center Point
Large Print**

**This Large Print Book carries the
Seal of Approval of N.A.V.H.**

Alice
I Have Been

Melanie Benjamin

CENTER POINT PUBLISHING
THORNDIKE, MAINE

This Center Point Large Print edition is published
in the year 2010 by arrangement with Delacorte Press,
an imprint of The Random House Publishing Group,
a division of Random House, Inc.

Alice I Have Been is a work of fiction. Any references
to historical events; to real people, living or dead; or to
real locales are intended only to give the fiction a setting
in historical reality. Other names, characters, places,
and incidents either are the product of the author's
imagination or are used fictitiously, and their
resemblance, if any, to real-life counterparts
is entirely coincidental.

The text of this Large Print edition is unabridged.
In other aspects, this book may vary
from the original edition.
Printed in the United States of America
on permanent paper.
Set in 16-point Times New Roman type.

ISBN: 978-1-60285-758-2

Library of Congress Cataloging-in-Publication Data

Benjamin, Melanie.
  Alice I have been / Melanie Benjamin.
    p. cm.
  ISBN 978-1-60285-758-2 (library binding : alk. paper)
  1. Hargreaves, Alice Pleasance Liddell, 1852–1934—Fiction.
  2. Dodgson, Charles Lutwidge, 1832–1898—Fiction. 3. Oxford (England)—Fiction.
  4. Large type books. I. Title.
  PS3608.A876A79 2010b
  813'.6—dc22
2009052536

To Nic, for leading me to
the Rabbit Hole

Acknowledgments

*I*T'S NOT OFTEN AN AUTHOR CAN SAY A BOOK truly wouldn't have been written without one person's influence, but *Alice I Have Been* would never have come about were it not for my dear friend and writing partner, Nicole Hayes. Gratitude doesn't even come close to expressing how I feel about her, but it will have to do.

My wonderful agent and friend, Laura Langlie, must also be thanked for her support, dedication, and unwavering belief. To Kate Miciak, the most enthusiastic, understanding, terrifyingly smart editor ever—thank you for loving *Alice* as much as you do.

I also have to thank Nita Taublib, Randall Klein, Loyale Coles, Carolyn Schwartz, Quinne Rogers, Susan Corcoran, Loren Noveck, and everyone else at Bantam Dell who has done so much for *Alice* and me. Also thanks to Peter Skutches, Tooraj Kavoussi, and Bill Contardi.

Judy Merrill Larsen and Tasha Alexander also deserve a big thank-you for putting up with my authorly angst.

Karen Schoenewaldt at the Rosenbach Museum and Library and Matthew Bailey at the National Portrait Gallery in London were very helpful in my search for images of Alice Liddell. I am also indebted to several books and websites concerning Alice Liddell and Charles Dodgson. *The Other Alice* by Christina Björk and Inga-Karin Eriksson (a charming picture book), *The Real Alice* by Anne Clark, and *The Lives of the Muses* by Francine Prose helped immensely in establishing biographical facts about Alice Liddell and her family. I found the website "Alice in Oxford" (http://www.aliceinoxford.info) to be very helpful as well. Also the Lewis Carroll home page (http://www.lewiscarroll.org/carroll.html), operated by the Lewis Carroll Society of North America, was useful, as was the site for the UK Lewis Carroll Society (http://lewiscarroll society.org.uk/index.html). *The Life of John Ruskin* by W. G. Collingwood was also of help.

Of course, I could not have written this book without re-reading Lewis Carroll's *Alice's Adventures in Wonderland* and *Through the Looking-Glass*.

Finally, I have to acknowledge my family—Pat and Norman Miller, Mark and Stephanie Miller, Mike and Sherry Miller; thank you all for the support and good wishes.

And as always, my love to Dennis, Alec, and Ben. Without you, none of this matters.

Alice
I Have Been

CUFFNELLS, 1932

But oh my dear, I am tired of being Alice in Wonderland. Does it sound ungrateful? It is. Only I do get tired.

ONLY I DO GET TIRED.

I pause, place the pen down next to the page, and massage my aching hand; the joints of my fingers, in particular, are stiff and cold and ugly, like knots on a tree. One does get tired of so many things, of course, when one is eighty, not the least of which is answering endless *letters*.

However, I cannot say that, not to my own son. Although I'm not entirely sure what I am trying to say in this letter to Caryl, so kindly inquiring as to my health after our hectic journey. He accompanied me to America, naturally; if I'm being completely truthful, I would have to admit my son was much more excited about the prospect of escorting Alice in Wonderland across the ocean than Alice herself was in going.

"But Mamma," he said in that coy way— entirely ridiculous for a man of his age, and I told him so. "We—you—owe it to the public. All this interest in Lewis Carroll, simply because it's the centennial of his birth, and everyone wants to meet the real Alice. An honorary doctorate from Columbia University." He consulted the telegram in his hand. "Interviews on the radio. You simply must go. You'll have a marvelous time."

"You mean *you'll* have a marvelous time." I knew my son too well, knew his strengths and his flaws, and unfortunately the latter outnumbered the former, and they always had. When I thought of his brothers—

No, I will not. That is uncharitable to Caryl and painful to myself.

Surprisingly, when the time came I did have a marvelous time. So much fuss made over me! Bands playing when the ship docked, banners everywhere, even confetti; endless photographs of me drinking tea—so tedious, but the Americans simply could not get enough of *that*. Alice in Wonderland at a tea party! Imagine! It was a miracle they didn't ask Caryl to dress up as the Mad Hatter.

However, to be feted by scholars—it took me back, in such an unexpected way, to my childhood, to Oxford. I hadn't realized how much I'd missed the stimulating atmosphere of academia, the pomp and circumstance, the endless arguments that no one could win, which was never the point; the point was purely the love of discourse, the heat of the battle.

Shockingly—and despite what I had been warned—I found everyone in America to be perfectly charming, with the exception of one unfortunate youth who offered me a stick of something called "chewing gum" just prior to the ceremony at Columbia. "What does one do with it?" I inquired, only to be told, simply, to chew. "Chew? Without swallowing?"

A nod.

"To what end? What possibly could be the point?"

The young man could not answer that, and withdrew his invitation with a sheepish smile.

Still, what was truly tiresome—what is always truly tiresome—was the disappointment, brief and politely suppressed, evident in all the faces. The disappointment of looking for a little girl, a bright little girl in a starched white pinafore, and finding an old lady instead.

I understand. I myself suffer it each time I consult a looking glass, only to wonder how the glass can be so cracked and muddled—and then realize, with a pang of despair, that it is not the glass that is deficient, after all.

It is not merely vanity, although I admit I have more than my fair share of this conceit. Other elderly dowagers, however, were not immortalized in print as a little girl, and not merely as a little girl but rather as the embodiment of Childhood itself. So they are not confronted by people who ask, always so very eagerly, to see "the real Alice"—and who cannot hide the shock, the disbelief, that the real Alice has not been able to stop time.

So, yes, I do get tired. Of pretending, of remembering who I am, and who I am not, and if I sometimes get the two confused—much like the Alice in the story—I may be excused. For I am eighty.

I am also tired of being asked "Why?"

Why did I sell the manuscript, the original version of *Alice's Adventures Under Ground,* printed by Mr. Dodgson just for me? (Lewis Carroll I did not know; they are merely words on a page—*written by Lewis Carroll*. They have nothing to do with the man I remember.)

Why would the muse part with the evidence of the artist's devotion? Even Americans, with their eagerness to put a price on everything, could not understand.

I look out the windows—the heavy leaded-glass windows, not as sparkling as I would wish; I'll have to speak to Mary Ann about that—of my sitting room, which overlooks the lush, heavily forested grounds of Cuffnells. Today the clouds are low, so the tempting glitter of the Solent is hidden from view. I can see the lawn where the boys played, Alan and Rex (and yes, Caryl); the pitch where they played cricket; the paths where they first learned to ride and where they strode home with their first stag, accompanied by their father, so very proud—and I know I made the only decision possible. This place, this is my sons' childhood, their heritage, and it's all I have left.

The other, the simply bound manuscript posted to me one cold November morning, long after the golden afternoon of its creation—that was my childhood. Only it had never truly belonged to me; Mr. Dodgson, of all people, understood that.

The clock on the mantel chimes twice; how long have I been sitting here staring out the window? The ink on the nib of my pen has dried. I find myself doing such idle, silly things so often these days, these days when my thoughts scatter like billiard balls into their respective pockets, these days when I am so very tired, unaccountably weary; I even find myself dozing off at the oddest moments, such as teatime, or late mornings when I should be going over accounts.

Simply contemplating my eternal weariness provokes a yawn, and I look longingly at the chaise in the corner, with its faded red afghan thrown over the arm. I manage to stifle the yawn and tell myself sternly that it is only two o'clock, and there is much to do.

I fold the letter to Caryl neatly in thirds; I'll finish it later. I open my desk drawer and remove a stack of letters bound with a worn black silk ribbon, letters that I have begun and not finished, for various reasons. I have learned, through the years, it is the letter not sent that is often the most valuable.

There, right on top, is the letter I began almost two years ago:

Dear Ina,

I received your kind letter of Tuesday last—

And that is all I have managed to write. Ina's kind letter of Tuesday last also is within this bundle; I remove it, adjust my spectacles (really, the indignities of age are *most* trying), and peruse it once more.

I suppose you don't remember when Mr. Dodgson ceased coming to the Deanery? How old were you? I said his manner became too affectionate toward you as you grew older and that Mother spoke to him about it, and that offended him so that he ceased coming to see us again, as one had to give some reason for all intercourse ceasing—

This is the letter that I long to answer, not the one from Caryl kindly inquiring as to my health. No, this letter, this ghost missive from my sister, dear Ina, dead now two years, almost. Yet the muddled memories she stirred up—the memories she always managed to stir up, or manufacture, as if she were a conjurer or a witch instead of a perfect Victorian lady—will not die with her.

Will they die with Alice? I often wonder. Before I am gone from this earth, before my bones lie in the churchyard, so far away from where those other bones lie, I do hope that others' memories will finally fall away and I will be able to remember, with a clarity of my very own, what happened that afternoon. That seemingly lovely summer afternoon, when between the two of us, we set out to destroy Wonderland—my Wonderland, *his* Wonderland—forever.

So yes, I do get tired; tired of *pretending* to be Alice in Wonderland still, always. Although it has been no easier being Alice Pleasance Hargreaves. Truly, I wonder; I have always wondered—

Which is the real Alice, and which the pretend?

Oh dear! I'm sounding like one of Mr. Dodgson's nonsense poems now. He was so very clever at that sort of thing; much cleverer than I, who never had the patience, not then, not now.

I remove my spectacles; massage the bridge of my nose where they pinch. My head is throbbing, *threatening,* and I do not like being in this state. The journey *was* exhausting, if I'm being entirely truthful. I am tired of being Alice, period; yet my memories will not let me rest, not as long as I'm reading through old letters, which is the surest sign yet that I have become a doddering old fool.

The chaise looks so inviting; it's such a cold afternoon.

Perhaps I will lie down, after all.

Chapter 1
OXFORD, 1859

O FF WITH THEIR—LEGS. THAT WAS THE curious notion I had as a child.

That certain people—queens, generally—lost their heads was understood to be a historical fact.

But in my world, legs were missing with alarming regularity as well. The men in their long academic robes, the women in their voluminous skirts; everyone skimming, floating, like puffs of cotton in the air—that is the first, and most vivid, memory of my childhood.

I knew, of course, that children possessed legs; yet the legs seemed to disappear as their owners grew up, and if I never questioned the logic of this it must be because, even then, I understood that Oxford was a kingdom unto itself. It was different from, and superior to, the rest of the globe (which of course meant Britain, for those were the years when the sun never set on Victoria's empire), complete with its own rules, language, and even time; all the clocks in Oxford were set five minutes ahead of Greenwich mean time.

Naturally, it follows that if Oxford was its own kingdom, then I was its princess—one of three, to be precise—because my mother was, as everyone knew, its queen.

Remarkable for a woman who bore ten children—one would have assumed she was perpetually in a state of bearing a child, or waiting for a child, or getting over a child—Mamma made certain that the Deanery was the social center of Christ Church, which was of course the social center of Oxford. No one dared give a party or a bazaar or a dance without her approval. At times she even graciously made room for other queens; Victoria herself once stayed with us, although not even her plump, imperious personage intimidated Mamma.

Papa was merely the Dean of Christ Church, responsible for the education and religious upbringing of hundreds of gentlemen, including the sons of that same queen. Even when I was so young that the only place I could look was up, for I was all too well acquainted with the ground, I knew that he was quite important. Instructors would bow to him, scholars would pale in his presence, princes deferred to him; entire halls full of young men would rise upon his entrance, as well as his departure.

While at home he could scarcely make himself heard; he was entirely eclipsed by Mamma, and entirely happy to be so. There was even a silly rhyme that made the rounds of Christ Church in those days—

I am the Dean, and this is Mrs. Liddell
She plays the first, and I the second fiddle

19

This did not reach my ears, however, until much later. For as the daughter of the Dean and Mrs. Liddell, I was sheltered, at least for a time, from most of the gossip that was the chief occupation of some of the finest scholarly minds of the age.

Privileged was how I would describe my early years, if only because I was told that they were such. I knew no life before Oxford, although Papa was, even then, a rising academic: domestic chaplain to Prince Albert, headmaster of the Westminster School in London. I was baptized in the Abbey, the fourth child, second daughter.

Ina was not baptized in the Abbey. I may have reminded her of this with some regularity.

While we still lived in London, an older brother, Arthur, died of scarlet fever. Papa had difficulty speaking of him later; his kind face, with the aristocratic nose and decided chin (which I, unfortunately, inherited) would grow quizzical, his brow furrowing, as if he—such a learned man—could not understand the simplest, most frequently asked question of all:

Why?

I don't recall that Mamma ever spoke of it one way or another. Although surely that can't be true.

When I was scarcely four—in 1856—we arrived in Oxford, upon Papa's appointment as Dean of Christ Church. By then the family included Harry, the eldest, followed by Lorina, myself, and Edith—the three princesses. Ina was three years older than I, Edith two years younger. All of us—along with servants, fine china, heirloom silver, imported linens, and all the other necessities of a distinguished household—moved into the Deanery, which Papa had arranged to be enlarged and remodeled to accommodate our growing family. Even so, it was never quite large enough for Mamma's ambitions.

It was in this world, this Oxford, that my first memories were made. It was a peculiar world for a little girl, in many ways; there were few children my age, as all the students and dons at the time were supposed to be celibate. Only the deans, the senior members of the college, were allowed to marry, and most of them were of an age where children weren't possible. Papa was rather the exception to the rule, and I believe that he was proud of the fact.

Perhaps that was why there were so many of us.

Each night, after I was snug in bed, Old Tom, the bell in the imposing tower that was the center-piece of Christ Church, tolled one hundred and one times (signifying the original number of students at the college); even as I struggled to remain awake for the first chime, I rarely made it all the way through to the end. Our home, the Deanery, was opposite the tower, our front entrance part of the pale stone fortress of buildings bordering the flat green Quad; we also had a private entrance opening up to the back garden. Quite literally, we lived among the students; I remember walking with Ina and Edith—three little maids all in a row, always dressed exactly alike, crisp white frocks in summer, rich velvets in winter—in the Quad with our governess, Miss Prickett, as young men removed their caps and bowed low, exaggeratedly, at our approach.

People in Oxford spoke in solemn, measured tones. Centuries-old traditions demanded to be followed, whether or not they made much sense. To me, still coddled in the nursery world of a proper Victorian childhood, they often did not; that is precisely why I wouldn't have changed them for the world. I was no ordinary little girl, I fervently believed, and Oxford only reinforced this notion. Every year on the first of May, we all gathered at dawn on the gray stones of Magdalen Bridge, sheltered by huge trees in the early burst of bloom, listening to the whisper of the river Isis down below. Magically, just as the first glow of sun painted the sky from purple to pink, a choir of pure, young male voices would float down upon us, singing ancient hymns to welcome summer.

My birthday was on the fourth of May; I cannot deny that as a child, I secretly believed this hallowed ceremony was somehow in honor of me.

Pricks—Miss Prickett—did not share this belief. She adored Edith, as did everyone; Edith was the most compliant creature on earth, and her swirls of russet red hair only helped endear her to

22

everyone she met. Yet Pricks practically worshipped Ina; as the eldest, the most refined, she could do no wrong.

As for me, in the middle—the only one with pin-straight hair; Mamma deplored how it hung on my neck like seaweed, so she chopped it off, short with a heavy fringe that made me feel as vulnerable as a baby bird before it grows feathers —I must admit, Pricks tolerated me. Barely.

"Alice, what on earth did you do to your frock? Look at your sisters—they haven't managed to get awful dirt stains on their hems! Whatever were you doing?"

"I was playing in dirt," said I, frustrated by my need to state the obvious.

"Playing in dirt? On your knees? In a white frock? Who would do such a thing—white *stains* so!"

"Then why do we wear it, when you know we're going out to the garden to play? Why don't we wear brown frocks, or green, or perhaps even—"

"Brown? Who ever heard of wearing brown in May? You'll wear white, as your mother wishes. Brown. What can I do with such a child?" Whereupon Pricks would throw up her hands to the heavens, as if God alone could tell her what to do with me.

I suspected He couldn't. I had once overheard Papa say that "God Himself broke the mold when it came to that one," and I knew, somehow, that he meant me. Even in a house full of children, I was the only one ever referred to in such a singular way.

I was rather proud of that, to tell the truth.

Pricks was prickly. That's why I named her Pricks; it had nothing to do with her last name. Pricks exclaimed a lot; she threw her hands up a lot. She bristled when I asked her the most natural questions, such as why the wart on her face had a hair growing out of it whereas the wart on her hand did not.

"Alice," Ina would murmur, patting her long brown curls. Oh, how I longed to have curls! The greatest tragedy of my life, at age seven, was that I had short black hair exactly like a boy. "That's simply not spoken of."

"What is?"

"Warts. Pricks can't help it. It's not very nice of you to talk about it."

"Do you think she slept with a frog when she was little?"

"I—well, perhaps." I could tell Ina was interested in spite of herself; she relaxed her pose—sitting on the windowsill of the schoolroom, hands folded properly in her lap, head bowed in perfect ladylike composure—and actually swung her feet to and fro. "Still, ladies don't talk of such things."

"You're not a lady. You're only ten."

"And you're seven. I'll always be older than

you." She clapped her hands with delight, while I scowled and longed to pull her hair. How unfair, how *tragic,* the world was; I would always be younger than her.

"But you'll always be older than me," Edith whispered, sliding her moist little hand in mine. I gave it a squeeze, as thanks.

"Oh, look, there's Mr. Dodgson!" Ina jumped up and pressed her face against the windowpane; Edith and I joined her, although Edith had to climb up onto the cushioned window seat in order to see.

The three of us watched—the windowpane, warm from the sun, smooth against my forehead—as a tall, slim man, dressed all in black from the top of his hat to the toes of his leather boots, wandered into view. He was strolling, hands in pockets, across the generous garden that separated the Deanery from the library. Stopping to examine flowers, hedges, he refused to walk in any sort of straight path, altogether acting like someone hoping to be discovered.

Just then Papa ran into the picture, gown flapping behind him like giant insect wings. He consulted his watch, dangling precariously on its gold chain, with a shake of his head; a huge book was tucked under his left arm. Papa was always running late. I held my breath as he nearly ran Mr. Dodgson down; fortunately, at the last possible moment he swerved around him, not even noticing when Mr. Dodgson raised his hat and bowed.

Mr. Dodgson looked up, then, and saw us in the window; Ina gasped and ducked out of sight, mortified to have been caught spying on him. Ina always behaved so oddly in his presence; she basked in his attention, schemed of ways to encourage it, and then, at the very last minute, always pulled back. Yet whenever I pointed this out to her, merely trying to be helpful, she had a tendency to pull my hair or pinch my arm.

That didn't prevent me from continuing to comment upon it, however. If she didn't want my help, that was her misfortune.

I shook my head at her and then tugged on the creaky sash of the window until it opened enough for me to stick my head out.

"Hullo, Mr. Dodgson!"

"Hullo, Miss Alice, Miss Edith." He bowed in his usual stiff way. I had recently informed him that he walked as if he had a poker stuck down the back of his jacket. He had thought about this, considered it gravely, and agreed that he did, but that he couldn't help it.

I thought this was a reasonable response and left it at that.

"Alice!" Pricks bustled over—no doubt summoned by Ina, who was standing well away from the window, her arms crossed over her chest, glaring at me. "What on earth are you doing?

26

Young ladies do not shout out of windows like monkeys!"

"Oh, I do wish I was a monkey!" I forgot about Mr. Dodgson for a moment; monkeys were my favorite animals, along with kittens, rabbits, hedgehogs, mice, and lizards. "Wouldn't that be smashing?"

"Alice! Wherever did you hear that word? Young ladies do not say 'smashing.'" Pricks reached over my head to push down the window. However, when she saw Mr. Dodgson smiling up at us, she hesitated. "Oh!"

"W-w-w-ould the young ladies like to join me for a pleasant st-stroll around the Quad?" He doffed his hat. "Accompanied by you, of course," he added hastily. I shook my head in sympathy; his stammer was worse than ever. Poor Mr. Dodgson! (Or—Do-Do-Dodgson, as it sounded coming from him.) Still, he never appeared too upset about it, unlike Pricks and her warts; she was always trying some new cream or lotion to be rid of them.

"Oh, well." Pricks smiled in that unexpected, scary way of hers; she bent slightly at the waist and twisted her face up almost as if she was going to be ill, but then, at the last minute, a smile appeared, a wide, snapping smile that revealed most of her teeth.

Patting her hair, smoothing her skirts, she swung around and surveyed the three of us, frowning at my dirty hem. "Alice, go ask Phoebe to change you at once. All three of you will have to change, I suppose—I might as well do the same."

"But why? I'll only get dirty again." Once more, I did not see why I had to remind her of the obvious.

"Because your mother will have a—will be quite disappointed, if I allow you out looking like that."

I was forced to admit that she had a point. Mamma would certainly make a fuss if she saw me, the Dean's daughter, outside in anything other than a stiff, freshly laundered white frock, the more frills, the better.

Pricks turned back to the window and whispered loudly, "We would be happy to accompany you, thank you so much, Mr. Dodgson. We'll join you directly."

"He can't hear, you know," I reminded her. "He doesn't hear out of his right ear. You have to shout."

"Oh, but I—oh, go ahead, Alice, but don't shout. Just—speak loudly."

I shook my head. Pricks was so exceedingly proper all the time, except when it came to Mr. Dodgson. Only he could make her behave in such a manner that I could almost, if I scrunched my eyes and tried very hard, imagine that she had once been a real little girl, like me.

"We would be happy to accommodate you," I said loudly, slowly, my voice as deep as Papa's when he gave a sermon. "We shall join you directly." Then I bowed.

Mr. Dodgson looked up at me, opened his mouth, and laughed. He was still laughing as he sat down on a bench to wait, after first taking care to pull his trousers up at the knees; men did this, I knew, to keep their trousers from creasing. I wasn't altogether sure why I knew that; it was one of the many bits of useful information I was just now aware that I possessed. When I was six, I had known nothing. Now that I was seven, however, I couldn't help but be impressed by how very wise I was growing.

"Come, girls!" Pricks clapped her wide brown hands. "Change quickly!" She bustled us out of the schoolroom, looking back at the blackboard with a sigh. "We really should get back to geography—it's such a lovely afternoon, though. We'll study botany instead. That will be a pleasant change." And she smiled, violently, suddenly, to herself.

I wondered again at the ability of adults to turn every single pleasurable experience into a lesson. Did they do this only for our benefit? Or when they were alone, at the dining table or gathered for one of Mamma's musical entertainments, did they, even then, stop to say, "This tea is very delicious. Are you aware that it comes from India, the subcontinent, which has been a part of the Crown since the rebellion of 1857?"

I believed I was on the cusp of discovering the answer, for I was starting to be included in some of the entertainments held here at the Deanery. Only a month ago, Mamma had allowed Ina, Edith, and me to perform "Twinkle, Twinkle, Little Star" for her guests. Mr. Ruskin, in particular, had pronounced himself impressed; he reached out to pat my hair as I walked past him, after we had curtsied good night.

Although he patted my hair, he had actually gasped at Edith's—"Look at those titian curls!" he exclaimed. I remembered to ask him what "titian" meant, during our last drawing lesson; he sucked in his breath and informed me my education was appalling but never did answer me. Not even after I pointed out that he had just missed an excellent opportunity to improve it.

"Alice, do hurry!" Ina grabbed my arm and pulled me down the wide gallery, lined on one side with the oil paintings of the English landscape that Papa so admired, on the other with an ornately carved banister crowned with ferocious lions at either end, as finials. "We mustn't leave Mr. Dodgson waiting!"

"Why ever not? He doesn't have anything else to do." I fervently believed that; while I knew, vaguely, that he taught mathematics at the college, I understood that this was not his chief occupation. No, he was ours more than the students'. He was our playmate, our guide on many excursions, our galley slave (he often took us rowing on the Isis, where we loved to pretend that we were Nelson and his men, while Mr. Dodgson did his best to maneuver us about as if we were at the battle of Trafalgar).

It was only recently so. My brother, Harry, along with Ina, had been his favored companions since the day he first made our acquaintance by seeking permission to photograph the Deanery from the garden; Mamma was fond of saying Mr. Dodgson showed up one day with his infernal camera and never really left. Edith and I were only summoned occasionally from the nursery, most often to be photographed. Harry went away to school this year, however, and Mr. Dodgson appeared, finally, to notice Edith and me, and to ask for us, along with Ina, when he called.

Ina did not appreciate this development, I knew. There was nothing she could do about it, and she never let Mr. Dodgson notice her resentment; she was, I had to admit, absolutely brilliant at presenting a sweet, simple face to the world, no matter her true feelings. Just as a lady should, Pricks never wearied of reminding me.

"You silly little girl. Of course Mr. Dodgson has other things to do. Loads and loads of things. He's a very important man." Pulling me into the nursery, Ina started unbuttoning the back of my dress, while Phoebe, our nurse, flew about, opening up cupboards until she found three identical white frocks, flounced with pink satin ribbons, the buttons covered in the same pink satin.

"I don't think so," I replied, remembering how Mamma had referred to Mr. Dodgson as "that nuisance of a mathematics tutor, a more obtuse man I have never met." Even though Papa corrected her—"Now, my dear, he is a *don*"—he had done it mildly. Papa was capable of standing up to Mamma, I knew, when he felt strongly about something. But evidently he did not feel strongly about Mr. Dodgson.

"Oh, Alice, why did you have to go and muddy your frock?" Ina was now stepping out of her own; her petticoats swayed to and fro as she crossed her arms over her chemise and glared at me. The way her eyebrows angled, high and disapproving, and the way her small mouth pursed, as if she was sucking on a lemon, made her almost always look cross, to be perfectly honest. "Those blue stripes on the bodice suit me so well! I despise the pink."

"I'm sorry." I genuinely was; I disliked getting dressed more than once a day. It was too much of an ordeal, what with all the buttoning and fastening and layer upon layer of stiff, scratchy underclothing. Chemise, pantalets, not one, not two, but *three* petticoats, stockings that I never could coax into staying smooth and high; my garters *always* came undone.

It would only get worse, I thought gloomily. One day I would have to wear a corset.

"C'mere, lamb," Phoebe said to Edith, who was kneeling in front of her dollhouse, a headless rag doll in her hand. "Let's get you into your fine feathers."

"It's so much fuss, simply to go outside." I raised my arms; Mary Ann, one of the maids, dropped the beribboned dress over my head.

"Are we ready?"

I turned toward the door; Pricks was standing there, in her new blue silk dress with yellow piping down the bodice that did not go well with her brown complexion, not at all. Still, she looked quite pleased with herself; she had even managed to add a pouf of false hair to the back of her head, so that it stuck out from behind her straw hat like the fuzzy tail of a bumblebee.

"Yes, Pricks," I said as Mary Ann buttoned up my last glove. Phoebe handed me a pink parasol. "Although what if Mr. Dodgson wants to take us to the Meadow? Perhaps to allow us to roll down a hill? I'll only stain my dress again, in that case."

"Mr. Dodgson won't do any such thing. He's a gentleman," Pricks said with a sniff.

Again, I wondered just what part of him Pricks and Ina could see that I could not. It was almost as if we knew two different people, both with the name Charles Lutwidge Dodgson. That was his full name; he had told it to me, after I con-

33

fided that mine was Alice Pleasance Liddell, which I found rather a long name to write. However, he pointed out that his was longer by one letter, and that cheered me immensely.

I suspected, in a deep, serious part of me no one else knew I possessed, at least so far, which was somewhat worrisome, that Mr. Dodgson was the kind of person who *would* allow me to roll down a hill. I felt he was the only person on earth, actually, who would; he was my one chance to do this, to do other things that I desired, even things I did not yet know but somehow, I felt *he* did.

I felt it most when he looked at me as he stood behind his camera, holding the cap to the lens, counting slowly, his eyes never moving from mine as he exposed the plate. There was something about his eyes—the color of the periwinkle that grew at the base of the trees in the Meadow, such a deep blue—that made me feel as if he could see my dearest wishes, my darkest thoughts, before they made themselves known to me. And that simply by seeing them, he was also giving me permission to follow them. Perhaps he was even showing me the way. For I wasn't very comfortable with the dark thoughts—muddled, nameless thoughts—that sometimes came to me when I relaxed my watchfulness.

I was always on guard, you see. One had to be vigilant; for what, I did not know.

"Alice, come!"

Pricks, Ina, and Edith—predictably clutching her parasol too high, in the middle of the handle; she was such a baby!—were already at the end of the gallery, descending the staircase; I ran after them and immediately felt my right stocking start to sag down my shin.

"Miss Prickett!"

The three of them froze; I took advantage of this moment to sneak into my rightful place, between Ina and Edith.

"Yes, madam?" Pricks turned, her eyes cast down. She curtsied as my mother walked slowly from the library down the front hall, confronting our little group at the bottom of the stairs.

"May I ask where you are taking my daughters?" Mamma smiled as she said this, but the smile did not make it up to her eyes; they were wide, wary—not inclined to believe what they saw, I knew from experience. Such as the time I broke the china shepherdess that always perched, much too nervously, near the edge of the library mantel. Even though I had the foresight to pick up a shard of china—the faded pink china bow of the shepherdess's apron—and plant it in Ina's shoe that night, hoping to incriminate her instead, I did not fool Mamma.

Perhaps there would be an advantage to having such a sharp mother someday; that's what she said, after she punished me by making me take my meals alone in the schoolroom for a week.

Still, even for a child so prone to daydreaming, I could not imagine the circumstances under which this could ever be true.

"We're going out for an expedition, madam. A little botany expedition. It's such a lovely day." Pricks raised her gaze to meet my mother's; she was always a trifle nervous around her but, unlike the rest of the household, had so far avoided being reduced to trembling tears. There was some hint of steel in her character, I had to admit, although she was careful to act completely obedient, always, to Mamma.

Mamma dabbed her upper lip with her handkerchief; it was warm for late May, and despite being tightly bound, a few strands of her black hair had escaped, lying damp and flat against her high forehead. She was fatter than usual because soon another baby would join us. I wasn't precisely sure what her being fat had to do with a baby, but that was how it was explained to me, and when I asked what the one had to do with the other, she would not say. She told me only that young ladies weren't supposed to ask such questions.

Still, I couldn't help but suspect that one very important piece of information was being withheld; I vowed, someday, to discover just what it was. Perhaps Mr. Dodgson would tell me.

"I don't suppose Mr. Dodgson has anything to do with this?"

I jumped; had Mamma read my mind? But no. She was talking to Pricks.

"Mr. Dodgson suggested it, yes," Pricks said without apology.

"The girls already took their exercise this morning, did they not?" Now Mamma singled me out with her black-eyed gaze; I felt her look me over, head to toe, searching for stains and tears as evidence.

Pricks could have lied, given how neat I looked now, but she didn't. "Yes," was all she answered, choosing to leave the rest up to Mamma.

Suddenly Mamma looked so tired; she closed her eyes, pressed her handkerchief against her forehead. I felt sorry for her. Babies must be very trying to get ready for.

"Oh, do go ahead. Just don't let the girls romp —and Alice, please try not to get dirty."

"I'll try, Mamma."

She smiled then, her eyes still closed. "Good girl." Then she slowly climbed the stairs, her wide skirts, in the jeweled red she favored, whispering as she brushed past us. As she went by me, she patted the top of my head.

"Now, girls." Pricks pulled her left glove up as high as it would go; it was rather a habit of hers, as she was always anxious to conceal that wart. Personally, however, I would have been more concerned about the one with the hair growing out of it.

Mary Ann held the door open for us, and we

walked outside. Adjusting my parasol, I blinked at the sudden brightness of the sun; inside the Deanery everything was so gloomy and muted, with heavy sculpted carpeting and oppressive flowered paper, dark wood paneling and banisters. It was always a shock to go outside.

"Miss P-Prickett, what a pleasure." Mr. Dodgson had walked around from the garden and was waiting for us. He removed his tall black hat, revealing his long brown hair, plastered down on the top of his head but with ends as curly as Edith's. He bowed; Pricks giggled, and I couldn't help but be embarrassed for her.

Ina must have felt the same, for she bit her lip and stared down at her shoes. Edith was too distracted by a butterfly to notice.

"Miss Liddell, Miss Alice, Miss Edith." Mr. Dodgson shook each of our hands, so solemnly that I had to laugh. As if the last time we'd seen him, he hadn't been standing on a chair in his room, swatting a mechanical bat with a broom and pretending to be Phoebe, who was terrified of anything with wings.

"What are we going to do today? I don't want to simply stroll about the Quad." I flung myself at him; his arms, as always, were ready to catch me. He held me close as I wrapped my arms about his waist; he was slender, so that I could reach all the way around him. I couldn't do that with Papa; I only got halfway around *him*.

Mr. Dodgson's vest scratched against my cheek as he bent down to meet me; he paused a minute to smell the top of my head. He was fond of doing that, I'd noticed lately. While I could perceive no harm in it, as long as he didn't have a cold, still I couldn't prevent a little shiver from chasing itself up and down the back of my neck. It wasn't a frightful shiver, such as the kind that stole over me whenever I had to walk down the gallery at night, past the ferocious carved lions, my candle weak and ineffective against the dark.

No, this shiver was more curious. As if it might lead me to some immense danger, or some immense delight, I couldn't decide which. One day I might want to know; not today.

He released me and turned toward Ina, who had been glaring at us. Suddenly she blushed, took a step back, hung her head, and smiled one of her maddeningly *teasing* smiles, as if she knew a secret she wanted you to find out.

I would never, ever ask her what it was, however. That would only be giving in.

Mr. Dodgson shrugged, hugged Edith, who had toddled over, bored with the butterfly, and then he straightened up.

"Any suggestions? I've the entire afternoon to be at your disposal."

"Can we go rowing?" I asked. "It's awfully hot!"

"No, I promised Mr. Duckworth we wouldn't

go again until he could join us, as he's heard me talk so much about our fun times," Mr. Dodgson said. "You wouldn't want me to break that promise, would you?"

"Oh, no!" I shook my head so vigorously that the ends of my hair tickled my ears. I did like Mr. Duckworth, who had a splendid singing voice; we had recently met him at tea in Mr. Dodgson's rooms, where he sang bits from an Italian opera for us. To be honest, I was surprised to meet him there, even if he was another fellow at college. I wasn't accustomed to seeing Mr. Dodgson with other adults, except on the rare occasions Mamma invited him to parties at the Deanery. "No, we mustn't break a promise to him!"

"I did tell Mrs. Liddell that I was taking the girls out for a botany expedition," Pricks said.

"Ah, b-b-botany. A fine excuse for an outing. Especially when accompanied by a mathematics professor."

Pricks laughed and took Mr. Dodgson's arm, which he offered to her after first stifling a small sigh, I noticed. I don't believe, though, that Pricks did.

"Would you like to go to the Meadow, my ladies?" he called over his shoulder.

"Oh, yes!" I jumped up and down, and I'm afraid I did shout, causing more than a few students, heads together in earnest discussion, to look my way. Mr. Dodgson only laughed, even while Ina and Pricks stiffened. "Might we roll down a hill?"

"I'm not sure what that has to do with botany, Alice," Mr. Dodgson said. "D-d-do enlighten me."

"Well." Frowning, I tried not to step on grasshoppers as I walked, as I knew from experience they made a mess when squished. "We would be rolling on grass, which is a plant. We could study the grass after, to see if it got flat or not. That would be scientific."

Ina laughed at me, and I resisted the urge to poke her with my parasol, but only because we were still in the Quad and Mamma might be watching from the window.

Mr. Dodgson did not laugh. He released Pricks's arm—she did not appear to like *that,* as she let out a sigh she didn't bother to stifle—and clasped his gloved hands behind his back. I wondered why he always wore gloves, inside and out, even when it was hot; I had to, of course, because I was a girl. Men, however, did not have so many requirements, so it made no sense to me.

Mr. Dodgson nodded slowly, giving my answer thoughtful consideration, which was one reason why I liked him so. He was the only adult who ever did.

"That is an interesting answer. I do wonder if the weight of a little girl would be enough, but then we must consider the f-force of the roll itself, as a factor."

"Exactly!" I was excited now, and pleased with

myself for coming up with such a brilliant experiment; I couldn't prevent myself from skipping a step or two, to Ina's great annoyance.

"Then again, there's another factor we must consider. Can you tell me what it is?"

"Bugs," crowed Edith happily. She loved bugs of all types and longed to have an ant farm in the nursery. Phoebe wouldn't hear of it, though, despite my many attempts to explain to her that ants did not have wings.

"No, not bugs."

"The wind?" Ina asked, in spite of herself; I resisted the urge to stick my tongue out at her.

We had crossed the hot, treeless Quad, passing the great fountain in the middle with its bronze statue of Mercury, and were now under the towering stone arch that marked the entrance. Turning left, we proceeded down the narrow, noisy street of St. Aldate's, with all its lovely shops. I did hope we would stop to buy sweets; I patted the tuppence in my pocket, just in case.

"No, the wind would not be a factor." Mr. Dodgson raised his voice in an effort to be heard over the clatter of carts and horses on cobblestones, the clang of bells on shop doors, the steady hum of conversation tickling my ears.

"The rain from yesterday?" I asked.

"No, not the rain—although, yes, I suppose on another day that could be a mi-mitigating factor. Not today, though; the sun is too bright."

"Then what? What is the other factor?" Despite my belief that lessons should never interfere with play, I was curious. So curious, in fact, that I didn't even notice we'd passed the sweet shop until we were two doors past, when a lady carrying a basket containing a large fish bumped into me. She apologized with a curtsy—the fish merely stared sadly up at the sky—and hurried away.

"No one has stopped to consider the effect of grass stains upon white—what is it? Cotton? Linen?" Stopping, he bent down and fingered the hem of Ina's dress; she stiffened, and I saw her shoulders tremble slightly.

"It is muslin," Pricks said with a patient smile. "Gentlemen never can tell the difference."

"Which is only as it should be. At any rate, grass stains plus little girls' white dresses equal a very—agitated—mother."

"True," I had to admit with a sigh. "Very true. Mamma did ask me, particularly, not to get dirty. And I did just get dirty this morning."

"As I'm sure you'll get dirty tomorrow. However, I do not wish to hasten the inevitable. So we shall not roll down the hill. Not today, at any rate," Mr. Dodgson said with a sad smile; all his smiles were just a little sad around the edges, as if he knew happiness never could last very long. Whenever he smiled, I wanted to pat his hand or lean my head against his shoulder to cheer him up.

"But perhaps someday?" I slid my hand in his and was grateful for his sympathetic squeeze.

"Perhaps." There was a sudden commotion; the lady with the fish dropped it in the middle of the street with a cry, and Edith ran toward it, eager to aid in its capture. I would have followed, but just as I started to go—right behind Ina and Pricks, who called out, "Edith, it's not proper to play with someone's dinner!"—Mr. Dodgson bent down and caught my elbow.

"But cheer up, my Alice. I do have a lovely surprise for you."

I stopped, my heart racing, both at the excitement of the fish, now flopping weakly in a gutter while a raggedy man poked at it with a stick, and at the tempting words Mr. Dodgson had uttered. His hand still caressed my elbow and I felt, at that moment, that I would go anywhere, do anything he asked, as long as it remained only the two of us, no one else allowed.

"Is it a secret just for me?" I whispered, unable to look in his eyes for fear I was wrong.

"Just for you," he whispered back. So I found that I *could* look in his eyes, his kind, loving eyes that picked me, out of three identically dressed little girls, and saw only me, despite all my many failings as recited daily by Pricks and Ina and Mamma. My heart was glad, so glad; it wanted to leap out of my chest and tell him so, but it had to content itself with my words.

"Oh, that sounds *so* nice! What is it? When will I know?"

"Soon. I'll send you a note soon, when the perfect day presents itself."

"But how will you know it's perfect?"

"It shall say to me, 'Mr. Do-Do-Dodgson, I command you to go fetch Alice, because this day belongs to her, it cannot belong to another, and the three of us—you, Alice, and myself—must spend it together, in order to remember it always.'"

"How can a day spend itself?" My head spun with the notion of Mr. Dodgson talking to the day; would he be addressing the sun, the clouds, the air itself? Just what did a day look like? Did it have a very deep voice? Or a merry voice, like the laughing tinkle of the little clock on Mamma's desk, the one with the ballerinas that spun around in a circle?

"Days are very mysterious things, of course. Sometimes they fly by, and other times they seem to last forever, yet they are all exactly twenty-four hours. There's quite a lot we don't know about them."

I did so want to know how a day spent itself, but I decided to leave it for another—day. Then I laughed, thinking I had made a pun, although I wasn't exactly sure; when Mr. Dodgson inquired as to why I was laughing, I shook my head, not wanting to explain.

He didn't appear to mind; he smiled and stood

up straight, still holding my hand, as we waited for Pricks and Ina to retrieve Edith.

"Oh, did she get anything on her dress?" I studied her anxiously; with Mamma's request weighing upon my conscience, I felt somehow responsible for the spotlessness of the entire party.

"Not a thing, thank heavens!" Pricks studied the bottom of her own skirt, which was now damp and muddy. "Oh, these streets! Mud and water and horses and fish and who knows what else!"

"Then let us hasten to the Meadow, where the fresh air will dry your skirt, Edith can chase butterflies and not fish, Alice can look at the hill but not roll down it, and Ina can sit prettily under a tree and look thoughtful."

Edith clapped her hands; Ina blushed and smiled; Pricks pulled her glove up high over her wrist and touched the false knot of hair sticking out from her bonnet.

I tugged on Mr. Dodgson's jacket. "What will *you* do?"

"I'll tell stories, I suppose. Don't I always?"

I nodded, happy. Yes, he did tell stories; intricate stories about us, about Oxford, about the people we knew, the places we saw every day, but somehow he managed to arrange them all into faraway places, lands we'd never seen before yet recognized all the same.

"Isn't that a sweet family?" I heard a lady say as we crossed St. Aldate's—Pricks raising her skirts with much exaggeration as she stepped over piles of fresh horse manure, as the dairy wagon had just passed—to get to the wide, tree-lined Broad Walk, which bordered the Meadow.

The lady was obviously not from Oxford; everyone here knew that we were the three Liddell girls. I laughed, even as Pricks gave a sudden start. She raised her chin, surprising me by looking very soft and almost pretty, with glistening eyes, a smile not quite so sudden and terrible; not all her teeth were showing. I wondered why she didn't correct the lady; I supposed it was one of those instinctive manners she was always going on about.

Ina almost said something; I could see her struggle as her face reddened, her mouth opened, and she looked at Pricks and Mr. Dodgson, as if seeking their permission. However, Pricks chose that moment to stumble and lean more heavily upon Mr. Dodgson's arm. I held my breath; she certainly was bigger than he, even without her swaying skirt, and I feared he might topple over. By some miracle he didn't; he grimaced a bit, but held on bravely.

Ina's eyes narrowed. I could see her storing this picture away, as she sometimes did; I knew my sister hoarded information the way squirrels hoarded nuts. Not useful information, either, such as why Phoebe always dipped her food into tea before she ate it (she said she had soft teeth and didn't want to lose them before she got too old to catch a husband).

No, Ina was more interested in quiet things, looks and sighs and passing touches. The way a man sat on a sofa next to a lady; the distance between them; the silence. She could find meaning in such things, and she sometimes talked about them with me, but mainly—as I never could understand what they meant, and didn't feel like trying very hard to learn—she stored them away. For some future use that I could not help but fear, as little as I understood it.

So we passed our afternoon companionably, doing precisely what Mr. Dodgson had predicted. Sheltered by the tall chestnut trees, Ina posed on a low stone bench, patted her curls a lot, and looked dreamy; Edith tried to catch every insect she saw; Pricks fanned her skirts out in a very energetic attempt to dry that one damp splotch. I looked longingly at a pretty slope, just the right height, with no dangerous tree roots sticking out; the grass was so very green and tempting, but somehow, I remembered my promise to Mamma. So I contented myself with picking buttercups for her, although I still ended up losing one glove and soiling the other.

Mr. Dodgson reclined on the grass—gentlemen did not mind stains as much as ladies; this was another important piece of information I now possessed—and told stories. Some silly tales, I soon forgot what they were; they were the same as all the other stories he told, long and winding and full of talking animals and people behaving strangely, although somehow recognizably. I felt I might know whom he was talking about really —the lecturing fish certainly sounded familiar, the way he droned on and on about heaven and the narrow path that leads to it—but in the end, I had to give up. It was too warm to think. I was too drowsy.

He did make me sit up straight, once, with just a look, a sudden, intense look, almost as if he were afraid I might disappear and he wanted to remember me. When I felt myself blush, wondering why I felt so strangely, he blinked, and I relaxed. With a smile, he put a finger to his lips, and I knew he was referring to our secret; my insides bubbled over with happiness, making me giggle out loud.

Immediately, however, I stopped. Ina's face pinched up; her small mouth set itself in a tight, disapproving line. Her eyes grew cold and still. They reminded me of Mr. Dodgson's camera lens, unblinking, unemotional.

Those eyes remembered, recorded *everything,* including things like secrets; including things like sympathetic hearts that were, as yet, barely noticeable even to those who possessed them.

Chapter 2

I WAITED AND WAITED FOR THE PERFECT DAY. I worried I wouldn't recognize it when it appeared. So I was anxious, always on guard, and wore on Pricks's nerves even more than usual.

"Alice, if you cannot sit quietly for five minutes, I will bind you to your chair with—with—butcher's string!" She looked around the schoolroom for some. Naturally, all she found were books and slates and papers, the huge globe that sat on a half bookshelf, a stuffed owl looming in a low, sloping corner. She scarcely bothered to look on her own desk, with its neat stacks of blotters in every kind of fabric, her favorite pen lying next to the inkwell, a sheaf of ruled paper full of lists written out in her neat, uninspiring hand.

"No, you won't," I explained, shaking my head once more; how could someone responsible for teaching me everything I was supposed to learn in order to be an educated lady be so very stupid at times? "You'd have to go all the way down to the kitchen to ask Cook for some, and meanwhile I'd escape. It wouldn't be difficult. I could climb out the window and shimmy down the drainpipe."

"I shan't resort to physical force, however tempted." With a sigh, Pricks turned to the blackboard. "But do try to act like Ina. She's behaving beautifully."

Ina simpered, adjusting her hands into another graceful pose, placing her left hand flat on her desk, folding the right one upon it, with a slight fluttering of her fingertips.

I wouldn't do that; I wouldn't act so sickeningly fake. I did try to sit quietly, though, for I truly did not want to be a nuisance to Pricks. She had not been feeling well lately; she was pale (as pale as someone with a nut-brown complexion could be), her hair was dull, and she had even stopped putting creams and lotions on her warts.

Ina, too, was acting strangely; noisy sighs and reclining poses, quick starts whenever there was a knock on the door.

And while I had believed myself to be ignorant of the feminine mind, a reason for their ridiculous behavior presented itself to me without much effort. Mr. Dodgson was the culprit. He had not been around as much as usual. Even more surprisingly, I thought I knew why.

Mr. Ruskin had alluded to it.

Papa said that Mr. Ruskin was a genius. Papa did not say this about many people, although many people said it about him. Papa and his friend Mr. Scott were always writing a book; the same book, a book with no end, apparently, like some of Mr. Dodgson's stories. Only this book was supposed to translate words from one language to another, from Greek to English. A lexicon, they called it, and even though I thought the entire

enterprise rather boring and not a little useless
—personally, I had never had reason to wonder
what the Greek word for, say, hippopotamus,
was—others did not. They always spoke about it,
and Papa, in hushed tones—while calling him a
genius.

Knowing that Papa never used this word carelessly, I had to admit that if he believed Mr.
Ruskin to be a genius, then he must be.

Only I thought Mr. Ruskin was a bore. He
wasn't part of Oxford, not truly. He only popped
in from London every few weeks to lecture and
give art lessons. Mamma made sure he came
round to the Deanery when he did, so that we girls
could have lessons, too, and while I did love to
draw, I did not enjoy doing so in the company of
Mr. Ruskin.

It wasn't that I thought he didn't like me; I was
quite sure that he did. He did not like me in the
same way as Mr. Dodgson, though, and I couldn't
quite put my finger on the difference between
them. Mr. Ruskin admired me; he tended to look
at me a lot, and smile down his long aquiline
nose at me, and pat me or touch part of my dress
whenever he had a chance. Still, unlike Mr.
Dodgson, he never seemed very interested in anything I had to say.

He would never allow me to roll down a hill.
He would never ask me about my thoughts,
either, for he did not seem to believe I possessed

any. Whenever I chanced to talk during our lessons, he always put down his pencil or chalk, sighed, and muttered, "The Medicis would have been easier to work for."

He did like to talk, just not with us girls. Mamma was his chief friend, at least whenever she was around; I did get the impression he wasn't so loyal when she was not. For Mr. Ruskin loved to talk about other people, the people of Oxford; who was on the outs with whom, who was writing love letters to a certain shopkeeper's young daughter, which son of a clergyman was rumored to have spent his entire allowance on wine and women—

Which mathematics lecturer was supposed to be paying court to the governess of the Dean's daughters?

"That's what they're saying, my dear," I heard him giggle to Mamma one afternoon while they were in the parlor, taking tea. I was on my way downstairs to the kitchen to see if Cook had any scraps to spare for my kitten, Dinah. Edith and I had dressed her up for a tea party, but so far, she wasn't cooperating. We decided it might be because kittens aren't partial to biscuits, and so I was on my way to procure some scraps for her, preferably fish bones.

"It's nonsense, of course," Mamma harrumphed. I heard the clink of china, as she must have placed her teacup in its saucer impatiently.

Stopping outside the door, I tiptoed back a few steps and flattened myself against the wall, very carefully, so my petticoats didn't rustle and give me away. It was nearly impossible to be an effective eavesdropper when one had to wear so very many clothes. Still, I persisted.

"Why nonsense? To the observer, it appears perfectly logical. He does spend a lot of time with her." Mr. Ruskin's voice was thin and high. It always sounded odd to me, coming from one with such an awful quantity of hair growing all over his head, even down the sides of his face; his eyebrows were so bushy they looked like caterpillars.

"He spends time with the children—they're the ones he comes to see. It's only natural that Miss Prickett accompany them on outings. I wouldn't allow it otherwise."

"Well, the sentiment is that he spends time with Miss Prickett, and the children are incidental."

"Nonsense," Mamma huffed. "More tea?"

"Yes, please."

There was a silence, during which my mind began to wander back up to the nursery. Had Edith been able to keep Dinah in her little dress? I did hope she wouldn't tear it with her claws; I had borrowed it from one of Ina's dolls.

Then Mamma spoke again.

"He is rather a nuisance, though. That man. Dodgson."

"Of course. Everyone says so."

"Always photographing them—the girls. Always taking them on outings, picnics, boating —it's as if he doesn't have any other friends. Does he?"

"I'm sure I don't know." Mr. Ruskin sniffed.

"What is his background? Only the son of a clergyman. No family to speak of. I continue to allow it because the girls are so young, and they do seem to enjoy his company and I'm sure it's a help to Miss Prickett. Otherwise they'd grow sick of one another. The photographs he takes are charming, I must say. The girls never seem to tire of posing—it's the only time I've ever seen Alice able to sit still."

The tips of my ears burned at the sound of my own name. I almost giggled but clamped my hand over my mouth just in time.

"I barely know the man," Mr. Ruskin said, sounding bored. "I don't imagine you'll be having many mathematics lecturers around when the girls are older?"

Mamma laughed. "Of course not! My daughters will not marry college professors. I have higher hopes than that!"

"Of course you do. I'd be disappointed if you didn't—they're pearls. And as such, should only be auctioned off to the highest bidder."

Now I was very confused. Only slaves were auctioned, and they had been outlawed long ago; Pricks had taught us this, when we were doing history.

"Oh, Mr. Ruskin. I do wish you wouldn't put it that way. It's vulgar." Mamma's voice grew icy, as only she could make it; on the surface she sounded more polite than ever, but it was quite like some of her smiles. You knew it was only for show.

I heard more china clinking, silver tinkling. The mantel clock chimed softly, and I was just about to leave for the kitchen when Mr. Ruskin spoke.

"So you're not concerned that people are talking about Dodgson and your governess?"

"It's nonsense," Mamma said again; I did wonder why she couldn't think of another word to say, as usually she had quite a lot at her disposal. "Particularly as he hasn't been around much as of late."

"That's because he heard, I'm sure, what people were saying."

"Then obviously it's not true, or else he'd make his intentions known. So there—I told you it was nonsense." I could hear the triumph in Mamma's voice; she did so love to be right.

"I never said it was true. I simply said it was what people were saying—although perception is reality, of course."

"I suppose so. It's such a bore. It's so difficult to find good servants, especially governesses and nurses. I imagined that this one would be different. It's not as if she's a beauty."

"No," Mr. Ruskin said, laughing. And while I would never, ever have confessed this to anyone, not even the Archbishop of Canterbury, I felt bad for Pricks just then. She couldn't help her warts, or the rough color of her complexion. However, she could help the silly way she acted around Mr. Dodgson, and I thought that perhaps I'd tell her so. Obviously, she needed my help in the matter. She had no idea people like Mr. Ruskin were talking about her.

On the whole, it appeared to me that Mr. Dodgson was acting sensibly by staying away, even if it meant that I missed him, too. I knew he didn't care for Pricks; anyone with sense could see that. Yet Pricks couldn't, and it puzzled me, since she did seem to know quite a lot about other things; boring things, certainly, but no one could say she wasn't educated.

My head grew muddled with it all; the silly ways adults acted with one another, never saying what they meant, trusting in sighs and glances and distance to speak for them instead. How dangerous that was! How easy it must be to misinterpret a sigh or a look. I was quite sure I'd never get it right when it came my time to grow up. Fortunately, that was a long way off. Unlike Ina, I was in no hurry to learn that particular, peculiar language.

Mamma and Mr. Ruskin then moved on to other subjects, subjects that held no interest for me. So I tiptoed down the hall toward the kitchen, where I did get a lovely little fish bone for Dinah, who ate it, even while giving me reproachful looks for putting her in the dress.

Meanwhile, I stored away all I had heard about Mr. Dodgson and Pricks. Until, trying not to fidget in the schoolroom, I observed Pricks jump at every sound, Ina flutter her eyelashes and sigh mournfully. With a shake of my head, I decided it was time to clear things up, for the very air was stifling, heavy with wishes unfulfilled—questions unasked.

I alone had the answers. I did not want to keep such impressive knowledge to myself.

"Mr. Dodgson hasn't been round much lately," I began. I kept my eyes trained on the blackboard, upon which Pricks had written some sums.

Pricks dropped her chalk and bent to retrieve it; I observed her lips tremble, ever so slightly, before she twisted them up into a scowl.

"I fail to see what that has to do with our lessons, Alice," she said firmly.

Ina, sitting next to me, had stiffened; slowly she turned her head to face me, her large gray eyes not blinking, so that she resembled nothing more than an owl with long curls.

"It's simply—I thought perhaps you'd like to know why he hasn't," I explained to Pricks, remembering what Mamma and Mr. Ruskin had said about her, and feeling myself soften just a bit; I honestly wanted to help her. "I thought it might make you feel better, because you're awfully jumpy lately. You haven't even been putting creams on your wa—on your skin."

Pricks yanked her left hand behind her back and covered her chin with her right hand—a reflex, to hide the offending warts. She glared at me. "Continue."

"Well," I said, kicking my legs, wriggling my toes so that my heels hung over the ends of my shoes; for once neither Pricks nor Ina told me not to. "I heard—someone—say that Mr. Dodgson was supposed to be paying court to you."

Pricks ducked her head, yet not before I saw how soft the light was in her brown eyes, how blurred her normally blunt features grew. Ina saw, too; she froze, staring straight ahead, her eyes unblinking, her face white.

"The thing is, though," I continued, anxious to clear up the situation, "he's not really, and that's why he's been staying away. Because of you, Pricks."

Ina gasped—then started to laugh uncontrollably. She held her hands against her ribs, as if in pain, and came perilously close to knocking over her inkwell. Pricks, however, did not laugh. Simply, startlingly, she sat down upon the floor where she had stood; it was as if her legs had been pulled out from under her. Encircled by enormous quantities of gray muslin, she continued to sink down into them until her crinoline popped up in front, revealing her petticoats. I couldn't help but notice some of them had fraying, yellowing edges where the lace was worn. She didn't bother to push the crinoline down, she didn't seem to care what I noticed; she appeared unable to move at all, except for her mouth, which kept opening and closing, though no sound came out.

"Don't laugh," I told Ina, genuinely shocked; she was the one who always went on and on about good manners, and here she was laughing at poor ugly Pricks. "It's not Pricks's fault she's no beau—well, that she has warts," I continued, remembering what Mamma had said. "Which is why Mr. Dodgson hasn't come around. He doesn't want people to talk about him and Pricks, because it's nonsense."

"You wicked girl!" Suddenly Pricks was standing over me; her eyes were red, her mouth wide and ugly, and she couldn't control her hands. They trembled, even as she grabbed the pointer from the blackboard and raised it over me. Ina stopped laughing then; she gasped and tugged on my arm, as if to pull me away.

I was frozen, my heart caught in fear; I couldn't breathe, even though every nerve was beseeching me to run. My skin actually tingled with the desire. But I didn't; I couldn't. For I could not imagine that Pricks—that anyone—would actually strike me.

I knew that some children were beaten regularly—the Little Match Girl from the story, for example. Yet never had anyone struck me, or Ina, or Edith. I could not believe Pricks would do this—so my mind told me it was ridiculous to run, for nothing would happen.

Nothing did happen; not at that moment, at any rate. Pricks glared at me with a cold, hard stare that made my stomach sink for what it might mean now and forever; with a cry, she dropped the pointer, hid her face in her hands, and ran to a corner of the room. Her voice all wobbly, she told us to please leave her alone; it must be time for lunch, and Phoebe would be wondering where we were.

Ina released my arm—had she been trying to protect me?—and seized Edith's hand, leading her from the room. I tiptoed over to Pricks but was stopped by her outstretched hand. So I followed Ina and Edith on trembling legs, for I truly did not understand what I had done.

I expected Ina to be angry—she always took Pricks's side in everything—but to my surprise, she actually hugged me.

"Oh, Alice," she breathed into my ear. "Are you all right? You're such a dear!!!"

I squirmed away; I did not like to be hugged, except by Papa and Mr. Dodgson. "What? Why is everyone acting so strangely?" My eyes filled with tears, for I knew something frightful had happened, and that somehow I was at fault, even though my only desire had been to explain things to Pricks so that life would be easier and so she wouldn't act foolishly in front of Mr. Dodgson. I knew it was selfish, but that was what I had wanted.

"You child! You don't know—but that's all right. It's perfectly all right. No one should know, not for a long time. Pricks needed to hear that. She was acting like such a fool!"

"I don't know what?" It felt to me that I did know, far too much, and none of it made sense.

"Never mind. But thanks to you, I'm sure now. Surer than ever. Oh, Alice!" She clapped her hands, hopping about in a merry dance; her long brown curls spun behind her, and her cheeks grew rosy, giving warmth to her eyes.

"Surer of what?"

"You're too young to understand. But I'm not! Oh, I'm not, I'm not! I'm so happy!" She took Edith's hand and swung it to and fro; I believed she might jump up on the banister and try to fly, she looked so wild, so unladylike, and while normally I would have informed her of this, I was much too confused at present.

"Why aren't we having lunch?" Edith asked, plopping down on the floor in a heap, her little black leather shoes sticking straight out in front of her. "Isn't that what we're supposed to do?"

"Oh, who can eat at a time like this? But do go ahead—I'll come with you. After all, we promised Pricks we would, poor thing. She needs us to behave, now more than ever. Her hopes are dashed, and I can't help but feel for her." Ina calmed down and glided toward the nursery with a ladylike sigh, her nose stuck in the air, her hands holding her skirts as if they were as long and voluminous as Mamma's. Of course, they weren't. Yet when I told her so, she refused to grumble or pull my hair or act in any way normal.

She merely smiled, one of her teasing, practiced little smiles. When I would not ask her why she was smiling—would not even hint that I knew she was thinking of something delicious, something she desperately wanted me to know, but would not, could not, bring herself to tell—she continued to smile all the same.

I did not want to know her secret, nor did I want her to know any of mine, particularly the one about the Perfect Day. Astonishingly, it was Mr. Dodgson who was responsible for all this, all these secrets and smiles and Pricks crumpled on the floor, her hands in her face, the pointer trembling above me, Ina's wild laughter, the fear, the confusion. The secretive gossip overheard in parlors.

Try as I might, I could not understand how one man—one shy man with a camera, a stammer, and an endless supply of stories—

Could be responsible for so much disarray.

Chapter 3

Dear Miss Alice,

The Perfect Day knocked on my window this morning. It said you were to be ready this afternoon, after your lessons, for an Adventure. Would you mind if your silly old Uncle Dodgson joined you, too? I don't know about you, but I am rather tired of being myself. Aren't you? Would you like to be someone else, just for today?

> *Yours,*
> *Charles Lutwidge Dodgson*
> *(22 letters, still, to your 21)*

*H*OWEVER DID HE KNOW? THAT TODAY *WAS* the perfect day for me to escape, unnoticed, and have an adventure? Also, that I was rather tired of being myself, clumsy, lazy, thoughtless Alice (to name just a few of the words that Pricks, Mamma, and Ina had used to describe me in the last few weeks)?

I paused only a second to marvel at his insight. Then I set about trying to plot my escape, which would not be difficult, as today was the day we were going to get the new baby and everyone was much exercised. Mamma was up in her bedroom;

she had not come down at all, not for more than a day. Phoebe was running to and from the nursery and the bedroom, carrying piles of freshly laundered towels and linens and bundles and bundles of candles even though the sun was bright; I'd never seen so many, not even in church.

Dr. Acland was in the hall outside Mamma's room with Papa; they were talking in low tones, occasionally laughing, and not looking very useful at all. Dr. Acland had brought with him several women, who were in Mamma's room. I imagined they were all having some sort of tea party while they waited.

Pricks and Ina were in a frightful state. Pricks declared a holiday from lessons today, as she felt we would make too much noise; the schoolroom was directly above Mamma's bedroom. She and Ina were supposed to be assisting Phoebe in getting the nursery ready, although I could not see that they were much help at all. Ina insisted upon placing fresh flowers all around—which Phoebe insisted upon removing, muttering that they smelled of outdoors and most likely were full of insects—while Pricks sat in the rocking chair, gliding back and forth with a dreamy smile on her face. She was back to her silly ways, now that Mr. Dodgson had resumed his visits.

Still, by the way she looked at me—always with a little intake of breath, as if simply seeing me reminded her of her own worst fears—I under-

65

stood that she had not forgotten that afternoon, when I told her all I knew. I had no real comprehension of what had transpired, yet I did know that it would linger, always, between Pricks and me, and that I would never try to help her again.

With all that was going on—really, I wondered at the demanding nature of babies; this one hadn't even arrived, and the household was topsy-turvy!—I had no difficulty stealing down to the front door (remembering to bring a compass, a handkerchief, and four chocolate-covered biscuits, tucked in my skirt pocket, because I didn't know what Mr. Dodgson had in mind, and I was resolved to be prepared) to wait.

Only one person noticed. The Mary Ann from the kitchen—Mamma called all maids Mary Ann; she said it was easier that way—came running past, carrying a hot kettle of water, the handle wrapped tightly in a kitchen towel. She stopped when she saw me, and some water sloshed out from under the lid, splashing her already damp apron. She frowned, her face as red and perspiring as all maids' faces generally were; her damp hair frizzed out from under her plain white cap.

"Oh, my heavens! What are you doing here, lamb? Won't Miss Prickett be wondering where you are?"

"She sent me out on an errand," I replied, surprised at how easily I told the lie, and wondering why I chose to in the first place. What did I have to hide? Nothing; something. "I'm to run to the stationer's to get some notepaper for the baby. The baby needs notepaper."

"Fine, fine," Mary Ann said absently. "Don't get dirty." She hurried upstairs, trying not to spill water on the carpet.

I sighed. Why did everyone—even maids—feel the need to tell me this on a daily basis?

I decided I ought to slip out now, in case Mary Ann ran into Pricks and told her my plans. Carefully I opened the door—it did have a tendency to squeak, like most doors, but today it decided to behave—and stepped out into the sunshine, shutting the door behind me. I surveyed the Quad; it was full of students, as the term had just begun. I wondered if I'd see the Prince of Wales. He'd just come down to Oxford, and it had been very exciting. Even as fat as she was, Mamma had insisted on holding the first reception; I had been allowed to stay up and meet him. He was very jolly, and shook my hand, and signed my autograph book, and told me my curtsy was very pretty, indeed, and that he had a brother my age named Leopold, who was a capital little fellow, and that I'd probably like him very much.

Then I was whisked off to the nursery, as usual.

Mr. Dodgson told me he'd asked if he could photograph him, but the Prince said no. I understood how posing for pictures could be tiring, but the Prince did not know Mr. Dodgson. He turned it all into a game, first posing us and then sitting down and telling us stories, sometimes drawing pictures; just at the point when we'd become absorbed in the stories, he'd run to prepare the plate, put it into the camera and tell us to hold very still, and remove the lens cover. He always counted out loud, sometimes as high as forty-five, but sometimes he did it backward, and other times he did it from the middle—starting at twenty-two and going back and forth until he said, "Forty-five, one—finished!" Finally, we could relax, and then he would continue the story.

He made it such a lark; not a bore, not at all. After the photograph was taken, we'd be rewarded by helping him develop the glass plate, and the combination of odors—of acid, chemical smells, and then the faint scent of cloves that always sur-rounded Mr. Dodgson, combined with the linger-ing smoke from the fire in his rooms—could make my head spin. Sometimes I imagined I got rather drunk on them. I didn't exactly know what drunk meant, only that often the characters in Mr. Dickens's stories got that way, and when they did, they acted peculiarly and talked strangely and made Papa laugh.

I did not see the Prince out today. Only the usual mass of students, some alone, others in groups, some walking backward to continue conversa-tions—all of them very intense about something. Even so, there were always a few fellows who were lazing about the fountain or swinging cricket bats, although this was generally frowned upon in the Quad.

At that moment, I was the only girl in sight. This wasn't an unusual occurrence, so it didn't trouble me. My presence did not appear to trouble them, either; I felt as safe there, surrounded by dozens of adult males, none of whom gave me even a second glance except perhaps to smile my way, as I did in the nursery surrounded by females. That the two—men and women—were different, of course, I was aware. Never did I feel, however, that one was more or less dangerous than the other.

"Miss Alice!" Mr. Dodgson was standing in front of me; I hadn't noticed his approach. He raised his black silk hat. "How is your mother?"

"Having a tea party, I suppose," I replied. "She and the ladies Dr. Acland brought with him. The baby should be here directly."

"Oh." Mr. Dodgson looked at me, a peculiar expression on his face, as if he was deciding whether or not to laugh. After a minute he simply nodded.

"Pricks and Ina are busy in the nursery, so they told me to go without them," I lied; once more, I wondered why I did so. My thoughts simply would not behave this afternoon!

"I supposed they might be busy today," Mr. Dodgson said. Surprised, I glanced up at him; was that why this was the Perfect Day—because he knew Pricks and Ina couldn't accompany us? (Edith I had left in the nursery, playing happily with her dolls.)

"What is it? What's the surprise?" I couldn't stop myself from jumping up and down; I'd waited so long—months, even! Months during which Mr. Dodgson had gone on holiday, although we hadn't, not this year; usually we summered in Wales, where Papa was going to build us a house. This year, Mamma was too tired to travel; she said the train was too bouncy. So I'd passed the summer at home in Oxford; such a quiet, lazy place during the holidays. Unlike during the school terms, when there was always a constant, catching buzz in the very air.

Even as I was prancing about, I was dismayed to see that in one hand Mr. Dodgson was carrying his camera, folded neatly in its wooden box; with the other, he held his tripod over his shoulder.

"That's the surprise?" My heart sank as I stopped in my tracks. Another photograph? That was what the Perfect Day had meant?

"Y-yes and no. Yes, I'd like to take your photograph, please. But this is going to be different. How would you like to walk on the grass in your bare feet?"

"Without my shoes?" I looked up at him, unable to believe what I'd heard. Walking—perhaps even running—on grass, simply feeling it against my bare skin, no fussy, confining layers of clothing or stiff shoes between me and the earth? It was one of my fondest desires, and I'd never, ever told Mr. Dodgson. Somehow he'd known anyway; his blue eyes, one slightly higher than the other, gazing down at me intently as if I were the answer to a question he could not bring himself to ask, told me so. He'd known, he *knew,* so very much about me.

"Without your shoes, just like a wild gypsy. Would you like to be a gypsy today, Alice?"

"That's what you meant in your note, about being someone else?"

"Of course."

"Oh, it sounds tremendous! Shall I take my shoes off now?" I desired so very much to please him; he looked at me wistfully, as if he was already imagining the gypsy me. Smiling, he set the camera down, bent slightly, in that stiff way of his, and stroked my cheek. His gloved hand was soft as the blanket I had placed, just this morning, in the new baby's bed.

"Not now." He jerked his hand away from me and looked over his shoulder, as if he feared someone was watching. "Let's go to the far corner of the garden. I've already brought my tent and case there—the light's perfect." I was no longer in his thoughts; now he was concerned with the photograph—would the light be favorable, the wind too strong, the chemicals spoiled, and the glass plates cracked? So many things could go wrong, I knew. I grew very anxious, thinking of them all.

"Do you think it will turn out right?" I proceeded to follow him through the arch that led round to the back of the house, to our private garden. Tripping on an uneven stone in the walk, I scuffed the toe of my shoe; my heart sank—already, I was dirty.

"Most likely. Who knows? It will be exciting to find out, won't it?"

I nodded. Of course it would. That was the jolly part about being photographed; one never really knew how it would turn out. There was always that moment in the chemical bath when the image first appeared on the glass plate, like a ghost swimming up from the past, and you didn't know if the image would be clear and sharp or remain a blur forever. My stomach always was in pleasurable knots at that moment. It was like opening a present, every time.

"Oh, but wait!" I stopped.

"What is it, Alice?" Mr. Dodgson turned around, so patient with me.

"Whatever shall I wear? I don't have any gypsy clothes!"

"Ah, but I have. An old gypsy herself lent them to me."

"Really?" I did so want to believe him; believe that an old gypsy woman, with rings and bells and scarves draped all over, had knocked on the door to his rooms and given him a little girl gypsy's dress.

Yet there was always that watchful part of me that asked, Have you ever chanced upon a gypsy woman in the Quad? On the High Street? In the Meadow? And how would she know where Mr. Dodgson lived? Why would she give him a dress?

Sometimes I despised that part of me.

"Truly she did, Alice. Don't you believe me?"

I sighed. I did so *want* to.

"You're an old soul, Alice. Did you know that? Most children your age would leap at the notion of a gypsy woman. But not you. You're too wise."

I didn't know what to say to him; he looked at me so dreamily, so hopefully. I knew that if I said a word, I'd disappoint him. So I merely smiled, allowing myself to be happy for this moment, this Perfect Day, and relaxed my watchfulness for now.

Opening the weathered gate to the garden, I shrank back from walking directly across it. I kept to the outer stone wall instead, even though it was much farther that way. Mr. Dodgson didn't ask why. Yet he knew. He knew I didn't want anyone inside the Deanery to see. I imagined—I *hoped*—that everyone was too busy to notice us. Still, Mamma would be very angry if she saw me as a gypsy girl in my bare feet. Perhaps even angry enough to drop the baby, and I certainly didn't want to be responsible for that. However, I was more concerned about Ina and Pricks. If either of them saw me alone with Mr. Dodgson—

my stomach fluttered uneasily at the notion. They hadn't been invited, and the longer they remained ignorant of this, the better for everyone, myself in particular.

"There are your rooms," said I, when we were halfway around the wall, far enough away from the Deanery—the windows looked like little half-closed eyes along the back of the house—that I felt safe. I pointed up toward the library, directly across the garden from the Deanery. "Did you see us playing croquet yesterday?" I knew he sometimes looked down at us while we played in the garden, but never before had I mentioned it.

"No, I'm afraid I didn't," was all he said, and I felt as if this was a subject we should discuss no further, although I was puzzled as to the reason.

It was chilly in the shadows of the garden, as it was October; I hugged myself to keep warm and wondered how cold I'd be in my bare feet. I determined that I would not let Mr. Dodgson see that it worried me.

At last we achieved the corner farthest from the Deanery, well hidden by trees showing off their autumn colors; this was where Mr. Dodgson had set up his equipment. There was his black leather chemical case, and a gauzy awning on poles, shading the corner where two walls met—he used this awning to filter the sun whenever he photographed us outside—and also his dark canvas tent, so cunningly small. It was just my height, so naturally Mr. Dodgson had to stoop very low in order to use it, which never failed to make me laugh.

"Where is my gypsy dress?"

"Behind the tent. But first, let's set you up and take a photograph of you just as you are."

"Just as me?" I couldn't conceal my disappointment; I did get so weary of being me.

"Just as you, but that's a wonderful thing. Just Alice." Mr. Dodgson smiled, and I felt somewhat better.

"I do despise my hair so." I didn't stifle my sigh as I shook my head, feeling the ends of my hair brush the back of my neck. I so longed to feel the weight of hair hanging down my back.

Mr. Dodgson laughed.

"Don't you know? Your hair is part of what makes you special! I could photograph every little girl in Oxford, and they'd all have the same kind of hair—long curls with bows. You stand out, of all of them. That's why I want to photograph you—only you could be my gypsy girl."

"Oh!" I hadn't thought of it that way, and the notion tickled my insides until I smiled. I beamed at him as he busied himself with the tripod and camera. However did he do it? How did he make me feel so special? I wondered if he had anyone in his life to do the same for him; I knew that he probably didn't. He did seem so very lonely at times.

"Your—your hair is very nice, too. And I like your gloves." I didn't, though. They were always either black or gray, as strange and off-putting as he himself often appeared to others. He did not appear that way to me, however, and so I vowed, from that moment, to tell him so as often as possible.

Every person, no matter how old, no matter how odd, needed someone like that in their lives, I thought.

Mr. Dodgson paused; his eyes widened, and his color deepened. I believed I saw his hands tremble. "Tha-thank you, Alice," was all he said. Then he busied himself with his camera, and while I was nearly shivering as I stood motionless, watching, he worked so energetically that eventually he removed his hat, his black coat, and placed them carefully upon a stone bench. He pushed his white shirtsleeves up as well, but never did he remove his gray gloves.

"Now, stand in the corner, please."

"Like this?" I posed, my hands by my sides, experience having taught me it was easier to hold still that way.

"Yes, but turn to your left—not that much! Just a little. Turn your head back toward me. Can you hold that?"

Steadying myself on my feet, I pressed my hands down upon my skirt. My neck already felt stiff, but I would not tell him. "Yes, I think so."

"Well done! Now relax a moment, but don't move. I'll just go prepare the plate." He dashed beneath the tent, although part of him—his rear part—stuck out. I didn't dare laugh.

Instead, I glanced back toward the Deanery to see if there was movement in any of the windows. The tree branches obscured most of the windows from view, which was a relief; if I couldn't see them, they couldn't see me. So I relaxed and allowed myself to wonder what the gypsy-girl dress looked like. I did hope that it had smudges on it, and that it might be torn.

"Now, back to your pose!" Mr. Dodgson emerged from the tent, the plate holder in his hand. Pushing it into the back of the camera, he waited for me to take a big breath. Then he removed the round lens cover and began to count. "One, three, two, four, six, five, eight, seven, ten, nine—" and I felt it was very unfair of him to be so silly when I had to keep still, concentrating on the lens, that round, unblinking eye. Finally he got to forty-five, and he placed the cover back over the lens; I let out my breath in a big laugh. He ran to embrace me—"There's a good girl!"—then hurried back to the camera, pulling out the lens holder and rushing it to the tent.

"May I bathe it?" I asked, shaking my arms and legs, twisting my neck. I did so enjoy washing the plate in its tray, waiting for the picture to emerge.

"Not this time, I've already started. Next one, I promise."

"Where's my dress? Shall I change?"

"Just on the other side of the tent. Go ahead, but try not to jostle it, please."

"I won't!"

I walked carefully around the tent and found a piece of worn, faded fabric draped across one corner. It took me a moment to realize this was the dress; there wasn't very much to it, not at all like my regular frocks with their flounces and layers—why, the sleeves of the frock I was wearing had three layers to them!

Holding this sliver of cloth—for that was what it seemed to me—my heart began to race. I was very certain that Mamma would not like me to wear this, especially not in front of a gentleman, even Mr. Dodgson. My nightgown had much more fabric to it.

"Shall I—shall I leave my petticoats on, anyway?" I couldn't control my voice; it warbled like a nightingale. A bug tickled the back of my neck, and I swatted at it. It felt peculiar back here, hidden in this corner by the tent, clutching a strange girl's dress; it didn't feel as if I was in my own garden at all. I might as well have been in deepest Africa, a notion that normally would have excited me. At that moment, however, it scarcely registered.

"Oh, no. Would a gypsy girl have petticoats?"

Mr. Dodgson's voice was muffled; I heard the swish of liquid in a container, inhaled the sharp smell of acid.

"I suppose not. What about my chemise?" Imagining myself clad only in this thin layer of cotton, I actually shivered.

"I don't—your chemise? I'm not sure—at any rate, I don't think a gypsy girl would have many clothes on except her dress, do you? So just the dress, please."

"Oh." I took the dress, held it up to me, then dropped it to the ground. Clutching my own skirt, I fingered the stiff, familiar lace like a good-luck charm. Then I realized something very important.

I realized I had never before undressed myself.

Phoebe performed that task, or one of the Mary Anns. All my buttons were in the back; every night I obediently turned around and waited for someone to unbutton all of them, help me step out of the billowing fabric, unfasten all my petticoats—again, all of which fastened at my back. Every night someone did.

Yet I couldn't let Mr. Dodgson down. So I resolved to do it myself; I reached behind my shoulder, feeling for the top button; I felt and felt but never did find it, although my shoulder began to ache and little drops of perspiration dribbled down my back. I relaxed, took a deep breath, and tried once more.

Finally I felt the top button, cold and hard, and

managed to push it through its hole. But there were so many buttons still to go! My eyes filled with tears, for I didn't know what to do, and I didn't want to bother Mr. Dodgson. Oh, what did little gypsy girls do when *they* had to get undressed? Suddenly that thin layer of clothing made sense; at least they weren't so dependent upon adults. I hadn't realized how helpless I myself was, really—no better than the new baby—until this moment.

Blinking my eyes—I resolved not to cry, as I knew my nose would get red and ruin the photograph—I tried once more. Reaching down the middle of my back, I groped and groped for a button, until I thought I heard the telltale rip of fabric splitting. I dropped my arm, panicked. How would I explain a torn dress to Mamma?

"Here, allow me to help," a kind, soft voice said. I didn't turn around; I squeezed my eyes shut, letting out my breath in a ragged, soggy burst; not quite tears, though. Then I felt hands— Mr. Dodgson's hands—upon my back. First one button. Then the next. He carefully—awkwardly—undid all my buttons from the top down, and as the bodice of my dress fell away, I felt the cool breeze tickle my shoulders, working its way down to my waist. Mixed with that breeze was warm, steady breath, and the combination made me shiver.

"Are you cold?" He sounded worried.

"N-no," I lied.

"You'll be in the sun soon enough."

"I know."

My dress was unbuttoned; I started to wriggle out of it but somehow became tangled up in the hem. Mr. Dodgson steadied me, his hands upon my shoulders; his hands felt both warm and cold at the same time. They felt different; they felt—

Bare. He had removed his gloves.

My mouth was dry, for some reason. I wished I had some lemonade. Or tea.

"Here, let's get you out of the rest," Mr. Dodgson said, his voice still very soft and patient. His hands, though, were not. They trembled, and twisting around I saw, as he unfastened my top petticoat, that they were stained, black on the fingertips; I hoped they wouldn't stain my petticoats as well.

"Is that why you always wear gloves?" I tried to ignore whatever it was that was worrying me; it was too vague, at any rate, to name. I did want to know the answer to my question, though, even as I realized, too late, that it might not be polite to ask.

"N-no, not really. It's from the chemicals," he explained, turning me around so that I faced him. And now that I could see him, see his kind, sad face with the soft cheeks, long eyelashes, as long as any girl's, I forgot the worry that had sat, uneasily, in the pit of my stomach. I was eager to help; we got my petticoats off in a flash, and it didn't appear to me that he had left his dirty fingerprints upon them. I pulled my chemise over my head.

He did look away then, passing his hand over his eyes as if he had a headache. Quickly, I tugged the gypsy dress down over my shoulders; its folds were thin and worn, soft as a caress against my skin.

"It's so torn!" It was; it hung over my shoulder in strips; most of my arm was bare. It was also quite short, scarcely covering my knees.

"Let's fix it," Mr. Dodgson said, starting to pull at the fabric with his clumsy, stained fingers. Suddenly, however, he dropped his hands, stood up, and told me, quite sharply, to rumple it myself. Then he went back round the front of the tent, to the camera.

I followed, tugging on the dress, but something did not feel quite right. Should I tear the dress further? Rub dirt in it? I didn't feel as unkempt as I had hoped; I still felt like myself. Like Alice.

"Oh, my shoes!" I realized. I sat down upon the grass, for once not mindful of stains; the ground was cool and damp against the back of my thighs, as the dress did not offer much protection. I removed my stockings and shoes, tossing them away in a heap. Then I jumped up, and I felt the dirt, the tickling grass, the hard little pebbles digging into the bottoms of my tender feet, and I wiggled my toes.

"It's wonderful!" I looked up at Mr. Dodgson. He was leaning on his camera, gazing at me, one of his sad, serious smiles on his lips. I felt my skin—my naked, vulnerable skin—warm under his gaze. "How do I look?"

"Like a gypsy girl. Like a wild little beggar girl. Go on—run about, run all you want, roll if you want. I know you want to!"

"Oh, I do, I do!" And I did; I jumped about, kicking at branches on the ground—they slapped at my toes, stinging a little; holding on to the trunk, I ran around a tree, rubbing against it, feeling it rough against my arms, tearing at my dress. I ran and ran, round and round, delighting in the freedom—I could lift my legs as high as I wished, for there were no petticoats holding them down; I could run as fast as I desired, too, because my dress was not tight against my waist. I could breathe freely, deeply.

Finally, I rolled. I rolled in the grass, like a wild creature. I rolled, every leaf, every twig sticking to my dress, my hair, and when I stood up I was so dizzy I fell right back down again. I did not care. Best of all, no one was there to tell me, "Alice, don't get dirty." "Alice, don't tear your dress." "Alice, don't lose your gloves."

Only Mr. Dodgson was there, watching me, always watching me, looking quite as if he wished he could roll on the ground with me, but that was too silly to contemplate. He smiled, and asked nothing of me other than that I enjoy this moment. And that he be allowed to share it with me.

"Do I look wild enough?" I shouted, digging up a handful of dirt and crumbling it between my fingers.

"Quite. Almost too wild—we'll have to get those leaves out of your hair."

"Oh!" I jumped up again, and started shaking my head. I was grateful, for once, that it was short and simple. I could scarcely imagine how difficult it would be to comb leaves and twigs out of Edith's mass of hair; it would take days, even using one of the stableboy's hay forks as a comb.

"You missed one." Mr. Dodgson pulled me close, bending down, brushing at my wispy hair. His hand—his dry, bare hand—lingered at my temple, and I closed my eyes and leaned into it. I was out of breath and content to rest in the palm of his hand. I believe he was content, too, for when I opened my eyes he was smiling, and while it was dreamy, it wasn't sad. His eyes, deep blue, brighter than usual, turned up at the edges for once. We stayed that way; somehow our breaths started to match until a bird flew overhead, throwing a shadow across us.

"The light will be going soon," Mr. Dodgson said then, looking up at the sky. "Are you ready, gypsy girl?"

"Yes, kind gentleman. The gypsy girl will pose for you now."

"Excellent. Why don't you stand in the corner, then—up on that ledge, see? Can you balance on it?"

"Yes." I did so, although the ledge was cold and a bit slippery, and I had to curl my toes around it.

"Now. Why don't you hold your hands out, in front of you—both of them?"

"Like this?" I turned my palms up and out, just like the poor urchins I'd seen in the streets, the last time we'd been up to London. There had been so many of them, so pale and thin and dirty, but Mamma had said we weren't to feel sorry for them. They knew their place.

I could not understand her meaning. Perhaps they knew their place, but they obviously weren't very content with it. Why else did some of them beg to be taken home with us?

"Yes, that's good. Can you hold that?"

I nodded.

"I'll just prepare the plate." He disappeared inside the tent once more; I stifled a yawn. Rolling on the ground was awfully tiring; so, too, was posing.

Mr. Dodgson returned, forcing the plate holder into the camera. Instead of hurrying to expose it, however, he walked over to me, moving my hands up, pulling one side of the dress down. He smoothed my hair, plucked another leaf out of it, then walked backward—very slowly—toward the camera. He did not take his eyes off me.

85

"Lower your head a trifle, Alice, then look up. Look up at me."

I did so.

"No, only your eyes—look at me with your eyes, Alice. Look only at me."

His voice sounded strange, thick and unsure. I looked up, keeping my head lowered, using only my eyes, waiting for him to remove the lens cover and count.

Only he did not.

"I dr-dreamed of you, Alice," he said, standing next to the camera, his arms hanging stiffly by his sides, his white shirt rumpled, his face flushed with strange emotion. "I dreamed of you this way. Do you dream, Alice?"

I looked at him, unsure what to do. Did he desire me to move or answer? If I did, I'd spoil the photograph. Yet he looked so strange, so lost, as if he had forgotten the camera was even there.

"Y-yes, I do," I answered slowly, trying to keep my head from moving.

"What do you dream?"

"I don't remember, not usually. Sometimes I dream of animals, or birthdays. I don't really remember."

"I dream when I'm awake sometimes," he continued, still not moving toward the camera; holding me upright through the power of his gaze. "I rarely dream at night. But during the day, sometimes—I get headaches, Alice. I d-don't tell people that. But I do."

"I'm terribly sorry."

"Don't be. I'm not, because of the dreams I get, beforehand. Do you know what I dream of?"

"No," I whispered. I was afraid to move; I was afraid not to.

"I dream of you," Mr. Dodgson whispered back. "Of Alice. Wild and charming and ever young, yet also old. I dream of you as you are—and you as you would like to be. As I would like you to be."

"Which am I now?" I tried very hard to understand what he meant, but his words *would* turn and twist, allowing me no clear path to follow.

"You're who you want to be. You always are."

"Mayn't I just be the gypsy girl now, please?" My legs were on the verge of trembling from holding the same position for so long; my shoulders wanted to twitch; every part of me desired to move. It was getting colder by the minute, and there was nothing between me and the brisk autumn air.

Finally Mr. Dodgson remembered the camera. He gave a little start, shook his head—which worried me, because I didn't want him to get one of his headaches—and looked at me again, but he only looked at the *outside* me. The position of my hands, the turn of my head. He did not, this time, see something else; *someone* else.

"Good, good. Look at me."

I did, and was relieved to see that he looked as usual. He removed the lens cover, made an amusing face at me, daring me not to laugh, and began to count, although just in the regular way.

"Forty-three, forty-four, forty-five. There!" He replaced the cover, removed the holder, and darted back under the tent without even a backward glance.

I slid off the ledge—the arch of my foot ached—and looked around. After the strange closeness of the last few minutes—it was almost as if Mr. Dodgson and I had been the only two people alive in the entire world—I felt abandoned. A sad little gypsy girl, left behind to fend for herself—how tragic! How unfair life was to wretched little girls forced to beg in the streets, at the mercy of gentlemen, kind gentlemen, but perhaps not so kind ones; for the first time, I wondered if some gentlemen might not be as understanding as Mr. Dodgson, which only made me miss him more. Even though he was merely a few feet away, I felt something gigantic, like an ocean or a universe, separated us. I wondered if we'd ever be that close again.

So bereft did I feel that when he emerged with the plate holder in his hand to pose me once more, I laughed out loud, a laugh of pure happiness. It must have been contagious, for he began to giggle as well; he threw his head back and laughed at the sky, a hearty laugh I'd never heard from him before. It sounded full and satisfied, as if it originated from someplace deep inside. We were both laughing, although neither of us could have voiced just why, when all of a sudden Ina was before us. Face pinched, hands trembling, eyes ablaze.

"Where have you been, Alice?" Her voice was high and strained; it sounded as if she was trying not to cry. "I've been looking all over for you."

"I stole her," Mr. Dodgson said with a smile for Ina, a conspiratorial wink for me. "I kidnapped her."

"You?" Now I believed she *was* going to cry; she blinked her eyes, over and over, and took a step back, just as Mr. Dodgson turned to greet her.

"I'm afraid so. It was such a lovely day, I sent round a note this morning."

"Just for Alice?" Ina managed to smooth her face, turning a deceptively placid gaze toward him.

"Yes, you see—I knew you would be such a help to your mother today, so I couldn't possibly have been so selfish as to send for you. How is she, may I ask?" He smiled at her, so unruffled; I had to admire him. I knew I couldn't have manufactured such a smashing lie on such short notice. I hadn't imagined him to be capable of deception; today had been a revelation, in so many ways.

"She—she's doing well, and we have a baby

sister named Rhoda, which is why I was looking for Alice."

Another sister! I already had two; I couldn't begin to think what I would do with another one. I didn't mind brothers so much; I hardly ever saw Harry anymore, but when he was home, Mamma and Papa were always so happy it was like having a holiday every day. Another sister was tremendously disappointing; I couldn't suppress a sigh.

"That's wonderful," Mr. Dodgson said. Ina simply shrugged, then turned back to me, snub little nose in the air, as if I smelled as distasteful as I must have looked to her.

"Alice, what on earth are you wearing?"

"Doesn't she look marvelous?" Mr. Dodgson said, before I could open my mouth. "I had an idea for an unusual photograph, as you can see, and Alice has been most cooperative."

They stood side by side, close but not together, and looked at me. Almost naked in my torn dress, I felt exposed, betrayed—and then, suddenly, alarmingly, powerful. It was I they were looking for; it was I they were looking at; it was I, clad in nothing but rags, whom Mr. Dodgson had dreamed of.

Not Ina.

Suddenly I was proud, I was defiant, I was *sure*. Sure that it was I who drew Mr. Dodgson to our house, time and time again, causing people to gossip, Mamma to fret, Pricks to sigh and be ridiculous—Ina to pale and quiver and act so maddeningly.

Ina was sure, too. Perhaps I should have been afraid of that, but right then, wild and powerful and *victorious,* I was not. I placed my hand on my hip, held my hand out—the little gypsy girl who wasn't to be pitied, after all.

"Hold it," Mr. Dodgson breathed, as he ran to the camera and shoved in the plate holder. "Don't move—that's perfect!"

I wouldn't; I couldn't. For I was looking right at Ina, standing next to Mr. Dodgson. Looking at her face, mouth open, face pale, eyes red-rimmed, entire body quivering. She stared at him; she stared at me. Storing it all away, she didn't utter a word.

Neither did I. I didn't have to. I had won.

"Forty-five," Mr. Dodgson said, and replaced the lens cover with a loud snap—happily unaware that he was the prize.

"I won't forget this, Alice," Ina hissed, blinking her eyes furiously, as he disappeared inside the dark tent. "I'm still older than you. You're only a child, after all. I'll make him see."

"He already does see," I shot back, understanding more than Ina, for once.

I held my breath as Mr. Dodgson packed away the glass plates, for they were fragile; I did not want the evidence of this day to crack or break or vanish in any way. I wanted to live on, always, as the beggar girl, *his* gypsy child, wild and knowing and triumphant.

What I did not understand, despite all my newly acquired wisdom, was that others might not see me—might not *want* to see me—that way, too.

Chapter 4

*A*S WISE AS I WAS AT AGE SEVEN, IT WAS nothing compared to how very much I knew as I passed eight, then nine; ten, then eleven.

At eight, I began dancing lessons, organized by Mamma with a few other Oxford children whom we weren't encouraged to otherwise befriend. However, learning to dance a quadrille would have been impossible with just the three of us.

At that age I also realized that even though spinsters were supposed to be treated kindly, in actuality everyone talked about them behind their backs and complained about how much money it cost to support them.

At nine, I began to learn French, courtesy of a plump don of languages who favored mauve vests and insisted upon kissing us on both cheeks, even though he always reeked of sardines.

It was around this age, too, when I discovered that it was useless to try to convince governesses that even if "little girls can catch more flies with honey than with vinegar," the truth is one can catch the most flies with horse manure.

Governesses, I was learning, were not concerned with practicalities.

At ten, I was started on Latin, taught by a don who was as musty and ancient as the language he taught; when he opened his mouth, I always expected to see cobwebs and dust come flying out.

I also realized, at ten, that somehow there was always a "servant problem." If only to provide ladies of a certain class a topic of conversation on which to agree.

At eleven—the age at which I started to learn domestic arts so that someday I might have a "servant problem" of my very own—I finally understood what Mr. Ruskin had meant that day in Mamma's parlor, when he said "perception is reality."

For Ina's perception became my reality. The one thing I had still to learn was that it could become other people's as well.

Yet before there was reality, there was Wonderland.

Those years, those growing, learning years, I was blossoming and blooming under the sunshine of Mr. Dodgson's faithful presence. What had happened that day in the garden was always with me; it was always with us. In his letters, occasionally he referred to me as his "wild gypsy girl." He also sometimes asked if I remembered how it felt to roll about on the grass.

I did remember, but I could not talk about it

with anyone, and I did not know how to discuss it in letters. Every time I tried, it always sounded too ridiculous—*Dear Mr. Dodgson, Of course I remember the feel of the grass against my back, while you watched.*

Then I would become confused. Why had he been watching? At the time, it seemed perfectly natural. The words on the page, however—there was nothing natural about them. They were unsettling, and had nothing to do with the Mr. Dodgson I knew or the happy, carefree moment we had shared.

Nervously would I cross the words out, crumple the notepaper, finally toss it in the fire, for I didn't want anyone to see. Because if I didn't quite understand what had happened, how could anyone else? So I would compose another—less candid—letter, merely asking how his headaches were, feeling as if I were letting him down.

I did not ask him if he continued to dream.

Even though he referred, often, to that day in his letters, he did not show me the photograph. I longed to see it; I longed to have evidence that once, I truly was a wild child. As time went on and my garments grew more confining, my skirts longer, I knew there would come a day when I would not be able to remember how the air felt on my bare shoulders, the grass between my tender toes. I felt that if I could only see it—see me—I would never lose those memories.

He neglected to show it to me; I do not know if it was because he assumed I might not be interested, or if there was some other, more complicated reason. Although I told myself there was nothing to fear—it was silly old Mr. Dodgson, for heaven's sake—I could not bring myself to ask.

It would be years before I saw it. By then, it was in someone else's possession.

Ina never once referred to that day. She simply waited, with a patience I had to admire, then pity—and finally fear. For I could sense her resentment simmering, like an ominous teakettle. I tried, so many times, to cause it to boil over, but it simmered on, until I was in danger of forgetting it altogether.

Meanwhile our outings continued, whenever we weren't needed in the schoolroom or he in the lecture hall. It is strange to recall how little we knew—or cared—about Mr. Dodgson's life away from us. It's as if it simply didn't exist. Naturally, we would see him at ceremonies and at chapel, in his black robes like all the other dons; spying him in a crowd never ceased to give me a little thrill of possession. He may have been part of the greater world, but he didn't quite belong. He only belonged—he only made sense—with us; with me.

For while Mr. Dodgson did not again single me out as he did that day in the garden—on the contrary, he was very careful to include Ina and

Edith, always, in our fun—I knew that I remained the reason he showed up, time and time again, at the front door of the Deanery. I knew by the way he smiled at me—or rather by the way, sometimes, that he did not smile when he looked at me. Moments when he appeared almost to be too sad in my presence; moments when he would pause in the middle of a story, Ina and Edith frowning up at him with impatience, and look at me, and lose the thread of the tale, stammering more than usual, his odd, uneven eyes clouded over with a dream, I knew. A dream of me.

No one else ever made him forget a story. No one else ever inspired one, either. It was on one of our rowing expeditions that he first told us the story of a little girl named Alice.

That day began like so many others; really, there was no reason to hold it special in my memory, except for all that came after. So I have often wondered if I do remember that one particular day or if my memory has conjured up a composite of all of them. I suppose I'll never know for sure. At any rate, if the day that comes to mind is indeed the "golden afternoon" so often remarked upon, it began in this way:

Mr. Dodgson sent Mamma a note asking if the three of us could accompany him and Mr. Duckworth on a boating excursion up the Isis to one of our favorite picnic spots, Godstow.

Godstow was a favorite because it was within

easy distance for two men who endeavored to teach three little girls the finer points of rowing. (Although Mr. Duckworth, who had proven to be great fun, a tireless singer, and a welcome, if infrequent, addition to our little group, was rather less patient than Mr. Dodgson. He tended to sigh a lot whenever one of us lost an oar.)

Godstow also had a lovely, wild low meadow full of all sorts of animals—cows and ponies and swans and geese—and gently sloping riverbanks dotted with haystacks. Nearby were the falling stone ruins of an old nunnery, where we girls liked to play even though Pricks always insisted it was haunted. Naturally, this only enhanced its appeal.

"Not again," Mamma said, frowning at the note. She was thinner than ever, for we hadn't had a baby in quite some time. And Mamma did look very handsome when she wasn't fat; she had lovely high coloring with shiny black hair and very strong features, almost like a painting of a Spanish empress. "Didn't you girls go rowing with him just a fortnight ago?"

"It was a month ago, Mamma," Ina said sweetly, if not entirely truthfully. It had been a fortnight, but fortunately when it came to unofficially sanctioned amusements, Mamma could be vague. She could remember the date and time of every party, every dinner or dance, as well as every single wardrobe detail, not just for herself but for all of us. Yet she sometimes paid only the haziest attention to what we children did out of the public eye. I understood. She was awfully busy, and what else had Pricks to do but be in charge of us? I couldn't see that she had any useful purpose, otherwise.

"A month, you say?" Mamma raised an eyebrow at Ina, who simply nodded, her eyes wide and innocent. I sucked in my breath and bit my lip, but however tempted, I was not about to tattle on her. Not this time, anyway.

"Well," Mamma continued, walking over to the drawing room window, which looked out upon the garden. Even so, the heavy brown velvet drapes scarcely admitted any sun. "The weather is lovely, and I do approve of Mr. Duckworth, even if he is at Trinity instead of Christ Church. Dean Liddell says he has excellent prospects, and may recommend him for a position in the Royal household; one of the princes needs a tutor." She gave the tasseled cord that summoned the servants a decisive tug.

"Yes, madam?" A Mary Ann appeared in the doorway with a curtsy.

"Bring me Miss Prickett," Mamma commanded.

"Mamma, does she have to go?" Ina ran her finger along the top of a polished mahogany armchair, her eyes downcast, a pretty smile playing upon her lips.

"Why do you ask?"

"It's simply that she hasn't looked very well

lately, and I don't suppose a day in the hot sun would be the best thing for her, do you?"

"What do you mean, she hasn't looked well?" Mamma turned to me. While I had little desire to aid my sister in her deception, I had even less to defend Pricks.

"Ina's right, Mamma. Pricks looks poorly, and I—I think she fainted after dinner the other evening."

"Fainted? Governesses do not faint. I'll not hear of it. Miss Prickett!"

Pricks, who was standing in the doorway in another one of her ugly dresses—even at ten, I knew that mustard yellow plaid didn't flatter a mottled complexion—looked startled. "Yes, madam?"

"Did you or did you not faint after dinner the other evening?"

"What—no, no, madam, not at all. I've never fainted!"

"Alice said you did."

"I said I thought she did," I corrected her. "I didn't say I saw her."

"All the same, the prevailing wisdom is that you fainted. May I ask why?"

"Madam, I did not." Pricks looked my mother in the eye firmly but politely.

"Hmmph." Mamma walked over to her, looking her up and down, almost sniffing her, like a hunting dog. "I do think you look frightful. So it's settled. The girls are going out rowing with Mr. Dodgson and Mr. Duckworth—the note specifically said there was room for only five in the boat, in any event. So be grateful that you have the afternoon off. I'll ask Cook to send you up a tray for dinner, so you shan't be disturbed."

"But I—"

"Thank you, Miss Prickett." Mamma turned her back on her. Pricks had no choice but to curtsy, her face flushed, her nostrils wide and quivering; in that moment she resembled, alarmingly, Tommy, my speckled pony. She turned to go, but not without one last, lingering glare at me, which I was happy to return.

I did despise servants so. Except for Cook, and Bultitude, the stableboy, and Phoebe. Also, the Mary Ann from the kitchen, as she sometimes snuck us up sugar cubes from the tea table, the ones with the candied flower petals on them that Mamma saved for only her special guests.

"All right, girls, do run up and get your parasols. And have Phoebe find you fresh gloves. Edith, remember to bring a pocket handkerchief —you tend to sniffle when out of doors."

Edith—who did sniffle, quite a lot during the summer and early fall, especially—merely nodded, obediently following Ina and me upstairs.

"Why didn't you want Pricks to come with us?" I asked Ina. We were united, for once, in a shared emotion, and I was more happy than I would have predicted; it had been so long since she had acted like one of us. To be quite honest, there were times lately when I missed her, even though physically, she was never far away.

"What do you mean?" Ina held her skirts up as she ascended the stairs, which was absurd; while they were longer, her skirts still did not touch the ground.

"Well, *I* didn't want her to spoil our fun by acting silly and making Mr. Dodgson wait on her hand and foot. That's why I said she fainted. Why did you?"

"I'm afraid I don't understand, Alice. I was truly worried, for I don't think she looks at all well." Ina shook her head with one of her new world-weary sighs. (I had caught her practicing them one afternoon in front of a looking glass, along with an entire repertoire of ladylike attitudes and poses.)

"But you don't give a fig about Pricks!"

"Alice, my dear child. When will you realize that I'm no longer interested in your infantile dislike of poor Pricks?"

My hand itched to reach out and yank one of her long curls. I told myself, sternly, that it wouldn't do any good, she would only yelp, and I'd most certainly get in trouble and not be able to go rowing.

I did it anyway. It was as if my hand had a mind of its own, for it raced out, grabbed one of her brown curls, and tugged, quite hard; her head snapped back.

"Ow! Alice! What the devil?" She spun around, eyes blazing, cheeks red.

"You stuck-up! That's not why you didn't want Pricks to go, and you know it. Why do you have to be so fake all the time? And make me feel so —so—stupid, for thinking that we were playing the same game—"

"What game, Alice? Unlike you, I'm too old for games. I have no idea what you're talking about, except for the fact that it's nonsense, as usual." Infuriatingly, she turned and calmly proceeded upstairs, pausing, just once, to slowly, dramatically massage the back of her head.

Why wouldn't she say anything? Why wouldn't she fight with me; why did she no longer *recognize* me as a worthy opponent? I knew she didn't want to share Mr. Dodgson with Pricks any more than I did, but she refused to acknowledge that we had any mutual feeling, any ideas at all, concerning him, concerning anything. I was too young to understand. That's what she thought; that's what she said all the time.

Didn't she remember I had already won, that day in the garden? It had been almost three years ago; did I need to remind her?

When I was thirteen, I vowed, seething as I stomped up the stairs—Edith trailing along, sniffling already—I would not be so cruel. I would not tell Edith she was too young to understand anything. I wasn't certain, however, about Rhoda. I suspected she might always be too young for me, as she still took naps.

We received our parasols and gloves from Phoebe; Rhoda trailed along in her short dress, with her fat little legs and arms, clutching at Phoebe's skirts whenever she stood still.

"I'll be so happy to have my own room," Ina said with a dreamy sigh, looking around the bright, whitewashed nursery. It was the cheeriest room in the house, I always thought, for here the windows were simply hung with starched yellow curtains, the floors bare except for a few braided rugs, the furniture comfortable and useful, not stiff and ornamental. "Mamma and I have already spoken about it. You children can remain in the nursery. She's making over one of the guest rooms for my boudoir."

"It appears to me," I said, a wonderful notion tickling my lips, turning them into a very mischievous smile indeed. "It appears to me that you're getting far too old, then, to play with Mr. Dodgson. If you're not careful, people will talk, just as they did with Pricks."

Ina turned to me, slowly, as she concentrated on buttoning up her left glove. She would not look at me, a tactic I was beginning to recognize as one she used whenever she most wanted to make a point. "I wouldn't be so concerned about *my* reputation, Alice. It seems to me there are others who have far more to worry about."

"What? Who do you mean?" I forgot I was angry at her; I truly wanted to know. I was afraid I was getting to be rather like Mr. Ruskin after all.

Maddeningly, Ina refused to answer, and at that moment a Mary Ann appeared in the doorway to tell us the gentlemen had arrived. So we left Phoebe and Rhoda—Pricks was, presumably, up in her room on the top floor, plotting some awful revenge upon me—and joined Mr. Dodgson and Mr. Duckworth, who were exchanging pleasantries with Mamma in the hall. They had a lovely hamper with them, and I was most anxious to see what was in it; Mr. Dodgson always did bring the best cakes. I hoped there was one with buttercream frosting, my favorite.

"I do hope the girls aren't too much trouble," Mamma said as we made to leave. "It is very kind of you to invite them."

"It's our pl-pleasure," Mr. Dodgson stammered; his stammer was always much worse around Mamma than it was around anyone else. "We-we always have such a lovely ti-ti-ti—"

"We have such a lovely time," Mr. Duckworth said with a fond smile for his friend. I very much liked Mr. Duckworth, with his patient eyes, jolly, plump cheeks, and muttonchops; he was so kind to everyone, the type of person who sought out the odd, lonely people of the world whom everyone else forgot. I was very glad he had sought out Mr. Dodgson; I did worry about him being lonely when I wasn't around. "Your daughters are such a credit to you—they're so well mannered and delightful."

"Why, thank you." Mamma looked pleased; her eyes matched her smile.

"Shall we, ladies?" Mr. Duckworth bowed and held open the front door; we all trooped outside, the two gentlemen in their white linen suits, straw boaters on their heads instead of the usual black silk top hats, carrying the wicker hamper between them. I heard the tinkle of china jostling inside.

"How many cakes are in there, do you imagine?" Edith whispered to me, evidently not very quietly, because Mr. Dodgson laughed and told her not to worry; we'd have enough left over to feed the swans on the river, most likely.

So we proceeded through town, crossing the crowded, narrow streets until we found the clear path to the river, following it to the end, right under the arched mossy stones of Folly Bridge, to Salter's Boat House. Mr. Dodgson politely asked Ina to pick out the perfect rowboat. Naturally, she took a long time doing so, walking up and down the riverfront, making quite a production of asking the boatmen how seaworthy each one was. Finally she picked one that didn't look any different from the others, and we all climbed in; the seats were damp, and I was very glad no one had told me not to get dirty because honestly, I couldn't see that I could help it. Mr. Duckworth and Mr. Dodgson manned the oars, and they asked me to man the tiller.

"Oh!" I took the thick knotty rope that steered the creaky tiller and pulled it over my head so that I could face them. My heart beat fast with the responsibility. "I do hope I don't make the boat go in circles."

"That is a fine thing to hope indeed," said Mr. Dodgson with a smile. "But it's a much finer thing to accomplish."

I agreed that it was. Then Mr. Duckworth untied the boat and pushed it away from the dock with his oar as we headed upstream, the air hot and still, perfect weather for rowing. Even so, the gentlemen did not seem in any hurry to exert themselves; the oars dipped lazily in the muddy water with a sloppy, regular slosh. I concentrated on keeping the tiller straight and sure; my hands grew tired of pulling at the rope, but I wouldn't have said so for the world.

Ina and Edith were crammed on either side of me, our identical white skirts overlapping so that it was impossible to tell whose was whose. Mr. Duckworth was in the far seat and Mr. Dodgson directly in front of us.

"Miss Liddell, I must say you are looking far too grown-up these days," Mr. Duckworth called out. He needn't have shouted so; across the calm water, his musical voice carried perfectly well. "Isn't she, Dodgson?"

Ina sucked in her breath and sat up straighter, trying very hard not to look at Mr. Dodgson as he replied.

"Quite," he answered, rowing steadily, thoughtfully, even as his strokes matched Mr. Duckworth's. "Far too grown-up, I'm afraid, to want to accompany us foolish old men much longer. Young swains will be more to her liking, I predict."

"You're—you're not old," Ina blurted, her face red, hands trembling, even as she kept them firmly folded in her lap. "I know you're only thirty."

Mr. Dodgson raised an eyebrow, while Mr. Duckworth suppressed a smile.

"Ah, I'm very old, indeed. Duck, however, is merely twenty-eight. I'll have to act as chaperone, I suppose."

Ina shook her head, blushing even more—and looking very pretty, I had to admit. Even though we still dressed identically, her skirts were longer, and her silhouette had more curves. My sister *was* a young lady, I realized with a pang; she wasn't merely saying it to spite me. I didn't know how to feel about that; was I jealous that I was not, or was I mournful because of all the changes I knew were just ahead, for all of us? After all, Mamma was already starting to talk about young men with "potential," and while I never heard her elaborate, I knew what she meant.

For the first time, I understood that childhood would end. In my eagerness to grow and learn, I hadn't, until this very moment, realized that the result would be the termination of my world as I knew it—sleeping under the same snug roof, three narrow beds all in a row, with my sisters; riding with Papa on the paths in the Meadow in the early mornings, the only time we ever had him to ourselves; endless days adrift on a river, journeys to places wonderful in their safe familiarity—

My eyes felt wet and hot, and my heart ached with loss. While I was surrounded by those who loved me—and yes, I even included Ina in that—already, I felt their absence.

"Wake up, Alice—we're listing to starboard!" Mr. Duckworth called out.

I shook my head and tightened my grip on the tiller rope, pulling until we straightened out.

"What were you thinking about, Alice?" Mr. Dodgson asked gently. "You looked like you were dreaming."

"Oh, just—I was just thinking how very *tragic* it is that childhood must come to an end."

Mr. Duckworth must have swallowed a bug, for he coughed, almost dropping his oars. Ina clasped her hand over her mouth and giggled. Edith kicked her plump little legs against the side of the boat and asked, "How much farther?"

Mr. Dodgson, of them all, looked as if he understood. For he nodded, his eyes blue and soft; his gaze was serious and sad, as serious and sad as my own.

"Oh, Alice, you're far too young to think about things like that!" Ina removed her gloves so she could dabble her hand in the water, just like an illustration in a novel.

"Dear little Alice, don't worry so—your sister is right. You'll have plenty of time to worry about all that later." Mr. Duckworth resumed his rowing.

"Would you like to stay forever young, Alice?" Mr. Dodgson asked. "Would you like not to grow up?"

"Oh, well—yes and no." I wasn't sure how I could prevent that from happening. "I don't want to have to keep having lessons with Pricks, and be made to memorize silly poems and lessons, and always being told by Ina that I'm too young." I turned to glare at my sister as she practiced her dreamy-eyed, thoughtful expression on Mr. Dodgson. (Who, I was very glad to see, was not paying any attention at all.) "But I don't want to wear a corset, and long skirts, and not be able to leave the house unescorted, and pretend I'm not hungry when I really am, and most of all I don't want to get too big to be taken out by you," I continued, surprised by my passion—I felt my eyes tear up again as I spoke faster and faster, louder and louder. Finally I had to hide my face in my hands, forgetting about the tiller so that the boat swerved sharply toward the bank again.

"Alice, Alice—don't cry!" Mr. Dodgson sounded so alarmed. I felt his hand upon my shoulder, patting it helplessly; the hamper was between us, and we were all so tightly wedged in the boat, it was impossible for him to get closer to me than that.

"I won't." I sniffed, and Edith passed me her pocket handkerchief so I could blow my nose.

We drifted for a long minute or so. Ina pursed her lips very disapprovingly, while I dabbed at my eyes and felt my face finally cool down so that I wasn't ashamed to show it again. Another boat passed us, two young men and two young ladies —accompanied by a stern-faced chaperone looking as if she longed to be anywhere but— laughing and singing a minstrel song. Even after they rounded the bend ahead, we could still hear a strong tenor voice singing *All the world is sad and dreary, everywhere I roam.*

"Who would like a story?" Mr. Duckworth finally asked, briskly taking charge of things— picking up his oars, nudging Mr. Dodgson with his boot, nodding at me to steer us back toward the middle of the river.

"I would! I would!" Edith clapped her hands. Ina—after leaning over and hissing, "Ladies do *not* talk about corsets, Alice!"—also sat up straight, an expectant smile on her face.

"Alice?" Mr. Dodgson asked, his voice low and kind.

I nodded, afraid to look up; when I did, I was rewarded with a look of pure love. I don't know how I recognized it. Was it the same look he had given me that day in the garden, when he told me he had dreamed of me? Perhaps, but that had been such a long time ago.

I knew only that, under his gaze, I felt—beautiful. Beautiful, and free to say whatever I wanted, think whatever I wanted, for I could make no mistakes. Not in those blue eyes.

"Yes, please, do tell us a story," said I.

And so he did.

"There once was a little girl named Alice," he began.

"Oh!" I couldn't help myself. Mr. Dodgson had told us hundreds of stories, stories with people in them we recognized, even if they had nonsensical—different—names. But never before had he named a character after one of us. I smiled up at him, waiting; Ina looked down upon her lap, glaring.

"Alice was beginning to get very tired of sitting by her sister on the bank," he continued, without giving that sister a name, to my everlasting delight.

So he continued his story, of a little girl named Alice, a white rabbit—who reminded us all of Papa, right down to the pocket watch; even Ina laughed at that!—a tumble down a rabbit hole, a crazy adventure with such curious creatures—

"Curiouser and curiouser!" I shouted, as the story wound itself around in circles and curlicues and love knots.

It took the entire afternoon to row to Godstow, but none of us was in a hurry, mesmerized, as we were, by Mr. Dodgson. His thin voice, just soft enough so that we had to lean in to hear him, which only made the story more exciting, rose and fell as the tale spun itself; even Mr. Duckworth was hanging on every word.

"Dodgson, are you making this up?" he interrupted once.

Edith cried out, "Shhh! Do go on!"

Mr. Dodgson turned and nodded. "I'm afraid I am," he said, although I wasn't sure Mr. Duckworth believed him.

Astoundingly, he made the story last the entire day. Just when he would seem to trail off, running out of words, one of us would cry out for more and he would be off again. He kept talking, taking breaks only when necessary, such as when we landed at Godstow and he helped us out of the boat, tied it up, and followed us girls (hamper in tow) as we raced about, stretching our legs from the long journey. We searched for the perfect haystack—there were always huge sheltering haystacks just far enough back from the river so that the ground was dry and the bugs weren't horrid—spread a blanket, and consumed the tea and cakes from the hamper. Mr. Dodgson drank gallons of tea—he must have been parched from all his talking—but then he picked up the story exactly where he had left off, right around the caterpillar.

So we spent that golden afternoon (we did break once, so that Edith and I could climb over the ruins of the nunnery; the tumbled stones, dark corners, and musty smell always gave me a thrill, even though I never once spied a ghost). Then we packed everything up and rowed downstream, back home; the light was fading by the time we crossed Tom Quad, exhausted, starving (the cakes long gone), still hanging on Mr. Dodgson's every word. He finally came to the end, where Alice's sister woke her from her dream.

When he stopped talking, then—we were in the middle of the Quad, by the quiet fountain full of lily pads—no one said a word. We couldn't; my mind, at least, was still filled with the images of the story. Also, with a melancholy. A story—like my childhood—was so fleeting. I thought of the hundreds of stories Mr. Dodgson had told us over the years; I couldn't remember a single detail from any of them. Yet once they, too, had filled my mind with pictures, notions—with dreams.

I didn't want this story to disappear; I didn't want the day to end. I didn't want to grow up.

"Write it down," I said finally, as we were gathering ourselves to say good-bye and go inside the Deanery, with its cheerful, welcoming lantern over the front door. "Please, could you—write it down?"

"What, my Alice?" Mr. Dodgson looked confused. He also looked very, very tired. His fine, curly brown hair was more mussed than I'd ever seen it, and his lips were chapped from the sun. When he was this tired, his eyes looked even more lopsided than usual; the left one drooped more.

"The story—my story. It is mine, isn't it?"

"If you want it to be."

"Oh, I do! I do!" Just like that, I reached out and took it, so bold, so sure that it was meant for me, as sure as I had been when he told me that only I could be his gypsy girl. And no matter how much older Ina was, she could never, ever be so confident, so certain with him; I knew she hated this about herself.

"Then it's yours," Mr. Dodgson said. "So you'll never have to grow up, in a way."

"But that's what I mean!" I could scarcely believe he understood so well what was in my heart; it was only later that I realized all he had to do was look in my eyes, to see. "If you write it down, I won't grow up—ever! Of course, not truly, but in the story. I'll always be a little girl, at least there, if you write it down. Could you?"

"I don't know—I'll try, Alice. But I'm not sure I can remember it all."

"Oh yes, you can! I know you can—and if you can't, I'll help!"

114

"Alice," Ina interrupted, taking Edith's hand. "We must go. It's late. You and Edith ought to be in bed, although naturally I'll be up for hours— simply hours!"

"Indeed," Mr. Duckworth said, knocking on the front door. "It's been lovely, ladies. A most enjoyable day. I do hope to see you again soon."

One of the Mary Anns opened the door as both Mr. Duckworth and Mr. Dodgson raised their straw boaters—somewhat limp after the long day in the sun—in farewell.

"Don't forget!" I twisted around to catch one last glimpse of Mr. Dodgson.

"I won't," he said, cocking his head and looking at me with a puzzled expression, before turning to leave with Mr. Duckworth. It was an odd request, I knew; one I'd never made before. I wasn't sure if he completely understood my urgency.

The door closed behind me before I could say anything else; I felt a rising bubble of panic burble up in my chest, but I tried to swallow it. I would see Mr. Dodgson again soon, I knew. I'd remind him then.

"He won't write that silly story down," Ina grumbled as we went up the stairs—Mary Ann gave us each a candle, as it was dark already. "What a rude request. He has much better things to do with his time."

"You're simply cross because he didn't tell a story about you," I retorted, sure of that, at least.

"What do you mean? I was the sister reading the book!"

"Perhaps." I also thought she was someone else: the dreadful queen at the end, who wanted to behead everyone, although I didn't dare tell her that. "Still, he named the girl after me, not you. He'll write it down, I'm sure of it."

"And if he doesn't? What? What will happen then?" Ina turned to confront me; her face loomed large and mysterious, the candle flickering and throwing off ominous shadows. "You'll have to grow up all the same. And then you'll be too old for him, too." Her mouth quivered while her eyes grew bright—with tears, I realized; wounded tears, spilling onto her hand as she clutched the pewter candleholder.

"No, I won't. I'll never be too old for him," I said, even though I knew it would hurt her. I tried to put my arm around my sister anyway. For even if I didn't completely comprehend what she was saying—how could any of us be too old for Mr. Dodgson, when he was always going to be so very much older than us?—still, I didn't want to see her weep. Ina never wept. I couldn't recall the last time I had seen her with tears rolling down her cheeks, smudged and dusty and pink from the sun.

"Yes, you will. You'll see—you will." Ina shook my arm off and stomped up the stairs. Edith had gone on up ahead, too tired to listen to us any longer.

I shook my head. Ina couldn't possibly understand that it was different with me. I was his gypsy
girl—his Alice, brave enough to stand up to
queens and kings and an assortment of odd, talkative creatures.

I did hope he remembered to write it all down.
For I feared it was the kind of story one could
easily forget, otherwise. Already, I was having
trouble remembering exactly what the tale of the
mouse had been about.

Chapter 5

*H*E DID NOT WRITE IT ALL DOWN.

Not the first time I asked, at any rate. Nor the
second. I asked every time I saw him—and as our
boat trip had taken place just prior to us leaving
for Wales and our new house that Papa had built
right on the rocky shore, I had to content myself
with asking him in the letters I wrote, every week,
during the holiday. Then the term started, and
life became an endless round of lessons and
manners, and Mamma got fat again. (I did wish,
this time, it would be a boy.)

Finally, Mr. Dodgson told me that he had
started to write it down. He said that he had been
thinking about it all the time, fortunately, so he
hadn't forgotten any of the particulars. He said
that writing it down was quite different; he had
published a few poems and short, silly stories

before, under a different name—Lewis Carroll—but nothing like this. Even though it was supposed to be just for me, not for anyone else, he thought it would take some time. When you write things down, he explained, they sometimes take you places you hadn't planned.

His meaning wasn't clear to me, but as long as he was writing it down, I didn't bother trying to puzzle it all out. I assumed I would understand what he was talking about once I read it again; once I saw my name on a page, as a little girl having adventures in a fantastic place underground. I knew I would keep the story with me, always. I thought perhaps I might put it in my mahogany box decorated with bits of sea glass, where I kept all my favorite things—the pearl bracelet Grandmother gave me when I was born; the perfectly black, round pebble I discovered in the Meadow one day; the pink silk thread I found wound through a bird's nest that had fallen from a tree in the garden; the teaspoon the Queen had used when she and Prince Albert came to the Deanery to visit the Prince of Wales. (To be perfectly truthful, I wasn't certain it was the actual teaspoon, but I found it on the tray that had been used to clear away the tea things after she left, so it *might* be.)

They take you places you hadn't planned.

If it was true in stories, it was also true in life, and it was exactly how I felt that winter;

unmoored, discontent, waiting for something to happen, without knowing exactly what it might possibly be. Everyone—*everything*—seemed to be waiting, too distracted to act properly; fires never behaved in their grates, servants walked out the door during meals, letters were posted but never received.

My family was not exempt from the general restlessness. Ina was now fourteen, established in her own boudoir with her own maid. She was tall for her age and extremely pale; when Harry came home for the Christmas holiday he acted very uneasy around her, as if he had no idea how to treat this strange creature who once had been his little sister. Harry generally had little use for us anyway—we couldn't play cricket and weren't interested in his stories about the "fine chaps" at school—but that year the divide appeared sharper. He stayed more with Papa, because Pricks had no idea what to do with him; she acted frightened of him, now that he was taller than she.

On the surface I felt as much like myself as ever, to my great relief. For I studied myself every morning in the looking glass, anxious to see signs that I was turning into a lady, and happy to find none there. My hair was, finally, just a little bit longer, and fluffier on the ends, but still I wore the same straight black fringe across my forehead, framing my dark blue eyes. My chin remained as pointed as ever, and while I was slenderer, I was not very tall. I did not fill out my frocks like Ina did, and I was very happy about that, for it meant I was spared having to wear a corset, at least for a while longer. (Although Ina never complained about hers, for she felt the tight lacing made her face even more pale, as was the fashion.)

Yet sometimes, lying at night in the nursery, listening to Edith's steady breathing, Rhoda's soft snores, Phoebe's gentle murmurings, I did envy Ina her own room. I longed for some privacy so that I might continue to study myself, not just my physical appearance but how I reacted to certain ideas, unfamiliar longings—and I did wonder, then, if that was what it meant to be growing up.

Edith, at nearly nine, was almost as tall as I was. She was becoming the acknowledged beauty with her thick russet hair and fair complexion. But unlike Ina, she didn't seem to care about how she looked; she wore her prettiness with ease; it fell upon her with the grace of a butterfly perched on her shoulder. She was as easygoing as ever.

Mr. Dodgson never did appear to change. I was conscious of that, more than before; conscious of his age, too. I would do silly sums about it, such as: If I was five the first time we met, that meant he must have been twenty-five. But now I was ten, almost eleven, and he was just thirty-one. For some reason, the difference between thirty-one and eleven seemed much less than the difference between twenty-five and five; I wondered why that was.

Physically, though, he was as ever—perhaps he walked a bit more stiffly, but that was it. As I made special note of his age, I also made special note of his appearance, constantly measuring it against other men of my acquaintance, as if they were all in some sort of competition. Mr. Dodgson's hair, for example, stayed long and curling and softly brown; comparing him to Mr. Duckworth, whose hair had started to be a bit thin on top, I couldn't help but think that Mr. Dodgson most resembled a hero of a romance novel.

Mr. Dodgson was also as thin as ever, but no more so; *slender* was actually the word I found myself using to compare him to Mr. Ruskin, who seemed to grow stouter each time I saw him. Mr. Dodgson, I could imagine upon a white horse—an idealistic Don Quixote on Rocinante, his slender torso leaning forward as he rode bravely toward ferocious giants. Mr. Ruskin, on the other hand, I could only see as Sancho Panza, his stubby legs dangling as he sat astride a flea-bitten mule.

Mr. Dodgson's dress, as well, remained the same —recently, I had decided that his constant glove-wearing was the sign of a true, refined character—but then gentlemen's dress usually did. It was only ladies who were forever changing fashions—that winter of 1863, skirts that had been merely bell-shaped a few years before were now positively pyramid-like; so wide that only one or two ladies might easily fit in a carriage, much to the disgust of Bultitude, who had been promoted from the stable to coachman. He had to make many trips in order to fetch ladies to and from parties.

Still, what I most remember about that winter was that Mamma was not at all well; I knew by now that babies somehow came from their mothers' bodies, which was why with every one she got so fat. Usually, though, she continued her activities almost until the very moment the baby arrived. Not this time; she stayed in her room for days, reclining on a chaise longue near the fire, very ashen, her hair dull and flat. While this naturally cast a pall over the household—it was surprising how much we relied upon her energy and decisiveness; without them, we appeared simply to list about, waiting to be told what to do—there was one benefit.

Mamma suddenly wanted to spend time with me.

I don't know why she singled me out. Of course she watched Ina carefully, as best she could from her dressing room; Ina was entering into the "dangerous years," Mamma told me: the years that would decide her future, for better or for worse, and Mamma was determined that it be the former.

While Edith was always a steadying, calming presence, needing nothing more than to be loved and cared for, it was, surprisingly, to me that Mamma turned whenever she wanted to talk, which was quite often. It occurred to me even then that there was a shadow across her thoughts about the coming confinement. She had already borne six children; did she feel the odds were no longer on her side?

At any rate, she often asked Pricks to send me down—even in the middle of lessons—to sit with her. I generally brought a book with me, although she had so many in her room, which was very unusual for the time. We had a great library, naturally, but Mamma said she liked to keep her favorite books near her. They comforted her, she said. I had never before imagined that Mamma might need comfort.

On one of these afternoons—it was gray, and sleet pounded the windows with a dull percussion—we talked of the future. The fire was burning brightly—Mamma was proud of the fact that the Deanery was always warm, no matter the season; she did not skimp on coal—and she reclined heavily beneath a red wool afghan, scarcely stirring, as it made her ill to move her head. She stared moodily into the fire as sparks danced on the hearth, and I wondered what she saw in them.

"Mamma?"

"Yes?"

"What are you thinking of?"

"Oh, so many things. There seem to be so many things left to do."

"Like what? Didn't Ina order dinner, as you told her to? I could go talk to Cook, if you wish."

"No." She smiled, a gentle smile, the smile she showed only to the family, and then rarely. "I didn't mean practical things. I forgot how literal you sometimes are."

"I'm sorry."

"Don't be, dear. Don't worry so much about all of us. You'll get a permanent frown—see how you look right now?" She motioned for me to go look in the mirror on her rosewood dressing table; I did, and saw that, indeed, I did have a faint V between my eyes.

I returned to the low velvet stool where I always sat, next to her. There was also a small marble-topped table that was full of the things she needed and wanted—a white etched-glass table lamp burning bright with oil, handkerchiefs, a carafe full of water, a magnifying glass keeping her place in a book (she said her eyes hurt sometimes), a silver bell to summon her maid, a smoky brown bottle of medicine drops.

"No, Alice." Mamma motioned toward the carafe; I poured her a small glass of water, careful not to spill. "I was thinking about the future. Yours, and Ina's, and Edith's, particularly. You're getting to be young ladies now—Ina already is. But so will you be, soon."

"Not too soon," said I, thinking—hoping—that if I kept saying it, it would be true.

"Before you know it," Mamma insisted, sipping the water, placing the glass on the table. She leaned back against her pillows and closed her eyes for a moment. "Oh, this one is different."

"This one what?"

"This child." She indicated her swollen stomach; the rest of her was so thin, while her stomach continued to grow. It seemed unnatural to me, as if there were a monster inside her, feeding off her flesh.

"I'm sorry, Mamma."

"Alice," she said with a drowsy smile. Then she opened her eyes, fixing me with a surprisingly fierce gaze. "You'll marry well," she whispered. "You will. It's your right—I've worked so hard for you girls."

"Please don't worry yourself—shall I ring for Yvonne?" Yvonne was her maid.

"No, no." She waved her hand impatiently, fretfully, as Rhoda sometimes did when she was too stubborn to nap. "You need to hear this, Alice. I'm relying on you—you have sense, child. I can see that. Despite your faults, you have a fine mind. You don't get distracted, like Edith, and you don't convince yourself that there are hidden meanings behind every single word, like Ina."

I was flattered but troubled. Normally I would

have longed to hear Mamma praise me—but not in this fevered, desperate way.

"Perhaps you should wait until you're better, and then you can tell me—"

"No, there may not be—there's no point in procrastinating, Alice. You always are one for that."

"I know." I sighed, happy to have her find fault with me again, wondering at the topsy-turvy nature of a world in which I would find my mother's disapproval to be a comfort.

"You need to ensure your sisters and you marry well. Good men, from fine families—but don't settle. You're worth something, all three of you. Never forget that. I've brought you up to be at home with kings and queens. I don't want you wasting yourselves on common men."

"Good men—like Papa?"

"Well, yes." She smiled. "Your father is a good man, and see what he has accomplished? There's none his superior at Oxford."

"What—what makes a man good, like Papa? Why did you—what made you want to marry him?"

"His excellent family, his established academic credentials, his unlimited potential." Mamma rattled the answer off so quickly, I wondered if she'd been made to memorize it. Then she smiled again, her eyes soft and thoughtful. "Of course, I loved him."

"He is older than you." I was very much concerned with age lately. For example, I knew that the Prince of Wales was only three years older than his betrothed.

"Yes, he's fifteen years my senior. Almost old enough." Mamma raised an ironic eyebrow.

"What do you mean?"

"Men need more time, Alice. They don't mature as fast as we do. An older man is an excellent match."

"Really? Perhaps—perhaps someone twenty years older?"

"Perhaps."

"How did you know you loved Papa? Did he tell you?"

"Merciful heavens, no! Men never know their own mind—we have to make it up for them. No, child, *I* told *him,* although of course, not until we were properly engaged. But I let him know, before. There are ways; you'll see. Pray remember, Alice—love isn't all. There is family, and education, and potential. Also property, of course."

"Oh." I wasn't sure what she meant; everyone I knew had some sort of property. Except servants, naturally.

"As well, there must be a—a mutual feeling, I suppose. That's the proper way to put it, a mutual feeling of respect, and kindness, and sympathy."

"Kindness and sympathy?"

"Yes. You'll know it—you'll see it in his eyes."

My heart beat fast, my face felt warm as I remembered eyes. Deep blue eyes, eyes that followed me wherever I went; I felt them on me even when I was alone. Especially—especially at night, while my sisters slept and I lay awake, on my back. In the nothingness of my cotton nightgown, not unlike a thin gypsy girl's frock.

I shook my head. I was not so watchful these days; thoughts could surprise me, shock me. I had no idea where they even came from, yet I felt perfectly capable of following them on my own.

"Poor Bertie," Mamma murmured.

"Who?"

"The Prince of Wales," she said. I relaxed, eager to think of someone else, for I suspected my own thoughts were dangerous even as I could not say precisely why.

"Why is he poor?"

"Because royalty never marries for love. Not that that's everything, of course—and I can't say that I approve of it being the only reason. But I know Bertie—he gave your father many a nightmare while he was in residence. He'll never be happy with a sweet little princess, no matter how beautiful."

"She is, isn't she?" I had admired the artist's picture of Princess Alexandra in the newspaper. She was stunning, with dark hair and beautiful big eyes and the tiniest waist I'd ever seen.

"Yes, but that won't be enough to keep Bertie in

tow. But that's not our problem, is it? The poor Queen—still in mourning."

I remembered when Prince Albert had died, more than a year ago. Mamma ordered the seamstress to make us up several winter dresses, either black or gray edged in black. I was very happy when we didn't have to wear them any longer.

"Mamma, how much property, exactly, must a gentleman own to be suitable?" I glanced over at my mother, prepared to do another sum. But her eyes were closed again, and she was breathing steadily.

Slowly rising—careful not to knock a thing over on the table with my wide sleeves—I bent down and kissed her on the forehead; it was clammy, so I blew on it, wishing I could dispel her troubled thoughts, as well. Then I walked over to the window and pulled the heavy brocaded drapes even tighter, trying to drown out the relentless drumming of the sleet.

As I did, I looked across the garden, toward the Old Library with its crooked roof and small windows, where Mr. Dodgson lived. I thought of the Prince of Wales, about to be wed.

It seemed to me—for I was caught up in the wedding fever, too, though I wouldn't admit it; an illustration of the Prince and his fiancée was currently folded under my pillow, where no one could see—that love was in the very air these days. Perhaps that was what we were waiting for, after all. It blew the bare limbs of the trees; it warmed the stones in the Quad on sunny days. I wanted to believe that happily-ever-after was possible, and not only in fairy tales or stories. Although not in the stories that Mr. Dodgson told—I realized, just then, that his stories were almost always remarkable for their lack of sentiment. Why was that? Did he need someone to—to *inspire* him, perhaps?

But surely, a storyteller like himself had to believe in happily-ever-after, deep down in his soul. Maybe he could put it into the end of *my* story; I blushed to call it that, but I did. Not out loud but in the quiet places of my heart. Perhaps it wasn't too late; after all, he hadn't written it down.

There was still time to change it, I believed; all I had to do was ask, for he had never denied me anything. Alice could be a tall, pale maiden with short black hair, a faint worried expression. She could walk into the sunset hand in hand with a tall, *slender* man with blue eyes, curling light brown hair, and they would live happily ever after, just like the Prince and Princess of Wales. Despite what Mamma said, I wanted to believe that they were very much in love. For if princes and princesses couldn't live a fairy tale, what hope did the rest of us have?

Did I see a light burning in a window across the garden? A light in rooms I had visited so many times, only to think of doing so again made my stomach tremble, my mouth grow dry, my head spin with notions of fairy tales and princes and love and good men? I shut the drapes quickly and turned to go—as if the creatures of the night could see me and read my thoughts.

As I did, I tiptoed past Mamma, the red afghan rising up and down steadily as she slept. I paused, just once, to look at her and guess at the dreams that mothers dreamed—

Wondering if happily-ever-after meant the same thing to them as it did to us.

ON MARCH 10, the Prince and Princess of Wales were wed. There was an explosion of celebrations in Oxford; Mamma was too ill to mind that she could not host any of them, and this malaise troubled me more than the strange confidences we had shared.

Still, she managed to dictate what Ina, Edith, and I were to wear at our one official obligation. We each planted a tree in honor of the marriage; mine was planted in memory of Prince Albert, and I gave a brief speech (which, according to Ina, no one heard, as my voice never rose above a whisper). After, we strolled through the narrow streets of Oxford with Papa and Grandmother Reeve, who was visiting to help Mamma, and we admired all the festivities—the bazaars and lawn games and dancing and music everywhere. I'd never seen so many musicians, many of them in military uniform, with faces to match the scarlet of their coats as they puffed away at their brass instruments. It was chilly despite the sun, but nobody appeared to mind, as there were bonfires on every corner, tended gaily by sweeps and ragmen wearing their very finest, shiniest black frock coats, top hats merrily askew.

Ina was not in a good mood, despite the infectious gaiety around her—strangers clasped hands in the streets, and young men boldly attempted to kiss young women, to Grandmother's audible horror. For Mamma was permitting me to stay up for the fireworks and illuminations that evening; not only permitting me but allowing me to invite whomever I wished to accompany me. Without hesitation, I invited Mr. Dodgson.

"You're much too grown-up to be out at night unchaperoned," Mamma had told Ina that morning—very crossly, as the baby was only a few weeks away. "Why on earth do you care if Alice goes?"

"Because I do want to see the illuminations! It's so romantic!" Ina flounced about the room; I held my breath as her skirts brushed Mamma's marble table, almost knocking over the carafe.

"Ina, do be quiet." Mamma looked as if she was about to be ill; she pressed her lips together and closed her eyes. Ina was startled into stillness.

"Do you want some water, Mamma?" I whispered from my post on the stool.

She shook her head, shuddered quietly, then opened her eyes again; they were dull with fatigue.

"Now." Her voice was weak yet decisive, an echo of her former self. It vexed me that Ina couldn't see how ill she was. I wanted to shake my sister until her teeth rattled—but only after we left Mamma's room. "Now. Alice has been a perfect angel to me and she deserves a treat. I fail to understand why she wants to go with Mr. Dodgson—Mr. Ruskin has made himself available, if she wants." Here Mamma looked at me, the question in her eyes underscored by the purple smudges beneath them. I wrinkled my nose and shook my head. Mr. Ruskin? Why on earth would he want to escort me? While I'd learned to keep my mouth more or less shut during our lessons, he still appeared to see me not as I was but almost as someone he had already decided me to be.

Also, I was no longer so sheltered from the gossip that circled like a dust storm about him wherever he went, not all of it generated by him, and much of it about him. There were whispers as to the true reason his marriage had been annulled, a reason that no one would actually speak but that caused many heads to nod sagely, even as it made ladies blush and gentlemen snicker. I had no desire to become further acquainted with him, despite the fact that I knew he very much desired to become further acquainted with me. This was not the first request he had made for my company.

"As you wish. Then Mr. Dodgson it is, although for the life of me I do not understand his appeal. If he weren't such a stammering fool! I suppose it's the Christian thing to do, to allow him his little friendship with you children. I'm sure he has no friends otherwise except for Mr. Duckworth, but that hardly counts. Mr. Duckworth is pleasant to everyone."

"See, then, Mamma?" Ina's fists were clenched, as were mine; neither of us liked to hear Mr. Dodgson run down like this. Why couldn't others see him the way we did? I marveled, again, at how one man could appear to be so different to so many people.

Ina's face, at least, remained smooth and sweet, just like her voice. "See how it would be the Christian thing, for me to go tonight, as well? As you said, he has few friends otherwise. We do seem to provide him comfort in that way."

"Stammering or not, he's a man and you're a young lady, Ina. You cannot be out at night together. Not even with Miss Prickett—but as her father is poorly and she's down at the cottage with him, that's impossible, anyway. No, you'll remain with me tonight, and Alice may enjoy the fireworks."

"Thank you, Mamma!" I forgot myself and jumped up, clapping my hands; Mamma grimaced. "Oh! I'm sorry!"

"It's all right. Now, please, girls, I need to rest. Enjoy yourselves today, but remember you're the Dean's daughters and act accordingly. Oh dear." Abruptly, she pressed her handkerchief to her mouth, waving us away.

We hurried out just as Yvonne burst into the room carrying a fresh chamber pot covered with a linen towel. I shuddered as poor Mamma summoned Yvonne over to her, her face ashen. Quickly, I shut the door.

"I'm never going to have a baby," I declared, feeling my own stomach turn in sympathy. "How horrid. And Mamma has had so many of them!"

"I think babies are perfectly lovely." Ina turned up her nose—but she paled a little as she heard Mamma's poor racking sounds from behind the door, and we hastened down the hall.

"Maybe they are, but getting them seems awful."

"Pray, how do you know about that?" Ina turned, folded her arms across her chest in perfect imitation of Pricks, and stared at me, her eyes narrow and suspicious.

"I—well, I—" Here it was; another thing I did not know, was too young to know, could never hope to know, but Ina, of course, did. I couldn't bear to see her standing there looking so superior, so I lied. "Of course I know about babies. I've known for ages."

"How, precisely?"

135

"Honestly, Ina, I can't possibly remember everything—"

"Did someone tell you?"

"Well—"

"Or did someone show you?"

"Yes! That's it—someone showed me."

"Someone older than you?"

"Naturally!"

"How long have you known?"

"How long have *you* known?" I countered, and was rewarded with Ina's startled look, a pink flush coloring her cheeks.

"I—well, I'm not quite sure—at any rate, I do know."

"Well, then." I brushed past her, as we needed to change for the tree-planting ceremony; Mamma had chosen new identical dresses of light blue taffeta, with black scallop edging up the front of the bodice and along the hem. "We both know. Imagine that, Ina—you're not the only one who knows something!"

"Oh, I wouldn't be sure of that, Alice." Ina followed, serenely; she paused in front of a gilded mirror hanging on the wall and smoothed her hair down with one of her secret smiles. "I know things, I see things. More than you do. I'll only say this—be careful tonight with Mr. Dodgson."

"What?" I stopped, confused. "What do you mean? Be careful of what?"

"I'm simply concerned for you, Alice. I'm your

elder sister, and I'm concerned about you, about this family—but mainly about you. Do remember that—remember that I'm always thinking of you."

"Fine, but—what did you mean about Mr. Dodgson?"

Ina continued to look in the mirror. Her reflected gaze caught mine, and for a moment it was as if a different person entirely was living on the other side of the gilt frame; a different—dangerous—person. Not my sister.

That person would not answer me, except to place a finger upon her lips and smile.

WHEN MR. DODGSON called for me that evening, accompanied by his brother Edwin, who was visiting, I remembered that smile, that sinister gesture. Despite my warm cloak, I couldn't help but shudder.

However, as soon as we left the Deanery—which had taken on a dark, sick atmosphere for me lately, I realized; Mamma's illness, and Ina's unaccountable actions and my own troubling thoughts, combined with the usual depressing gray of an Oxford winter—I felt my spirits lighten. The night was ablaze with spectacle; music was still in the air—I wondered if the musicians had paused for a moment's breath or at least for dinner—and the possibility of love was everywhere. The Prince of Wales was married! There would be more little princes and princesses, someday a new King and Queen. England would never die; it was the greatest nation on earth, and Oxford was the crown jewel. I was so proud of my country, proud of my home. There was nothing to fear, only everything to celebrate.

"Edwin, may I present Miss Alice Liddell?" Mr. Dodgson gestured to his younger brother, a pale, blurry copy of himself. They had the same lop-sided eyes, but Edwin's were more so; the same small mouth that curved slightly down at the ends, only Edwin's appeared to hang slightly open.

By now, I had met several of Mr. Dodgson's siblings; two of his brothers, Skeffington and Wilfred, were undergraduates and had sometimes accompanied us on rowing trips. (Neither of them sang, though, and they *both* sighed, extremely loudly, whenever I dropped an oar.) Once two of Mr. Dodgson's sisters came to visit him, and I thought them awfully fat and nosy. (The fattest one, Fanny, had asked me if my mother dressed me in silk petticoats!)

I was a bit doubtful about Edwin then; although I told myself that one should keep an open mind.

"I'm very happy to meet you," I said, borrowing one of Ina's fake smiles as I curtsied.

"It's a pleasure." Edwin bowed.

"Where shall we go first, Alice?" Mr. Dodgson took my hand—both of ours were gloved, but still I could remember how his hand had felt that day in the garden, dry but soft, cool yet warm.

I clung to his hand tightly, as if I could feel it that way again. "Every college has an illumination —I'm told Merton is especially nice."

"Can't we simply wander? I don't want to be in any hurry."

"That's a perfect plan. We shall wander and enjoy the night and wi-wish the Royal Couple much happiness."

We crossed the Quad—there were more than a few students teetering on the curved stone edges of the fountain, slick with moisture, and I did hope one of them might fall in, but regretfully, none did. As we passed through the great iron gate separating the Quad from St. Aldate's, we found ourselves in the midst of a noisy, pushing crowd. We had no choice but to follow it.

"Alice, don't let go," Mr. Dodgson instructed me.

"I won't," I told him. Edwin grabbed my other hand, too, and I was glad, for I was afraid I might get swept away only to be kidnapped by a gang of child thieves, just like Oliver Twist, although I'd never once heard of a gang of child thieves in Oxford. Still, the crowds were so enormous— looking about, I didn't recognize anyone, which was so unusual as to be slightly thrilling—that I felt tonight, of all nights, it might be a possibility.

Just as I was warming to the idea—if I were kidnapped by a gang of child thieves, I was certain that eventually I'd be found out to be a lady, just as Oliver had been found out to be a gentleman, although hopefully not before being coached on the finer points of pickpocketing—we turned the corner into the High Street, and the crowd had room to spread out. I took a deep breath, just as everyone looked up at once and started exclaiming. Directly overhead, high above the steep, uneven roofs, there were rockets and flares sizzling so that the very sky looked about to catch fire. A sharp scent burned the insides of my nostrils, like a thousand matches all lit at once.

"Oh!" I halted in my tracks, causing Mr. Dodgson and Edwin to stumble. But then Edwin let go of my hand, and I was holding on only to Mr. Dodgson.

"Isn't it grand?" he asked, following my gaze. I could only nod. I'd never seen the sky so brightly lit, not even in London; enormous rushlights were in every conceivable location—hanging on sides of buildings, affixed to the sides of horse troughs, even stuck in the ground—and they were all burning so intensely, I could feel the heat as I passed each one.

Suddenly a flaming pinwheel careened across the sky, showering sparks all over the crowd. There were shrieks and laughter, and one lady shouted, "Arthur, me skin's on fire!" and Arthur shouted back, "Ain't it always, love?" Then there was more laughter.

Mr. Dodgson gripped my hand more firmly. "Let's move on, shall we?"

"But the poor thing's on fire—" I craned my neck, trying to see who might be aflame. Mr. Dodgson pulled me through the crowd with surprising force. Edwin followed, his face a bright scarlet; I wondered if he was hot because of all the fireworks.

The crowds tonight were different. Earlier, everyone had been very stiff and proper in their finest clothing, even the poor people, some in dreadfully old short jackets and unfashionably narrow dresses. But tonight everything—*everyone*—was more relaxed; limp collars, wrinkled skirts, broken hat feathers that dangled tiredly. This morning the crowds had been happy but restrained, almost trying to ape the dignity of royalty; tonight people were shouting their joy, slurring their pride, dancing their congratulations to the Royal Couple.

There were bold romantics, too. We passed a couple in a darkened doorway; the man was kissing the back of the lady's neck. She had her eyes closed so that I couldn't determine if she was enjoying it or not; she then turned to him, lifting her lips to meet his, her arm arching gracefully about his neck. No one saw them but me, and I felt responsible for their secret; my heart began to swell with the importance of keeping it. Yet I couldn't stop myself from looking back; somehow the sight of the two of them, pressed together in the doorway, caused my skin to burn more hotly than any fireworks.

"What is it, Alice?" Mr. Dodgson, his hand still in mine, looked down at me. Edwin was a few steps ahead.

"Nothing, it's simply—it's simply that everyone's in love," I blurted, unable to keep the secret, after all.

Mr. Dodgson raised his eyebrows but smiled. "Romance is in the air, as they say?"

"Everyone's so nice tonight. Everything's so nice. Isn't it? Isn't it perfectly lovely?" I felt giddy with the beauty of it all. The fireworks, the music—every band seemed to be playing a different Viennese waltz—the illuminations filling every open space. Some were dancing light-filled displays of pictures of the Prince and Princess; others had names or sentiments spelled out with blazing candles in different colored glass lamps.

Most of all, I was enchanted by all the couples strolling arm in arm, sitting in happy conversation on benches—standing in darkened doorways, eyes closed.

"Perfectly. You should see yourself." Mr. Dodgson's voice sounded dreamy; as dreamy as it had been that day in the garden, which was, I realized with a sudden awareness of the passage of time, the last day we had been alone together—until now. "Shining hair, shining eyes, shining heart."

I didn't know what to say, because it was exactly what I wanted to hear. I yearned to be part of the magic of this night, too. I yearned to be special, I yearned to be beautiful—I yearned to be loved.

For some reason, I resisted showing him how happy he made me; I looked down at my shoes instead. Miraculously, my stockings were still up and my black leather shoes unscuffed. Another sign I was changing, growing; lately, my clothes, my hair, my entire appearance, managed to stay more or less intact.

"Soon I'll be a young lady," I murmured, immediately hating myself for sounding exactly like Ina. Why on earth did I say that? It simply popped out.

"Yes." Mr. Dodgson steered me over to an empty bench; he pulled out a handkerchief to wipe the seat, as there was a half-empty glass of ale perched on the arm. He put the glass on the ground, and we sat down. Edwin had wandered on ahead, toward a booth that was selling commemorative cups and trinkets.

"That's what Mamma said, anyway," I continued—desperately wishing I hadn't, unable to stop myself. "I'll be eleven, you know, this coming birthday. Almost old enough for—" I couldn't finish my thought, for it wasn't completely formed. My head spun with so many choices; what *wouldn't* I be old enough for?

"Old enough? Can one ever be old enough? Or will there always be something just out of reach?" Mr. Dodgson smiled, looking amused at himself, and while normally I would have followed along with his game, tonight I felt impatient with it. It seemed ridiculous, when there were so many more serious things to discuss. For a moment, I could almost see him through Mamma's eyes: an odd man, living in his head, speaking nonsense.

But only for a moment. He caught his breath, as if he'd only just realized what I had really said. Then he shut his eyes; when he opened them they were startlingly blue and clear and focused, seeing only me. I had to turn away, for I knew he was looking at me differently now, and even though this was what I had wanted, I was frightened of the change. "Old enough, perhaps, to think of l-l-love? Like the Prince and Princess of Wales?"

Our knees were touching; I was aware of the warmth and sturdiness of his body through his woolen trousers. Still, I couldn't look in his eyes.

"Yes, I do think that—I mean, well, tonight one can't—one can't help it."

"It's natural, then, isn't it? For one to imagine, to hope?" he asked so softly that I had to look up, because I needed to confirm he had said it. He wasn't looking at me now; he appeared to be talking to someone else. Yet there was no one else to hear him; only me. "It's quite natural to dream."

"Like before? When you talked of your headaches, and your dreams of—of—" Something prevented me from saying it out loud; inside,

144

however, a bold, surprising part of my heart was whispering, *me.*

"Yes, in a way." He did turn to me, finally; his eyes were soft and shining, and magical lights were reflected in them—the flickering candlelight of the lantern behind us, the stars, the multicolored fireworks punctuating the sky above.

"My dreams are different now," he continued, his voice a monotone, so unlike the way it had sounded on the river the day he began my story. "They frighten me at first. But then I see them as they really are, so pure and sacred, as love truly is, truly can be, and I think—I hope—that it can be that way, but then I'm frightened again."

"You mustn't be afraid," I said impulsively, wondering how often he was; aching because I could never be there for him in his darkest moments.

"I mustn't?" His eyes—they were so hopeful; they studied my face, looking for an answer I wasn't sure I possessed.

I shook my head. "I do wish I could help you." I felt tears in my eyes, tears of frustration, for never being able to truly help the ones I loved.

"Dear Alice." Mr. Dodgson smiled, a crooked, sad smile, sadder than usual. "Do you know how very much you help, simply by being?"

"I do?"

"Yes. Simply by being, by never growing up, by remaining my wild gypsy girl."

"But I am growing up—I just said so. *You* just said so. I'm almost a young lady."

"But you won't change, will you, Alice? Not like the others? You're different—you were old when you were young, so it makes sense that you'll be young when you grow old."

I couldn't reply. To follow his logic was to allow myself to follow a dream of my own, a dream I wasn't sure I was permitted. Instead, I took his hand—his gloved hand; I could make out his long, tapered fingers. I longed to touch his fingers with my own, trace them, see how much longer they were than mine. I played with his hand, turning it over, laying my palm against his palm, soft leather against soft leather, yet through the layers both of our hands felt warm and alive. I heard him swallow, as if his throat was suddenly dry; I felt his pulse beating, brushing up against my own, but still it wasn't enough. Why were there so many barriers between us, always? Barriers of clothing, of etiquette, of time and age and reason. Yet wasn't I his wild child? His dream gypsy? Before, I had needed permission to roll in the grass, to feel life against my naked skin; no longer.

I bent my hand back, ever so slightly; our wrists touched. Flesh against flesh. He caught his breath in a ragged gasp.

I did not. Marveling at the sight of our bare wrists touching—mine was pink and tender, his

146

pale and sinewy, with soft brown hairs that tickled—I was amazed at my boldness. I couldn't help wonder—what else could I do? What else could I win? Once again I felt victorious, for I possessed something; I possessed a man's heart, as well as his hand. I knew it, as surely as I knew that the Prince and Princess of Wales would live happily ever after. I knew, in that moment, I could say anything I wanted and he would believe it. I could do anything I wished, and he would only applaud it. I could ask for anything I wished, and he would have to grant it. Knowing this, I did not seek permission any longer.

"Wait for me," I whispered, naming my dream.

Mr. Dodgson's mouth trembled; so did his hand. I simply covered it with my own and pressed down until he stopped.

"W-what?"

"Wait for me."

"I don't—what is it you're asking—"

I removed my hand from his. I placed it back in my lap. Then I looked up at him with no fear, no worry, no childish doubt. I met his gaze evenly, for the first time not waiting for him to tell me how I felt, what I should do, how I should act. His eyes were full of tears; his heart was full of wonder. I knew, because mine was, too.

"You do know," I whispered. But I wouldn't, couldn't, say it out loud; say that he must wait for me until I was older, then we could be together always in the way that men and women were together. I didn't know exactly how, but he had already touched me with hands that trembled; had already seen me wild with abandon; had seen me gentle and ladylike, too. While I knew that each instance had been entirely proper and harmless, still, I felt again that others might not see it that way. Not when I was almost eleven, and he was thirty-one.

When I was older, however; when I was fifteen and he thirty-five (there—I was doing sums again!), no one would care. No explanations would be needed. We would be free.

"Oh, Alice," he whispered—resting his head upon mine, his breath warm against my forehead. I closed my eyes, just like the lady in the doorway.

"Alice? Mr. Dodgson?"

Mr. Dodgson gasped, pushing me away, as we both looked up, only to see—

Pricks. Who was staring down at us, her breathing labored, her nostrils flaring.

"Miss Prickett!" He tugged on his waistcoat, bolting up; his face was scarlet, the ends of his hair alive and electric, and his hands gripped his hat so tightly I worried he might crush it. He bowed too hastily, nearly hitting his head on the back of the bench.

"Hello, Pricks," I said coolly. Why was I so self-possessed, so calm—so like Ina? I had no idea; I only knew that somehow, I was stronger than Mr.

Dodgson at that moment. "Is your father doing better?"

"Quite." Pricks looked from me to Mr. Dodgson, her little eyes—like a pig's, I realized in my detachment—wide and afraid. I could sense her fear, even as I didn't understand it; she was fidgeting, tugging at her wide skirt, pulling up her gloves, fingering the buttons on her threadbare cloak.

"I'm sorry—is your father poorly?" Mr. Dodgson had recovered somewhat, although he now appeared to be very intent on not meeting my gaze, or Pricks's. He looked everywhere but at either of us.

"Thank you very much for asking. Yes, he was, but he appears to be improving. I decided to come home tonight, in order to see some of the celebration. It was very quiet down at the cottage, you know. We're quite isolated." Pricks smiled desperately at him, that violent, openmouthed smile.

"How fortunate for us," Mr. Dodgson said automatically. "Now we'll be four."

"Four?"

"My brother Edwin is with us. Oh, here he is—Edwin, please allow me to introduce Miss Prickett, Alice's go-go-governess."

Edwin, his arms laden with commemorative cups and ribbons and a tea cozy, came strolling up. He bowed, grinning as he indicated his hat, unable to remove it.

"It's my pleasure," Edwin said.

"Shall we see more of the illuminations?" I stood, buttoning the top button of my wool cloak, for the air had a definite chill to it now.

"I don't wish to intrude," Pricks began, lowering her head—looking up at Mr. Dodgson through her pale, thin eyelashes.

"Nonsense. It's an honor," he said flatly.

"Yes," I agreed, stepping over to Mr. Dodgson and sliding my hand in his. He grasped mine firmly, tucking it under his arm.

"Edwin, let me help you with your bounty— what on earth did you buy?" He turned to his brother.

Edwin grinned again, and I liked him in that minute. He seemed so easy to please, and I envied him his purchases. I hoped Edwin might offer to give me something, even as I realized it wouldn't be good manners to accept. Still, I did think the cup with the Prince and Princess's initials on it was lovely.

"Just a few novelties. I couldn't help it— everyone was selling them."

"Well, Alice and I will help carry, so you may escort Miss Prickett," Mr. Dodgson said, handing me the tea cozy with the Princess's face embroidered on it.

"To tell the truth, I'm rather tired," Pricks said. She did look it; her shoulders slumped, and her mouth drooped. "Thank you very much, Mr.

Dodgson, but I think I'll return to the Deanery now. Alice, perhaps you should accompany me? It's very late."

She tried. She tried to behave like my governess; she knit her brows together, cocked her head in that schoolroom way of hers, as if she was waiting for me to conjugate a verb. She was not my superior tonight, however; she wasn't even my equal. I knew something she did not—and it was the most important thing in the world.

I knew how to make Mr. Dodgson tremble. I knew how to make him wonder. I knew how to make him wait.

For he would, surely. I knew it as we waved good-bye to Pricks, who weaved her lonely way in and out of the crowd, past couples strolling arm in arm, past couples standing motionless, simply gazing at each other. She clutched her ugly green cloak about her, hugging her own elbows for warmth, or for companionship. I did pity her.

I was not alone; I would never be alone. Mr. Dodgson and I resumed our walk past the illuminations, stopping to marvel at one in particular that had been erected in the small quad in front of the stone edifice of the Examinations buildings. It spelled out, in a blaze of colored lamps, *May They Be Happy*. As we admired the flickering spectacle—not a flame on the enormous platform was extinguished, and there were clever little mirrors nestled among the lamps and leaves of the garlands, which created a magical halo effect around the entire thing—I heard Mr. Dodgson whisper, "May we all deserve happiness."

"Oh, but we will!" I looked up, my cheeks radiant from the heat of all the lights. In that moment, holding the hand of my chosen, I was so confident, so wise; my heart felt ready to break with the joy of my new understanding of the power of love, and its astounding ability to make the strong weak, and the weak strong.

Instead, my heart nearly broke at the look on Mr. Dodgson's face as he gazed down at me, his eyes dark in the amber glow of the dancing lights. He did not reflect back our shared joy; rather, the corners of his eyes, his mouth, his chin, even, seemed pulled down with sorrow. He stared at me as if I wasn't standing right there beside him, my hand in his; instead, he blinked at me as if I was a dream—and he was about to awaken.

"Will you write my story now?" I asked wildly, suddenly afraid. So afraid, I needed to remind him of how tied we were together, and that was the first thing that came to mind. "Do you remember how it begins?"

"That's not the problem, dear Alice," he said with a sad smile. He brushed a square of burned paper—the air, the ground, was filled with scorched scraps—from my shoulder. "The problem is knowing how it will end."

I shook my head, exasperated but indulgently so. This man! Why did he worry over our story? The thing to do was simply write it, live it; be it.

I turned back to the illumination. One of the garlands had caught fire, and a man was busy throwing sand on it; in his hurry, he had knocked over several of the lamps. The "Happy" was slightly askew, apart from the other words.

It didn't look as if it belonged anymore.

Chapter 6

*I*N EARLY APRIL, MAMMA HAD A BABY BOY named Albert. In early May, I turned eleven. In late May, Albert died.

So much happened in such a short time. Naturally, we were joyous at the arrival of a new brother; I was so relieved that Mamma was soon up and about and ordering everyone around again. We were very proud, too, when the Prince of Wales agreed to be Albert's godfather.

However, by my birthday Albert was very ill; so ill there was no birthday celebration, although I told myself that at eleven, I was far too grown-up to mind. Mamma and Papa walked around with worried expressions, Dr. Acland was at the Deanery all the time, and Phoebe wouldn't leave the nursery for a minute. Rhoda did not understand what was going on; she simply cried all the time for Phoebe. I did feel sorry for her. Up until then, Phoebe was Rhoda's world. Now she had to suffer under Pricks like the rest of us.

Then Albert was gone. We hadn't had any time to get to know him—he was so tiny and weak that no one was allowed to hold him. All we knew was a wrinkled, pale face wrapped up in a white crocheted blanket, with lips that were almost blue, his tiny mouth opening up for feeble, raspy cries, like a baby bird.

Papa cried so very much. At night he would trudge up to the schoolroom, where he scarcely ever went otherwise, and wrap up the first child he saw in a great hug, weeping openly, his tears wetting the tops of our heads.

Mamma did not say a word. I tried to be good; I tried to be there for her as I had been before. Yet when I knocked on her dressing room door one evening, a week after the funeral, she opened it with a look of surprise.

"Alice! What do you want?" She was thin again; her hair shiny and tightly bound, with two severe waves off the top of her forehead, like raven's wings. There were a few new lines around her eyes, but the sickly purple smudges were gone. Her dark eyes saw me but kept me at bay; they looked sharp and suspicious as before.

"I thought—I thought you might want me to sit with you."

"Whatever for? I'm perfectly fine. You, on the other hand—" She took a step back and surveyed me as if she was trying to figure out how much I might fetch at an auction. "That dress is too short."

"It's one of Ina's, from when Prince Albert died." I tugged at the waist, which was a bit snug, and attempted to pull down the skirt. The black wool itched and was too warm for May, but we hadn't gotten our new mourning dresses back from the dressmaker's.

"Ask Mary Ann to let it out."

"I will. But—Mamma, I thought—if you wanted to rest, I could—"

"I'm perfectly fine. There's such a lot to do, and your father isn't much help right now. I need to go over the list for the Prince and Princess of Wales's visit in June. They're staying at the Deanery, and they sent a long list of requirements, and I don't know how I shall get everything done. Now, go along, child, and I'll see you in the morning." She gave me a peck on the cheek and shut the door before I could say a word, her black skirts swishing with the sudden movement.

I stood there, staring at the closed door, the brass knob shiny and polished. I placed the palm of my hand against one of the raised panels, feeling the cool walnut. The door was only a few inches thick, yet the barrier between my mother and me was much greater, impenetrable. It was as if we hadn't spent those long, intimate winter evenings together at all. Only the fact that my heart stung with mourning for them made them real. I felt tears roll down my cold cheeks, and I realized I hadn't once seen Mamma cry; I wondered if she was even sad about the baby.

I wondered if she'd ever cry for me, as I did for her.

Then it was summer. Commemoration weekend with all its ceremonies, made more special this year due to the Prince of Wales's involvement, was upon us. Mamma was in her element, happily brusque and efficient despite her mourning attire; the Deanery was abuzz with excitement, full to the brim with Royal servants and retainers. I don't recall where they all slept, but I was forever tripping over a uniformed gentleman wearing a sash and looking as if he hadn't anything to do.

I did not trouble myself too much about them. For through it all—the sadness of baby Albert's death, and the happy, frantic times of the Royal visit—Mr. Dodgson was a constant presence; I never had to wonder, when I opened my eyes to greet a new day, if I would see him. He was simply always there, stepping into the void that Mamma and Papa had left: Papa by his grief, which had now taken him to a far, lonely place; Mamma by her frenzied social responsibilities.

Truly, I cannot think of those months, those eventful months, without thinking of him. It was as if we both sensed some acceleration of time and chance, and agreed, without a word, to make the most of it. Mamma was too distracted to notice how often he showed up without sending a note beforehand or asking permission. Normally she detested this casual familiarity. Now, however, she didn't comment upon it, not even to go on about that "nuisance of a mathematics tutor."

Pricks didn't protest, either—but neither did she seem to look forward to his visits any longer. She dully accompanied us, sitting quietly, reading a book or working on her knitting, not even rousing herself to remind me to behave like a lady.

Ina was unnaturally silent, as well. She sat apart, like Pricks—but unlike her, she did watch. Her unblinking gray eyes did notice, particularly when Mr. Dodgson would pause in the midst of a story, or a game of croquet, or an afternoon in the garden spent drawing nonsense animals (*hippopotahorse, crocoduck, kangalion*), and look at me. He looked at me often, and I him; when we caught each other's gaze, he would often tremble, as if catching a sudden chill. He would then look away, very abruptly.

I did not tremble; I did not look away. What was there to fear? We could enjoy our time together now, and look forward to our time together later. Knowing that my future was settled, I relaxed my watchfulness and allowed myself to think only of the moment, a child once more.

• • •

ANOTHER GOLDEN AFTERNOON; another trip on a river. I believed there would be many, many more like it. Why should I not?

This was a large party; ten of us, including Mamma and Papa, which was very unusual. More unusual, still, was the fact that Mamma actually called on Mr. Dodgson beforehand, requesting that he organize the entire excursion. Yet when it came time for the party to gather at Salter's, where an enormous four-oar boat had been procured, it was obvious that she intended to treat him more like a servant than a guest. That honor was reserved for Lord Newry, a new undergraduate.

Lord Newry was a dashing, vivacious Irish nobleman with black curly hair and drowsy eyes, one of those students who believed that the rules of Oxford did not pertain to him, and in this he was encouraged by Mamma, who was prone to having favorite students, usually those with titles.

What drew such an unlikely group together on that last afternoon? Lord Newry and his friends were loud and boisterous, passing along pocket flasks, scarcely even bothering to conceal this activity, and constantly threatening to upend the boat. The rest of us were still in mourning for Albert; our black muslin dresses looked dreary and cumbersome, like rain clouds, among the white linen suits of the men. Mr. Dodgson somehow found himself in the middle; neither subdued family nor carefree young man. I tried my best to make him feel comfortable, and during the trip downriver I asked him to tell a story, but he refused.

Upon landing at Nuneham—with its landscaped parks, the pale stone manor house, Nuneham Courtney, just in view beyond a hill dotted with trees (Edith always vowed she would live in a house as grand as that someday)—Mr. Dodgson silently but effectively made himself useful. He assisted Mamma in choosing a pleasant site beneath a tall oak tree; he tended the spirit lamps for tea; he frightened away bugs and spiders from the assembled feast. Once we were all gathered for our repast, reclining on gay quilts, he sat quietly apart from the other men. Without thought, Edith and Rhoda and I settled near him, balancing our plates in our laps.

Mamma invited Ina to sit next to her, which happened to be next to Lord Newry. I knew, then, why he had been asked; surprisingly, Ina did not appear to understand our mother's motives. She chose to sit near Mr. Dodgson as well.

"Lord Newry, please favor us with your impression of your first year at Oxford," Mamma commanded with a dazzling smile. "We're eager to hear how you young men are getting on, aren't we, Dean Liddell?"

"What? Oh, yes, indeed, indeed," Papa said, pulling his gaze away from the river for a moment. We could hear other parties in the distance, laughing and chatting among the trees; Nuneham was most popular during the summer, as the Earl of Nuneham Courtney very graciously opened the grounds to picnickers every Thursday.

"Your charming hospitality has been a welcome surprise," Lord Newry began, his eyes sparkling with some suppressed emotion—amusement, I suspected, as his friends caught his gaze, then immediately busied themselves with their plates, piled high with cold poached chicken and lobster in mayonnaise.

"Thank you," Mamma replied.

"The architecture of the city is, of course, every bit as breathtaking as I had heard."

"Indeed, indeed." One of his friends nodded, overly enthusiastic; he nearly knocked over a bottle of lemonade.

"And the pubs are the best I've sampled," another of his friends burst out, while the others laughed heartily and patted him on the back.

"Really?" Mamma's voice, as well as her spine, grew rigid.

"Gibson!" Lord Newry frowned at his friend, while his eyes danced. "I do apologize for Gibson, madam. It seems he hasn't been himself of late."

"I'm sorry to hear that," Mamma replied. "Is he ill?"

"No, not exactly." Lord Newry suppressed a grin.

"No, madam, I'm fit as a fiddle," Gibson sputtered through a mouthful of lobster. "In body, at any rate; I'm not sure about my mind."

"Yes, the poor devil's been quite mad ever since he left his heart in a doxy's bed the first week of term," another friend snickered, falling over with glee and tipping into my lap; I caught a sour whiff of liquor on his breath.

"Sir!" Mr. Dodgson leaped up, pulling me to my feet, putting himself between the young man and me. "Apologize to the ladies."

Everyone froze. Peeking around from behind Mr. Dodgson's back, my heart beating with the twin thrills of being in the company of a bad man (the likes of which I was, regrettably, much too meagerly acquainted with) and being defended by the most noble gentleman on earth, I had to suppress a giggle. For the young man lay on his back, as helpless as an insect at Mr. Dodgson's feet, even as there was an amused, superior smirk on his face, shiny and red in the heat.

"Mamma?" I asked, unsure what to do. I buried my face in the scratchy folds of Mr. Dodgson's white waistcoat; his slender back rose and fell with quick, short breaths, and his gloved hands clenched in fists. I'd never seen him quite so angry; then it occurred to me that I'd never seen him angry, period. That he was so on my behalf filled me with a romantic thrill; I was Dulcinea to his Don Quixote. Ina may have been older than me, but she had never had her honor defended. Turning around to catch her eye—she and Edith and Rhoda were staring, mouths agape, like little monkeys—I made note to remind her of this later.

"I'm very sorry, Mrs. Liddell, Dean Liddell, girls." Lord Newry rose. He faced Mr. Dodgson and bowed, one gentleman to another, although he did not speak his name. "Come, Marshall, let's walk it off, shall we?" Lord Newry helped his friend to his feet, and they and the others sheepishly took off for a little shelter of saplings, about half an acre distant.

"Mr. Dodgson, I very much appreciate your actions," Mamma said as she and Papa rose. They both stood looking after the young men. "Would you mind helping the girls? I need to speak to Dean Liddell." She took Papa's arm; he had remained so oddly silent during it all, so detached. For the first time, I wished that he had just a little of Mamma's hard, brittle energy; I was impatient with his grief, and feared he might remain lost in it forever.

Mamma led Papa away, speaking very energetically, while Papa barely nodded, acquiescing to whatever she said. Then he put his hands in his pockets and sat down upon the ground, his short legs in front of him, staring at the river.

Mr. Dodgson, Ina, Edith, and I attempted to tidy up as best we could, but with Rhoda trying to help—she broke two plates, at least, before I stopped keeping count—it took rather longer than usual. When we were finished, I walked over to Papa and laid my cheek against his, feeling his scratchy whiskers, not as luxuriant as they once were; he reached up and patted me, but I didn't think he even knew which one of his daughters I was. I kissed him anyway, and walked back to the others.

"Well," Mamma said, pursing her lips in disapproval. "I must say, those young men's manners are appalling. Still, he is a lord, and one must make allowances. I think, however, it might be best if you girls return home another way. Mr. Dodgson, would you be so kind as to escort them home by way of the railroad? Abingdon Road station isn't very far, although perhaps too far for Rhoda. I'll keep her with me."

"But, Mamma!" Rhoda stamped her foot and shook her glossy brown curls. I liked her more and more each day; I perceived she would become an exceptional ally in my ongoing war with Pricks. "I want to go with Mr. Dodgson!"

"Nonsense." Mamma raised her formidable eyebrows, and Rhoda subsided with a pout.

"It will be my p-p-pleasure." Mr. Dodgson bowed in that stiff way of his. "I'm happy to b-b-be of assistance."

"Yes," was all Mamma said, already forgetting about him as she glided off to find Lord Newry, her long black skirt trailing in the dry grass, leaving a circular pattern in the flattened stalks.

The four of us—Ina, Edith, Mr. Dodgson, and I—grinned at one another; suddenly the sun took on a happy glow, and the air blew soft with the perfume of wildflowers and new grass. We bade farewell to Papa with affectionate hugs, then trooped our way across the fields, to the narrow lane that led down to Abingdon Road station, a journey of almost two miles. We did not hasten, even though we didn't possess a timetable; I don't believe we would have minded if we'd missed the last train altogether. For the day was ours at last; earlier, we'd been only borrowing it.

Did Mr. Dodgson tell us another story that lovely, last day as we strolled along a dusty country lane picking flowers, blowing dandelion fluff, chancing upon nests of rabbits and mice? He did, although it frustrates me that I can't recall what it was about. It did prompt me, though, to remind him of another story.

"Have you written it down yet?" Breaking a branch off a tree, I dragged it along behind me; it made a satisfying swishing sound in the fine pebbles of the road.

"Written what down?" Mr. Dodgson removed his straw hat, wiping his forehead with his handkerchief. It was rather hot, particularly in my mourning clothes; even though it was late afternoon now—the sun had drifted behind the trees —it felt as if the accumulated heat of the day was trapped within the folds of my black frock, which persisted in sticking to my skin, weighing down my petticoats. Rivulets of perspiration snaked down the front and back of my bodice, my pulse pounded, and my skin felt baked. Looking at my sisters, I knew they were as hot as I; Ina's curls had lost their spring, while Edith's had taken on new life, frizzing about her head like lightning.

"I imagine that it's cooler on the river," Edith said without envy.

"Have you written my story down?" I persisted. "The Alice story?"

"It's not the Alice story," Ina hissed. "It's just a *story*. Any old story."

"I am working very hard on it." Mr. Dodgson acted as if he had not heard Ina; he had such proper manners! I was very taken with them all of a sudden, given the events of the afternoon. "I assure you, my Alice, it will be done, and you shall have a nice little memento of a lovely day."

"I told you he would," I taunted my sister.

"I'll believe it when I see it," my sister taunted me.

"Girls," Mr. Dodgson interposed, automatically. "Let's play Grandmother's Trunk. I'll begin. I went to my grandmother's trunk and I found an —antipodean aardvark. Now, Edith, your turn."

"I went to my grandmother's trunk and I found an antipodean aardvark." Edith couldn't stop herself from giggling at the thought. "And a bumblebee," she added, as one had just alighted upon her hat.

"I went to my grandmother's trunk and I found an antipodean aardvark, a bumblebee, and a catapult," Ina continued.

"I went to my grandmother's trunk and I found an antipodean aardvark, a bumblebee, a catapult, and a dragonfly," I replied, choosing another stick from the side of the lane, as the one I had been using snapped in two.

I was so content in that moment; those horrible men were gone, I was with my sisters, and with the person who loved me and knew me best in the entire world, I was sure of it. After the tumult of the last few months, swinging so wildly from exquisite highs—the night of the wedding of the Prince and Princess of Wales—to heartbreaking lows—Albert's death—it was good to have this; this sweet, unhurried reminder that there would be, still, simple days in the sun for us all.

So we trudged along the road playing word games, telling stories; soon enough we rejoiced at the sight of the little white clapboard station, where we knew we could get a cool drink from a bucket and wait for the train in the shade.

After about a quarter of an hour, it slid up with a gentle hiss and a clang, wheels groaning in protest as the brakeman performed his duties; Mr. Dodgson paid our fares, and we climbed aboard a first-class carriage.

"Shall I put the window up or down?" he asked.

"Oh, up! I do hate to get cinders in my eye," cried Edith.

We settled in on the stiff horsehair-covered seats, Mr. Dodgson sliding in next to me, even though Ina had purposely sat opposite, forcing him to choose. While the journey to Oxford wasn't long—only five miles or so, less than an hour's time—almost as soon as the train pulled away, I felt my head nodding, heavy with heat and sleep, gently rocked by the rhythm of the steady train. Ba-*dump*-ba-*dump*-ba-*dump*! it went, over the railroad ties.

My eyes *would* close, despite my best efforts; I blinked and attempted to focus on Ina, who shifted in her seat and turned toward the window so that her clean, perfect profile was in view, should anyone wish to admire it. Soon, very soon, I did not see her, for my eyes had shut for good, and I was falling, falling—down a rabbit hole? I giggled, murmured an answer to Mr. Dodgson's gentle inquiry, which I could not quite understand.

I continued falling, falling, finally landing, ever so softly, in a dream. A dream of happiness, a dream of sunshine; of drifting waters and babies snuggled into tiny blankets, rows and rows of them, perched on stalks just like sunflowers, nodding and sleeping with happy smiles on their faces. Soon a great man, gray of hair and short of leg, holding a watch just like Papa's, was walking along a curving lane, touching each and every one, whispering that it was too soon, too soon for them to go.

Then another man, a slender man with a tall black silk hat, gray gloves, a stiff way about him, was walking along that same lane. It was night now; the babies were gone, replaced by shops and darkened doorways, and there were fireworks splashing the sky with color. "May they be happy," he said over and over. I thought he meant the babies—until he turned and looked down, his blue eyes sad and brimming over with tears, and in that instant, I knew he meant me. Glancing over his shoulder, I saw a couple in a doorway. She arched her arm, gracefully, about his neck, bringing him closer and closer to her upturned lips.

"Alice," the man in the hat said, tenderly. "Alice, be happy. Be happy with me."

"Of course," I said with a happy sigh. "Of course."

"Alice?" I felt warm breath upon my forehead, scratchy fabric pillowing my cheek. "Alice, dear? Alice, wake up." An arm was about my shoulders, gently shaking me.

Did I feel lips in my hair? I nestled my face deeper and deeper, trying to hold on to my dream.

"Alice, wake up," he said. Reluctantly, my eyes opened; looking up, I saw his face, large and pink and near, so near; soft brown hairs curled over his ear, eyelashes brushed cheeks that were red from the sun, a faint line of perspiration dotted his upper lip. His breath was warm and a little sour, yet it did not repulse me. On the contrary, it made him real—too real for a dream; real enough for a man.

As I searched his face, his lips asked a question, or said my name—either way, the answer was the same; my ears felt hot, full of a sound like the pounding of waves, the roar of a mighty current, or a riptide; my eyes were full, too full to see anything but his eyes, his nose, the down on his cheek.

Arms reaching, gracefully; lips moving, to seek and give the only answer possible.

A man who fancied himself a child and a child who thought she was a woman turned to each other on a hot summer day, mindful of nothing, no one, but each other—not even the sister who sat opposite, watching; the sister who sat silently, remembering.

Meanwhile, time did not stand still for any of them; the train pulled into the station where other people were waiting, too; where other people were watching.

As with a jolt, a clang, a final high, lonesome whistle that pierced the air, sending shivers down everyone's spines, the train reached the end of its journey.

OVER A YEAR LATER, I received, in the morning post, a green leather-bound copy of a story.

Alice's Adventures Under Ground. I opened it to see the dedication—"A Christmas Gift to a Dear Child, in Memory of a Summer Day," printed in very ornate script. Chapter one began, *Alice was beginning to get very tired of sitting by her sister on the bank. . . .*

I turned to the last page; after the final paragraph of the text, framed by flowers and curlicues, was a photograph of me, cut out from a larger photograph and pasted in. Not a photograph of me as I was, nor even as I had been—Alice, his Alice, his wild gypsy girl.

Simply a portrait of myself in a high-collared white dress, taken when I was seven. I looked at this child with dark circles under her innocent eyes, a decided chin, scraggly hair like a boy's, and I did not recognize her at all.

I shut the book, took it upstairs to my bedroom, and put it in a drawer.

I did not open it again for a very long time.

Chapter 7

OXFORD, 1875

*I*S IT TRUE THAT YOU'RE ALICE IN Wonderland?"

"I believe you know the answer to that, Your Royal Highness."

"Don't call me that."

"I believe you know the answer to that, then, Leopold."

"No. Say it. Say what I want to hear."

"I believe you know the answer to that." I stopped, blushing; I had to look down at my gloved hands, folded gracefully in my lap, as I whispered, *"Leo."*

"That's better." He placed his hand over mine; his hand was white, as soft as a child's, with jeweled and crested rings on the long, slender fingers. Yet there was a strength in it; the strength of possession.

From the front of the room, Mr. Ruskin paused in his lecture to give us a look from beneath his bushy eyebrows. He stroked his chin, and then continued. "The gospel of the insolent and idle became the gospel of the painters of England."

I hastily retrieved my hand from the one who had possessed it; His Royal Highness, Prince Leopold, who looked at me with round, sensitive blue eyes framed with long golden lashes, and frowned.

We sat in feigned attention to Mr. Ruskin for several minutes. Mr. Ruskin—who was now more or less permanently installed at Oxford as the first Slade Professor of Art—was giving one of his famous lectures, this one the first in a series of studies of the twelve discourses of Sir Joshua Reynolds.

Mr. Ruskin's lectures drew enormous crowds,

and often were given in the vast expanses of the Sheldonian Theatre or the Museum. As this series was supposed to be for students only, it was held in a large lecture hall in the University Galleries instead: rows and rows of hard oak benches, gaslights flickering on the walls. I was seated near the back of the crowded room. It seemed to me that every year Oxford welcomed more and more students; Great Britain was in the midst of an unprecedented period of peace and prosperity, as we hadn't been at war since the end of the Crimean conflict in 1856. I suspected many young men who might have sought a military career felt there was really no future in it.

Naturally, there were no female students. More and more ladies did, however, attend lectures, particularly Mr. Ruskin's lectures. Despite Mr. Ruskin's public grumblings concerning this new practice—"I cannot bear to look out and observe the ridiculous costumes in that revolting green and purple plaid so many ladies are fond of, not to mention hats with dead birds upon them"— privately, he did not mind in the least, and was known to boast about it at parties. Still, I knew he did not countenance disruptions from either sex; his lectures were more like theatrical performances as he gesticulated and paced about.

Dutifully, I attempted to follow his words; as the daughter of Dean Liddell, my presence at any lecture was always noted and, I felt, appreciated.

Yet how could I pay attention with Leo—my heart sang, to call him that!—by my side? I lowered my head to gaze at my lap—no revolting green and purple there; instead, a scalloped sky-blue taffeta, pulled tightly back into a bustle, which provided a welcome cushion to the hard lecture chair—and attempted to look at Leo with a sidelong glance. He sat easily, his plain black robe, identical to all the other students', concealing a perfectly tailored coat and trousers, a rich gray vest, in which, I knew, resided a gold pocket watch with minia-tures of his sister, the Princess Louise, and his dear dead papa. One graceful white hand rested on a simple ebony walking stick. The other hung lazily—tauntingly—over the arm of his chair, just within reach. While he appeared to be extremely interested in Mr. Ruskin, somehow he managed to convey his attention to me as well. It was in the way he reclined, leaning ever so slightly in my direction, his head tilted my way, while his body remained turned to the front of the room. I was aware of his soft, steady breathing, his occasional, gentle clearing of the throat, the way his Adam's apple moved up and down as he swallowed; the blinking of his eyes, even. For the room was tightly packed, and we were by necessity seated more closely together than we had ever been.

Resolutely, I gazed back at Mr. Ruskin, who now appeared to have thrown away his prepared notes and was pacing about the front of the room.

"English society has fallen lower and lower, and therefore, now its nobles are gradually abdicating their ancient seats and leaving them to manufacturers."

"I'm afraid I am unable to understand what Mr. Ruskin's opinions of the decline of English society have to do with the teachings of Sir Joshua. Perhaps this lecture should be called 'The Rambling and Egotistical Discourses of Mr. John Ruskin,' instead," I whispered to Leopold.

"I wager half a crown you would never say that to him in person," Leopold replied, stroking his neat mustache.

"Sir, I am scandalized! Wagering with a lady?"

"It's entirely your fault; you're corrupting me. I was a wide-eyed innocent before I made your acquaintance."

"Naturally. It's only women who have the power to corrupt," I murmured slyly, as Mr. Ruskin cleared his throat and looked our way, this time more pointedly. Naturally, all other heads turned to see who he was looking at; I suppressed a giggle and looked down at my lap, while Leopold merely nodded, a true Royal, and smiled at Mr. Ruskin, who bowed and continued.

At long last, the lecture ended to thunderous applause, to which I did not contribute. Looking at the admiring faces around me, I couldn't help but believe that were Mr. Ruskin merely to stand in front of a lectern and belch the alphabet, he would be so rewarded—and likely asked to repeat the performance later.

Prince Leopold rose and helped me to my feet; we followed the crowd out the back door to the anteroom, where my maid and his valet were waiting to hand us our cloaks. The back of Sophie's hair was flat and unruly; I wondered if she'd been napping while she passed the time. I would have to speak to her about this later.

"Miss," she said with a curtsy, handing me an umbrella. "I believe it's raining now."

"Oh, bother," I said, turning to Leo. "We'll not be able to have our stroll."

"Sir, I was going to venture that perhaps you should go back to Wyckeham House and rest," his valet—an older military man who had served Prince Albert—said firmly.

Leo sighed, a look of frustration mingled with resignation crossing his face, even as he could not disguise the bitterness in his voice. "I must be the only undergraduate at Oxford who has to have a lie-down every afternoon."

"You know you have to conserve your energy," I consoled him. "You're so dear to all of us, to Mamma and Papa; it would be unkind of you not to rest. Whatever would we do if you were to take ill? You're being very selfish, you know." I smiled, trying to coax him out of his mood before it began. A lifetime of being a semi-invalid had not encouraged him to bear his cross without

175

some complaint. Matters were not helped by the Queen, who wrote daily expressing her suffocating concern for her youngest son, who had been born with hemophilia. Leopold considered it a miracle of Papist proportions that he had been allowed to attend Oxford at all; it was due only to the influence of Mr. Duckworth, his former tutor, that the Queen had consented to let him live beyond her protection.

The stories he had told me about his childhood—the servants whose only tasks were to constantly follow him, ready to catch him if he fell; the loneliness he suffered as the only boy among a household of women, as his brothers all went off to school and military careers; the stifling atmosphere of the Queen's continual mourning, a strange world where Prince Albert's clothes were laid out every morning, brushed and pressed, only to be put away again at night— broke my heart. I could not imagine how he had emerged so cheerful, really; I knew I must allow him his small complaints.

"I'm dear to your parents? Am I not dear to you as well?" Now Leo did smile, taking my arm and trying to tuck it under his. I persisted in retrieving it, uneasy at his public boldness. We walked out into the hall properly, a respectable space between us; the hall was full of students hoping to talk to Mr. Ruskin. As we passed, a narrow path opened up before us as students murmured and bowed quickly and respectfully to the Prince.

He did not appear to notice, however; he gazed at me with a steady, expectant expression, until I was forced to answer.

"Of course you are," I murmured, not wishing anyone to hear.

"You never did answer my other question." Now there was a mischievous glint in those light blue eyes, a twitch of the soft yellow mustache.

"I'm sorry?"

"Earlier. You never did confirm that you are the real Alice in Wonderland."

"Oh, Prince—Leo, you know very well all about that." I sighed, impatient—perhaps even irritated.

"So it's true, then? Duckworth told me, before I came down, that I'd meet the real Alice. You realize it is one of Mamma's favorite books? She is not one for reading, but she is exceedingly fond of your story."

"That's very flattering," I said automatically, with that polite detachment I had practiced for so long to cultivate concerning the subject. Had I ever been proud to call it "my" story? Once, long ago. But so much had happened since then.

"Although I admit, I was surprised not to find you with long yellow hair." He reached up and fingered a wayward strand of my plain black hair with a smile.

I slapped his hand away with a look. I sometimes felt that his illness made him too reckless, as if he believed he could not afford to move at the pace that propriety demanded. "Yes, well, I didn't actually pose for the illustrations, of course. Those came later. Originally, it was intended simply to be a story shared by two—by two friends." I concentrated on keeping my voice steady, unconcerned. "Naturally, I'm very happy that it turned into something much bigger, and that it has brought joy to so many people."

"Are you happy that it has brought me to you? That's how it seems to me now. That it is all part of some greater plan." Leo paused as his valet rushed ahead to open the entrance door. We walked out into the foggy October afternoon, both of us opening our umbrellas and holding them aloft. They offered just enough protection from the steady drizzle, although we had to raise our voices to continue our conversation.

"What do you mean?"

"Well, isn't it interesting that Duckworth became my tutor? It's as if it was all leading to you and me, in some mystical way. That he was there, with you, when the story was told, and now here I am, with you. Do you mind, Alice? Do you mind very much that I'm so happy to be with you?"

He leaned close to me, so close that his head was beneath my umbrella; I felt his breath blow warm upon my face. He smiled down at me, such a sweet, earnest expression in his eyes, and my heart surged within my breast, contained only by my tight bodice. I could not hold his gaze; I was no longer as bold as I had been as a child, when I was not afraid to claim the things I desired.

"No, I don't mind," I whispered as timidly as any lady; even Ina would have approved. Yet I also couldn't prevent a happy, sure smile from escaping.

Perhaps I was not the lady either of us believed me to be, at that.

Satisfied, Leo returned to his own umbrella and took my arm, as any gentleman would under the soggy circumstances, guiding me firmly across the puddles that were gathering between the cobblestones. We were on St. Aldate's now; Sophie and his valet followed, a proper three steps behind.

"It's so odd, to realize that Dodgson is Lewis Carroll. Before I came here, I imagined that Lewis Carroll was a kind older-uncle sort. Jolly, plump, with whiskers. To find that he's simply a fussy mathematics professor—and not a very good or popular one at that! Although Duckworth always speaks fondly of him; they're great friends, aren't they?"

"Yes, I believe they still are, although I haven't seen Mr. Duckworth in years, not since he went up to London." With effort, I slowed my breathing; with every passing reference to Mr.

Dodgson, it had sped up so that it was matching the accelerating raindrops on my umbrella. Even so, I couldn't prevent myself from shivering.

"Old Duck's the same as ever—oh, my poor dear, you must be freezing!" Leo stopped, looking at me in alarm.

"I am, rather."

"Then you must go right home. Come, I'll escort you." He made as if to shepherd me across the street, to the entrance of the Quad.

"Oh, no! No—you need to rest, and it's so wretched out. I'll be fine. You'll be home much more quickly if we part now."

"Will I see you tomorrow night?"

"Of course!" I flashed him a reassuring smile. "Mamma is delighted that you're coming. She got the whole evening up just for you."

"Then, tomorrow." Leo took my hand, pressed his lips against it, and bowed. I curtsied and watched as he walked away, a slight, jauntily commanding figure beneath his large black umbrella, trailed by his somber valet, who was bareheaded, his thin hair plastered to his skull by the rain.

Sophie and I crossed the street, pushing our way through a sea of umbrellas—there was no hope for it; my skirt was now thoroughly drenched, as well as my shoes, and felt as if it weighed twelve stone. Just before we reached the entrance to the Quad, I looked up at windows north of the tower. There was light, shadows of objects behind curtains, but I didn't see any movement there.

Still, I couldn't help but feel as if I was being watched, as I'd been watched ever since I was a little girl playing croquet with my sisters in the garden. Only I wasn't a little girl anymore. And my games were much more complicated.

"SO, TELL ME," Mr. Ruskin purred, taking my arm and pulling me into a corner. "Will I be addressing you as Her Royal Highness anytime soon?"

We were in the dining room of the Deanery, brightly lit by two enormous chandeliers, the candles flickering gaily; refreshments were being served between musical acts. Mamma, her dark hair shimmering with a few threads of silver now, was hovering, handsome as ever in emerald green satin, with a boldly low neckline showing off her formidable décolletage. She was eyeing the refreshments, set out upon the table and sideboard—platters of cold tongue, pyramids of fruit in two low brass epergnes, delicate china plates of jellies and ices, and great cut-glass bowls of punch. She looked up anxiously, and moved a platter of tongue precisely as a dollop of wax was about to drip onto it.

Papa was holding court just outside the room; he was in the middle of a story about little Lionel, only six, and showing much academic promise. At long last, Papa had a son whose intellect could be hoped to match his own. Harry, kind and generous as he was, had not lived up to that expectation.

Mamma had survived her childbearing years, and our family was now complete with the addition of Violet, Eric, and Lionel. Complete, and now, also, expanded; Ina had married last year, to a nobleman from Scotland, William Skene. His family held many estates, to Mamma's everlasting delight, while William was also an academic close to Papa's heart. He had been a fellow at All Souls College when he met Ina. Thus, they lived in Oxford for part of the year.

"Mr. Ruskin," I murmured. "If that were true, you would be the first to know it."

"Deception, Miss Alice, does not become you." He looked at me from beneath those unruly eyebrows, his blue eyes glittering. "I would be the last to know it."

"From my lips only; to be sure, you would hear it from some other. One of your sources, perhaps?" I smiled wickedly, moving away from the table into the hallway, to the staircase, which was draped with picturesque couples. The ladies were in jewel-toned evening dresses of the current fashion (tightly fitted bodices and front skirts, pulled back to beribboned bustles cascading with lace and bows; low necklines, tiny puffs of sleeves, and short gloves of lace or net). The attending gentlemen—holding dinner plates for their partners—were in black tailcoats, white vests, and white shirts with the new winged collar. The round-globed gaslights, recently installed in the Deanery, threw off hazy yellow light against the dark flowered wallpaper, although Mamma still insisted upon candles being lit as well.

"Don't be coy with me, Alice," Mr. Ruskin grumbled, following so closely that he stepped on the train of my peacock-blue Worth gown, a birthday present from Ina and Mr. Skene. "I observed the two of you at my lecture. Very cozy, you were. I wonder if the Queen is aware?"

"I'm confident that Leo—the Prince—hides nothing of importance from her."

"Leo?" Mr. Ruskin's eyebrows shot up to his hairline.

"The Prince," I repeated firmly, my face burning at my mistake.

"Hmmph. So the Queen approves?"

"I said he hides nothing of *importance*. He and I are friends; that is all." With a great effort, I swallowed my rising unease and favored him with a coquettish smile, one I knew had a soothing effect upon him. I used it often during our art lessons, whenever he leaned too closely over my shoulder. While I still enjoyed painting, I continued my lessons, dutifully accompanied by Edith, who did not share my talent, simply because they remained the only course of study open to me. The end of my schoolgirl years was marked by my Grand Tour; even as I was traveling through Europe with my sisters, unaccompanied, for the first time, by either of our parents, I worried how I would occupy myself once we returned. I was grateful to be in Oxford, at least, where young ladies attending lectures and reading books wasn't quite as shocking as it would have been in a more fashionable place, such as London.

However, my pursuit of art meant that I was thrown, more and more, into the company of Mr. Ruskin. Hence my reliance upon certain coquettish smiles and playful phrases.

This evening, unfortunately, he was having none of them.

"You and the Prince are merely friends, my dear? I find that very hard to believe. How can any man ever content himself with friendship?" Stepping off my train, he pressed close against me so that his breath blew chills across the back of my neck. "Especially when it comes to Alice in Wonderland? Do you think the Queen knows all about *that* business?"

"I do wish you wouldn't call me that," I hissed, squirming, attempting to get away. He had pressed me into a corner behind the stairs; I had no choice but to confront him. "And pray tell me what you mean by 'that business.'"

Mr. Ruskin smirked, his generous mouth tipping up at the corners, half concealed by his unruly sideburns, which were heavily perfumed with a sweet, overripe fragrance; I turned my head, nauseated.

"Now, Alice, don't look like that. We're friends, you and I. We have much in common, and I believe I can help."

"Help?" I looked down at him; he was starting to stoop with age, and I had grown tall in these last years. Surveying his figure—filled out in the shoulders, at the hips, yet strangely slim at the waist, suggesting a corset—I managed to conceal a smirk. "I wasn't aware I was in need of rescue."

"Dear Alice—dear, innocent, naïve Alice." He chuckled, sounding like the benign scholar so many people believed him to be. "Is Mr. Dodgson aware of your new *friendship*?"

I stiffened, drawing myself up to my full height; I was my mother's daughter, after all. I rapped my fan against Mr. Ruskin's shoulder, pushing him away.

"I have no need for deceit. I'm sure that Mr. Dodgson, like all my friends, would only wish me great happiness. That is, were there any occasion for it, which there is not."

"How bewitching," Mr. Ruskin purred, stepping aside, releasing me. "That you believe, even now, in Wonderland. It's one of your many charms, my dear."

I whirled around, about to contradict him, for I had long since stopped believing in a land where reality could not intrude. Then I paused. Since Leo had arrived, had insinuated himself into my

185

life, my heart, I realized I had allowed myself to believe once more.

His Royal Highness, the Prince Leopold, had appeared in a swirl of ceremony, one more Royal pupil for my father to welcome to Christ Church; I was mildly curious about him, as I remembered the Prince of Wales telling me of this youngest brother when I was very small. Mindful of the past and heeding Mamma's warnings for the future, at first I was resigned to remain in shadows, watching with amusement as she pushed Edith toward the dapper young Prince, seating them next to each other at dinners and concerts, arranging romantic musical evenings like tonight.

The Prince, however, did not play his assigned role. He saw me in the shadows, ignored my mother—who was not used to being ignored—and insisted upon pulling me into the sun. Where I realized, to my great surprise, that I still wanted to believe in fairy tales, after all.

Yet how could they come true while I remained here in Oxford, trapped by my past, trapped by my very name, even? Trapped by eyes, eyes everywhere; eyes once kind. Now, however—I did not know. I didn't want to know. I wanted only to forget.

"Alice, where have you been?" Edith came gliding up, her hair—a darker auburn now—arranged in cascading curls held off her smooth white brow with diamond clips. Her deep green eyes took in my discomfort at once; she placed her hand on Mr. Ruskin's arm and dimpled prettily at him.

"Mr. Ruskin! I've been looking for you everywhere! I'm very angry at Alice for monopolizing you!"

"Dear girl! Dear, dear girl!" He preened and twittered like a malicious magpie. Stroking his sideburns, he allowed himself to be steered away by Edith.

"Oh, Alice! Ruskin! There you are!" Prince Leopold joined us, unfortunately before Edith could succeed. Leo's smile, when he saw me, was pure happiness; I wondered, not for the first time, what he saw when he looked at me to make him smile this way.

"Your Royal Highness." Mr. Ruskin bowed, as Edith and I curtsied.

"Oh, do stop it. We see each other with too much frequency here at Oxford; we must dispense with such formalities."

"I don't recall your brother, the Prince of Wales, expressing himself so when he was a student, Sir," Mr. Ruskin replied.

"No, Bertie wouldn't," was all that Leopold had to say about the matter. "I'm so very glad I caught the two of you together," he continued with an impish grin. "I made a wager with Miss Alice here—yes, I am a very corrupting influence— and I must see it through."

"Oh, Prince Leopold!" I shook my head, laughing—attempting to pull him away from Mr. Ruskin.

"Come now, Alice. I'm no welsher."

"What? You two made a wager concerning me?" There was no use for it; of course Mr. Ruskin's considerable vanity was now involved. I shook my head at Leo, who was watching me with laughing—innocent—eyes.

"Mr. Ruskin," I began, my voice as light and merry as I could make it. "As you observed, I had the pleasure of attending your typically *brilliant* lecture yesterday. Somehow, I fail to see what your opinion concerning the current, declining state of English society—which, after all, is hardly an original opinion, at that—has to do with Sir Joshua Reynolds's valuable discourses. There. Where is my half crown?" I held my hand out to Leo; he laughed, reached inside his pocket, and tucked a coin into my palm, folding my fingers over it with a lingering, possessive gesture. Mr. Ruskin's sharp eyes did not fail to observe this discreet ceremony.

"Well, as usual, it's delightful to hear a lady's —hardly original, in its own way—opinion about a scholarly subject." Mr. Ruskin did not quite manage to conceal his contempt with a smile. "Miss Alice, would you do me the pleasure of further enlightening me? I would very much like to continue our conversation." He raised his bushy white eyebrows. "Tomorrow afternoon, perhaps? In my rooms, for tea?"

"Oh dear! I believe I have a dressmaker's appointment?" I looked at Edith, who nodded much too vigorously; she was not as skilled a liar as her elder sister.

"Yes, I'm sure of it, Alice. I remember it's been scheduled for days."

"I think you can postpone it for an old *friend,* can't you? You, who have so many old friends scattered about?" Ruskin bowed, finally allowing Edith to drag him away—but not before he whispered in my ear, as he brushed past me, *"Alone."*

I shivered, turning to Leo, longing to grab his hand and run away to—where, exactly? There was no place for us to go; there were so many eyes upon us. Mamma's eyes, too, worriedly watched the two of us; I could see her brow knit, her lips press themselves tightly together as she stood in the doorway to the dining room. I looked away. I did not want to see my thoughts confirmed in my mother's face.

"Strange fellow. Whatever did he mean?" Leo watched as Edith skillfully steered Mr. Ruskin back toward the refreshment table.

"I couldn't say."

"Alice, are you ill? You look pale."

"No, no, I'm perfectly fine. Although I'll never hear the end of it from Mamma if I monopolize you—she so wants to enjoy your company."

"I sat next to her all during the Bach quintet. I brought her a glass of punch. I promised her I'd be her guest of honor at a winter ball. Now I must claim the reward for my patience." He stroked the top of my satin glove, pressing my hand against his chest; I allowed this liberty only long enough for me to feel his heart beat against the palm of my hand, before I gently pulled it away.

"Oh, Leo," I said, wishing I could hide my face against his shoulder; hide my shame, my past, my fears.

"What? Alice—are you crying? Whatever is wrong, my darling?" He pulled me to him, looking into my face, his eyes round with alarm. One strand of dark yellow hair fell across his forehead, giving him such a youthful look.

I shook my head, blinked away my tears, and glanced around the room, desperate to find something amusing to lighten my thoughts.

But I did not find such distraction, and knew we had lingered too long in our private alcove; with calm determination, I moved toward the hallway, which was lined with family photographs, particularly of the three identically dressed Liddell girls when they were very small.

"What a tableau!" Leo paused in front of one photograph; it was of the three of us, Ina, Edith, and me, in identical short lacy dresses with pantalets and ankle socks, strumming tiny guitars, or *machetes*. Of the three of us, I was the only one looking right at the camera—or rather, right at Mr. Dodgson. Yet I did not remember taking the photograph; it must have been in his rooms, probably at the instigation of Mamma.

"Mamma was fond of dressing us up and having us photographed," I told Leo now. "She did not mind Mr. Dodgson at those times."

"Mr. Dodgson took the photographs?" Leo still gazed at the picture, and I smiled, wondering what he saw in my younger self.

"Yes, he's very skilled."

"A man of many talents. And a man of obvious discernment, choosing you as his muse again and again!" Still looking at the photograph, Leo slipped his hand in mine, and I allowed it to linger there for a moment more than usual before I moved away.

"I'm not sure about that, it was simply convenient back then as we all were such great friends, living practically next door to each other," I murmured, watching Mamma start to make her way toward us.

"I wish to have a photograph of you." Leo turned to me just as Mamma joined us. She bowed—but paled, as she must have heard what he said.

"Sir?" she asked, somehow making it appear as if she was smiling at both of us, although she never once looked my way.

"I was saying to Alice I wish to have a photograph of her. I don't have one, and I'm just now aware that there's a gifted photographer right in our midst! Would you be so kind, madam, as to arrange for Mr. Dodgson to photograph Alice? We could make it a party—I'm terribly fascinated by the whole process. I have a camera myself, but I'm rather clumsy with it."

"Sir, I'm happy to arrange for my daughters— for I'm sure you meant to include Edith, naturally—to pose for any of the wonderful photographers we now have in Oxford. Surely you've heard of Mrs. Cameron? The girls have posed for her before—in fact, there's a lovely photograph of Edith in the library, if you'll allow me to show you?" With a sure yet respectful hand upon his arm, Mamma gestured down the hall toward the library.

"I'd consider it a great favor if you asked Mr. Dodgson," Leo replied firmly. "I cannot pass up the opportunity to have Alice in Wonderland photographed by Lewis Carroll."

I was frozen, a polite smile plastered on my face. I felt utterly helpless. I could not bring myself to meet Mamma's accusing gaze, nor could I try to cajole Leo out of his whim; not here, not in front of her.

"I understand, but you have no idea how beautifully the girls photograph with Mrs. Cameron—"

"I said Mr. Dodgson."

I had never heard Leo speak so imperiously

before; neither had Mamma. But she recognized a Royal command when she heard it. She had no choice but to curtsy and hurry away, announcing to all the company that the musicians had returned, and everyone was to take their seats.

During the rest of the evening, while sitting next to Leo—Edith resided on his other side, placed there with scowling determination by Mamma—I pretended to enjoy the delicate trills of a Mozart quartet. My heart, however, remained heavy, and the back of my head burned with the heat of Mamma's accusing glare. I knew who she would blame for this latest reminder of *all that business,* as Mr. Ruskin so carelessly called it.

Was there no escape from my past? As long as I remained here, I knew there was none. But I could not escape Oxford on my own. I needed someone to spirit me away; I had a notion of myself, tucked into a trunk or valise, being carried out the gate of Tom Quad, hidden from eyes, those prying eyes.

Leo's hands were too slender, I feared. Too slender, too unaccustomed to the burden of carrying someone else.

Particularly someone so burdened herself.

THAT NIGHT, AS I undressed for bed, there was a knock on my door.

"It's only me," Edith's voice called softly.

"Come in!" I smiled, relieved; Edith's presence was so restful, so assured. Surely she could calm my jumbled nerves, for I had not been able to shake off the unease Mr. Ruskin had left behind after he took his leave with another arch reminder of our "lovely tea" on the morrow. "Sophie, you may go," I told my maid, who curtsied and gathered up my fallen finery—bustle with its network of tapes, corset, petticoats, drawers, silk stockings, satin dress. She staggered under the load, as she was a mousy little thing with a forever frazzled look about her. Wrapping myself in my dressing gown, I opened the door to let her out, and Edith in.

"I couldn't sleep." Edith's hair was a bright electric cloud released from its pins and clips. She plopped down in the middle of my four-poster bed, jostling the rose brocade curtains. "Did you have a nice time tonight?"

"Yes." I sat down at my dressing table and started to remove the pins from my own hair, dropping them with a clatter in a little scalloped china dish. Then I began to brush it out, although it didn't take long; even though my hair was not as thick as Edith's, and still pin straight, I never tired of the heavy weight of it down my back.

I looked at my sister in the reflection of the gold-framed mirror. "Why do you ask?"

"I was merely curious."

"You mean concerned, don't you?"

"Alice, you're getting to be extremely suspicious in your old age." Her eyes grew big and bright, her mouth strangely set, as if she were holding a handful of pebbles in it.

"I've always been extremely suspicious. And you've always been a terrible liar. Mamma sent you in here, didn't she?"

My sister swung her white legs over the edge of my bed and sighed. "You're too sharp for me, Alice. You take after Mamma that way."

"Much to my regret." I placed my hairbrush down on my dressing table and joined my sister on my bed. Grabbing her hand, I pulled her down with me, so that we were both staring up at the canopy above. "What is her concern this time? Did I spill my punch? Tear my dress? Betray the location of the family vault?" I knew what my mother's concerns were, naturally, but I simply wanted to make Edith laugh.

She didn't disappoint. "Alice!" Edith giggled, musically, joyfully; she sounded like a little girl again, which was what I had wanted. And so I had to giggle, too; her laugh was so infectious.

"Isn't this nice?" I asked with a melancholy sigh, when we had tired ourselves out.

"Yes, very." Edith leaned her head upon my shoulder with a contented smile.

"As if we were little girls again, up in the nursery with Phoebe, dear Phoebe. She's so old now. However does she keep up with Violet?"

"I don't believe she does. Violet has the run of the place. She's quite the little tyrant."

"True. I am loath to say it, but I almost wish Pricks was here. She'd straighten her out in no time."

"She asked about you the other day, you know," Edith said, after a moment.

"How could she?" I twisted my head around to stare at my sister; we were so close, I could count the faint freckles on her nose—ghost freckles, I called them, for they were almost translucent, hardly noticeable to the casual eye.

"I went down to the hotel, to visit. Pricks enjoys seeing us—well, seeing me, and Rhoda."

"An innkeeper's wife. How fitting."

"She always speaks well of you, Alice."

"As well she may, now that she's done her damage." I rolled over, my arms crossed against my chest. "She's a ridiculous figure, and it's a wonder she ever snagged a husband at her age, the way she positively threw herself at—well, at those who had better taste."

Edith did not comment; she simply waited for me to roll back over and take her hand, so she could give me a comforting squeeze.

"You haven't told me what your mission is," I said with a sigh, finally steeling myself to hear it. Mamma rarely spoke to me directly these days; indeed, she hadn't in years. It was as if she couldn't trust herself not to speak what was truly in her heart. Or perhaps she couldn't trust me not to do the same.

"I'm not going to carry it out," Edith declared, happy and proud in her little act of defiance. I had to smile, turning my face toward hers, breathing in the summer smell of rosewater that always lingered in her hair.

"She wanted you to tell me to be less attentive to Prince Leopold, didn't she?"

"Yes, but I don't want you to, unless you feel the need for secrecy yourself. Oh, Alice, you seem so happy with him! I don't care that Mamma had her eye on him for me—I wouldn't want him, anyway, for I am—am fond—of another. Truly, I see your happiness, the light in your eye, the smile, and I'm so glad, for I haven't seen that in you in such a long time!"

I wrapped my arms about my sister, tears springing to my eyes; they dampened the shoulder of her pink lisle nightgown, but she didn't appear to mind. She was so dear! So unselfish with her love! She was the only person in my life who still treated me as I was before the breach. For that was how I viewed my life; it was as if the first part had been spent in a land of pure contentment, a land of gingerbread houses and spun-sugar clouds and lemon-drop sun. But one day a giant quake tore the very earth away from my feet, and cast me up on the shore of a darker, foreign place.

I knew it was ridiculous; no childhood could be that uncomplicated, and I knew my memories couldn't be trusted, for wasn't that what everyone said? Yet forever, I viewed my life as divided into two different parts, or lands; before and after.

"I'm so very glad you're here," I told Edith, speaking what was in my heart, for once. "Now!" I brushed away the tears on both of our cheeks and sat up, fluffing a pillow—shooing away the tiny white feathers that escaped from it—and leaning up against the headboard. "Tell me who has won your heart, for I know you're not simply fond of this gentleman. Fondness has no place in your vocabulary."

Edith dimpled, rolling over so that her head was propped up on her slender hand. "Do you remember my childhood dream of living in a house as grand as Nuneham Courtney?"

"Yes, but—Edith! You don't mean to say you're in love with Aubrey Harcourt?"

Edith blushed, but her green eyes, as bright as stars, confirmed my guess.

"Oh, how wonderful! He's a kind young man, and of course, all that property, including Nuneham Courtney! Mamma will positively swoon! Do you love him, truly?"

"Yes," Edith said, twisting a strand of hair about the fourth finger of her left hand, until it resembled a wedding band. "He's no prince, of course—I leave the truly spectacular match up to you—but he is fond of me, I think. Ever so fond. And I of him."

"Then I shall think fondly of him, too. Although

I can't bear the notion of giving you up." I reached toward her, grabbing her hand as if I could grab on to my childhood, as well. How quickly we all had grown, after all.

"You won't have to, not for ages, not until the summer, at earliest. I'll be the one who will have to part with you, I fear. Fear, and hope, both?" She smiled at me, joining me at the top of the bed, nestling under my arm.

I didn't answer. There was both fear and hope within my heart, true. They did not mix well together, I discovered, placing a hand upon my breast, trying to quiet the tumult within.

"I don't know," I finally whispered to my sister, voicing the fear, hoping that by hearing it out loud, it might not feel so real. "There are many obstacles in the way, I'm afraid."

Edith nodded, forced to agree; she was a sweet little optimist, my sister, but no fool. She understood instantly what I meant.

"Did Mamma mention anything about being photographed?" I asked.

"Yes. By Mr. Dodgson, you mean?"

I nodded, unable to look my sister in the eyes.

"It was an odd request, was it not? By the Prince?" Edith's voice was very gentle, very careful.

I nodded again.

"I would think, then, that no gossip—no talk, I mean—has reached his ears. I believe that is why Mamma has decided to arrange for a sitting; she seems to view this as an opportunity."

"An opportunity to humiliate me in front of the Prince?" I couldn't help it; I flew off the bed and paced around my room, tying and untying the sash of my dressing gown, not knowing I was doing so until I found my hand wrapped tightly in a knot of silk.

"An opportunity to show that there is no basis to—to what some may have said, in the past." Edith remained on the bed, her legs dangling over the side, watching me.

"And what some are still saying." I remembered Mr. Ruskin, and his summons.

"Which is all the more reason to do this, Alice. The Prince truly loves you—I can see it!"

"The only reason Mamma is consenting is because of you—you're the one she desires to see happy. Not me."

"That's not true, Alice."

"Yes, it is. The Prince is not intended for me; if she's eager to show the gossips that the Liddells are not afraid to associate with Mr. Dodgson, it's not to restore my reputation—I'm too far gone for that. It's to clear the family name for you."

"But don't you see that the result will be the same? One less obstacle, as you say?"

"No, I don't. Because I don't know what will happen—how we can possibly return to that—to him—to—oh, I don't know. I don't know!" I threw myself back upon the bed; my head somehow found itself resting on Edith's lap, as she smoothed my tangled hair. Eventually my breathing slowed, my limbs grew heavy, and, yawning, I began to feel the lateness of the hour.

"Alice, Alice. I know it's been terribly difficult for you, but I believe good times are just ahead. You're strong—so strong! So much stronger than I am."

I looked up at her sweet, worried face. "You're just as strong. We're both our mother's daughters, for better and for worse."

"I do believe she wants you to be happy, Alice. I truly believe so."

"I know you do."

"As do I. I pray, very hard, every night, for your happiness," she whispered, before gently kissing me on the cheek and pushing me off her lap. Then she ran out the door, back to her own room.

"May we be happy," I murmured, not quite understanding what I was saying, only that the phrase seemed familiar to me. A ghost missive from the land of childhood, I mused drowsily, getting up to blow out the candle on my dressing table. I stopped there and gazed at my reflection in the mirror, looking for some trace of the child I'd been—before.

I still wore my hair in a fringe; I still had a rather decided chin. But other than that, I could see no trace of the triumphant girl in the pale, somber-eyed maiden that stared back at me. What did Leo see in that maiden, then, that enchanted him so? What goodness, what innocence, did he find? I could not recognize it; I saw myself only as others did, as my mother did. Should I pray that he see me that way, too, so that he could absolve me with his love? Or should I pray that somehow I could miraculously shed the past and become who he believed me to be?

"May we be happy," I repeated, frowning at myself; I blew the candle out. Climbing back under the down quilts of my bed, I wondered if Sophie would have the sense to bring up a bed warmer, as the nights were growing colder. "May we all deserve happiness," I murmured into my pillow.

Then, with startling clarity—and a cold, sick dread that spread over my limbs—I remembered when I had heard those words, after all; I remembered who had spoken them to me.

I knew no copper bed warmer would give me comfort tonight.

Chapter 8

*T*HE NEXT AFTERNOON I DRESSED IN MY most somber dress, a wine-colored wool with tightly buttoned sleeves, high neck, and lace trim; I pinned my plainest hat in place and left the Deanery—Sophie trotting behind me—rejoicing that I did not have to walk across the Quad, where I was sure to feel his gaze upon me with every step.

Mr. Dodgson had moved to different rooms some years previous. He no longer lived across the garden from the back of the Deanery; he now had larger quarters across the Quad from the *front* of the Deanery.

Our meetings, in the years since that summer day, had been few, always strained, always in public—and always commented upon by others; Mr. Ruskin was considerate enough to inform me of *that*. Yet they were inevitable, as long as we both lived in such close proximity. For Oxford was, despite its deserved academic reputation, simply a village, after all. The students might come and go, society as a whole might change all around us—a new, bustling middle class was rising out of the ranks of the poor, demanding to be taken seriously—but the established citizens of Oxford remained the same. Prone to the same quarrels, the same jealousies, the same social maneuverings as any hamlet one might read of in the novels of Mr. Trollope.

Mr. Dodgson had aged, finally; considerably. He was a graying, stiff-limbed figure now, thin, with a pronounced limp. When we met in public, as was inevitable, we were always polite. Never did our eyes truly meet, though, except from across a greater distance; across the Quad, across a crowded lecture hall, across the packed congregation in the cathedral. And always I felt his eyes upon me when I walked to my own front door; I felt them pick me, once again, out of all the people in the Quad and follow me until I reached the safety of the Deanery. No longer did this bring me happiness, make me feel special and loved; now I was afraid. Afraid that he could see me, after all—see the real me, as his camera had done so often—and know the truth.

And I watched, myself. I watched him go on picnics with other little girls. I watched him escort them to his new rooms, accompanied by their governesses. I watched him take them rowing on the Isis, and I couldn't help but wonder—did he tell *them* stories? Capture their souls, their desires, with his camera?

Did he feel my eyes upon him, too?

I had no idea. The only thing I knew for sure was there was no escaping him; with the publication of *Alice's Adventures in Wonderland,* which was what Lewis Carroll decided to call *Alice's Adventures Under Ground,* our lives were seemingly bound together for eternity. The book was an instant classic, and Mr. Dodgson dutifully sent me every edition, including foreign printings; when he published *Through the Looking-Glass,* he sent me that, as well. In his odd, indirect way, he persisted in dedicating both books to me.

What was I to make of that? That I remained,

forever, a child of seven, courtesy of the man who had caused me to grow up sooner than I had ever wished? I'd spent years trying to figure out this last, most confounding, puzzle of his. I doubted I'd ever be able to solve it.

Still, he haunted me. Everywhere I went; everyone I met. His eyes, his words, were upon me always. Alice in Wonderland. I would never be anything but.

Not even to Leo, I thought with a sigh. That was who he came to Oxford ready to fall in love with, I knew. An invalid all his life, shut off from the world until now, wasn't it natural that he fall in love with a girl spun from dreams, from words, from pictures; not from flesh and blood and dubious experience?

Sometimes, I wondered—did he dream of me as I was, the pale young woman with straight black hair, cut in a fringe? Or did he dream of me as a girl in a pinafore with long yellow hair? I could never ask him; I was afraid to know the answer.

"Sophie, do keep up," I snapped, marching down the path in front of the library, turning right onto Merton Street, much narrower and less crowded than the High or St. Aldate's; there were few shops, mainly university buildings. I despised the necessity of being chaperoned wherever I went, but I, of all women, could not risk censure, no matter the circumstances. Fortunately, Sophie was a simple creature, and easily distracted by servant gossip; the promise of tea and a cake with Mr. Ruskin's equally gossipy housekeeper would keep her occupied while I met with the eminent scholar himself.

Quickly I attained Corpus Christi, the small college adjacent to Christ Church—both colleges bordered the Meadow—where Mr. Ruskin's rooms were located. The heel of my boot rapping sharply against the walk, I headed down an intimate little rectangular stone quad to the Fellows building, the largest building in Corpus. I always thought the façade resembled Buckingham Palace, with the pitched roof at the center above faux columns.

I paused, although I was not out of breath despite my tightly laced stays, and readjusted my hat. Sophie, however, was mopping her brow with the sleeve of her coat. "Miss, how quickly you do walk!"

"You're simply out of condition. Now go on, quick, up the stairs and knock on the door."

"Yes, miss."

I followed her up a staircase to the first floor; she knocked on the door and was admitted by a plump, red-faced housekeeper with a comical air of regality.

"Miss Alice Liddell, to see Mr. Ruskin!" Sophie exclaimed, breathless.

"Do come in," the housekeeper intoned.

Brushing past, I handed her my card, removed

my hat and coat and bestowed them upon Sophie, and waited to be shown into Mr. Ruskin's drawing room. "Sophie, as it is teatime, I'm certain that you won't mind stopping in the kitchen and having a bit of cake with Mr. Ruskin's housekeeper."

"Oh, thank you, miss! That will be lovely!"

"Well, then." I nodded at her as the housekeeper opened the door to the drawing room with a stiff curtsy.

"My dear little friend!" Mr. Ruskin rose from an easy chair in front of the fire and met me halfway across the room. He was wearing his usual attire: outdated black frock coat, bright blue tie, rough tweed pants.

"Pray, don't act so surprised. I believe this was a command performance, was it not?" I allowed him to kiss me on both cheeks, in the continental fashion, while wondering just when he had acquired this habit. It must have been on his last trip to Italy.

"Just when did you get so very suspicious, my lovely? You remind me of your dear mamma more and more each day." He chuckled with pleasure and gestured toward another chair near the fire. There was a table set up between the two chairs, laden with tea things: two fragile cups of distinctly Italian decoration, a matching teapot, plates, silver, and delicate cakes.

Removing my gloves, I surveyed his drawing

room. I'd managed not to be coerced into visiting here in the four years he'd been in residence; Edith and I took our lessons at the Deanery. Yet I admit I had been curious to see his rooms, as I'd heard so much about the odd décor. Indeed, this was a singularly eclectic room; overfilled with books, etchings, and especially paintings and photographs, on easels, hanging from walls, on the floor, slanted against furniture. In addition, there were two cabinets full of rocks of every shape and hue, each carefully labeled. In short, the room resembled nothing more than a museum exhibit.

With a smile—for there was something oddly charming about the juxtaposition of cold, scientific artifacts and the abstract, light-filled Turner landscapes he loved so well—I made to sit down. Before I could do so, I froze.

For there, in a simple silver frame on a low round table, was the photograph of me as Mr. Dodgson's beggar girl.

"Where did you get that?" With shaking, suddenly icy hands, I picked up the photograph. Staring up at me was the picture of myself, at age seven, clad in the torn gypsy girl's dress. One hand was on my hip, the other lazily extended as my younger self gazed at the camera with a defiant smirk, the triumphant glare of a child who has discovered herself to be a woman.

Closing my eyes, clutching the photograph to my chest—it was cold and heavy against my breast

—a rush of memories overtook me, causing the room to spin with their fury. Unlike that other photograph, the one that charmed Leo so, suddenly I recalled every detail of this one. I remembered the chill autumn day, I remembered changing behind the tent, far from the eyes of everyone except Mr. Dodgson; I felt, once more, his bare hand upon my shoulder, my waist; the grass between my tender toes. How long ago it seemed! How little I knew then of the ways of the world, but looking into those glittering dark eyes—so different from the eyes that stared warily back at me from the looking glass every morning—I saw that I had imagined myself to have known so very much. About men, about women, about dreams and desires; about the future.

His letters—the letters that he wrote, after that day; unbidden fragments of thought, of dreams, came to me: *Do you remember how it felt, to roll about on the grass while I watched?*

Those letters, those dreams, were long gone now. I'd seen them burn with my own eyes; they burned in the grate of the nursery hearth, bitterly torn and prodded by the poker in Mamma's hand as she railed and wept and forbade me to do the same.

Yet here was the picture, the one tangible relic that remained. I had so longed to see it, before; I recalled how I had never been able to bring myself to ask him for it. In my childish innocence,

I had believed it would remain in his possession. The creation of this image had been so intimate. I had not wanted strangers' eyes—Mr. Ruskin's eyes!—to see the result.

I had wanted to live forever as a gypsy girl; I had wanted to live forever as a child, tumbling down a rabbit hole. I had been granted both wishes, only to find immortality was not what it had promised to be; instead of a passport to the future, it was a yoke that bound me to the past.

"Yes, that's you," Mr. Ruskin said.

"I know—I'm merely startled, that's all, to see it after—after all this time."

"Charming, isn't it? I was taken with it the first time I laid eyes on it."

"When was that, pray?"

"Oh, years ago. Not long after it was taken, if I recall."

"He—Mr. Dodgson—gave this to you?"

"He had many copies printed. You're quite famous, my dear, among lovers of photography."

"Others have seen it?" I looked up in alarm; I fought an impulse to shield myself as if it were I, at twenty-three, standing half clad, vulnerable, and not the image of my seven-year-old self.

"Why so surprised?" Mr. Ruskin looked down his aristocratic nose at me and smiled. It was not a kind smile; it was the expression of a cat that had cornered a mouse, and was not yet decided whether to play with it or devour it.

"I don't know, it's ridiculous, I suppose—of course, I had to have known he intended others to see it."

"Don't be angry, Alice." Remarkably, it was he who now appeared hurt; he lowered his head in a pout, looking up at me with his beseeching eyes. Apparently, his theatrics were not limited to the lecture hall. "I had no idea you would be so upset. If I had, I would never have accepted the photograph. But you and Mr. Dodgson are such good friends—or rather, I suppose, past tense is more appropriate?"

"I believe you know the answer to that already." I was in no mood for his games; I forced myself to place the photograph down, dispassionately, without further histrionics. I was becoming quite the bashful maiden, after all. Ina would have been delighted to observe how close I'd come to a proper swoon.

As I returned the photograph to its place, I noticed a small painting next to it. It was of a young girl with arched eyebrows, light blue eyes, reddish yellow hair. Her pale, ethereal face was almost otherworldly. I suspected I knew her identity; it was an open secret among everyone at Oxford.

Mr. Ruskin had his own dark past, his own scandalous affair. The circumstances were heart-breaking—the young woman whose childhood portrait I beheld had recently died, insane; she was a religious zealot, it was rumored, and had spurned Mr. Ruskin for God. Yet somehow, I could not find it in my heart to pity Mr. Ruskin. I could never convince myself of the sincerity of his emotions; he was too eager to draw on every aspect of his life, no matter how tragic, as a means to further his fame.

"Sit, Alice, and please do me the honor of pouring out." He took his own seat and watched as I did the same.

"It will be my pleasure." I picked up the teapot and poured two cups, adding lemon to his, as prompted.

"There," he pronounced, settling into the depths of his high-backed wing chair; the sides of it were so deep, a person could completely disappear from view. "Isn't this cozy?"

"Quite." I stirred my own tea and sipped quietly; it was fine tea, slightly spicy, bracing. I could not fault him on his hospitality. He certainly knew how to set a stage.

"We are old friends, you and I, are we not?"

"If you say so."

"If I say so? Alice, why will you persist in being so enigmatic? Ah, but that is part of your charm, of course. Still, I sometimes wonder if you like me, even just a little?"

"Surely someone of your fame and influence need not question the devotion of one such as me?"

"Again with the prevarication!" He slapped his knee in delight; I smiled demurely into my teacup, now sure of my hold over him. "Alice, I cannot deny that I find you most charming. I also feel compelled to tell you that I see much danger in your current path. There—finally, an honest reaction! I see the hesitation in your eyes. Would you like me to continue?"

I set my teacup down and folded my hands in my lap. Staring into the mesmerizing flames of the fire—they were dancing with the hypnotic motion of a snake being charmed—I pondered his question. Would I like him to continue? No, certainly not. Still, he found me charming—I had always known this, ever since I was small—and as such, might behave in the manner of a spurned suitor if I did not listen. And there was no denying that he had great influence, not only here at the university but with the Royal Family; several of them were patrons of the new school for drawing he had just established. Leo himself was a trustee.

I glanced at him, perched so benignly in his chair. There had been rumors, many rumors, concerning my friendship with Mr. Dodgson, the source of the obvious breach between him and my family. Rumors that had not, thus far, reached Leo's ears, or the ears of his courtiers; last night had confirmed that. And who was the source of most of the rumors flying up and down the hallowed halls of learning?

The man sitting next to me, stirring his tea, spilling it on his trousers, shaking his head at his own foolishness—all the while grinning like a certain cat from a certain cherished children's book.

Would I never be rid of the thing?

"Proceed," I said with a regal nod.

"There's a wise girl!" Mr. Ruskin stroked his whiskers, releasing a whiff of perfume. "First, let me be so bold as to satisfy a curiosity of long standing. Is it true that Dodgson asked your parents for your hand, all those years ago?"

A shock went through me; my heart pounded so hard, I could hear nothing but the roaring of my own pulse in my ears. I had not reckoned on him being quite so blunt; that was not the way we spoke to each other.

He saw my distress yet did not attempt to alleviate it. He simply remained in his chair, watching me with eyes that glittered with the firelight. He reached for a tea cake and popped it into his mouth, chewing with gusto.

"I—that is, that is very rude of you to ask such a thing!"

"I know, I know, and I do apologize. But I cannot help you if I do not have all the facts."

"Facts? Facts concerning what?"

"Concerning your past, my dear. Don't be a fool. Do you think that you could possibly enter-tain the notion of marrying a son of Victoria's without inviting scrupulous attention to your previous actions?"

"I have told you, I entertain no such thing. Prince Leopold and I are simply very good friends."

"I give your formidable mamma much more credit than that. I cannot imagine that she would let a catch like Leopold slip through her capable fingers without a fight."

"I believe it's well known that the Queen seeks only Royal matches for her children," I replied, finding strange comfort in one of my greatest fears. While I did not want to believe this to be true, it was quite useful in deflecting attention from my—friendship—with her youngest son.

"With Leopold's dreadful infirmity, not to mention his being so far down the line of succession, I cannot help but think that Victoria might relax her standards in this case. Your mother certainly knows this. As do you, I'd venture."

My cheeks flamed, hearing my dearest heart spoken of in this manner, so coldly, so surgically. I didn't mind Mr. Ruskin gossiping about me— at least, within the privacy of this room—but I deplored hearing him gossip about Leo. Leo was too fine, too pure, to be caught up in one of Mr. Ruskin's verbal snares.

"I daresay, Edith would be better suited for such a match—were it being considered. Which, I assure you, it is not." I sipped more tea. My throat, my tongue, my lips, even, were unquenchably dry.

"True, were it not for the fact she loves another, and he her." Mr. Ruskin's eyes sparkled with triumph.

How did he know about Edith? Even Mamma didn't suspect. "I tell you, once more, there is nothing between Prince Leopold and myself," I repeated; as if restating that one simple sentence, over and over, would convince him, although I knew it would not.

"I see you neither confirm nor deny your sister's plans. Mamma has taught you well. All right, it's obvious that you will not concede your position willingly. I cannot pretend to be surprised, so I'll get to the point. Relax, my dear, close your eyes —I can see you're tired, your left eye is twitching—and listen while I propose my little plan."

Touching my left eye—he was correct; a little muscle at the outer edge of it was pulsing against my fingertips—I decided to do as he said. I needed to know, finally, what I was up against.

"Now. The facts are thus: You are in love with Leo, and he with you. Don't continue to protest," he said, as my hands rose, once more, in response. "I have eyes; despite what you so obviously believe, I have a heart."

My eyes flew open, surprised. Perhaps, after all, he did.

"Yes, my dear—I see your astonishment. I

could go into details, if you wish, of my own recent—disappointment." He glanced at the table, at the miniature of the young woman. With a great effort—a visible stiffening of his shoulders, an intake of breath—he continued. "Indeed, in time, I imagine I will. But first I need to know about your own. Did Dodgson ask for your hand, as it is rumored?"

"I don't know," I said, shaking my head, trying, once again, to find the truth of that afternoon and all that came after. Yet always it was hidden from me. I was too young, everyone insisted. I had no way of remembering.

I wished that one day, when I was far away from here—with Leo, the one person in my life who offered me hope, not regret—I would be able to recall, and know, the truth. A truth of my very own.

"I honestly don't know," I repeated, looking up at Mr. Ruskin, speaking plainly, finally; hoping he would do the same, for my head ached, the light was fading, and I longed to be alone with my tangled thoughts. "You would have to ask Mr. Dodgson, for I was so very young, and Mamma refused to let me talk with him, or correspond with him."

"I did ask him."

My heart raced; I felt on the verge of knowing, at last, and I was both afraid and excited at the same time. I leaned forward eagerly, as if to embrace my own history—or to run from it, as fast as I possibly could.

"What—what did he say?"

"He said I would have to ask you."

"What? No! How could he? How could I possibly know? Do you actually believe my mother would tell me such a thing, if he had? Do you actually believe we talk about such things? I shouldn't even be discussing them with you!"

"No, I don't believe that, but perhaps Mr. Dodgson does."

"Then—then he does not know my family, after all."

"That's no surprise; he has never been one to dwell in the land of reality."

"It doesn't matter," I said tiredly, not believing my own words. "It's been so long, I only wish to be allowed to find my own happiness. What does it matter anymore?"

"It matters if you truly love your young prince. Can you not see that even the slightest whisper of rumor or scandal would ruin that happiness?"

"Of course. Of course I see—what do you take me for, a simpleton?"

"No, I would never do that."

He rose and walked over to me, standing behind my chair so that I could only hear his voice, not study his expression. "I do wish you happiness, Alice. You must believe me. Even if the facts of your—little drama—are unclear, they still matter.

Perception is reality, especially when it comes to affairs of the heart."

Another memory stirred. "You're very fond of saying that," I told him.

"Well, it's true. Now, I quite understand why you're unwilling to confess your romance to me. You're wise to keep it secret, although I must advise that you do a better job of it than you did the other day at the lecture. The Prince is not accustomed to being out in the public, not as his siblings are; the Queen did an admirable job of keeping him protected while she could, but I'm afraid the result is he's not as cautious as he should be. I doubt he's ever been in love before, you know—poor chap never had a chance. You must be the sensible one."

I bit my lip, conceding his point.

"Here's what I propose. I can make certain that your young prince remains in the dark, concerning any—secrets—you may have. Should anything reach his ears, I can negate the effect—as I said, the Royal Family holds me in esteem. I can also make certain that Dodgson remains ignorant, too; he's the most obtuse man I've ever met. I can hardly imagine that he sees the romance that is blossoming in front of his very windows."

I was silent. I couldn't allow myself to believe that; not with those eyes upon me, always; not knowing, as Mr. Ruskin did not, that soon I would be back in his rooms.

"You've been very cautious up until now, I have to admit that. Staying in the background, when Ina was out, and then married. You've been very wise."

"You're not, if you believe that was all of my own doing. I wasn't allowed much freedom until very recently. Packed off to the Continent like a disgrace—oh, of course it was all very proper, the three Liddell girls on their Grand Tour, just like every other fashionable young lady! But Mamma would have been very happy had I found some quiet count in France and not come back. Yet I did, and I suppose she realized she couldn't keep me shut up in the attic like a lunatic; I had to emerge eventually. So." I took a sip of tea, flush with my confession. Why I chose to deliver it to Mr. Ruskin, I could not imagine; his frankness must have disarmed me.

"I truly had no idea," he said. He was silent for a long moment; the only sounds were the creak of the boards as he paced the floor behind me, the snap of the fire in the hearth; the distant laughter of Sophie and the housekeeper, the soft *tick* of a mantel clock. Finally I rose, put my gloves on, signaling the end of the interview. I was determined to return matters to a businesslike footing: no swooning for me.

"So, tell me what you desire, in return for your discretion. That is what this interview is about, isn't it?"

"First so coy, now so blunt. I'll never be able to predict your behavior, my dear Miss Liddell."

"I'll choose to take that as a compliment. Now, tell me what my debt will be."

"Only yourself."

"Me?" I laughed; it was so very predictable. "I will spare us both the cheap novel melodrama of assuming you want to seduce me."

"Oh, Alice, you do amuse me." Mr. Ruskin chuckled admiringly. "No, I don't wish to seduce you. I merely desire your company. We have a great deal in common, you and I." Here he glanced, once more, at the small portrait on the table. "Both of us have past friends with whom we can no longer commune, share the best parts of ourselves." He trailed off, still staring at the clear-eyed maiden.

"Rose La Touche," I stated. It was no longer a question in my mind. "There are few secrets here at Oxford. Even about you." Despite my vow to remain as detached as possible, I could not help but place my hand upon his arm when I saw the tears brightening his eyes.

"She was my Alice, in a way. Men like me, like Dodgson, we need a muse, a way to stay young, and vital. We're no good on our own."

"But I'm—I'm no longer a child. How can I help you now?"

He turned to me, his eyes cloudy with tears and sadness, veiled with a lost dream, and I knew that he was not looking at me; he was looking at—he was looking *for*—someone else.

"Come to me," Mr. Ruskin whispered. "Simply come to me, now and again, and sit by my fire, and let me gaze at you. Let me talk. And then—" Finally he shook himself, shook off his demons, with a tremor of his head; it appeared to start from his feet, moving up the entire length of his stooped, beaten body. "And then, I will help you with the Prince. I give you my word."

I was silent. I could not see my way; it was as if I were trapped in a maze of trees, a dark, oppressive forest, only the trees were my past— and now, Mr. Ruskin's past. They stopped my progress at every turn as I strained to find my way out of the dark and into the light, where Leo was waiting to carry me, finally, away.

What other choice did I have? Leo would graduate in the spring; it was only a little while that I had to pose as Mr. Ruskin's friend. And as a friend, he would be helpful; as an enemy, he would be maliciously destructive. That much I knew.

"I will," I said finally, my voice flat, expression-less. "I will come to you. As a friend. Nothing more."

"That is all I ask." He smiled sadly, leaning in to kiss my cheek, his lips dry and rough. I shut my eyes against him, although I could not shut my senses against his sickening perfume—a combination of lavender and rose and heliotrope, more flowers than a bride would wear.

"Till next time." I pushed him away—gently—and gave him my hand; he took it, clasped it warmly, then lifted it to his lips, kissing it with a passion that startled me; it was as if my hand offered salvation, and he was a dying sinner.

"This time next week," Mr. Ruskin said, releasing me with the same passion; turning away to stare moodily at the small table, where my photograph and Rose's portrait sat like twin sirens.

Hesitating, I waited for him to show me out, but he did not move. Finally I turned and crossed the floor with a heavy step, a heavier heart.

I knew I would grow to despise this room and all that I had so recently found charming in it. I knew I would grow to despise Mr. Ruskin.

I knew, also, I would grow to despise myself.

Chapter 9
JANUARY 23, 1876

Dearest Heart, I am wretched with worry over you. I must maintain a detached, dignified air, outwardly expressing mild concern, for naturally, as the daughter of the Dean, I would be properly anxious to hear word of your welfare.

Yet "properly anxious" does not come close to revealing the anguish in my heart. I ache to be by your side; I envy the doctors who have the privilege of caring for you. O, were it my hand that mopped your brow, held your hand, brought you nourishing soups! Can you see, then, how wild I am? Can you imagine Miss Alice Liddell actually carrying in a tureen of soup with her lily-white hands?

I would do more, were it possible; were it my right. I would launder your bed linen; I would slaughter the chicken myself, grind it up—is that how it's done? I have no idea!—to make the soup; I would walk any number of miles to fetch you the finest medicine. If only I were allowed.

I am not, however. I must content myself with hearing, from Papa, the infrequent updates—for they would be frequent enough only if they were every minute!—your secretary so kindly sends. I must go about my business here in Oxford, smilingly, willingly, in the grand manner Mamma has so assiduously culti-vated, as if I have nothing more pressing upon my mind than what frock to wear, which carriage to summon.

You must know that my thoughts, my heart, are not here but in Osborne, where you lie, and that every second of every day I long to be there in the flesh as well.

You will improve; you must. And when you do, I will be here, certain to make a most undignified fool of myself when I throw myself at you, and weep, and beg for your kiss, your caress.

Until that very satisfactory, if rather sentimental, time, I remain yours, as always.

Yours only, in fact. You've quite spoilt me for anyone else, so you see, you must get well or else I'll become a tragic spinster, and I'm sure you don't wish to be responsible for that!

> *Please come soon,*
> *my dearest heart.*
> *Your Alice*

BLINKING MY EYES—FOR I WOULD NOT allow a single splash of a single tear to spoil my words—I took the heavy bronze blotter and carefully applied it to the notepaper. I then folded the letter neatly in thirds, reached inside my desk, and produced a packet of similar letters, bound with a black silk ribbon. Pressing it to my lips— ridiculous, I knew, but I needed to indulge my feelings this black, cold winter day—I slipped this newest letter into the ribbon and placed it back in my drawer.

One day I would share with Leo these letters, these photographs of my heart, my despair. But I could not risk doing so now; I had no idea if he was well enough to read his own correspondence or if his secretary must do so for him. I only knew that he lay ill with typhoid fever at Osborne House, the Queen's home on the Isle of Wight, where the Royal Family spent Christmas; that he had taken ill prior to the holiday, and that his condition had not improved in weeks. So far there had been no indication that his hemophilia played any part in his current illness, but like a shadow, it was in the back of all our minds.

I dipped my pen in the bronze inkwell, reached for another sheet of notepaper, ready to begin the letter that I would actually post. But instead of putting my pen to paper, I found myself gazing at the small frame on my desk: the photograph of Leo that Mr. Dodgson took that afternoon in November when we all sat for him.

The photograph was a good likeness; he was seated, clasping his walking stick, his face turned slightly away from the camera, tilted up. The round eyes, the neat mustache, the trim figure—all were well represented. But there was no life in them. Leo was all spirit, all bravery in the face of his illness; that was his charm, and no photograph could capture that.

Then again, the photograph of me from that afternoon—the photograph that I couldn't help but hope was at Leo's bedside as he lay ill, although I had no way of knowing—was just as flat and dull. Although Leo refused to admit it; even so, I knew he had been disappointed by it.

How could the result have been otherwise?

Mr. Dodgson had warned Mamma that the year was late, and so the light would be weak; though he had recently persuaded the college to build a rooftop studio for him, complete with skylights, he could not guarantee the outcome. Leo, however, insisted on going through with the plan anyway. So it was that on a rare sunny November morning, four of us—Mamma, Edith, Prince Leopold, and myself—found ourselves climbing the dark, narrow stairs in the building across the Quad from the Deanery, until we reached a black door with the words "The Rev. C. L. Dodgson" painted upon them.

Edith reached for my hand then; I squeezed it gratefully, for my chest felt as if my corset had been laced too tightly, my heart was pounding so. I had not been in Mr. Dodgson's rooms since I was eleven; then, I used to run to his rooms, throw myself in his arms without thought. Now— I felt so many memories, both good and bad, clear and confused, swirling about me, constricting my breath, my vision even, that I wasn't sure my legs would even carry me over the threshold.

What was Mamma thinking? I could not tell, for she would not look at me. She had, however, kept up a loud and merry conversation with the Prince ever since we left the Deanery; our visit had not gone unnoticed by anyone in the Quad. I knew that Mr. Ruskin would pepper me with questions on the morrow.

Leo rapped on the door with his walking stick; a harried-looking housekeeper opened the door and showed us in, taking our cloaks until she was no longer visible beneath them, and then Mr. Dodgson himself appeared, leading us toward his sitting room.

I had a sense of many rooms, off both sides of the hall; this arrangement was certainly larger than his old rooms over the library, where I remembered the lone sitting room being cramped and overstuffed with objects.

The sitting room I found myself in now was not cramped; it was large and spacious with an inviting red sofa and a large fireplace surrounded by red and white tiles depicting the most unusual creatures—dragons and sea snakes and odd Viking-like boats. There was room for all of us to sit easily, yet I stood, awkward as a child at a stranger's birthday party, unsure what to do.

"Pl-pl-please sit down, Miss Alice," a hesitant voice said softly, and looking up, I briefly met his gaze. The eyes were just as blue, the one slightly higher than the other, now framed by cobwebby lines, the hair curling although shot through with gray. He still wore the black frock coat of his youth; he still wore gray gloves.

Gesturing with those gloves, he showed me an empty chair, and I sat on it. Biting my suddenly trembling lip, I stared at my own hands, clenched tightly upon my lap.

"My dear Mr. Dodgson, it's a pleasure to visit you at home. I'm afraid we've seen too little of each other since I've matriculated, but that's the way it often is, isn't it?" Leo sat next to Mamma on the sofa, his arms resting expansively across the top, as if these were his own rooms. His manner was always so easy; he was at home wherever he went.

"Sir, it's an honor." Mr. Dodgson bowed stiffly, and I was reminded of how often I teased him, when I was young, that he walked as if he had a poker stuck down the back of his coat. What a rude little girl I had been! However did he put up with me?

Just then Mr. Dodgson caught me staring at him; his cheeks reddened, and I wondered if he had been thinking the same thing.

I turned away, intent upon my surroundings, while Leo engaged Mr. Dodgson in small talk concerning the university. Mamma chimed in, as if there was nothing more on her mind than academic politics; this obviously startled Mr. Dodgson, who seemed, at first, stunned by her loquacity. Edith smiled and nodded, throwing occasional anxious glances my way.

While they chatted, I surveyed the room. Even though it was large, it was a bachelor's suite, pure and simple. The few tables were uncluttered, their surfaces bare, not covered with fussy doilies; the backs of chairs were bereft of antimacassars.

There were not many adornments other than a black vase of peacock feathers near the fireplace, some small watercolors, mainly of the university. And one framed print of the frontispiece of *Alice's Adventures in Wonderland,* hanging on a wall; it wasn't very big, and certainly not in any place of honor. Indeed, it seemed rather lost, as if there were supposed to be other prints surrounding it.

It was a fastidious, scrupulously clean room, but despite its size, there was something stifling about it. In its very fastidiousness I recognized, with a surprising pang, that there was no room here for anyone else. Had he ever intended to share his home—his life—with a woman? Any woman?

However, I soon understood that if there was no room for a wife, there was definitely room for a child—or rather, children. For after closer inspection, I saw that the room was stuffed with toys, just as his old sitting room had been. Now, however, they were not out in the open, strewn about, but rather piled tidily in cupboards, lined up with precision on a window seat, peeking out of hidden corners. China and rag dolls, stuffed animals, a wooden Noah's Ark, music boxes of all shapes and sizes. One in particular I remembered from my childhood: a square contraption with a large handle, rather like a hand-cranked organ. There were a variety of tunes it could play, I recalled; he used to keep the circular music cards in a separate box, neatly categorized.

"The Last Rose of Summer" had been my favorite song; I had a sudden wild desire to look for the box to see if he still had it.

So his rooms had not changed with time. Had he? That I could not answer. For I was afraid to study him closely; afraid to speak to him, for fear of finding out. Yet I felt his eyes upon me more than once as I surveyed his room; was he trying to see me here as I was now, or as I once had been? Did I look out of place to him, now that I was grown? Or did I look familiar, achingly so—like a dream?

The air was oppressive, and I longed to open a window.

"Alice?" Someone was speaking to me. With a small shake of my head, I turned to find Leo looking at me with a slightly puzzled expression; I was so happy to find him here—I believe I had forgotten all about him—I nearly burst into tears. Instead, I simply smiled at him, feeling my heart slow down, my head clear of memories; I recognized myself in his eyes, the woman I was now. Not the little girl I used to be.

"Yes, Sir?"

"I was just saying how extraordinary it is that Lewis Carroll and the real Alice live practically across the street from one another! It's so odd that neither of you speaks of the book, yet surely it's a pleasant association?"

"Allow me to answer for Alice," Mamma said,

and I had no choice but to do so. Quickly I glanced at Mr. Dodgson; he had busied himself with straightening a painting, his slim shoulders unnaturally hunched and tense with the effort. "Sir, it's a fine tribute, of course, but naturally we don't speak of it outside of the family. It's simply not done, to call attention to Alice in such a public way—of course you understand, being a gentleman! As for Mr. Dodgson, well, I'm sure I cannot speak for him." Although Mamma did look as if she wanted to, for she fixed him with such a glare that I was surprised Leo didn't comment upon it.

"I will always remember our day on the river fondly, and be grateful that Alice urged me to write the story down," Mr. Dodgson said softly, still not looking at us. "I have many pleasant memories of our fr-fr-friendship. The books are but one memento." Finally he turned around; I would not look into his face, would not look at his sad smile that I knew so well. I couldn't; my own vision was blurred with tears that I tried to blink away before Leo saw them. What caused my heart to ache so? Was it loss? Regret?

Or guilt? For despite the toys, the music boxes, there was such a lonely emptiness to these rooms; betrayal, frozen in time, chilled the very air. Being a child, I had had no choice but to grow up, while he remained exactly as he had been. Before.

"And now may I propose we take the photographs? I do fear losing the light," Mr. Dodgson said, leading the way down a narrow passage to even narrower stairs. We all followed, climbing the stairs until we found ourselves in a light, airy space—I had to blink at the unexpected brightness.

This was his studio: a wall of windows on one side, brick on the other, skylights in the ceiling. There were the trunks of costumes, just as I remembered them; there was the brown leather valise in which he carried his developing chemicals; there was the camera. The same camera made of rosewood with that same large, unblinking eye that had once captured my soul.

There was also another room, the door shut tightly: his darkroom, I assumed.

He had accumulated more props—sofas, chairs, tables, ladders, and even some painted backdrops, perhaps left over from college theatricals. Obviously he was still pursuing his hobby; with a slight itch of irritation, I spied a small pink satin slipper—turned up at the toe in the Arabian fashion—peeking out of one of the costume trunks. Who was his favorite subject now? I wondered.

"Who would like to sit first?" Mr. Dodgson asked, removing his frock coat, rolling up his shirtsleeves—and pulling off his gloves. The sight of his hands, pale, slender, with those dark smudges still on the fingertips, caused my stomach to flutter, my legs to tremble. I sat down abruptly upon a chair, mindful of Mamma's suspicious glare.

"I'm sure His Royal Highness would love to see Edith sit first, as she photographs so beautifully," Mamma said, turning away from me, and for once I did not mind her presumption. Although I saw that Leo—with one golden eyebrow arched in exasperation—did.

Mr. Dodgson motioned for Edith to sit down upon a leather high-backed chair; he arranged her just so, and the photograph was taken; he counted to forty-five softly, almost under his breath, and I remembered how he used to be so silly about it when we were young. Mamma then urged Leo to sit with Edith for a photograph, which he did with politely concealed impatience; then Mr. Dodgson requested a photograph of Leo alone, for his own collection.

"Now Alice must sit," Leo said eagerly, when Mr. Dodgson emerged from the darkroom with a newly prepared plate. Mr. Dodgson nodded, concentrating upon fitting the plate into the back of the camera, and nearly dropping it.

I walked to the chair, slowly; I felt all eyes upon me, and wondered what they were all looking for, what they were all waiting for me to do. I sat upon the chair, turned to Mr. Dodgson, and awaited his instructions.

"C-c-could you—per-perhaps, if you will—I'm

not certain, bu-bu-but I believe if you j-j-just—"
For the first time in my memory, he could not
control his stammer; finally he simply stopped
trying to talk and shook his head. He was unable
to tell me what to do; he was as terrified as I was.

I wanted to go to him and tell him it was all
right—just as I had when I was a little girl and I
ached at his sadness and knew only I could save
him. But it wasn't all right between us, and it
never would be again, and the reason for that
hung heavy on everyone's minds, all of us
gathered in this odd rooftop space fitted with
strange costumes and unnaturally colored
painted backdrops of make-believe places.

There was only one person who did not feel
the unbearable weight of the past in that room.

"Why don't you lean back?" a voice suggested.
Blindly, I turned in its direction and saw, despite
hot tears, that it was Leo. Leo who walked over to
me, placed one hand upon my shoulder, and
with the other brushed a strand of hair back
from my face tenderly; I closed my eyes, leaning
into him, and wished the two of us were somewhere—anywhere—else, alone.

Mamma cleared her throat, and my eyes flew
open—catching Mr. Dodgson's surprise as he
stared at the two of us. Surprise, and some other
emotion that I did not want to understand; my
face burned, and I gently pushed Leo away. With
a steadying breath, I straightened in the chair,

tilted my head down, and looked up—seeking some safe, anonymous spot on the wall behind the camera upon which to concentrate.

Look at me, Alice. Look only at me—the words echoed strangely in my ears, and I wasn't sure who had said them, or if I was remembering another time and place. So I kept my eyes trained on the wall and willed myself not to move.

Mr. Dodgson removed the lens cover and counted to forty-five, his voice soft, monosyllabic. With a swift movement, he removed the glass plate and hurried it to the darkroom. I exhaled—I must have been holding my breath the entire time—and rose. Our group was suddenly silent, awkward, without Mr. Dodgson. Even Leo did not seem to know what to do.

"That's it, then," Mr. Dodgson said, emerging from the darkroom. He limped over to retrieve his frock coat and gloves and put them back on while we all mutely stared, still waiting for something. Had we done what we needed to do? Was there something missing? Something unsaid?

Of course there was. The air was oppressive with what was not being said; the unspoken words—accusations, pleas, reasons, questions—bounced around the bright space until I longed to cover my ears. Even Leo seemed to sense it now, as he shifted his weight awkwardly from one foot to the other, clearing his throat softly.

"I no longer print my own pictures; I send

them out," Mr. Dodgson finally said. "As soon as I get them back, I'll send you all copies."

"Fine, fine—I can't thank you enough." Leo recovered his self-possession with evident relief. Laughing heartily, he shook hands with Mr. Dodgson. "I do so look forward to the photographs. And we must see each other more; perhaps at one of the many enjoyable evenings at the Deanery?" He turned to Mamma.

"Naturally," she replied, her voice as smooth and cold as ice. Mr. Dodgson bowed, but his faint, wry smile betrayed that he did not expect any such invitation to be forthcoming.

We left him in his sitting room, standing in front of the fireplace, his back toward us as he warmed his gloved hands in front of the flames. When the photograph arrived a week later, I held my breath when I pulled back the brown paper: What secret part of me had his camera captured this time?

The sad, lost part of me; the part that needed rescue. My dispirited eyes did not meet the camera, my face was pale, my mouth a small, grim pout. I could not share Leo's enthusiasm for it, although I was happy to know that my likeness would reside in a silver frame on his desk, just as his resided in a silver frame on mine.

And now I could not help but wonder if it was all I would ever have of him; with a jolt, my thoughts returned to the awful uncertainty of the present, where fear was as oppressive as the unspoken accusations of the past. Still, I cleared my disorderly thoughts with a stern shake of the head, gripped my pen firmly, and began the letter required of me, the measured, circumspect letter from the daughter of the Dean to a favorite student.

HIS ROYAL HIGHNESS,
THE PRINCE LEOPOLD

Dear Sir,

I write with much concern, inquiring as to your health and telling you that your friends here at Oxford miss you dearly. The holidays have been a bleak affair, indeed, as the knowledge of your illness hung over every celebration. I must tell you that Papa is very worried and was heard to mutter, "Dear fellow, dear fellow," the last time your secretary posted a letter about your condition

"Alice?" With a soft rap on my bedroom door, Edith opened it, popping her head inside. "Am I bothering you? I felt as if you might want company."

"Are there any letters? News?" I jumped up— nearly flinging my pen across the room before I collected myself and placed it back in the inkwell. I ran to the door and pulled Edith inside, my hand gripping her arm so tightly she exclaimed.

Gently, she removed my hand and placed her arm about my shoulders. "No, I'm sorry, dearest, Papa has received no letter yet today."

"Oh." I allowed my sister to steer me toward a soft chair by the hearth; she pushed me down in it, kneeling beside me, taking my hands in her own.

"Alice, your hands are like ice!" She began to rub them vigorously. "Have you eaten today?"

"I don't know." Dully, I stared into the fire, not truly seeing, aware only of the soft popping of embers. My thoughts would allow me to see nothing but Leopold lying on a bed, his face pale, his beautiful, sympathetic eyes closed, his luxurious yellow lashes grazing his cheeks; dying, perhaps, or already—

I shut my eyes, twisted my head, and could not prevent a small moan from escaping my heart. Every nerve, every bone, felt raw, rigid, from trying to contain my true feelings for so long. Why could I not be there? Why could I not simply commandeer a carriage—no, a train!—and fly to Osborne, steal a boat, row myself out to the island, and march right up to the house, demanding to be taken inside?

Heartsick. I truly knew the meaning of the word, for my heart *was* sick, ill, wrung with worry; I felt, at times, as if I simply could not go on living, for the poor instrument would give out, unable to absorb any more of my fear and longing. My voice must be mute, but my heart was not; it cried out with every beat.

"Mamma desires you to come down for dinner tonight," Edith said softly, still stroking my hands.

"Desires?"

"Commands, if you will. She will not hear of you staying in your room another evening. You know how she feels about that, and I'm afraid—I'm afraid that she refuses to see your distress, as she is unwilling to acknowledge your true feelings for the Prince."

"Naturally. I suppose she wishes me to do a merry dance for everyone's amusement, as well?"

"Alice," Edith soothed, laying her cheek against my hand. "At least your wit is intact. You're not so far gone as I feared."

I smiled at my sister, her face so sweetly furrowed with concern. "No, I'm not so far gone as that. I know it does no one—least of all, Leo—any good to mope about in my room. But, oh, I do so long to be with him! Why am I never allowed to be with the ones I love when they suffer? I can't bear to think of him afraid, in pain, without me—what if . . . what if he needs me, cries out for me—I'm stronger than he is, oh, so much stronger, I would give him my strength, if only I were allowed!" My heart rose up, choking my throat, flooding my eyes with tears; I couldn't stop them; I allowed them to wash over me, unburdening my heart, giving voice, finally, to my fear and longing. I held my sister close—she was so warm, alive in my arms—and allowed myself to weep until I was empty, finally, relieved of my silence. It was a blessing, despite the pain. I felt a strange sense of calm wash over me as I wiped away my tears.

"Oh, I wish I could give him my strength as well," Edith said, wiping away not a few tears of her own as she wriggled out of my arms. She pulled the other chair closer to me and sat down—but still, she held my hand. "I would, you know."

"I know." I smiled; Edith was the picture of health, rosy-cheeked, prettily plump in a country dairymaid way. I was inclined to thinness, unfortunately; my features were much too sharp, and my unwillingness to eat these last few weeks had not improved my looks. If—*when*—Leo did return, I would certainly scare him away. There were purplish smudges under my eyes that even candlelight could not disguise.

"What is the time?" I asked, suddenly aware of the gathering darkness outside my window.

Edith consulted the diamond watch pinned to her dress. "Four-thirty."

"I must go." With an effort, I pushed myself out of my chair and walked over to my dressing table. Pinching my cheeks, smoothing my hair, and pinning up a few strands, I did the best I could to make myself presentable. Then I rang for Sophie.

"Alice, do you have to go today? Wouldn't

241

he—wouldn't he understand if you sent a note saying you were ill?" Edith's eyes grew darker, clouded over with worry; suspicion, too. I turned away, so she couldn't see my face.

"No, Mr. Ruskin is a demanding taskmaster. He feels I am not working as hard as I might with my sketching. But truly, it's a welcome distraction. When I'm there, I—I don't think of Leo at all!" Spinning around, I smiled tightly and faced my sister once more.

Yet I did not deceive her; shaking her head, she placed her hand upon my arm, just as Sophie knocked on the door and entered, bringing my fur wrap, hat, and muff.

"Alice, wouldn't you like me to come with you today, at least? Mr. Ruskin enjoys my company," Edith said, her voice low and concerned.

"Of course he does. But it's simply a private drawing lesson, and there's no need for you to be bored." I turned around while Sophie buttoned my wrap, and heard my sister's stifled, worried sigh.

"Well, do try to enjoy yourself, if you can. I'll come get you if there's any word from Osborne."

"Oh, do, please! Thank you!" I flung my arms around her, kissed her on the cheek, and hurried out, leaving Edith standing near my dressing table, her face troubled.

As I flew down the stairs—Mr. Ruskin did not like me to be tardy—Mamma suddenly appeared at the foot of the staircase. It was uncanny how she did that, how she sometimes managed to simply appear, no sound, no whooshing of her skirts or creaking of her corset, to give her away.

"Alice."

"Yes, Mamma?"

"I trust you're feeling better?" She tilted her head, studying me with her cool, appraising eye.

"Yes, Mamma."

"Good. I don't approve of young ladies eating alone. You'll be down for dinner, then."

"Of course, Mamma." I brushed past her, pulling on my black leather gloves; Sophie tiptoed past, and I could sense her trembling. I'm not sure she had ever said one word to Mamma in all the time she'd been with me.

"Alice—wait."

There was a catch—a hesitation—in my mother's voice that startled me, and persuaded me to pause just as I selected an umbrella from the massive Chinese urn beside the front door. "Yes?"

I didn't turn around; I stood there, my heart beating wildly in some kind of hope, some kind of anticipation, as I heard Mamma take a step toward me.

"Will you—that is, I wanted to tell you that we've not had any updates from Osborne this afternoon. In case Mr. Ruskin were to inquire."

Tears sprang to my eyes; I longed—I ached—to run to my mother, throw myself in her arms, and be folded up in them, rocked gently, loved.

I wanted to be a little girl again, her sole trouble a scrape upon her knee that could be healed only by a mother's kiss.

Yet—when had I ever been that girl? When had my mother ever given me such comfort? I was remembering someone else's childhood, not my own.

"Thank you, Mamma," I whispered. Then I left, not daring to look back.

Chapter 10

UNREAL. DREAMLIKE. AN OPIUM HAZE.

With each afternoon spent in Mr. Ruskin's drawing room, I grew more and more uncomfortable, yet strangely mesmerized. It was as if, once installed in the high-backed chair by the fire—pouring out tea as instructed, dispensing the cakes, the linen napkins—my thoughts, my very limbs, would be blanketed by a numbing, reality-altering opiate.

Once, as I sat there watching him laugh hysterically at a notion that had just seized him, I thought, "So this is what the Mad Hatter's tea party was like."

But unlike the other Alice, I could not simply get up and leave. I was bound by my word to remain; to return, even, week after week.

At first, Mr. Ruskin cozily chatted about his day, or his work, or the newest gossip. Our afternoons would pass quickly, and while I never looked forward to them—there were times when he seemed displeased to see me, as if it was I who was insisting upon visiting him; other times he would berate me for being one minute late or leaving one minute early—still, my duty seemed easy to discharge. And there was no denying the amazing breadth of his knowledge about art and architecture; even his commentaries on society were interesting, although I could never reconcile his professed love for the emerging middle classes with his practiced love for the finer things in life.

Even in those early visits, however, there was a sinister element, an unspoken debt to be paid; it was evident in his eyes, studying me even as I did the most ordinary things—stirred my tea, paged through a book, asked about the provenance of a painting. I tried to flatter him, always, and never did I feel as if it was enough; I knew he was waiting for something more.

Then, sometime around late March, Mr. Ruskin's moods grew even more changeable; oddly, this coincided with Leo's return to Oxford.

When I first received the letter telling me, in his own strong handwriting, only the brevity of the message betraying his weakness, that Leopold was recovering splendidly and that the only recuperation he required was to hold me on his knee, stroke my hand, and be allowed to tell me quantities of undignified yet romantic sentiments,

I sank to my knees in my room and wept for joy. Then I wiped my eyes, wrote a letter echoing his desire, and posted it, careless of who else might read it, my only wish to let him know, in the most direct way possible, that our hearts were of one accord. As I watched the footman carry the letter away, I felt such relief, both at the knowledge that he would recover and at my disregard, for once, of the need to conceal my true feelings. My sleep that night was one of utter peace; when I awoke, the circles under my eyes had vanished.

We had arranged the exact hour of his return to Oxford; I was waiting for him at the door to the Deanery, pulling him inside before any servant could see. He was shockingly thin—I could not hide my despair at the way his collar hung so loose about his neck, at the suddenly prominent bones holding up the fine flesh on his face—but his spirit, his vivacity, had not diminished. There was a new sense of purpose in his blue eyes, and I felt certain I was behind it. For upon our reunion he was the one to wrap his arms around *me,* spirit me away to a dark corner in the front hall, and kiss me, passionately; my words of greeting were vanquished upon my lips.

His lips were soft but insisting, seeking answers, promises I was more than eager to give; I kissed him back, awakened, finally, from the torpor of the last few weeks. I could not have enough; he tasted of salvation, just as I had hoped;

we pressed close together; I had never before been so aware of the many layers confining us, separating us, but somehow I still felt *him,* his passion, his warmth, and I longed, *longed,* to feel his hands against my skin, my bare skin—

Abruptly, I pulled back. I could not catch my breath; it came shallowly, too fast, and my head grew light; the room began to spin. Leo reached out to me—I saw, after all, that his hands were strong enough to carry me away—and grabbed my upper arms just as my knees buckled.

"Alice!"

"I'm all right, truly. You took my breath away!" I was able to laugh as I sank down into a small chair. "Sir, I must protest! I had expected a recovering invalid, not a—a—"

"Lover?" He knelt beside me, taking my hand; his round blue eyes danced with satisfaction, with delight, even though his face was so thin now, his mustache looked much too big for it.

"Leo!" I lowered my voice to a whisper; Mamma's and Papa's footsteps were heard in the gallery above, headed for the stairs. Papa called, "Is that the voice of the Prince I hear?"

"This is just the beginning, Alice, I warn you. I mean to make each moment I have left at Oxford more memorable than the last, and that includes the time I have with you. Commemoration is in just a few weeks, and I have so very many plans, my darling! Mamma has been most touchingly sweet and accommodating since my illness, and I have reason to believe she simply can't deny me a thing right now. Anything—anything I ask. Do you know what that means?"

"I believe so." I couldn't look at him, but my mouth—as if tied by a thread to my soaring heart—turned up in joy. This was the first time he had alluded to the future and to the possibility of the Queen's blessing.

"It means that we will be together, I promise. I have been away from you too long; I never mean to be away from you again."

"I am yours, you know. Oh, Leo, if you only saw the letters I wrote to you! I didn't dare post them, but—oh, you would laugh, I was so foolish! But that's all in the past now. You're here, and you're well, and there's nothing more I need in the world." I searched his eyes for my reward: my reward for keeping silent, for not giving way to my fears, for not giving Mamma any reason to scold or lecture; for submitting to Mr. Ruskin.

I sought, and I found; his eyes bright with tears, Leo put his finger to my lips, kissed my forehead, and murmured, "And there's nothing more I need, for I have found my true love. My Alice; my heart can speak no other name."

I closed my eyes and knew I would never be happier than I was in that moment; that moment when I allowed myself to deserve happiness, after all.

"Leopold! Is that Leopold?" Papa was rounding the last stair step; Leo and I jumped up and managed to release each other just as he came into view. "My dear boy, my dear boy! I am so happy to see you well and strong!" With a cry, a hasty wipe of a tear, Papa bounded toward Leo, who likewise moved toward him. They clasped shoulders, shook hands, and I was so happy to see their obvious affection for each other.

Mamma joined them; she, too, had a welcome smile on her face, although she could not prevent herself from searching me, for—what? I no longer knew what she was looking for when she studied me this way: signs, scratches, everyday wear and tear? Betrayal?

I did not have time to linger, however; it was nearly five o'clock, and I was expected elsewhere. I bade farewell to Leo; when he kissed my hand, I could not prevent myself from imagining him kissing me elsewhere; my throat, the back of my neck ached with the desire. With a great effort, I managed to withdraw my hand and say good-bye. Then I hurried off to Mr. Ruskin's, Sophie in tow.

"You've been kissed," he said immediately upon greeting me. He thrust his lower lip out in a sulk and stomped over to his chair.

"Indeed, I have. Rhoda kissed me on the cheek this morning, when I lent her my new green riding habit." My face was flushed, my lips still throbbing from Leo's kisses, but I managed to take my seat with a demure smile, pouring out, as usual. The tea looked exceptionally hot today; the porcelain pot was very warm to the touch and stung my hands.

"That's not what I mean. This tea is too hot." He tasted his, made a face, and set his cup back down upon the table with such force that the tea splashed out, ruining a cake.

"Now look what you've done." I began to mop it up with a napkin.

"Don't scold me. I'm not a child. Nor am I infirm," he grumbled, his face reddening so that he did, indeed, resemble a small boy holding his breath to have his way.

"Nor are you acting sensibly. Do behave."

"There you go again! Do this, do that. I tell you, you've been kissed, that's what. You have that look about you—bruised, ready, and ripe for plucking. Who is he? Who?"

"I will not continue this line of conversation," said I, feeling ice surge through my veins, cooling my skin, allowing me to gain control of the situation. "I neglected to give you your lemon; that will cool your tea."

"It was him, I suppose, wasn't it?" Mr. Ruskin grumbled, blowing on his cup so that his whiskers practically stood on end.

I couldn't suppress a smile, remembering the passion of Leo's greeting; I felt my skin suffuse with heat.

"Aha! I thought so. Lucky devil. Just look at you, all rosy and twittering like a bird. A lovely little bird. Why him? Why him and not me?" Again he set his cup down on the table, this time so hard that he shattered it. Tea was everywhere: on the table, the flowered rug, splattering the fire screen, splashing my skirt.

"What on earth?" I looked at him, aghast. He did not resemble a little boy any longer; his eyes were hard, his brows thunderclouds, his mouth twisted up in a horrible grimace.

"Why him? Because he's younger, is that why?"

"Why would you ask such a thing?"

"Ah—see, look at you! I was right. You've been kissed by him, that man—Dodgson! Haven't you? Don't deny it, my pet. I'll not have that."

"Mr.—Mr. Dodgson?"

"Yes, Mr. Dodgson. Why him and not me?"

"What are you talking about?" I froze, halfway out of my chair; too many thoughts, memories, rushed through my mind; lips and hands and hopes and dreams, summer days, the look in Leo's innocent eyes when he told me I was his, just minutes ago, could it possibly be?

"Dodgson. Why him, why allow his kisses, when you know I want to pet you, too? Ever since you were a little girl, I watched you. Alice, Alice, lovely Alice in Wonderland. What is it about him that charms you so? He's a stuttering fool, but you chose him."

251

"I don't know what you're—that is, he's not—Mr. Dodgson? What can you possibly mean? I told you he's no longer—I thought you were referring to, to—" But I could not say Leo's name.

"Little girls and their charms," he sneered, his hands gripping the arms of his chair. "So innocent, they seem. Yet seductive, too. You wanted his attention—you asked for it, just as you're asking for it now. You knew what you were doing that summer afternoon, didn't you?"

I shut my eyes against the memories—the rhythmic swaying of a train, the velvety blackness of heat-induced sleep, the confused awakening. Ina's eyes, round and unblinking, seeing what she wanted to see; what I wanted her to see—

"No!" I shook my head. "No! I was too young! I can't possibly remember—I was too young!"

"That's what she said, too." Still he sat, glaring at me.

"Who?"

"Rose. My Rosie, my pet, my puss. On a summer afternoon. Always, always it's a summer afternoon, isn't it? She's too young, she says. She won't walk with me, she says, even though I ask and I ask and you won't talk. Your parents won't permit it. Why?" Now he was standing, pacing, his hair wild, as wild as his eyes. There was a tremor in his hands that he did not bother to hide.

"My parents? Whatever do you mean? Why would you ask them?"

"Because I'm a gentleman, that's why!" He shouted it, shocking me out of my frozen state; finally I was able to rise from the chair, shaking out my stained skirt with trembling hands; on trembling legs I began to inch toward the door.

"Mr. Ruskin, I'm afraid you're not well today. I should leave you to rest—"

"No!" Abruptly, he stopped, blocking my path; he swung around, staring at me with anguished eyes, clenched fists. I jumped back, my heart pounding, my skin prickling with fear. "No! Not when I've got you here—got you back! You're always leaving, always slipping out of my grasp, first Alice, now my puss, my pet—Rosie, please don't go! I'll be good now; I'll do whatever you say. Please." Great, slow tears rolled down his suddenly sunken cheeks; he wiped them with his coat sleeves, sniffling, shuffling, as forlorn as a little boy.

With a shock, I comprehended the situation. He was sick. Sick, tired, confused; I took a step toward him, holding out my hand, as one would do to a wounded animal.

"Mr. Ruskin, please, I'm not Rose. I'm Alice. Alice Liddell. Don't you remember?"

He stared at my hand, his gaze moving up my arm to my face. His great white brows furrowing, he glared at me.

"Of course I remember. What do you mean? Where's the tea? Alice, I believe I asked you to pour out. Look at you—did you spill it? Let me ring for Mrs. Thompson."

He rang for Mrs. Thompson, who hurried in, took one look at the hearth, and scurried back out, returning with a pail of water, a rag, a dustpan. With efficient cheerfulness, she cleaned up the spill and brought in fresh tea.

While she was on her knees picking up the pieces of the shattered cup—it had a pattern of dark blue forget-me-nots—she paused and looked at Mr. Ruskin. He was staring out the window toward the Meadow, which was pale green in its first blush of spring; the days were lengthier now, so it was no longer dark at teatime. Mrs. Thompson then looked at me. I was standing, useless, in the middle of the room, unable to do anything but watch her try to put everything back together again. She caught my gaze, furrowed her brow, as if trying to piece together a difficult puzzle, and gave me a cautious, careful smile. Then she finished her task and left without another glance.

"Now, pour, please, and do a better job of it this time. Tell me, when is Edith going to announce her engagement? Poor Aubrey is beside himself." Mr. Ruskin returned to his chair, rubbing his hands together briskly as he looked at the cakes on the table beside him.

Slowly—moving as if underwater, against a heavy current, sights and sounds strangely muffled and distorted—I returned to my chair. Everything around me seemed perfectly normal, remarkably undisturbed: the fire dancing in the hearth, fresh new tea things on the tray, Mr. Ruskin looking at the cakes in anticipation. The only clue that something bizarre, something unsettling, had occurred was the sight of the ugly splotches of tea, still wet, clinging to my light wool skirt.

"There's a good girl," Mr. Ruskin said, as I poured the tea out once more—feeling quite as if I had only *imagined* doing so earlier. "I must say, Alice, you look pale today. I supposed you'd be practically blooming with the return of Leopold, which I understand took place this afternoon at a certain Dean's residence, heh?" He chuckled softly. "I must caution you not to get caught up in the excitement; it's imperative that you two remain discreet. But you can trust me; I'm on your side. I'm always on the side of romance." He sipped his tea, his manner easy and expansive.

I attempted to do the same, although I couldn't taste mine; it might have been scalding, it might have been cold. My lips, my tongue, were too numb to tell.

"What do you say to a game of Beggar My Neighbor? I'm rather in the mood for cards today, as my head aches. I find that mindless games are best for a poor head, don't you?" With a bright smile, he nodded toward the cabinet where the cards were stored; I rose, retrieved them, and returned. He shuffled, I cut, and he dealt.

I said not a word the rest of that afternoon, but he didn't appear to notice. I sat before his fire, playing a child's game with the eminent Mr. Ruskin, who laughed happily, greedily, when he took my cards.

When I left to go, he asked me to give Leopold his best and kissed me on the cheek with the careless affection of a kind uncle. And were it not for the stain on my skirt, the extra care with which Mrs. Thompson bade me good evening, I could scarcely believe that anything odd had happened, after all.

Yet when I left the building, I glanced up. Mr. Ruskin was standing in the window looking at me, the portrait of Rose La Touche in his hands; turning away, I began to run as fast as I could.

I was nearly to Merton Street, not caring if Sophie had managed to keep up, as I bent my head toward the ground, struggling to collect my thoughts and arrange them into a manageable packet that I could tuck within my bodice, out of sight, when I heard my name.

"Alice—Mi-Mi-Miss Alice, tha-tha-that is, is that you?"

I looked up; I had nearly run into a man. A tall, slender man with blue eyes, one higher than the other; he wore nothing more than his usual frock coat and gray gloves, even though the air was still chilly with the memory of winter.

"Oh!" I couldn't prevent myself from taking a step backward, discovering a sniffling Sophie to be much closer than I had anticipated. "Hello, Mr. Dodgson."

He raised his hat and bowed. "I trust I'm not keeping you; you appear to be in a hurry."

"No, not at all. I'm on my way from Mr. Ruskin's, where I—I had a drawing lesson." Across the street, a gentleman opened the door to a pub; light and music briefly spilled out in the gutter, and I shivered suddenly at the gay tinkling of a piano.

"Are you well?" Mr. Dodgson asked, alarmed. I saw him reach his hand out, as of old—ready to help, ready to comfort; with a shock of confusion I recalled his habit of bending down and sniffing the top of my head when I was small.

I took another step away even as he snatched his hand back and hid it behind his waist. "Yes, I'm fine, and I do hope that you are, as well," I murmured, embarrassed for us both.

"I am, thank you. Tell me, have you had word of Prince Leopold? He's such a great fa-favorite here. We're all eager for his return."

His soft voice was hesitant, devoid of any archness or duplicity. Steeling myself to look, finally, into Mr. Dodgson's eyes as I had not been able to do in his rooms, I raised my head.

His eyes were blue and kind and without suspicion, I felt. Yet I told myself I did not know him any longer. We had both changed so much.

"It's very good of you to ask," I said finally, for that was the truth, at least. "Indeed, the Prince has just arrived back at Oxford this very afternoon." Was it just this afternoon? What very mysterious things days were—what had Mr. Dodgson once said? *Sometimes they fly by, and other times they seem to last forever, yet they are all exactly twenty-four hours. There's quite a lot we don't know about them.* "Do you remember—?" I began, then stopped, catching my breath. There could be no comfort in shared memories for the two of us.

"Well, I'm very happy to hear about the Prince. Truly, I am."

Again I steeled myself to search his eyes; again I found nothing but kindness there.

"Thank you. I'll be sure to let the Prince know you asked—that is, I'll be sure to have Papa do so. Now, if you'll excuse me, I'm expected home from my drawing lesson."

"Good evening, then." Mr. Dodgson stepped aside, allowing me to proceed. With a grateful smile, I nodded and hurried on a few steps—until his voice stopped me once more.

"W-where is your sketchbook, Alice?"

I paused, looked at my hands—my muff my only possession, Sophie certainly not carrying anything. I bit my lip, cursed my stupidity, and turned around with one of Ina's coy smiles upon my lips.

"Oh dear, I must have forgotten it! Sophie, do run back to Mr. Ruskin's and fetch it, will you?"

"But miss, you never—"

"At once, Sophie."

With a gasp and a start, she trotted back down the path we had just walked, her faded red coat barely visible in the gathering darkness.

I shrugged and turned to go with a disapproving click of my tongue at the mindless ways of servants, when Mr. Dodgson called after me once more.

"Do-do-do be careful, Alice. Whatever game he's playing with you—he's not entirely *reliable,* if you understand."

I froze, unsure to whom he was referring. Leo? Mr. Ruskin?

"I'm sorry, I know it's none of my business," he said hastily. "Please forgive me."

"No—that is, there is nothing to forgive. I appreciate your concern, but pray don't trouble yourself further. It's not as if I—it's not as if we're—it's simply not necessary."

"It's not as if we're friends any longer, is that what you mean?"

His voice was gentle, coaxing, sad. I knew there would be sadness in his eyes, too; sorrow in the way his smile turned down at the ends.

But I did not turn around to see. I simply continued on my way home, faster than before.

Eager to put more distance between myself and my past.

Chapter 11

I RETURNED TO MR. RUSKIN'S THE NEXT week, and he was himself—by turns gruff and garrulous; petulant and dignified. He called me by my own name and never once referred to the past, his or mine. Then he left for a visit to his home in the Lakes, and I was free. Free to indulge myself in long talks with Leo about topics grave and topics small, it hardly mattered; our minds were so well matched, as well matched as our hearts, that we simply enjoyed the conversation, regardless. Between the two of us, we knew, we could solve the world's problems. All we needed was enough time.

There were moments we didn't talk; often he would sit and watch me while I sketched the river, or the new flowers in the Meadow, and once I even tried to reproduce his likeness. But my hand—usually so steady with a pencil—would not behave; while I managed to capture his eyes and his nose passably well, his mouth was impossible, for I could not look at it without wanting to feel it upon my own. I had to give up, finally, and tell him that his mustache needed a proper trimming before I would sketch him again.

That spring the air was always soft and warm, the flowers in bloom more fragrant than ever before, the promise of summer so poignant, so tangible, it brought tears to my eyes to think of it. I slept every night with my window flung open, as if to let summer—to let God, even—know that I was ready, waiting, for all the goodness, the promise, to come.

Yet when Mr. Ruskin returned and summoned me once again, I found that in his drawing room, at least, winter still resided. His windows remained shuttered against the fresh air, and his fire burned as bright as ever. The room was stifling, so hot I felt as if I were being suffocated by my own clothing. Despite my pleadings, he would not open a window.

"It'll do you good to keep inside where it's warm. All that traipsing about in the woods, the Meadow—I know, I see. So you've decided to forgo my advice about discretion?"

"We have decided not to hide our feelings for each other, true. Although there is no need for further speculation."

"Hmm. And the Queen?"

"Her Majesty has been most anxious about her son's health and is happy to hear that he is in such fine spirits. Now, how was your visit to the Lakes? I'm sure it was quite lovely this time of year. I do hope you were able to rest some; you've seemed rather—tired, of late."

"I'm fine, I'm fine." He waved his hand at me in dismissal; he was kneeling before a cabinet along the wall, searching for something.

I shut my eyes against the fire, the too-familiar tea things. I was weary of this room, weary of these visits—I could not see that he got much pleasure out of them, despite his insistence— but I was afraid to ask when my duty might be considered discharged. He seemed agitated this afternoon—scarcely drinking his tea, jumping in and out of his chair like a jack-in-the-box— although I told myself it could also be merely that he was well rested and energized after his holiday.

"Ah! Here it is!" He leaped up, a large black leather book in his hand. Opening the front cover, he flipped through a page or two, then brought it over to me, dropping it in my lap without warning.

"What is this?" The heavy thing nearly slid off my skirt, but I grabbed it just in time; it was an album. A photograph album.

"Look! Look inside!" With a strange laugh, he started to pace back and forth behind my chair.

I sighed, then opened the album. On the first page was pasted a copy of the photograph of me, as the beggar girl. I shut the album. "I've seen this before."

"No, no—you have to continue! Look!" He leaned over my shoulder and opened it again. "Keep going!"

Pressing my lips together, I turned the page. On it was a photograph of a young girl in a cape; from an open window, she was descending a rope ladder. The next page showed another young girl, this time reclining on a sofa, a sofa I recognized. It was Mr. Dodgson's sofa, from his studio.

I continued turning pages. The photographs were all of young girls—all about the same age as I had been when the beggar-girl photograph was taken. I recognized them all, not by the subject—I had no idea who most of these girls were —but by the photographer. No one but Mr. Dodgson could persuade children to pose like this.

Looking at these other photographs, of these other girls—one of whom was wearing the pink slipper I had spied in Mr. Dodgson's studio—I felt a rage slowly boiling up inside me; a rage of jealousy. Had he told *them* of his dreams? Had he spoken of happiness in that sad way of his, had his eyes grown soft with desire? Now, as a woman, I could at last recognize it for what it was, for I recognized it in my own eyes, reflected in Leo's. I recognized it, too, in the gypsy girl's eyes, glittering from the photograph.

I was his dream child, alone; only. No matter that he himself had outgrown my dreams; I needed to believe I was still the only one who haunted his. I'd spent my entire life believing it, despite the wreckage that had followed in the dreamers' wake.

I shoved the album off my lap; it fell to the floor with a thud, as behind me, Mr. Ruskin cackled with delight.

"Ah—you see it, don't you? You see how he is? You thought you were the only one, didn't you, my pet? I wager you even convinced yourself you were special, that your friendship was sacred. Yet he's spent the rest of his life trying to replace you, and he has—you see! You see it in the photographs. What do you think of that, then?"

"I think it's very odd of you to show me this. What is your purpose?" Impatiently, I launched myself out of the chair, too angry, too confused, to sit any longer; despite the heat, I stalked the floor, childishly desiring to kick all the odd objects that cluttered it—artifacts, footstools, paintings—out of my path. "What can you gain by showing me these photographs?"

"I simply wanted you to see him as he is. I wanted you to see yourself. He used you. Don't you see?"

"Yes." I did see; I'd always seen, in a way. My story, for instance—certainly, he'd gained from that, at my expense.

"You were merely an object—a charming object, but an object nonetheless. It will be your downfall, and you aren't even aware."

"What do you mean, my downfall?" Spinning around, I faced Mr. Ruskin, unafraid to speak my mind, for I was sick of him; sick of his—

Games. Mr. Dodgson had been trying to warn me. He was watching over me, still.

"I mean that you've spoiled yourself for a man

who didn't deserve you, and now you're unfit for one who does. That's your greatest fear, isn't it?"

I didn't answer. Once, I would have agreed with him. But these last few weeks had seemed like a rebirth, a second chance; I was beginning to see myself through Leo's eyes.

"Ah, I'm correct, of course. I'm always right in these matters!" Still, Mr. Ruskin could detect even my smallest doubt; his eyes glittered in triumph.

"I am not spoiled, as you call it—I am not! I would never have encouraged Leo if I believed that, for I think much too highly of him. Why do you say such things, such awful things, about us all? You keep me coming here on the promise of friendship, that you will protect me."

"And I have. I just want you to see how different I am from him. I'm constant. My love is pure. I never tried to replace you with another. You're my only, my pet, my puss—can't you see, Rose, that I'm not like the others?"

"I'm not Rose." I tried to control my voice—I did not want to summon Mrs. Thompson or Sophie—but I needed to make myself heard, once and for all; I needed to make myself *known*. "I'm *Alice*. Not the beggar girl, not the girl in the story, not the girl in the portrait you are looking at now, instead of me!" With a cry, I swept Rose's image off the table; it fell to the floor, the little wooden easel on which it resided snapping in two.

Mr. Ruskin dropped to his knees, making a

sound like an animal howling. He grabbed the canvas and held it to his heart.

"Why would you do that? Why would you try to destroy the one thing I have left? Rose, my Rosa, my little puss—why do you grieve me so?"

"I am not Rose!"

"Don't say that—don't say that. I need you to be her, don't you see? I need you to be my Rose, she is you, she lives in you, you are one and the same, just as Dodgson and I are. You're no better than us, at that; we're all a group of sinners. Even Rose, pure, sweet Rose—she sinned, and she died."

"You're not the same as him. And I will not be *her*. I will not let you bring me down to your level, your shame. I will not be like that."

"You are already," he sneered; I felt his accusation like a dagger, plunging deep within a heart that tried, for once, to reject it. Because of Leo— Leo was so kind, so good; he saw the goodness in me, too. He would not love me if he did not see.

"No, you're wrong." I knelt beside him; he was rocking with the portrait still clutched to his chest; it was pathetic, but he smiled so viciously, I could not have pity for him. "Mr. Ruskin, you must stop this—you don't know how cruel you are! Rose is dead, and I'm not her. I'm Alice. And I don't deserve—"

"Alice in Wonderland!" he taunted; now I saw that his eyes were opaque, confused, his clothes

266

slightly askew; his vest was buttoned wrong, his shirt had a yellow stain around the collar. His whiskers were more unruly than usual; they did not reek of perfume but rather of stale food.

"Oh, Mr. Ruskin—you're—you're truly not yourself. Let me help you—"

"What did they tell you?" Abruptly, his eyes hardened; he dropped the portrait, stood without my assistance, and leered down at me. "What did they tell you about me?"

"I don't know what you're—"

Grabbing my arm, he pulled me to my feet with a vicious sneer. "I know what they told you. Effie, Effie told you, didn't she?"

"Effie? Your wife? I've never met her!" I tried to pull away, but despite his frail appearance, he was stronger than I. Much stronger.

"Did that filthy whore tell you filthy lies? Did she?"

"Do not speak to me this way. Please let me go."

"Did that filthy whore tell you about our wedding night? Did she tell you I couldn't satisfy her? Did she? Because it's a lie, a damned lie, and I can prove it. By God, I can prove it—" Releasing me, he began to remove his coat.

I was horrified—terrified—wanting to leave yet feeling I could not, not when he was in this state. How could I ever face him again if I allowed him to continue to debase himself, debase me?

Just as he threw his coat down, muttering,

"Whores lie, they lie standing up and they lie on their backs, it's all the same," I set my jaw, took a determined step forward, and slapped him across his face. My hand stung from the force of it; he drew back, his eyes glittering dangerously; he made as if to grab my wrist, but then, all color draining from his face, he sank down upon his knees. He buried his face in his hands and began to sob; I remained standing, willing my breathing to slow down; my stays felt tight as a vise around my lungs, but I would not allow myself to entertain any thought of fainting.

"I'm sorry," Mr. Ruskin sobbed, not trying to hide his shame. "I'm sorry. Alice—please forgive me."

"Forgive you for what? For nearly assaulting me? Or for calling me a sinner?"

"For both. For everything."

I was silent; I could help him, but I would not be his salvation.

"Please?"

"You understand I cannot come back here?"

"No!" Anguished, he walked over to me on his knees and grasped my hands. He pulled them to his lips, kissing them passionately. "No! I will behave, I promise. This—this was simply because I've been so tired. I will not take advantage of you in this way again, you may be assured. But I've grown so fond of our afternoons, and I'm so very lonely at times—"

"No. I cannot. You are tired, I can see." I pulled my hands away from his, with a great effort; his strength, once more, surprised me—and frightened me enough to stand firm in my resolve. "You need to rest. The term is nearly over; Commemoration is soon. You must go back to the Lakes and rest. But I will not return."

"I have done nothing but rest, and still my mind tortures me. I need you, don't you see? I need you to tell me these things so I can get better. You need me, too, or don't you recall? What was it you called it—your debt for my discretion? I have been discreet. You are near to landing your Prince. I would not wish anything to prevent you your happiness, Alice."

"And it's precisely because of our friendship that I cannot return. Further visits would only cause your mind greater distress, until the time when you might say—or do—something that would cause us both great harm. Greater harm than anything you might threaten. You don't wish for that to happen, do you?"

"No." His brow was furrowed; his voice low, considering. "No, I would not wish for that to happen."

"I place all my trust in your discretion, as you may with mine. I will not tell a soul of your recent—illness." With a calm I did not feel, I smiled at him. "And I place all my hope for happiness in your continued friendship."

"I am most appreciative of your trust. I am most touched."

Suddenly it dawned on me that he was still upon his knees. Embarrassed, I turned away while he rose. I gave him time to gather himself before turning back, willing myself not to run out of the room as fast as I could but to linger over my farewell, as any—friend—might do.

"I will see you quite soon, I'm sure of it. We'll meet at the Commemoration ceremonies, and naturally, Papa and Mamma will have you over to dine, as they so often do."

"Yes, I would think so. The Deanery's hospitality is never wanting."

"Good afternoon, then, Mr. Ruskin?" Why I felt I needed his permission to leave, I do not know. I sought it, all the same.

"Good afternoon, Alice." With a cold stare, a furrow of his brow, he—reluctantly—bestowed it.

He bowed, I curtsied, and then I left his room forever, feeling his gaze follow me out the door, then down the narrow quad. I longed to run home, propelled by the soft breeze, for I could not shake the feeling that he might follow me and try to lure me back, ensnaring me further. I did not run, however; to Sophie's surprised relief, I walked as prim and proper as a Quaker going to Meeting, careful not to draw any attention to myself.

When I arrived home, I quickly ran up to my room. I changed my clothes, washed my hands, tried to rid myself of any trace of him and his sick, wayward thoughts, his intent.

Then I sat at my dressing table, staring into the looking glass for a very long time. My eyes grew red, raw with the strain of searching my face; searching for the goodness I prayed that Leo would still find there.

I sat there until day turned into night, and then night turned back into day. Yet try as I might, I could no longer see it.

Chapter 12

*Y*OU LOOK LOVELY—THAT ROSE TULLE OVER the tarlatan is perfection! Oh, I do wish I was going!" Covering her face with her handkerchief, Edith coughed fitfully and then fell back against her pillows, her hair a tangled mess of curls. Her face was nearly as red as her hair.

"Yes, you'd be a perfect vision, with all that coughing! I know it's unfair, and Aubrey will be vexed, but you know what Dr. Acland said. You're to stay in bed for a week, at least."

"It's so unlucky! And for once I thought I'd be the belle of the ball instead of you! Papa was going to announce the engagement tonight." Edith smiled weakly, and turned her head to sigh over the beautiful blue taffeta gown hanging in the cupboard.

"I'm never the belle of the ball when you're

present, so I relish the chance tonight. May I borrow your diamond star clip for my hair?"

"Yes, of course—it'll look wonderful with your diamond earrings!"

I smiled my thanks and rummaged around in her jewel case until I found the clip; dancing over to the looking glass above the mantel, I pinned it in my hair, just above my left ear. "Is this right, do you think?" I turned.

"It's perfect. Oh dear!" And Edith was off on another coughing fit again.

"Poor darling! I'll ring for the nurse—Dr. Acland said we weren't to get too close, in case it's measles. I do wish I could give you a kiss, though, before I fly. I'm rather excited for tonight—silly, but I am! How many Commemoration Balls have I attended?"

"None like tonight," Edith managed to choke out, between coughs. Finally they subsided, and she fell back against her pillows once more. "Do you think the Prince will propose, then?"

"I really don't know, but perhaps he—might." I was too superstitious to say more, even if I could not stop myself from smiling in anticipation. We had made so many plans in these last few days, as his time at Oxford drew to an end; some were quite unattainable (I doubted, for instance, that the Queen would countenance Leo's idea of moving to America in order to organize the recently emancipated slaves into helping the

British recapture the colonies), but others more down to earth. I knew he had also spoken to Papa. Yet there remained the matter of obtaining the Queen's permission, and I had not been able to ask if he had written her.

Still, I sensed it, my future; it was close, so close I could wrap my arms around it; wrap my arms around *him*. Perhaps, tonight, he would simply waltz me out of Oxford, right under everyone's noses.

Giggling, I began to waltz around Edith's room, holding my skirts up, showing off my new silk dancing slippers. Edith giggled, too—as best she could—but when she began to cough again, I stopped.

"Oh, I'm making you much worse! I'll finish my toilette in my own room. You rest now, darling, and I'll save you a program and tell you all the gossip in the morning."

"Oh, I do wish I could go!" She couldn't help but shed a tear, even as she beamed at me from the depths of her pillows, looking like a dyspeptic angel in her white nightgown. "Keep Aubrey company! And I can't wait to congratulate you in the morning!"

"Good night!" I blew her a kiss, then hurried out of her room, shutting the door softly behind me. Downstairs, outside the front door, I could hear Bultitude stomping his feet and grumbling; the carriage must have arrived. Where on earth was Sophie? She was supposed to have brought down my gloves and wrap ten minutes ago. I headed back to my room to retrieve them myself; I did hope she had remembered to dress in her good black silk, and pack her needle and thread in case I needed repairs later.

"Alice!" Mamma was gliding down the hall, handsome in her new ruby red silk gown, the bustle a cascade of white satin ruffles dotted with black velvet bows.

"Yes, Mamma?"

"I need to talk with you before we leave."

"About what, Mamma?"

"This business with Prince Leopold. Your father spoke to me about it this evening."

"He did?" Perhaps Leo had heard from the Queen, then? I couldn't hide my hope; I couldn't, wouldn't, stop myself from beaming, even as I blinked away a surprising tear of joy.

Mamma, however, pretended not to notice, as she merely sniffed before continuing. "Yes. He's a fool, your father. He's blinded by his affection for the Prince. But he does not view the situation with clear eyes."

"I see." My eyes were dry now. I met my mother's gaze directly. "And you do?"

"Yes, I do. Despite what you believe, I do."

"What I believe? I'll tell you—I believe that you cannot view the situation with anything but jaded eyes, Mamma. I believe that you cannot look at me without seeing—without seeing what you want to see, which is that I'm not good enough for a prince. Confess it, Mamma. Confess that you think that Leo is too good for me." My voice was rising, the back of my neck was bristling, just like an animal engaged in mortal combat, but I did not care. Finally, I would make my mother look at me, talk to me, treat me as an equal—even if it was by challenging her to speak a truth I did not want to hear.

Her dark eyes glittered, even as her eyebrows shot up in their triangular way, and I think she admired me, in spite of herself; she knew so few true adversaries. Still, she shook her head dismissively. "I know the world in a way which you do not. I know the Queen. I know there might—there will be inquiries. But instead of accusing me of thinking less of you, have you ever thought that I might be protecting you? Protecting your heart from getting hurt? I once thought you the most practical of my daughters, Alice, but now I wonder. You seem so desperate lately. So reckless."

Why was it, whenever I tried to shape my own destiny, I was considered to be acting recklessly? Was that the fate of the unmarried woman? I had to believe it was so. "Well, then, I *am* desperate! And if that makes me reckless, so be it! I'm desperately in love, I'm desperate to get away from here—I'm twenty-four, Mamma! Twenty-four! I should be married, I should have a home of my own, but I've been kept out of sight, put up on a shelf. And Leo found me there, and rescued me! I know something about the world, too—give me some credit, at least. I've taken measures to protect myself." I thought of Mr. Ruskin, that last horrible day in his drawing room, and I shuddered.

"Alice." My mother's face softened; her eyes shone with what I could almost believe was understanding. I remembered that long-ago winter before Albert came, when she had asked for me, and only me, to keep her company; I had seen that same expression in her eyes then. Although never since. "Alice, I do wish for you to be happy. I wish for you to have your own family, your own home like Ina, like Edith will soon. I merely wish that you and Leopold—tell me this, Alice. Do you truly think *he'll* keep quiet? Do you truly think he'll stand by and not say a word, while you plan to marry another man, particularly a prince?" Her mouth twisted up, as if she couldn't bear to even think of him, and I knew she was referring to Mr. Dodgson now.

"I think he'll want me to be happy," I answered defiantly, speaking what was in my heart, for it was what I truly wished for him.

"You do?" Mamma raised an eyebrow. "Then you're a bigger fool than I took you for."

The words stung, like a slap across my face—

had she called me ugly, I wouldn't have minded, but I realized I had long set a great store in the fact that Mamma thought me sensible—but I would not let her see my pain. "I'll join you in the carriage in a moment, Mamma. I must find Sophie first." Without meeting her gaze, I brushed past her and headed to my room.

Before I reached the door, I heard her say, once, "Alice." It was not a command; it was more like a prayer. A mother's prayer? I wondered. I could not know, for I had never once heard my mother ask God for anything. I ignored her and entered my room, shutting the door behind me.

I found Sophie sitting like an obedient child at my dressing table; I told her to hand me my wrap and gloves, and to try, for pity's sake, not to crush my nosegay on the drive to the ball. Then I ran to the mirror for one more look—had I ever stared at myself more than I had this evening? Holding my reflection in my gaze, I forced myself to shake off the effects of Mamma's words; I slowed my breathing down, felt my cheeks lose some of their heat, blinked my eyes so the tears would not fall. I tried to recapture the giddy joy I had felt in Edith's room; but I knew I would not recover it except in Leo's arms.

Suddenly I could wait for him no longer; I ran from the room, Sophie struggling behind, and flew down the stairs, scarcely bothering to wrap my shoulders in my cloak. Joining Rhoda,

Aubrey Harcourt—looking very pale and morose without Edith—and my parents in the carriage, I leaned forward as we rumbled away, as if I could will the horses to fly. Mercifully, the journey was short. In no time we drew up to the entrance of the new Corn Exchange behind the Town Hall, where the Oxford Commemoration Ball of 1876 was being held.

I had to fight off the urge—truly, it pulsed through me like a fever—to run out of the carriage, calling Leo's name.

Instead, I demurely walked down the steps, the folds of my dress gathered in my clenched hands, and followed my parents into the building, waiting to be announced, one more time, as "Miss Alice Liddell, daughter of the Dean and Mrs. Liddell."

"YOUR ROYAL HIGHNESS, I believe many young ladies are staring at you, hoping against hope that you will sign their program for even one turn about the floor."

"Are they? I have no idea, for I cannot look at anyone but you."

"You will tire of that someday, you know," I teased, not believing my own words. "You will look back upon the days when you could have danced with any number of young ladies with longing, and possibly regret."

"I believe you're talking of yourself, after all!

Now, 'fess up, Alice: You want to dance with one of those hopping young undergraduates—see that pack of them, over in the corner, the ones who look as if they've borrowed their fathers' waistcoats?—instead of poor me. You're the one who fears regrets, not I!"

"Oh dear, you've found me out! I can't hide anything from you!"

Laughing, Leo spun me about—not quite in step with the orchestra—until I grew dizzy, but I didn't mind. Looking up into his smiling face—finally he was filling out, so that his cheekbones weren't so prominent—I surrendered myself to his sure, confident embrace as he guided me across the crowded dance floor. It was such a relief to have him steer me about so; tonight, I didn't want to think, I didn't want to worry. I wanted only to laugh, and smile, and dance, and, yes—perhaps even flirt. But most of all, I wanted to love, and be loved.

And in his arms, feeling the burning imprint of his hand upon my waist even through the hard shell of my corset, I found not only the joy I had sought earlier but the realization, without a doubt, that I was.

The Corn Exchange—normally a huge, drafty place with soaring ceilings, broad exposed beams, sawdust-covered wood floors—had been transformed. Tonight the floors had been scrubbed and polished to a sheen with beeswax; the cavernous walls were hung with velvet maroon drapes, great gilded brackets holding dripping candelabras, and bouquets of flowers tucked into swaths of lace and cord. A very welcome addition was an enormous stack of ice blocks near the back, which did help cool the room from the heat of the candles and the warmth of the dancers.

While my gown was, naturally, one of the most elegant, there was no shortage of finery on display. The young ladies wore gowns of the lightest material—whispery muslin, delicate lace, rustling tarlatan, gauzy tulle—in colors of the gayest spring, bustles lower this season, more trailing than bunched; the men were elegantly slim in their close-fitting black trousers, skimming dress coats to match, showing broad expanses of white shirtfront studded with diamonds or gold. Naturally, everyone wore white kid gloves.

The ballroom was a feast for the senses: a rainbow of colors swirling, merging, parting; the beguiling music of the orchestra, the low, mellow instruments keeping time while the melody swirled about courtesy of the violins; the honey-sweet aroma of burning beeswax combined with the hothouse fragrance of a thousand flowers all mixed together. And hovering above it all was the rise and fall of ballroom conversation; teasing, taunting, laughing, occasional serious undertones of earnest lovemaking.

"I do love balls." I sighed, content to be simply one fair maiden among many tonight.

"That is the least profound idea I have ever heard come from your delectable mouth, and I love you for it." Leo laughed indulgently, even paternally—and I allowed him to do so with a bashful, very maidenlike smile.

"Am I too serious for you at times? Would you prefer it if I only chatted about gloves and bows and parasols instead of books and art and ideas?"

"Not at all! I've spent far too much time in the company of such perfect ladies—"

"So I'm not a perfect lady?" Arching my back, I pulled slightly away, feigning outrage with a pout.

"No, no—oh dear!" He began to laugh, help-lessly, his slim shoulders shaking with mirth. "This is one of those conversations which I will never survive. Suffice it to say you're perfect in every way, and I don't want you to change one whit. There—am I forgiven?"

"I suppose so." I tried very hard not to smile, but I couldn't help it. He looked so appealingly con-fused, like a small boy; still, when he gazed at me with that sparkle in his eye, I knew I was his equal in every way, and that he admired me for it.

The music came to an end with a violin flourish; the dancers applauded, and Leo bowed while I curtsied. Somehow we had ended up in the center of the ballroom, all eyes upon us, and I decided that, after all, I did not want to be one among many. I wanted to be the sole prize upon the arm of Prince Leopold, admired, studied, envied.

Holding my chin high and proud, feeling my cheeks blaze, knowing my eyes sparkled, I rejoiced that I was the talk of the ball. I had known notoriety, of course, but this was different; this was intoxicating, and I'm afraid I rather encouraged it by laughing just a little louder than usual, touching Leo's arm, as he led me off the dance floor, just a little more often than necessary. Tonight, I did not care who saw me.

"Alice, my dear Alice! Let me look at you!"

Suppressing a small sigh, I turned around to face my elder sister, just arrived from Scotland. She was attired in a silver blue taffeta gown, with rows of tiny pink silk rosebuds sewn vertically up the front of the bodice in an artistic attempt to draw the eye upward, not out, although there was no way to obscure the obvious; Ina had grown stout. There was no other word for it; my sister had grown stout and matronly after the arrival of her first child.

Her husband, William Skene, was a tall, thin man, kindly, with an air of endless patience. I was fond of my scholarly brother-in-law. He was a man very much like Papa—living in his head most of the time, although he had a certain hard practicality about him, too. My sister was a woman quite like my mother. They were a perfect match; dreamlike men always benefitted from energetic women.

"You look wonderful, darling." I embraced my

sister. "What a lovely frock! Wherever did you find that silvery shade of gray? It almost matches your eyes!"

"London, of course; we can find nothing up in Edinburgh. I told William I simply *had* to dart down to London before the ball."

"I'm sure you did," I said with a quick smile, remembering many, many times when Ina had bossed me about in the same way. "It was worth it; the dress is beautiful."

"Mrs. Skene, it's a pleasure." Leo bowed to her, taking Ina's plump hand, lifting it to his lips. She blushed, curtsied, and began to fan herself furiously, one of her teasing smiles upon her lips, although the effect wasn't quite the same as it had been when she was fourteen.

"Your Royal Highness, how lovely it is to see you again. I'm very happy to observe that you've recovered fully from your illness."

"Thank you. Of course, I had a great incentive to do so." Smiling, Leo took possession of my left hand, tucking it under his arm. Ina's eyebrows shot up, her mouth pursed, and I saw her exchange a look with Mamma, who was standing in the doorway to the small anteroom that had been furnished for the Prince's private party.

Catching Ina's look, Mamma came rushing forward, practically dragging Rhoda by the arm. "Sir," Mamma said with a worried smile. "I do hope you won't mind dancing with dear Rhoda

—she has an unexpected opening on her dance card, and she was so hoping for a polka."

"I'm afraid I'm rather booked," Leo said, glancing at my dance card, dangling from my wrist.

"But surely Alice won't mind sitting this out, in order to give her sister the pleasure of just one dance?" Mamma continued to smile, more ferociously than before; she looked at me, her eyebrows nearly to her hairline. I felt the blood simmer in my veins, but I would not give way to my anger at her meddling.

"Of course," I said, through gritted teeth. "I don't mind in the least. Do go on."

Poor Rhoda—who obviously was not pleased to be used in such a way, as she had remained scowling at the floor through the entire exchange—curtsied as Leo bowed, then they repaired to the dance floor just as the orchestra started back up.

"That was very subtle, Mamma," I said, turning to meet her disapproving gaze. "What's next? Are you going to throw Ina at him, to keep us apart?"

"Alice, of course I can't dance," Ina huffed—even as she looked longingly at the dancers swirling about to the music. "I'm married now."

"I was being sarcastic, Ina."

"Alice, I'm merely acting in the Prince's best interest," Mamma replied smoothly. "It is unchivalrous of him to dance so often with just one partner. We wouldn't want word of his poor manners to get back to the Queen."

"Even if Leo danced by himself in the middle of the floor, no one could accuse him of poor manners. The truth is, I don't believe you would mind at all if that sole partner wasn't me."

Mamma did not answer; she simply made a grand, sweeping turn and rejoined Papa and all their friends greedily partaking of Leo's hospitality, as his private room was furnished with superior refreshments.

"Don't vex Mamma so, Alice," Ina murmured, patting the perfectly round sausagelike curls tickling the back of her neck—their chestnut brown not *quite* matching the rest of her hair, although I refrained from pointing this out. "You're awfully impertinent these days."

"I? Impertinent?" I looked at my sister, my deceptively placid paragon of a sister. Her gray eyes returned my gaze unblinkingly.

"I daresay the Prince's attentions have gone to your head, Alice."

"I wonder that there is only one person in this family who wants to see me happy. Dear Edith, I do wish she were here tonight!"

"So do I," said an unwelcome voice at my elbow; suddenly the cloying scent of cheap perfume filled my nostrils. Turning reluctantly—my limbs suddenly blanketed with dread—I came face-to-face with Mr. Ruskin.

I had not seen him since that nightmarish last afternoon. Observing the way his eyes glittered dangerously beneath his white, thundering brows, I knew he was remembering that day, too. While, to my great relief, he looked as usual—his clothes were neat, his abundant whiskers freshly groomed—I still feared for his reason. What name would he call me tonight? I had never known him to attend a ball before, as he declared them a ridiculous waste of money and time; what had brought him to this one?

"Mr. Ruskin." Ina curtsied.

"My dear Ina. Now, if only Edith were here, I could behold the lovely Liddell girls all over again. Ina, Alice, Edith—such pearls you are, still."

Ina—hardly a pearl; more like an oyster—simpered and blushed. I could not find it within me to flirt and carry on, as I once would have done; I had too much to fear of him. Too much to lose.

"Alice, my dear, you are simply a vision." He glanced at me, up and down—and I felt naked, vulnerable beneath his cold, boldly needful gaze.

"Thank you." Despite the heat of the room, I shivered.

"You and the Prince make such a lovely pair."

"We do?"

"Yes—you're like a flower on his arm. A lovely flower."

I could not reply; my heart was beating too rapidly against my tight stays.

"A rose, I would say." He leaned toward me, so that his breath was tickling my neck. "You look like a beautiful—*rose*." He whispered this last; placing his hand upon my arm, he stroked it, up and down, lightly, as if I were a blossom, opening to his touch.

"I—that is, I must—Prince Leopold!" For he was suddenly beside me, having led a flushed Rhoda off the dance floor; I hadn't even noticed the music had stopped.

Laughing, gasping, I reached for his gloved hand; he took mine, pulling me to him, and I felt safe once more.

"Mr. Ruskin!" Leo shook his hand with apparent delight, surprising familiarity.

"Sir." Ruskin bowed.

"I must tell you, once again, how grateful I am for your—assistance in that matter." Leo's smile was wide and genuine; his eyes danced with the delight of a happy secret as he looked at me, then back at Mr. Ruskin.

"It is my pleasure. I am only too happy to provide what little help I can. I only wish it is of value to you, after all."

"I have great hopes that it will be. Great hopes."

"What secrets are you two keeping from me?" I tried to make my voice light, my face untroubled, but I could not ignore the heavy stone of dread settling in the pit of my stomach. I did not enjoy knowing that both Leo and I were engaged in some sort of secret dealings with John Ruskin, of all people.

"Ah, but that is not for you to know just yet!" Leo reached down and studied the dance card dangling, by a slim gold thread, from my wrist. "Hmmm. I wonder, who is this 'Prince Leopold' fellow?" And before I could say anything more to Mr. Ruskin, Leo had swept me up and back out on the dance floor with so much speed—he was turning me about in such tight circles I was dizzy—I could scarcely catch my breath.

"Leo! What on earth? The orchestra has barely started!"

"I could wait to have you in my arms no longer, I'm afraid!" His face was red, his eyes blazing with suppressed emotion; all I could do was follow him, allow him to propel me across the dance floor—bumping into other couples, stepping on trains, not even stopping to apologize—until somehow, we were all the way to the opposite side, and he was leading me through a small door.

He finally stopped then, and I could catch my breath for a moment and try to put myself back together; my dress was crumpled, and I knew the lace on my bustle must be in tatters. Finding ourselves suddenly alone, the music muffled on the other side of the door, Leo and I simply looked at each other and laughed. It was as if we shared a secret or had gotten away with some amazing deception, like two naughty children.

"Alone at last, my darling!"

"Leo, you take my breath away!"

Without warning, he swooped down and kissed me on the lips, grabbed my hand, and started pulling me down a passage.

I had held Leo's hand many times; I had felt his arm about me, looked into his eyes. But never before had I been so aware of his confidence, his sureness, his boldness. For I felt something different in the way he touched me, shepherding me down the hall past servants who flattened themselves against the walls as we hurried by; I felt the possession of a lover—perhaps a husband?—and my heart thrilled, every nerve strained and tensed, for I longed to submit, to be possessed.

"Sir, I do not jest—you leave me, quite literally, breathless!" I laughed, but I was serious, for he was walking so very fast I could hardly keep up, despite the firm grip he had on my hand.

"I'm sorry, my dear!" He slowed, turning to smile at me—he was so eager, his smile seemed to take over his entire face. "I quite forgot that ladies' clothing is so devilishly—well, so devilishly *constraining*. Although I do think you look lovely tonight—have I told you?"

"Several times. But I'll never tire of hearing it."

"Be careful what you wish for!" With another smile—another twinkle of his blue eyes—he turned down a different passage; it was unlit, narrow, the floor uneven, and I could not see my hand before me. All I could do was trust in Leo to guide me, and I was glad to do so.

"Watch your step!" I heard the creak of a door, then stubbed my toe up against a small stair. Following him blindly, I stepped up, then out—into the night. Blinking at the relative brightness—the moon was not quite full, yet it shone purposefully down upon us—I found that we were in the large open-air market behind the Council Hall. It was empty tonight, of course, although the ground was still scattered with straw, and there were a few permanent wooden stalls as well as several benches. Leo led me to one, and laughed as I sank down upon it, finally able to catch my breath.

"I'm sorry, truly, but I was so eager, you know, to have you entirely to myself!"

"Sir, I am most gratified, but do we dare it? We're quite unchaperoned!" I smiled up at him; he was no longer laughing. The solemn look in his eyes chased away my own smile; I studied him with the same gravity, for I knew I would want to remember this moment for the rest of my life.

"Alice." He knelt beside me; I wondered, oddly, if he would dirty the knees of his trousers. "Dearest Alice, please give me your hand."

Trembling, I did as he asked.

"Darling, I had the most amazing communication this evening from Mamma. She sends her best wishes, naturally."

"How very kind of her," I said automatically, wishing he would get to the point while also, strangely, happy to linger in the sweet anticipation of the moment; just to see the love light in his eyes, those hopeful, thoughtful eyes, filled all the aching, empty places of my heart up with a quiet joy.

"Yes, well—she knows, now, how very—fond —I am of you. I've taken great care in telling her. I'm afraid I've been rather a boring correspondent, as I've had just one single subject. You."

"Oh, is the Queen very tired of me?"

"I daresay—particularly as I even enlisted others in my cause."

"You have?"

"Yes—I didn't want to trust our happiness to my own feeble pen. That was what I was referring to, with Mr. Ruskin. I asked him, as well as Duckworth—your old friends, of course—to write to her, also. She respects them, and she knows their great regard for your father, their long association with your family. I felt that would be the wisest course, don't you agree?"

Did a cloud veil the moon, or was it fear that darkened the night, chilling my bones? Yet I told myself that Leo would not be on his knees beside me if the Queen had not given him reason to hope. What could Mr. Duckworth say, after all? He was a good man. He was also Mr. Dodgson's closest friend.

But Mr. Dodgson was kind, I had seen it in his eyes; he wanted me to be happy—*may we be happy*—

"Oh, Leo!" My heart fluttered, sickeningly, to my feet. And why hadn't Mr. Ruskin mentioned this to me before? If he intended to aid us, would he not have told me?

"What is it, dear? You look so distressed—is it the cold? Here, do take my coat—I forgot about your wrap." With a sweet, worried shake of his head—entirely in the manner of one delighted to find himself suddenly responsible for another —he removed his jacket and placed it about my shoulders.

"Thank you," I said, looking up at him; his hands lingered upon my shoulders as he bent down to kiss me, gently, almost reverently.

But then his lips—his soft, full lips—sought more; he sank down beside me on the bench, wrapped me in his arms, and took my love as insistently as I could give it. I sought, too—pulling away with a little gasp, my limbs limp, only his arms holding me up, I suddenly needed more; I met his lips, tasted his tongue, with a hunger of my own. My arm arched gracefully about his neck—a strange liquid thrill shot through my womb, and I cried out, even as I sought more.

And he was eager to provide it; he leaned into me, pressing down upon my body almost until I could no longer hold myself upright; I sank down, down, down until my back nearly touched the bench.

"I—I—oh, darling!" Suddenly he sprang back, wrenched away, and pushed at my shoulders, his hands trembling. Leo shook his head, as if to clear it; I searched his face, still wanting more; still wanting to possess him, possess him so absolutely that nothing he could hear—not from the Queen, nor Mr. Duckworth, nor Mr. Ruskin —could ever keep us apart.

"Yes, Leo?" Struggling to sit upright, I felt my hair falling down the back of my neck, and I saw Edith's diamond clip sparkling on the ground near the bench. I studied him anxiously; wanting so very much to please him.

"I'm afraid—that is, we mustn't do much more of—that, at least not now. Not until—not until later, my dear." He clenched his hands into fists, holding them tight for a long moment before finally relaxing them and turning back to smile at me. I noticed, however, that he was still breathing heavily.

"Oh! Yes, of course, I quite understand." I did understand that it was different with men; their passions were more difficult to control.

"Although I must say, dear Alice, you do kiss quite well. Almost as if you've been kissed before, many times!" Now he was teasing me, I knew; his eyes glittered and coaxed, until I was forced to smile, despite my sudden queasiness.

"Well, I have been—you've kissed me yourself!"

"Ah, I'm much more accomplished than I've been led to believe." He—very gingerly, as if I might be too warm to touch—placed his hand upon mine and sat quietly for a moment, until his breathing came more regularly.

"Now, then, you've quite gotten me off track. I do believe I was speaking very seriously about a matter of great importance to us both."

"Yes, of course—do go on." I tried to match the lightness of his tone, even as I fought off a rising bubble of panic. Had I been overeager? Had I scared him away? I had always been confident around Leo, knowing I was his equal in so many ways. Suddenly, I was very unsure of myself. I did not feel on equal footing, not at all; I was so close to my heart's desire that I was unable to think, to choose, to act, for fear of chasing it away.

"As I said—before I was so spectacularly interrupted—I've written Mamma, and she understands where my heart lies. With you, of course, my Alice. And this afternoon, then, I received a letter from her, a most encouraging letter—"

"Alice! Alice!" It was a strange voice calling my name; startled, Leo and I both looked up. Someone was running toward us, across the great expanse of the marketplace.

"What? Who's there?" We rose, and I tried to

make out the approaching figure, sprinting, as if to a fire, calling my name.

"Alice—there you are! We've been looking everywhere! Come quickly—we must leave right away!" It was William Skene, his shirt untucked, his coat half off his shoulders; he bent over, hands upon his knees, struggling to catch his breath before he looked at me—I saw, even in the moonlight, that his face was deathly pale.

"What? What is it?"

"Edith. It's Edith—quick, we must go back to the Deanery. Your parents have already left with Ina and Rhoda—I'm to take you in my carriage."

"Edith?" I could only repeat her name, for it did not register in my brain. Edith? Edith was home, in bed; I had just waltzed around her room, getting ready for this night. "What about Edith?"

"She's ill—very, very ill. Dr. Acland has gone, too. Come—we can't tarry. Prince Leopold, help me!"

I did not understand what he meant, but somehow Leo was pushing me—gently, yet forcibly—toward William, who was hurrying back across the market square. Then I was in front of the Corn Exchange, being lifted into the carriage—I heard my brother-in-law yell to his driver to hurry, there was no time to waste—and somehow I found the presence of mind to lean out of the carriage window and look, one more time, at Leo as the horses pulled away. I realized, too late, that I was still wrapped in his jacket; it smelled like moonlight, like warm breezes, faded jasmine. My own scent, I realized; it had mixed and lingered with his. I smelled myself upon his coat.

Leo was standing at the curb, just under a streetlamp; the light shone down upon him, making his hair a golden halo but obscuring his face so I could not see his eyes. He raised his arm in farewell, opened his mouth as if to speak.

We rounded the street corner before I could hear what he said, but I was sure that it was just one word—

Alice.

Chapter 13

PERITONITIS. MEASLES. PERITONITIS.

Dr. Acland could not make up his mind as to the cause of Edith's sudden decline. He felt her pulse, looked at her dilated pupils, and palpated her stomach, even cut her wrist to study her blood. In the end, all he could do was shake his head and try to make her comfortable. Yet he could not even do that. In her half-conscious state she moaned, she writhed, she gasped and pleaded with words that did not make sense even as they pierced the heart.

I sat next to her; I would not leave her for a minute. Mamma sat on the other side of the bed. But the men—Papa, devastated; ashen Aubrey—

could not take it. They stood outside the room and talked in low, unbelieving murmurs, while Ina officiously declared that she was there to tend to them, for there was no place for her in the sickroom.

During my vigil, I did not weep. Neither did Mamma. We sat, silent sentries, and did not speak, not to each other; we did both try to comfort Edith, try to soothe her, try to bring her back from her purgatory of pain, but there was no reaching her. The poor, pale face—there were some outbreaks of spots, but not many—was drenched in sweat, her hair, dark with perspiration, spread out over her pillow; her entire body seemed twisted, wrung out like a wet dish towel. She rarely opened her eyes, and when she did, they were a dull, muddy color, clouded over with pain. I know she did not see us. All I could pray for was that she *felt* us; felt my hand in hers as I tried so very hard to pass my strength on to her frail, tortured body.

Even during my vigil—did I sleep? Eat? I do not recall—I was aware of one thing.

I was aware that Leo had not called.

I had expected him to be here; if not here, precisely—knowing his own tendency to sickness—then at least sending me notes of comfort and hope. I had expected him, at the very least, to call asking about Edith, for he was very fond of her, as was everyone who knew her gentle spirit.

His absence was conspicuous; I even heard Papa, outside in the hall, remark upon it.

Mamma did not. She spoke to me only once, after a particularly anguished spell during which Edith's limbs went rigid, her back arched off the mattress in agony; I pressed my lips together, holding in a cry of my own to see my sister so. I asked, finally, for God to put a stop to it, however best He saw fit; I vowed I would never ask for anything again—for what else would I need, if Leo were by my side?—if only she didn't have to suffer.

After Edith went limp again, unconscious but mercifully out of pain, Mamma sagged in her chair, pressing her handkerchief to her mouth and giving way to a heartbreaking moan. When I looked over at her, with eyes too full of my sister's agony to truly see anything else, she removed her handkerchief and said, "Why couldn't it be you? You've never brought me anything but pain, while she has brought me nothing but joy."

I knew she spoke the truth as she saw it; I also knew I would remember her words, and cry against their cruelty later. Later, when I had emotion, strength, to spare for myself.

But at that moment I could only listen, and stare at my mother, and be grateful, at least, that here was one child she would truly mourn.

The second day of our vigil, I was told, very sternly by Dr. Acland, that I must get some fresh air or else there would be another patient on his hands. So I rose—my neck was stiff, the small of my back ached, and I felt, immediately, dizzy upon my feet—and somehow stumbled out of Edith's room, pleading with Dr. Acland to come get me the minute she awoke, or—

I would not give voice to the alternative; I would not. I shut my eyes but could not prevent the hot, tired tears from rolling down my cheeks. I drifted down the stairs—I do not know how, for my legs were as numb as my other senses—and found myself outside, in the garden. It was a beautiful day, I thought automatically, looking up at the bright sun, the blue sky, noting that the roses were almost in bloom. I must fetch Edith, for she would enjoy it so—

Falling down upon a stone bench, I buried my face in my hands and allowed my fears to take over, driving all hope from my heart. How could she recover? I knew she could not. Yet it was too cruel to contemplate, my sister being taken just as her life was starting; I recalled the wedding dress she had recently ordered, the excitement in her eyes as she sketched out the flowers she would carry in her bridal bouquet. My heart could not bear it, but I could not stop trying, somehow, to understand; she was healthy, she was strong, she was in love. How could this happen? Wasn't goodness—wasn't love—enough for God?

My stomach lurched, pushing bile up in my

throat; I retched, although nothing came up but sobs—huge, racking sobs that shook my very bones, rattled my weary heart. I could not bear to lose my sister—I already felt an empty ache in my chest where she should be, as if I'd carried her around with me always, and I knew, of course, that I had. Who would I turn to if she wasn't there? What would I ever do with all that emptiness? My sister was my only friend, except for Leo, and he was not here, either. Where was he? What could his absence mean? I couldn't bear to lose him, too—oh, I could not possibly bear any more!

And then he was standing before me. I looked up, blinking through my tears, not at all sure it was him—it could have been an apparition, a dream of him, so golden was his hair as the sun shone through it—but then my arms were about his neck, my head upon his shoulder, and he was stroking my forehead, murmuring my name.

"Leo, Leo, where were you? I needed you so —but you're here now." I was babbling, too exhausted to try to collect my thoughts; every nerve was raw, worn to a frazzle.

"Dearest, I'm so sorry. I—I had—that is, how is she? Tell me, how is Edith?" Gently, he lowered me to the bench and sat beside me, my head still upon his shoulder. I closed my eyes, felt his strength and his protection, and I wanted to remain there forever. If I did, then everything would be all right; Edith would simply be waiting for me in her room, pouting about not being able to go to the ball. And Leo and I would always be together, and the burden of being myself—watched, watchful, and so very, very careful—would be lifted from me.

"She's—oh, Leo, she's so ill! She's delirious, burning with fever, racked with pain, and Dr. Acland won't say it, but I know—I know—he despairs!" Each word was wrenched from my heart, until it could give no more and I had nothing left but tears, steadily shredding the remnants of my poor heart apart.

"Shhh, shhh—don't speak," he whispered.

We sat for the longest time, until my sobs subsided, leaving my ribs aching, my chest in spasms. There was a warm breeze ruffling the thin flowered muslin of my dress; I looked at my sleeves in wonder, not knowing just when I had changed from my ball gown.

As I continued my observations—to my astonishment, I heard carriages clattering in the distance, horses neighing, a bell ringing from far off; time had not stopped, after all, and outside of Edith's room the world was continuing its business—I saw that Leo had changed, too. Not simply his attire—he was wearing an ordinary white linen suit, already crumpling from the heat of the June day—but also his behavior. While he held me, it felt almost like an obligation;

there was a hesitation in his manner. He had not looked into my eyes once.

Pushing myself away from him, patting my wayward hair, I searched about for a handkerchief but found I had none; without a word, he handed me his own, and I attempted to dry my eyes.

"What is it?" I asked, my voice thick; my eyes felt raw and hot. "What happened? There is something strange in your behavior."

He didn't answer. Instead, he turned away, passed his hand over his eyes, and sat staring at a far-off tree—a willow—for a few moments. When he turned back to me, finally, I saw that there were tears in his eyes.

"I cannot—I cannot bear to add to your distress at this time," he said, his voice anguished, his face twisted up as if in pain. "I cannot."

"Yet you must." It was not a question. The dread that had been in my heart—my poor, battered heart—for weeks, heightened by his absence these past two days, settled over me, numbing my senses, dulling my voice.

"Yes, I'm afraid I—I must." He clenched his fists, stiffened his body; I saw that he was making a great effort not to fall apart himself. Despite my own pain, I was touched.

"You heard from the Queen."

"Yes."

"She does not approve of our—of me."

"Please don't keep—please let me speak, let me

shoulder the burden of this, at least, for you've had so very much to bear!" Again he turned from me, unable to control his voice.

I could only nod, wishing I could shake this strange detachment; realizing it was probably a blessing that I could not.

"Mamma has decided it's best for me to look to royalty for a match, like my siblings. I had hoped that my—circumstances—might have persuaded her otherwise, and she did give me reason to hope that. The other night, at the ball—I had received a letter earlier indicating this reason. Ultimately, however, she felt she must not deviate from her plans." Now Leo's voice matched my own in dullness; he had obviously rehearsed this speech, or memorized it word for word from her letter.

In my odd detachment—there was a barrier between myself and the rest of the world, I felt; as if I were encased in tin, or glass—I asked the question I would not have been able to otherwise. But I desired information, in the place of emotion.

"Was there mention of some past business of mine, perhaps? Involving Mr. Dodgson?"

With a strangled cry, Leo buried his face in his hands and nodded.

I longed to put my arm around him, to comfort him, for he was in such despair; he was not protected from his pain, as I was. I felt such pity for him.

"Tell me, who brought it up—Mr. Ruskin or Mr. Duckworth?"

"Both—both made mention of some—confusion, regarding a break with Mr. Dodgson. Mr. Ruskin was rather more forthcoming, to my surprise; I had not imagined him to have any concerns, given his enthusiasm for my request. Yet he swore that he was acting in your best interest, too, for he feared a renewal of old gossip. But it was put to Mr. Dodgson, to confirm or deny, just this morning."

"And?"

"He did neither. He would not speak of the subject."

"He was silent?"

"Yes."

"Oh." With a jolt—an oddly mechanical click, as if a missing piece of machinery had finally fallen into place—I remembered. Out of all the things I could not recall of that afternoon so long ago, now, at last, here was one.

I remembered silence. My own silence, in the face of similar questions. Understanding—or perhaps hoping—that I could not trust my own memories, as words and images of the past filled my eleven-year-old mind with conflicting emotion, I simply took refuge in silence. It was that silence, I knew—that much, now, I knew, despite the kindness I thought I had seen in his eyes—that had wounded Mr. Dodgson forever. I *had* wounded him, so that when it came his time to clarify, he could not bring himself to speak, either. So, in the end, he might destroy my happiness, as I had destroyed his.

Wonderland was all we had in common, after all; Wonderland was what was denied the two of us. I had denied him his; he had denied me mine.

"I'm so very sorry," I told Leo, finally. Turning to him—steeling myself to receive his pain and rejection—I placed my hand upon his shoulder and accepted my punishment.

I was not spared it, for his eyes were anguished, large, and reproachful; his mouth was twisted, as if trying not to accuse me of anything further. There were gaunt hollows under his cheeks, and I had the burden of knowing that I had caused him more pain than typhoid fever had done.

"No!" With a cry he grasped my hand, like a drowning man would a strong rope; he pulled it to his lips and kissed it passionately. "No, I will not believe any of this. You're still my Alice, my heart—I may not be permitted to have you, but I will not allow myself to think that you are not the woman I know and love. Please tell me that, at least. Please!"

I knew that no matter what I said, it would not be enough; when you're on the other side of the looking glass, nothing is as it seems.

"My love for you is unchanged; my heart—the heart you hold, that you will always possess—is unchanged. I can't undo what's been said, what's been done. I could have—I could have allowed myself to be—used—in order to preserve Mr. Ruskin's silence, for he is not the friend to either of us that you believe him to be. But I could not do it—and because I could not, you must know that I am the woman you love!"

Shutting his eyes—either against my words or against the pain they caused—he bit his lip, as if to prevent himself from asking the question that, in the end, would burst out anyway: "Did he—did he ever touch you?"

"Mr. Ruskin? No."

"Then—Dodgson?"

Hands, upon my shoulders; lips, upon my—

"I can't recall—you must believe me! I was just a child—and I don't—I didn't understand what I was—what was happening. I only know that he was forbidden to see me, after a time. And that I've not been five minutes in his company since, until he took my photograph for you."

Stifling a moan, Leo put his finger to my lips, pulled me to him, forgiving me with this gentle act; briefly I felt the peace of lying upon his breast and hearing his heart beating, calling my name. "What will I do?" he whispered, his lips upon my hair. "What will I do without you?"

"And I you?" Now my protective layers were cracking; I thought of tomorrow, and the next day, and the next day after that; weeks, months, years when I would not be allowed to see him, to hear his voice, to know his thoughts, his heart. I would never again feel as loved as I did in that moment; knowing this, I could not prevent my mind from racing ahead, reminding me of all I would miss. His habit of patting his mustache with two fingers, when he was deep in thought; his merry laugh—as innocent, as pure, as a child's; his unabashed enjoyment of life, the easy way he gave of himself, his humor, his love.

The way he said my name—simply Alice. No other words were necessary. I was not "Alice dear," "Alice my pet," "Miss Alice"; I was simply his. *His* Alice.

"I can't go. I can't leave you." Leo tightened his arms about me. "I don't have that strength."

"Nor do I." I began to weep, quietly now, tears of benediction. An almost peaceful sadness had overcome me, stealing over my limbs; I longed to linger, to sleep in his arms, until the moment I had to be wrenched from them.

"Here." Still holding me against his shoulder, he reached into his breast pocket and then held out his hand; whatever was in it sparkled, catching the rays of the sun.

"What is it?"

"Your hair clip. It fell, the other night when— when we were—at any rate, I went back to get it for you."

I took the small silver clip, decorated in a starburst of tiny diamonds, and closed my fingers over it; it was cool and surprisingly heavy.

"It's Edith's," I whispered, shutting my eyes. "She lent it to me. I was so happy—she was so happy—"

Then I heard a cry from across the garden.

"Alice, come quickly! Oh, Alice—come before it's too late!" It was Rhoda, standing at the garden gate, gesturing wildly.

I shot up, every nerve and muscle suddenly energized; my heart raced, and I knew what lay before me; I knew what I had to do.

I began to run. Leo held on to my hand until the very last moment, until my fingertips touched his, and then there was nothing between us; nothing but the truth. I heard him call out, "I'll wait for you, oh, do hurry!"

"No!" I could not look back. I could only look ahead, my hand tightening about the diamond clip until I felt the sharp end bite into my palm, and even so, I clasped it tighter. The ground was skimming before me, the gate still banging in Rhoda's wake. "No, don't wait—for God's sake, go now, while I can bear it!" For this instant, I could; as soon as I ran through the door of the Deanery—already I heard voices from inside the house, urgent, loud voices, doors slamming, a desperate wail—I knew I would not have the strength to watch him leave me, too.

And my heart, at that moment, split in two; I

gave one half to Leo and one half to my sister and, saying good-bye to both, knew that I would never be whole again.

MY SISTER EDITH WAS buried on a magnificent June day; the sun was so brilliant, the birds in such full-throated song, one felt either the cruelty of such a day or the comfort of it. She was laid to rest in the wedding dress that had arrived the day before. Rhoda, Violet, and I followed behind her casket, wearing the bridesmaids' dresses she had chosen. A bridal bouquet rested on top of the casket instead of the usual wreath. Aubrey Harcourt was the chief mourner; his sobs could be heard throughout the service.

Among the pallbearers was Prince Leopold, the black silk armband on his left arm. Many of those present commented upon how pale and grave he looked, and remarked upon his touching devotion to the Dean's family.

Only once did our eyes meet. After the pallbearers had placed the casket at the head of the cathedral, he walked back to take his seat. But before he did, he paused, turned to me, and gazed down into my face. I absorbed the sorrow in his beautiful blue eyes, the wordless grief upon his face, and knew for whom he was truly mourning; still gazing into his eyes, I raised my fingers to my lips, kissed them, and finally turned away, my eyes too full of hot tears to see anything but the glorious light shining in through the stained-glass windows.

My love walked down the aisle, away from me. And I knew I would never see him again.

Chapter 14

CUFFNELLS, 1914

*A*LICE, LISTEN TO THIS. CHAP HERE IS WRITING a book about the late King. Says that the poor old Queen allowed Mrs. Keppel to visit him on his deathbed. What do you think of that?"

Lowering the front page of the *Times*, I raised an eyebrow and stared across the table at my husband, who was hidden by his own copy, freshly ironed by his butler. I continued to stare at him until finally he lowered his paper and met my gaze with a sheepish grin. "The Queen was always most understanding about all that—business," he said. Then he quickly hid his face from me once more.

"Yes. Isn't that touching? The Queen was so very understanding about the King's mistresses—all of them. A most gracious woman, Alexandra."

"Would do some people good to emulate her," my husband grumbled from behind his paper.

"What's that, Regi?"

"Nothing. Always did admire the Queen, that's all."

"Yes." I sniffed, remembering. "She is a saint, and Mamma was right. Bertie never was satisfied with a sweet little princess."

"Your mother was correct about a great many things. Wise woman, she was."

"Hmmm."

"Always got along so well with her, I did."

"Yes."

"Not like your father, though."

"No."

"Listen to this! New Forest walloped Hampshire! Could really use a good off spinner, poor chaps!"

"Mmm-hmm." I paid scant attention to him now that he was going on about cricket; still, I glanced over at his plate and saw that he had finished his kippers. Pressing my foot down upon the electric buzzer—neatly hidden by the Brussels carpet—I waited for a maid to appear.

"Mary Ann, Mr. Hargreaves would like more kippers. And I require more coffee."

"Yes, madam." With a short bob—not a proper curtsy; really, the cheekiness of servants these days!—she left the room, and I went back to the paper. Turning the page, another headline caught my eye; it caught my heart, also, in an icy grip.

Kaiser Threatens Czar.

"Regi," I said, interrupting him in the middle of a description of an especially exciting innings. "When is Alan home on leave?"

"Don't know. Imagine later this month, don't you think?"

"I have no idea. That is why I asked you."

"Right. Well, sorry."

"I was just reading this headline about the Kaiser and Russia. Do you—do you believe it will come to war, then?"

"Couldn't say—oh." Finally he lowered his paper and gaped at me; he was white of whiskers now, wrinkled of brow, with the ruddy face of the typical English country gentleman. Realization dawned as visibly as always—starting with his forehead, moving down to his arching eyebrows, slowly comprehending eyes, finally to his mouth, pulling it up in a simple, understanding grin. "Say, you're worried, aren't you? About Alan? Well, I imagine it won't last long, regardless. And he's a captain now, he'll be tucked away somewhere safe and sound. After all, he's no young lad anymore; he's what? Nearly forty?"

"Thirty-three. Our eldest son will be thirty-three in October."

"Right. Good God, has it been that long?"

"Yes, it has." I couldn't suppress a smile; his emotions may have been slow in coming, but they were always touchingly honest and transparent. He looked simply dumbstruck at the passage of time.

I resumed my perusal of the paper, but my thoughts did not follow. Good God, indeed. Yes, it had been that long.

I had been sitting across the breakfast table from Regi for thirty-four years, since 1880; four years after Edith died. Four years after I saw Leo for the last time, at her funeral.

In those four years, left behind by those I loved, I felt myself stagnate, mired helplessly not only in their shadows but in the shadows of the tall, graceful spires of Oxford itself. I also grew older while, around me, the undergraduates grew younger. I was no longer the beautiful princess of Christ Church, the belle of the Commemoration Ball; I saw the glances, heard the whispers. Bluestocking. Spinster. Old maid.

Mamma finally lost a tick or two of her phenomenal energy when Edith died. Or was it when Leo left? To be truthful, I wasn't sure which was the precipitating factor; I know only that when I alone remained, Mamma stopped trying so hard. Ina was married, Edith was dead, and I was "disappointed"—for that was the proper term for a jilted lover in those days; the three little princesses were no more. Neither Rhoda nor Violet ever seemed inclined toward matrimony, for some reason.

Ultimately, those four years were a blessing. For during them, memories faded, people left, hearts mended. Mr. Ruskin finally broke down, shouting obscenities during a lecture, and had to be forcibly removed from the hall. No one cared about what had happened on a long-forgotten summer afternoon between a fussy mathematics don and the bluestocking daughter of the Dean. The Queen had no more princes left to educate at Christ Church.

Alice in Wonderland, however, lived on; new editions of the books, theatrical productions, toys and blocks and games. No one seemed to care— or even know—that the real Alice had grown up, was on the verge of growing old, alone.

Certainly Reginald Gervis Hargreaves, Esq., did not care. Regi Hargreaves did not care about books at all; in fact, he had such little regard for them that it took him six years to matriculate at Oxford, instead of the usual four.

When did I first meet Regi? I cannot recall, although he insisted it was at that fateful Commemoration Ball of 1876. He claimed he saw me on the Prince's arm, and that he had never beheld a more beautiful creature in his life. He was in awe—but knew there was no way he could compete against a prince. So he bided his time, and did not seem to notice that I was a fruit rather past my ripeness. He simply hung around until I fell off the tree for good, and he was there to scoop me up.

Regi was a sportsman, a cricketer, the usual English country squire type; I admit that at first, I found this was refreshingly different and not a little thrilling. He had no title but enough property to impress even Mamma. His family had made money in trade; in textiles, only a generation previous, which of course was slightly scandalous. Rather, it would have been for anyone else but me; in my case, Mamma was willing to overlook this lapse.

He was tall, broad-shouldered, good-looking, with soft brown hair he parted carelessly in the middle, ruddy skin, a slight overbite that he hid with a bristly mustache. I knew I would never love him the way I loved Leo; I knew I would never be able to converse with him in the same way, laugh with him, tease him. Regi did not, even then, display much of a sense of humor; I learned quickly to keep my more biting, sarcastic observations to myself, or else risk spending half an evening trying to explain them.

He proposed in July, after Commemoration, on a rowboat in the middle of the Isis; his proposal was typically Regi:

"I say, we row together awfully well, don't we?"

"Yes, I suppose."

"What say we row together always, then? Talking of marriage, I mean. You know."

"Oh. Well, yes. I suppose we might as well."

"Capital!"

Despite the comical brevity, I was touched; he had at least tried to be poetic, and given the number of times he repeated the exchange to friends, I could tell he was very proud of himself.

We were married in September, in Westminster Abbey at my insistence, instead of Christ Church

Cathedral. Two days before my wedding—an elaborate affair that amused more than engaged me, but I viewed it as my farewell gift to Mamma —Leo sent me a brooch; a small diamond horseshoe, for luck. I wore it on my wedding dress of silver brocade and white satin; I wear it still, to this day.

Regi, far from being jealous, was proud that the Prince thought so highly of his bride that he would send her such an intimate gift. He was so awestruck by royalty that I do not think he would have minded if Leo—or better still, the Prince of Wales himself—had offered to deflower me on our wedding night. Indeed, I believe Regi might even have taken out an advertisement in the *Times* proclaiming the fact, and preserved the room in all its consummated glory, after.

Mr. Dodgson, too, sent me a wedding gift; a small watercolor of Tom Quad. It was a very accurate likeness that I could find no reason not to display, unlike many of my wedding gifts. While feebler artistic attempts grace the walls of the servants' quarters, that particular watercolor resides now in my bedroom.

Over a year later, Leo married a rather plain princess from a minor European province. He named his first daughter Alice; I named my second son Leopold Reginald, although we called him Rex. Two months before his second child, a son, was born, Leo died from internal hemorrhaging after a fall while staying in France. Mr. Duckworth had the kindness of heart to telegraph me right away, before I could read of it in the newspapers.

When word of his death reached me, I had to retire to my bedroom and shut the door against Regi and the boys and their untroubled harmony; they had no idea that the sun had just fallen from the sky. For while I had known I would never see Leo again, still I rose every morning taking comfort that he was in the world, awakening to the same rosy dawn, sleeping under the same night sky. We rarely corresponded, and when we did it was always extremely polite and impersonal; but I felt as if he was in my life, and I in his. I felt it because I knew, when I looked at a painting, read a book, observed a rare bird or delicate flower, that he would have looked at it in exactly the way I did; our hearts, our minds, were so sympathetic. So that merely by going on and enjoying life, I was sharing it with him.

When he died, I was no longer whole. That was it, pure and simple. Regi might hold me, kiss me, claim his right as a husband, and he was not ungentle in that way, but he was never *of* me as Leo was. When he was gone from this world, I was less.

I don't wish to indicate that I was not fond of Regi. I was. He was a consistent soul whose only fault was that he was not Leo; a gentle man who rarely gave me reason to quarrel. If he did occasionally indulge himself in the way most men of his class and generation did, at least he did it more or less discreetly, and always made up for it after with a trip to the jeweler, with whom I had an understanding. (Regi's tastes tended to the gaudy, unfortunately—he once bought me a turquoise ring; imagine! Mr. Solomon, however, soon learned to steer him toward more understated gems, such as amethyst and emerald.)

I could not complain overmuch; God knows I was not the most affectionate wife, although I was, truly, grateful to him for rescuing me.

For finally, his were the hands that spirited me far away from Oxford, to a Wonderland where no one knew me except as Mrs. Reginald Hargreaves. Regi afforded me a fine country house, Cuffnells, in the village of Lyndhurst, right in the middle of the Hampshires; 160 acres belonged to us, and the house was situated in the middle of lush, fertile earth with a view of the Solent from the upper floor. We even had a small lake, fully stocked; the boys loved to camp out there during summer holidays and skin and fry the fish themselves for breakfast.

The house itself was grander than anything Mamma could have wished for, even if the first time she saw it, she merely sniffed and told me I had done fairly well for myself. I cannot deny that I gloated a bit when I showed her the two stories of pale stone, the balcony running along the upper floor; the huge orangery, impressively wide staircase, billiard room, library, and cavernous dining room; the drawing room decorated with a frieze of peacocks painted by an Italian artist. All of this was mine, simply for agreeing to marry a man I did not love but who was, in the end, the only man who had ever asked.

It seemed a fair exchange, on the whole.

I was in charge of a large household staff—finally I could boast of my own servant problems!—and it took a great deal of my time, for which I was secretly grateful. It was very quiet in Lyndhurst; the days seemed to pass more slowly here. There was no constant buzz in the air, like at Oxford; more like a somnambulant snore. There was too much time, if one was so inclined, to reflect—upon the past, the present, the future.

I was not so inclined. So I threw myself into entertaining, making Cuffnells a gay, vibrant center of culture and sophistication to rival Mamma's efforts at Christ Church. She might have a string quartet playing on the landing of the Deanery; I arranged to have an orchestra perform in the orangery, musicians hidden among the illuminated trees like so many sprites. She might have entertained the Queen for tea; at Cuffnells, I took great delight in showing my guests a room, furnished entirely in gold—gilded furniture, gold brocade curtains, carpets —in which King George III stayed for one night, and which has remained untouched, to preserve the privilege for future generations.

While Mamma had to content herself with arranging rowing parties on the Isis, I once out-fitted a schooner with fairy lights and had my guests dress as characters from Shakespeare for a Midsummer Night's cruise across the Solent, culminating in a midnight picnic on the Isle of Wight. Even Ina was charmed by that evening, although she insisted upon dressing as Titania, resembling nothing more than a plump bumble-bee instead of an ethereal Fairy Queen.

Regi, being so sociable, was happy to fund my extravagances even if he would have preferred quiet hunting weekends to Shakespearean fetes; he was, in his simple way, proud to have such a socially accomplished, intellectual wife.

Thirty-four years, gone in the blink of an eye, a blur. I could recall details of talks with Leo, walks we had shared, minute images that still appeared as vivid to me as the day I saw them—the odd stone path we discovered once that led away from the river, for instance; all the stones were of the same white color, the same circumference, and had been placed with great care, yet it ran for only about ten feet, ending abruptly in a ditch.

My life with Regi, by contrast—and despite our extravagant entertainments—seemed all of one color, one speed. At times, I wondered if I could even remember what he looked like if he didn't happen to sit across the table from me day after day.

With a sigh, I folded up the newspaper and placed it neatly beside my plate, for I could not focus on anything other than the distressing number of headlines related to the chances of war. Moodily, I sipped my coffee. "Regi, will Alan come home for leave, then? If there is talk of war, I would hope that he would, instead of going off doing some reckless, foolish thing like racing pigs in India or whatever he did last time. Don't you agree?"

"My dear, you're really worried, aren't you?" Again, he looked so childishly surprised, yet that did not prevent him from throwing down his paper and attacking his fresh kippers with gusto.

"I am, rather. We already went through the Boer War with him; I thought we had reached an age where we would not have to worry about our sons anymore, and then this comes along. Of course if Alan is mobilized, what will happen to the other boys? It would be entirely like Rex to join up just to vex me." I stirred my coffee with such force it nearly splashed onto the saucer; Rex had been doing his level best to vex me ever since his birth.

I sometimes reflected how ironic it was that one of the three little princesses of Christ Church had borne three little princes of her own. Alan, Rex, Caryl; three little men, all in a row. So used to the company of my sisters, I wondered, at first, what on earth I would do with *boys*? Sportsmen, hunters, reluctant scholars, just like their father?

Yet Alan, the eldest, the sturdy leader, gave me little trouble; Caryl, the youngest, was so anxious to please as to be slightly irritating, but he was easily placated with a smile or a look. But Rex! Oh, Rex; the middle child, the one of whom my father had said with a fond chuckle, "God Himself broke the mold when it came to that one."

The child who was, to my mother's everlasting amusement, as she never wearied of pointing out the resemblance, exactly as I had been at his age.

"Whatever can I do with your cowlick? It simply won't stay down," I found myself saying nearly every Sunday when he was small, as we stood waiting for the carriage to take us to church. "I should cut it all off and be done with it."

"Go ahead," he would reply with an unconcerned shrug. "It's only hair. Although I'll look like a convict, which I'm sure I wouldn't mind a bit. In fact, I think it might be quite interesting. So go ahead, if you don't mind."

"Of course I mind! Only hair? A convict? I think not! Go inside and wet it as you should have done. This instant!" And Rex would do so —after first giving me a look of such ill-concealed amusement, I had to ball my hands into fists so as not to run after him.

322

Or another time—

"Rex, how on earth did you manage to get plaster in your shoes?" I stared at him, aghast, as he calmly sat upon my best Chippendale side chair and removed a sodden, heavy shoe with a triumphant smile, watching as the gooey bits of plaster rained down upon my Aubusson carpet. "How does this even *happen* to a child?"

"I don't wonder that you wouldn't know," he said with a small, worldly shake of his head. "I can't imagine you ever were a child yourself."

"That's a very impudent thing to say, young man, and I assure you I most certainly was—but do not change the subject! Answer me!"

"He was trying to jump over the new wall that the men are building in the garden, and got stuck," Caryl, who had been watching the scene with interest, piped up helpfully.

"Rat," Rex retorted with a sneer.

"Rex! Apologize at once, and go up to the nursery and change—and for heaven's sake, don't take off your other shoe until you're upstairs!" Whereupon he slid off the chair—leaving mud stains—and grinned like a little devil, saluting me sharply and running off before I could sputter anything further; running off before I could give in to a sudden, wild desire to laugh out loud. The child always prompted such conflicting emotions in me! Why couldn't he simply behave like his brothers, Alan in particular, who always managed to keep his clothes so neat and clean—

Pressing my lips together, clutching the folds of my skirt as if to physically restrain myself from chasing Rex up the stairs, I would survey the ruined chair—or broken vase, or torn drape, or whatever havoc he had managed to wreak this time—and ring for Mary Ann to clean it up. Then I would flee to the refuge of the drawing room, where I would attack a petit point pillowcase with my needle until I nearly shredded the fabric, not entirely sure with whom I was angrier—Rex, or myself.

I nearly shredded my breakfast napkin now, remembering. Try as I might to fill my life with activity, I found that lately, with the boys all grown, I could not always keep the past at bay. Nor the future; it suddenly occurred to me that if Rex enlisted, wouldn't Caryl surely do the same, just to keep up?

Then I would have three little soldier boys, all in a row.

Sensing my anxiety—I must have sighed—Regi actually set aside his fork and knife to reach across the table and grab my hand with his rough, dry mitts. "But they're not young men, remember —not as young as the military likes them. Don't imagine they'll see much of the show."

"You don't?" Rarely did I need my husband to reassure me of anything, but I did at that moment.

"I don't. Also, it can't last long! Feller down at

the club tells me that the Germans all hate the Kaiser and there'll most likely be a civil war, instead."

"Really?" I didn't believe that; it sounded exactly like the kind of preposterous hope a man would offer to a woman just to keep her calm. But I so wanted to believe it that I nodded anyway, trying to convince myself.

"Really. Now, why don't you go order a new dress or hat or something? That'll perk you right up." He beamed at me, so pleased to have come up with a remedy for my distress.

I did not quite manage to stifle a sigh. "I don't believe the purchase of a new frock will prevent the Kaiser from invading Russia, unfortunately."

"Never said it would," Regi grumbled, his face falling. I felt an irritating little prick of guilt. He was being very kind; he was trying, in his own uninspiring, typically Regi way, to distract me from my worries.

"But I do thank you, nonetheless. Now I must talk to Cook about dinner, and then I'm to meet the committee about the flower show. You don't imagine anything will happen by then, do you? I would hate to have to cancel it; the villagers do so look forward to spending an afternoon here at Cuffnells and viewing the grounds. It's such a treat for them."

"Well, I'll be damned if I'll let the old Kraut cancel my flower show! No, go on. We'll have it, no matter what. But I don't think anything will come of this, after all. Don't fret so—you're getting that little pucker between your eyes again. Can't have my girl looking worried now, can I?"

"No, you can't. Shall I order lamb for dinner?"

"Capital!"

Rising from the table, I started toward the door. I paused, however—that little prick of guilt was still lingering, as if looking for a more permanent residence—and turned around. Swiftly I walked back to my husband and kissed him on the cheek. He looked up; surprise, then delight filled his cloudless brown eyes. "Well, what's the occasion, Mrs. Hargreaves?"

"I do not require an occasion to kiss my husband," I huffed—but smiled down at him, unaccountably touched at how happy this little gesture made him.

"Not going to complain, I'm not," he mumbled, reaching for the paper, a satisfied grin upon his face.

Turning to leave, I considered making a vow—perhaps a bargain with God?—to be nicer to my husband. It did not take much to make him happy, after all; nothing that was not already within my power to bestow.

But then I recalled that God had not been very good at keeping His end of bargains in the past. And surely the Kaiser would stop his ridiculous posturing; he and the Czar and King George were cousins, for heaven's sake. Bargains and vows were for the weak and unfocused; not for me.

I pushed through the dining room door without a backward glance; as I strode down the hall with a sure step, servants flattened themselves against the wall, well out of my way. I could scarcely wait to hear Cook's excuse for last night's venison; it was ghastly—as dry and tough as an old straw hat. If she was planning on doing the same with the lamb tonight, perhaps she should start advertising for a new position.

"REX, I DO WISH YOU wouldn't wolf your soup so. There are many courses left, you know. Or don't they dine as well as we do in Canada?"

"Mamma, please. Can we not go one day without you finding fault with that poor dominion? I might add you are the one person at this table who has never traveled there."

"I do not need to see a place in order to know whether or not I approve of it. Red Indians and trees and bears—I do not see what the appeal is, or why you should have to spend so much time there."

"Mamma is getting on her high horse," Alan teased, looking quite like my boy again now that he was out of his intimidating military uniform and in an ordinary suit and tie, his hair soft and loose, flopping into his eyes.

"Queen Alice has joined us for dinner," added

Caryl, absently reaching into his breast pocket for a packet of cigarettes—and catching my disapproving eye before sheepishly putting them back.

All three boys were home for the flower show; a rare event these days. Alan's career in the Rifle Brigade kept him so far away from us that his leaves could not always be spent traveling back to England. So to have him back home—my tall, dark-haired boy; he was the one who most resembled me physically, I could see myself in his eyes—was a special treat.

Rex, the spitting image of his father, was in business, and had offices in Canada, where he spent a great deal of time. Yet he, too, made a point of being home this late July; I was delighted to see him, although I managed to mask it in my disapproval over the rough beard he was growing, and the coarseness of his clothes (it appeared there was no decent tailor in all of Canada). I knew, naturally, why he had made the effort; it was the talk of war that brought him back, not the prospect of sitting beside me on the dais as I presented Best in Show to old Smithson of the Post for his lovely azaleas.

As for what Caryl did when he was away, I could not say with any confidence. My youngest son dabbled in a great many things and mastered none of them. He lived in London, coming home for weekends, often with undesirable friends, such as artists and musicians, in tow. Smaller, slighter than his brothers—his hair neither golden brown like Rex's, nor black like Alan's, only some mousy color in between—it was almost as if he was a poor copy of them, down to his valiant little mustache; the resemblance was there, but the hand that had created him was not so steady and accomplished. I could allow that, even as I acknowledged that it was my hand that was responsible.

I did not linger on such feelings tonight; the dining table was full again, and I was far too content to eat, which was a blessing. I had quite forgotten what quantities young men in their prime could put away!

"Oh, do stop it, all of you," I said, but I was not upset about their teasing; I enjoyed being the center of attention, the sole female. Unlike Regi, I did not fret about the lack of daughters-in-law and grandchildren. There was still plenty of time for that.

"Boys, you are irritating your mother, and I'm the one who always pays that price. Do stop. Alan, tell me about the last polo match. How's your pony holding up?"

"Fine, sir!" Alan's face lit up, and he looked so young; my heart suddenly ached with an unbidden memory—the day he brought home a tiny owl that he found on a fallen branch in the woods, begging to be allowed to keep it. His face looked the same now as it did then; shining and earnest with good intent. "Mamma," he had said, so worried and serious, his voice very husky for such a little man. "Can't I keep him in my room? I promise I won't neglect him, and I'll make Rex help me catch mice and things for his meals, so you won't have to."

Had I allowed him to keep it? I couldn't recall, although for some reason, it suddenly seemed very important to me to know. It was on the tip of my tongue to ask—for surely he would remember? But I did not; I swallowed the question, knowing how ridiculous I would sound for asking it. What on earth did it matter? It was twenty-five years ago, at least. The poor owl was long gone by now, regardless.

Sternly, I gave my head a little shake, sipped some wine, and forced myself to join in the general conversation. It was about nothing, really—Rex's latest business deal involving some innovative method of pulping trees for paper; Alan's new sublieutenant, who had a wife who insisted he write her three times a day and enclose a lock of hair with each letter, so that now the poor chap was looking quite bald; the dinner party a friend of Caryl's had thrown at Simpson's, although the host managed to leave before the bill arrived, prompting Caryl to magnanimously take care of things—Regi's eyebrows popped up to his receding hairline when he heard *that*.

All in all, we were determinedly, *frightfully*, gay and lively, avoiding the one topic that was upon everyone's mind. Until Regi rose, praised me for the meal, then proposed port and cigars in the billiard room; my boys followed him, abruptly quiet and somber, each one stopping to kiss my cheek on his way out of the dining room.

It was then, alone, drifting through my quiet home—the only sounds those of the servants clearing up dinner—finally settling in the library, where I summoned a footman to light a fire, that I did wish I had daughters-in-law, after all. It would be a comfort to have someone to share this quiet time with; it would be nice to have someone to distract me from my thoughts. It was times such as this when I missed my sisters; I missed Edith, in particular, although at that moment I wouldn't have minded Rhoda or Violet or even Ina, who was in a London flat now that William had died and her son had taken over the estate in Scotland.

I suppose I could have demanded an end to the custom of port and cigars, and become a suffragette in my old age—although as a whole, I had little use for Mrs. Pankhurst and her kind. What coarse, vulgar women they were, always trying to get their photographs in the newspapers! Still, the thought, while fleeting, did cross my mind. However, considering it further, I knew that I had absolutely no desire to talk about ponies and cricket and motorcars, the usual things men discussed.

When they were not discussing war, that is.

I walked about the room, adjusting lamp-shades, wondering if I should play the gramophone but deciding against it because the only discs I could find were Wagner arias, which I despised; so very indulgent, with all those histrionics! Caryl must have left them out after his last visit home. I then ran my finger along the bookshelves, as was my habit (the upper shelves could use a dusting; I must speak to Mary Ann in the morning). We had an impressive collection of books, some from Papa's library in Oxford. Many were my gifts to Regi, in the hope that he would perhaps open one up and actually read it. The hope had been in vain, although he was quite proud of his library and enjoyed showing it off to guests on the way to the billiard room.

After selecting an old favorite—Mr. Twain's *The Innocents Abroad,* for I was in the mood for a laugh—I settled into a chintz chair by the fire, yet long moments passed before I could turn to the book, and when I did, I couldn't open it.

Instead, I found myself tossing it aside and skimming across the room, to a low glass-enclosed bookcase tucked under a window; I fell to my knees beside it, opened the glass doors, and took out a book.

Alice's Adventures in Wonderland. I held the small, old-fashioned book in my hands—the leather, while still stiff and hard, not worn with use, had turned a dark, purplish red. The pages were yellowing as well; they were heavier than the pages of modern books, and had the ragged edges signifying they had been cut by hand. I supposed I must have done so, although I had no memory of it.

All my editions of the *Alice* books were stored in this cupboard; Mr. Dodgson had faithfully sent me each and every one, specially bound and inscribed: foreign editions, nursery editions, reissues. At first I simply stored them away in a drawer in my room, eager to keep them out of sight; as the years went on, and I grew more aware of their value as family heirlooms, I had this small cabinet made, as it kept the dust out.

I had never intended to read the books to my sons when they were small; I could not see the point of it, as they had a nursery full of books, which more than satisfied them, especially as they grew and fell more under Regi's influence. I had not shared with them much of my childhood; had never told them of that afternoon on the river when Mr. Dodgson first told the story —*my* story. I don't believe it was a conscious decision. It simply never came up.

However, one summer afternoon when the boys were on holiday from school—it was the end of Caryl's first year, I remember; he looked so small yet dapper in his uniform, even though he was still in short pants—I went into the library to check on the flowers. Mary Ann was always quite lazy about refilling the vases.

"Leopold Reginald! What on earth are you doing now?" For Rex was sitting cross-legged on the floor beside the open cabinet, a book in his lap, other books scattered about him, crumbs crushed into the carpet as he casually munched on a chocolate biscuit.

"Reading," he replied calmly, not even pausing to look up. "What else would I be doing with a book?"

I twisted my lips up, fighting an inconvenient desire to laugh at his ridiculously reasonable response. "You know very well what I mean. Why aren't you outside? It's a lovely day, and you know I don't approve of little boys staying indoors when it's not raining."

He shrugged. "I decided I might as well improve my mind. You said I ought to, after my report last half-term."

"Well, you've made quite a mess in the process," I said, drawing up a low stool. "As usual."

"Yes," he said with an understanding sigh. "I'm sure I have."

"What are you reading?"

"This." He held up the first edition of *Alice's Adventures in Wonderland*. "I've heard of it before. At school. Some of the chaps have it."

"Oh."

"Mamma," he said, his little face all wrinkled up, as if pondering a great and profound matter. "I need to ask you a most unusual question."

"Yes?" I tried not to smile, but he looked so very serious.

"Is this the same thing?" He held up the green notebook-bound, hand-drawn copy Mr. Dodgson had first sent me: *Alice's Adventures Under Ground.*

"Well, it is, in a way." I sat perfectly still, studying him, waiting. My heart beat fast with excitement and fear. It was as if we had been playing hide-and-seek in the garden and I was about to be discovered.

He paged through the smaller book to the very last; he studied the pasted picture of me at age seven, and then he looked up. His soft boy's hair—wispy brown, with two cowlicks on either side of his forehead—was all rumpled, as if he'd been scratching his head. His eyes were big and dark, as solemn as only children's eyes can be. "The thing is, Mamma, I believe this is you!"

Although more laughter bubbled up at the deadly serious tone of his voice—almost as if he was scolding me—I did not laugh. I managed to keep my face as solemn as his, and I nodded.

"Yes, I'm afraid it is."

"I thought so. There is a picture like it at Grandmamma's. However did you get to be in a book?" Now he seemed relieved; I wondered, later, if he had thought himself quite mad, to believe that his mother could ever be in something as important as a book.

"Well, you see—" I hesitated, looking at my son, who was waiting, so patiently, for an answer. Was it right to share this with him? Would it become a burden for him as it had been, so long, for me? But there was no going back; he knew that the little girl in the book was me, and I could not undo that knowledge. "I was quite a little girl—slightly younger than you—and I knew a gentleman who loved to tell stories. One day he took me, and your aunt Ina, and your aunt Edith—remember, I told you about her?—out on a river, near where Grandpapa and Grandmamma live. And he rowed us up the river and told us a story, and the story was about a little girl named Alice, just like me. Afterwards, I begged him to write it down, and he did, and that's the small book you're holding. But later other people read it and asked him to make it so every little girl and boy could read it, too, and that became the other book you're holding. The one the chaps have at school."

As I spoke, Rex inched closer and closer to me until he was in my lap, which was a startling sensation; I couldn't recall holding him so closely before, not since he was an infant. He snuggled further against me until he was heavy and warm against my chest. For a fleeting second I bent my head to his and inhaled; he smelled of earth and flannel and warm milk.

Then he opened the book—the actual book, not the hand-drawn notebook—and pointed to the first word. He sat so very still, almost as if he was afraid to breathe. Almost as if he was afraid I wouldn't understand what he wanted.

But I did. And suddenly I was the one who was afraid to breathe.

"Chapter one," I began in a whisper; I hadn't heard these words in years. Not since—I cleared my throat, which was suddenly parched; licked my lips, which were suddenly dry. My heart was racing again, and this time I knew it was from fear: fear of hearing these words, hearing this story, and finding out the truth. The truth of my childhood, of who I was and who I was not, for if I wasn't the little girl in the story, then who was I? Yet what was most frightening was my suspicion that I *was* the little girl in the story. And that the entire world—all those foreign editions Mr. Dodgson had sent to me!—knew it, knew of all my desires, my wants, my actions that had led to so much confusion and, yes, destruction.

All my actions—for they were mine, and mine alone; Mr. Dodgson had been only the recorder of them—that had led me to this place, so very far from Oxford, so very far from where I had loved and been loved; that had led me to this house, this child, seated on my lap, innocently wanting to be read a story.

My story.

Rex shifted in my lap, his chubby forefinger—dirty under the nails, I thought with odd detachment; I must speak to Nanny about that—still pointing to the words, written by Mr. Dodgson, on the page. *"Down the Rabbit Hole,"* I tried again, but my entire body was shaking, causing my voice to wobble, catching in my throat.

Rex knew my fear; how could he not, since he was trembling, too, from the force of it? So he tried to be helpful, this child; my child. He gently put his hand to my mouth to silence me, and began to read himself.

"Alice was beginning to get very tired of sitting by her sister on the bank. . . ."

"No," I said suddenly—firmly, my voice finally steady and clear. I shut the book so decidedly that the sound startled Rex, who jumped. "No, I—I'm afraid I don't have time today, perhaps another time—" Abruptly, I pushed Rex from my lap. He turned around and gazed at me with such a confused, hurt expression, his dark eyes bright with tears, his round little chin trembling; my heart felt pierced as if by arrows of my own design, shot with my own hands. Mercifully, the sudden onslaught of my own tears obscured my vision, so that I could no longer see my son's disappointment.

Although nothing could prevent me from understanding it, far too well; I remembered standing outside my mother's bedroom door, wondering why she would not open it to me.

"Mamma, I was looking all over for you!"

Suddenly Caryl was in the room, panting, face red and shiny with exertion. "Did you know that Rex knocked over the new shrubbery with his velocipede?"

Rex inhaled sharply and moved farther away from me; I realized then what he had been doing indoors. I also realized, with a sick flutter of my heart, that he was not only disappointed in me but afraid of me.

I was silent for a moment, staring at the closed book in my hand. I then looked up at Caryl, whose eyes glittered with triumph.

"Don't tattle, Caryl. It's not gentlemanly. Do go along and make yourself useful elsewhere."

Rex looked up at me, his eyes wide with wonder, his hair standing up all over his head, and while I did not smile at him, I did not frown, either. I simply started to gather up the books, while he quietly began to pick up the biscuit crumbs; we worked together to clean up the mess while Caryl ran from the room, his face scarlet.

Not a word was said between the two of us afterward, regarding that afternoon. Although I do know that he somehow informed his brothers that I was Alice in Wonderland, and that they took the news gravely, as if this bestowed some enormous, almost royal, responsibility upon our family. Caryl, in particular, was fond of informing all his playmates, and total strangers, also—I had to cure him of *that*!—of the fact that his mamma was Alice in Wonderland, "all growed up."

Just when each read the book on his own, I did not know, although over the years enough was said in reference to certain details of the story that it was obvious that they had. But I never asked, and none of them ever volunteered the information.

My sons may have thought they knew who Alice was, but they never knew the Mr. Dodgson of her childhood. After my marriage I received a few letters from him—letters that were, finally, mine to keep, although now I did not want them. For the most part, they were merely polite descriptions of the newest editions of *Alice*. Then in 1891, prior to leaving for Oxford for Papa's retirement ceremonies, I received the following letter:

My Dear Mrs. Hargreaves,

I should be so glad if you could, quite conveniently to yourself, look in for tea any day. You would probably prefer to bring a companion: but I must leave the choice to you, only remarking that if your husband is here, he would be ~~most~~ *very welcome. (I crossed out most because it's ambiguous; most words are, I fear.) I met him in our*

Common Room not long ago. It was hard to realize that he was the husband of one I can scarcely picture to myself, even now, as more than 7 years old!

> *Always sincerely yours,*
> *Charles Dodgson*

Your adventures have had a marvelous success. I have now sold well over 100,000 copies.

I pondered the invitation; Regi had indeed met him a few years previous. He said that Mr. Dodgson had been quite odd and could not stop from staring at him, in Regi's words, "As if I had my drawers on my head!"

I put off responding to his letter. When we arrived in Oxford, the entire family under the Deanery's roof for the last time, I found that I could not bring myself to go to tea, with all the polite formality and length of time that would entail. However, one morning I did take the boys out, on the pretext of visiting Edith's grave—but first, we made a stop across the Quad, climbing that narrow staircase.

Before I knocked on the door, the words "The Rev. C. L. Dodgson" now chipped and faded, I turned and faced my sons, fidgeting in identical sailor suits; Rex's scarf was already undone, and I bent down to tie it. "I think it might be best if we don't tell Grandmamma about our visit here," I said in a carefully unconcerned voice.

"Why ever not? Doesn't she like Mr. Dodgson?" Caryl asked, pulling at the waistband of his pants, as if they were too snug; had he grown overnight?

"Don't tug so. And no, Grandmamma isn't particularly fond of Mr. Dodgson." I decided, at that very moment, that perhaps honesty in the face of dishonesty was the best policy.

"You want us to *deceive* Grandmamma?" Alan was genuinely alarmed; two scarlet patches appeared in his cheeks as his dark eyes studied me intently.

"Not deceive, exactly—simply don't bring it up. That way you—we—won't have to deceive her," I said, suddenly nervous—and extremely irritated at myself. What did it matter, after all these years, if I did decide to take my sons to meet an old friend? Still, once under the Deanery's roof—so crowded now, with all the children and grandchildren gathered for Papa's farewell festivities—I could not help but revert to long-held habits. The day before, I had found myself quarreling with Ina over who got the largest biscuit at tea.

"I won't tell, Mamma," Rex said with a conspiratorial grin. "I understand perfectly. After all, there are a great many things I don't tell *you*."

"Thank you—what? What kinds of things?"

Rex's answer was to reach past me and knock on the door; I fixed him with a glare, then tried to plaster down his cowlicks, but the parlor maid opened the door before I could do anything but pat him, rather vigorously, on the head.

I had sent round a note the day before, so Mr. Dodgson was right behind her, very flustered as he led us to the parlor. Dressed in black as always—in the old-fashioned frock coat of his youth—he had white hair now; his voice was quite high-pitched, and I thought that he seemed much deafer than before.

"Well, well, this is a wo-wo-wonderful thing, to see you again. Do-do make yourself at home. Oh—and what a treat to make the acquaintance of your chi-chi-children!"

I stepped into his rooms once more as an adult, my sons—not my sisters—following behind. It seemed like a lifetime ago, yet if I closed my eyes I could still see us, Ina, Edith, and me, dressed exactly alike in those short, wide skirts—how absurd they seemed now!—lace pantalets, quaint, old-fashioned parasols.

If I closed my eyes I could still see *him,* as he was—but no. I did not need further remembrances of my childhood with this man, for I did not know what to do with the ones I already had. So I kept my eyes open and observed him now.

Instead of bending down to shake hands with my boys, he stood stock-still, his gloved hands behind his back, and nodded warily at each one as I introduced him. Caryl bowed formally when he was presented, as if at court.

"So, you're the man who put Mamma in a book," Rex said pleasantly; Mr. Dodgson nodded but didn't elaborate.

"I imagine it's quite a good book, even though I don't usually like to read," Alan said as he put his hands in his pockets and thrust his nose in the air—in perfect imitation of his father. "There weren't really any games in it, other than croquet. You might have put a polo match in; that might have helped."

"I—that is, polo?" Mr. Dodgson looked at me, blinking his eyes, obviously confused; was he no longer used to the frank conversation of children?

"Alan," I said sharply. "That's not very polite."

"Well, I did say it was a good book." He colored as he realized what he had said. "I'm very sorry, sir. Please accept my apology."

Mr. Dodgson did not reply; he simply stood there, staring at my son until Alan turned away, still bright red, and pretended to be interested in a jade plant perched upon a table. Mr. Dodgson then walked over to the window, fumbling to pull up the shade. (The room was exceedingly dark and dusty; I had a good mind to talk to the parlor maid on my way out.) Motioning for the boys to take a seat, I walked over to him and placed my hand upon his arm as he struggled with the cord; I was surprised to find he was trembling, and in that moment I knew that he was afraid. As afraid as I had been that day in the library with Rex.

What were we so fearful of discovering, the two of us?

"Please," I said impatiently, as he continued to fumble with the cord. "Do not trouble yourself so for us. We can't stay long. Sit down." I'm afraid I rather commanded him to do so, but he seemed happy to obey; he plopped down in a high-backed chair with a sigh.

"We can't stay because Grandmamma doesn't know we're here," Rex explained. Mr. Dodgson looked at me, a question in those uneven, watery eyes; I decided not to answer it, choosing instead to congratulate him on the 100,000 copies of *Alice* sold.

"Does that mean you're very rich?" Caryl asked.

"Caryl," I said, but Mr. Dodgson did not appear to have heard; he cocked his head and put his hand up to his right ear. One look from me convinced Caryl not to repeat his question.

Mr. Dodgson looked from boy to boy, shaking his head as if he was quite unable—or unwilling—to acknowledge that I could be a mother. "No, it will not register. My Alice with children of her own? How strange the world has grown! Oh—they simply won't sit still, will they?"

"Neither did I, when I was a child." I smiled

but felt myself growing irritated as he continued to gape at my sons, shaking his head; it wasn't as if he'd never been around children before. Why was he behaving so strangely with mine?

"No, you little girls were very well behaved, always sitting together so pleasantly, I have such fond memories of those afternoons—oh dear! The boisterous one is going to upset that table!"

Rex wasn't even close to the table, but I grabbed him by the arm anyway; this gesture seemed to placate Mr. Dodgson. "Do tell me what you've been up to lately," I said, determined to have a pleasant conversation.

"Not very much, except of course for your adventures. As I mentioned in my letter, they keep me tolerably busy, which is a blessing, for I'm so alone otherwise."

"They're not—they're not really my adventures, of course. They're yours, now. I'm simply a country wife and mother, with no time to chase after rabbits—although chasing after boys is rather the same thing!"

"You don't chase after us—you never! You're much too old," Rex said with a resigned shake of his head. "Although if you did, I'd most likely let you catch me, just to be nice."

"That's very gentlemanly of you," I replied, smiling wryly at Mr. Dodgson, trying to draw him into my world. But he continued to stare at my sons as if they were noisy apparitions, and when he looked at me, his eyes clouded over, his mouth slightly open, I knew he was seeing a ghost as well; the ghost of a little brown-haired girl in a crisp white dress. A little gypsy girl. A long-forgotten dream.

Stirring in my seat—he was quite mistaken, for I was rather a squirmy child, I suddenly recalled, remembering how tight and itchy all those layers of clothing had felt upon my tender skin—I was unable to meet his gaze as I once had been able to. So I looked around the room, instead. It even smelled like a haunted place: stale, musty, airless, *old*. Even the toys were ancient; Caryl picked up a threadbare stuffed animal and tossed it aside with a sigh; Rex shook an old china doll, and dust filled the air as her head nearly came off her unfashionable body. I had told them of all the treasures Mr. Dodgson used to keep in his room for children, but now I saw that these were no treasures. Not for modern children, anyway.

Not for little boys used to cast-iron soldiers and merry-go-rounds and fire pumpers.

Mr. Dodson suddenly snapped at Rex to put the doll down, and while this angered me—had he ever told me or my sisters to stop playing with a toy?—at least he had stopped staring at me so mournfully. As I watched him fuss and flutter about, I tried very hard to keep a pleasant smile upon my face but could not succeed. When had he become such a nervous old man?

He implored Caryl to pick up the stuffed animal, and continued to fret over the passage of time. "What a sad, sad thing it is to grow old! I've grown too old, too old for my friends now. Too old even for you, I'm afraid—or am I? No, don't tell me! Instead, let's remember more pleasant times. Don't you recall when you—"

"And how are your sisters? Well, I hope?"

"As well as can be expected, for we've all become such a feeble lot. Alice, my dear, do you remember how nice and neat you and your sisters used to be? Do you remember?"

I did not want to remember; that was not why I had come. Because if I were to remember, there were other things that might come to mind.

So, why had I come back to these rooms, then, if I did not wish to reminisce? If I couldn't even read the book, why had I brought my sons to meet the author?

I could not say. I knew only, as I watched Mr. Dodgson rush to straighten a lampshade that Caryl had scarcely even touched, that it had been a mistake. I was angry at him; angry at myself, for coming here in the first place, for tempting the past.

I was not, for once, angry at my sons; they were behaving admirably, and I was proud of them. That was why I had come here, I suddenly realized: to show off my boys. To show Mr. Dodgson—and perhaps, remind myself—that my life was full, that I had moved on. But he refused to see, and worse—he was determined that I see that he had not.

"I don't wish to detain you any longer," I said, rising. Far from looking relieved, as I had expected, Mr. Dodgson's face fell.

"Oh, but do you have to go so soon?"

"I'm afraid we do."

"But—all my child friends grow up and leave. You were the first to do so, and I despise it. Bu-but we're different, aren't we?" He leaned down to look at me—he was not nearly as tall as he once was, nor was I so small; our eyes were almost level. Still, I had to look up—as I had done when I was a child.

"Different?"

"We'll always have your story. You'll never have to grow up, then."

"I'm afraid that's not entirely true." I wished he could see me, truly see me, as he had once been able to do better than anyone else—or so I had thought. Now, however, I wasn't sure; had he ever seen me as I was? Or had he always been this blind?

"Oh, but it is. We'll always have Wonderland." His dark blue eyes were dreamy now, almost filmy, as he gazed down some distant path I had no desire to follow. I wanted to shake him, shake the cobwebs out of his mind, the dust from his shoulders, the clouds from his eyes. I had no patience for such a man; it was a wonder that I ever had.

For so long, all my dreams had begun and ended with him; even my dreams of Leo. I could not imagine these feeble, trembling hands—still clad in gray gloves—holding anything so precious of mine, now.

"Yes, well, that's a nice thought, isn't it? Wonderland? I'm glad it gives you comfort, at least. Now we really must go." I reached out to shake his hand in farewell, although I did not want to touch him; his grip was weak, and I could feel the clamminess of his skin through the fabric of his glove. I quickly withdrew my hand, fighting a childish impulse to wipe it on the back of my skirt.

As I turned to go, I heard him ask, in a voice I remembered, a soft voice thick with longing, "Will you remember me, Alice?"

"Pardon?"

"Will you? Do you?"

"Oh, Mr. Dodgson, I—"

"Come, Mamma," Rex said impatiently, tugging on my hand.

"Just a moment, Rex."

"My name is Leopold! Leopold Reginald!" he shouted, stamping his foot; I stared at him, for he disliked his given name, and never before had I heard him claim it.

Mr. Dodgson gasped when he heard the name; I could not meet his gaze. My cheeks grew hot, and

I felt as if my most secret thoughts were suddenly on display for all—the boys included—to see.

"Oh, Alice—I—I've never been able to f-f-forgive myself, all those years ago, you must understand why I—"

"Don't," I said, warning him. My head snapped up, and I met his gaze full-on. "Don't try to rewrite the past. Leave it be. My life is very full now, as I wish you were able to see." Once I had questions—so many questions! Now all I wanted was to get on with my life; we were expected back at the Deanery for a faculty tea, and we hadn't yet been to Edith's grave. "We must be going. Thank you very much for your hospitality."

"You see why I'm not so fond of little boys, my Alice?"

"I am not—" I struggled to control my voice, my anger; I was not his. "Whatever do you mean?"

"Because they have to grow up to be men. Men like me," he said with that sad, sad smile that used to tug so at my heart. Now, however, it only enraged me. He was older than I was. Why, then, did I always feel as if his happiness was my responsibility? It wasn't fair for him to burden me with that. It had never been fair.

"No, they don't. Not all of them," I snapped, my voice low, for I did not want the boys to hear. "Not mine."

Three small, sticky pairs of hands clutched at

my skirts, eager to drag me out of the past, into fresh air, into my life. I was eager to follow them. I turned to go before he could say anything further; I never saw him again.

Charles Lutwidge Dodgson died in 1898; I could not attend his funeral, for my father was dying as well. He passed away four days later. And with their passing, I had no reason ever to return to Oxford.

"MAMMA?"

I looked up; for a moment I was startled to see a tall man with brown hair—still sporting those twin cowlicks—and a mustache. So caught up in my memories, I had expected to see the little boy with the dirty face, instead.

"Yes, Rex?"

"We thought we'd find you here." Caryl and Alan were standing behind him. I allowed my son to reach down and help me rise; I'm afraid I did not *bend* quite as well as I used to.

I straightened my narrow skirt, ending just above my ankles, as was the fashion these days. I smoothed my hair, patted the brooch—Leo's brooch—fastened at my throat, and looked at my sons. Not one of them could meet my gaze, and in that moment I knew.

"So. You're enlisting, then, are you not? Caryl and Rex?"

"Yes, Mamma." Alan, the leader, spoke for them

all, even though his future in uniform was not in question.

"I thought as much. I assumed that was what you were sneaking off to the billiard room to discuss. Really, the impertinence of you men! As if I were too delicate for the conversation?"

"I'd never think you were too delicate for anything, Mamma," Caryl was quick to say.

"Nor would any of us. It was Father—he wanted to talk some things over, and he didn't want you to have to worry yourself," Rex explained.

I surveyed my sons, all standing tall and sturdy; in that moment I wished Mr. Dodgson could see for himself what fine men they were, how brave. Alan was more assured—for he had the military experience, after all; Rex more eager, for he was the most adventurous; Caryl more unconcerned, as if it was simply another jolly party or prank cooked up by one of his friends.

They were not asking my permission to go; they were far too British for that. Yet they did appear to be seeking my blessing, and I knew I had to bestow it in the only way that would allow them to do what they had to do without regret. I would not burden my sons, as I had been burdened myself.

"Worry?" Frowning, I shook my head, as if they had been caught in a minor infraction, such as raiding the biscuit tin. "That was sweet, if misguided, of your father. I'm perfectly capable of talking about all this—I suppose you were going over wills and such? Entirely sensible; it's something we should all do now and then. I would hope you'd do it even if there wasn't any war. I should go over my own, now that I think of it. Well, do you have any idea what regiment you'll join, Caryl, Rex? Not the Rifles?"

"No," Alan said hastily, as Caryl opened his mouth to speak. "I've learned a few things in my career, and I do not believe it's wise for brothers to be in the same regiment. It gets rather—complicated, if you will. A bit risky, too."

"Naturally—that's very wise of you. Well, then?" I faced Rex. I was so rigid my jaw ached, but I would not fall apart; I would not act as if I was asking for anything more important than if they wanted kippers for breakfast, or kidneys.

"I think I might give the Irish Guards a whirl," he said casually, as if he was talking about a dance.

"Very good. Caryl?"

"I rather fancy the Scots Guards," Caryl replied, in earnest imitation of his brother's easier, breezier attitude.

"Yes, I think that's a good choice." I nodded approvingly; Caryl needed that more than his brothers did. "Quite a busy day, then, hasn't it been? And tomorrow's the flower show. If you'll excuse me, I believe I'll retire, as there's so very much to do. You'll all be up early to help?"

"Of course, Mamma." Alan smiled very indulgently, as if he knew how desperately I needed to get to my room just then—and he broke my heart. When did he become such a wise, understanding man? It was not right; he should not have to comfort me.

"Lovely. I'll see you all in the morning, then." I walked quickly past, afraid to touch any of my sons; afraid that if I did, I would not be able to let go. I managed to leave the library, walk down the hall, attain the stairs, speak to one of the Mary Anns about breakfast—I decided on kidneys—and climb the long, wide staircase without touching the banisters, even as with every step I climbed, my eyes filled with more tears. Finally I reached my bedroom—I heard Regi across the hall in his, with his door open, calling out my name, but I could not come to him just then—and closed my door, reaching my bed before the first tears fell; I sat silently, feeling the tears upon my cheeks but not really thinking, not seeing anything—

Until I looked down at my lap, surprised. For in my hand was the copy of *Alice's Adventures in Wonderland*; I had been holding it all this time.

"Oh!" I clutched it to my chest, holding it tight, as if I could keep it safe in this way—knowing that I could not do the same for my own sons. Why hadn't I read it to him? I thought wildly, remembering that moment in the library so long ago. What had I been afraid of? What did I even know of fear, then?

Now war had come. The little boy was a soldier now. And it was too late for us both.

I opened the book and turned to the first chapter. Blinking, I studied the page through swimming eyes; I focused and focused until the words finally were clear enough for me to read them.

"Alice was beginning to get very tired of sitting by her sister on the bank," I read aloud. When my voice caught in my throat, I stopped, took a breath, blinked again, and continued. *"And of having nothing to do; once or twice she peeped into the book her sister was reading. . . ."*

I shut the book again. I waited until my eyes were dry.

I'll read it to them later, I told myself. When they come home. I'll read it to them when they're all home safe and gathered around the dinner table, teasing me, irritating their father. After dinner I'll insist that they join me in the library and I'll read it to them, and I won't mind that it's foolish, absurd, for a mother to read to her grown sons. They won't mind, either; they'll understand. Somehow, they'll understand.

I nodded to myself, at the faded book in my hand with my own name on the cover, and I repeated the words, softly, almost like a prayer—

I'll read it to them when they come home.

Chapter 15

*I*T'S SUCH A COMFORT TO BE AWAY FROM London just now. They say there could be air raids at any time. Those vile zeppelins! I think they're horrid."

Ina wrinkled her pert nose, pursed her small, sour mouth as of old; but she was not a little girl any longer, and her simpering manners verged on the comical. For Ina was white-haired now: still plump, but a softer plump than before, and very few wrinkles, which is one of the benefits of the fuller body in advancing years. The dear girl was also a bit jowly, and her chin now looked to have melted into her neck.

I was stringier with age; while my figure remained slim, my hair was more dark than gray, my wrinkles were more evident, and my bones more prominent. My eyes were still as wide and watchful, still framed by the fringe of my hair, but I had need for spectacles now. Particularly when doing close work, such as knitting, as I was at the moment.

Ina and I were in the drawing room of Cuffnells; it was an early May morning, so the hearth was cold. Outside the French windows—open to the soft, fragrant spring air—the flowering trees were in full bloom; great pinkish white petals on the tulip trees, the brilliant pink blossoms on the cherry trees, the softer white clusters of the crab apples. Even on an overcast day such as today, the blooms brightened the landscape, standing in vivid relief against the more sedate green of the oaks and maples and pines.

Inside the drawing room, even without a fire, the décor was cheerful; I had had enough of the oppressive Victorian upholstery and wallpaper and carpets of my youth. In this room—which was more mine than Regi's—I had chosen lighter carpets of buff pink, chintz in bright blue and pink and white for the furniture, and had had the paneling whitewashed. Vases of apple blossoms dotted the many small tables, filled with photographs and small paintings, mostly watercolors.

"We are happy to have you, of course," I told Ina, not quite truthfully; Regi had made quite a fuss when she wrote asking to come.

"I cannot stand that woman," he stated flatly. Ina was the only person I knew who could incite such a warmth of feeling in him. "Let her go to Scotland and stay with her coward of a son."

"Moncrieff is doing war work, Regi, even if he's not at the front," I reminded him weakly; it was difficult to be sympathetic to those working here at home, when all of our sons were still in the midst of the fighting.

Alan had already been wounded, only a month or so after war was declared, in October. He had been invalided home, and while I was so thankful to have him that I slept those first few nights in a chair outside his room in case he needed me, after the first couple of weeks it became evident that he was not happy to be here. He had already changed; he was thinner, with a haunted look in his eyes as if he saw ghosts at every turn. He was also impatient, almost fretful; he spoke constantly of his men, worried about them, and desired to know more than he was capable of knowing from the vague dispatches in the newspapers. I will not say it was a relief to see him go back; on the contrary, I felt a piece of my heart tear itself apart and go with him. I actually had to place my hand upon my chest, as if to keep the rest of it intact.

As much as I yearned to keep him safe and sound under our roof, however, I knew I could not. I realized he would not be happy, would not be sound, as long as he was away from the front. He actually looked more like himself—or rather, like the earnest little boy he once had been—for the first time right before he left.

As we stood on the front drive, the car warming up while the driver loaded his kit into the trunk—he would be driven to Lyndhurst station, then journey on to the front—Alan hung his head bashfully. "Mamma, I do apologize for my frightful behavior. I know it hasn't been easy on either of you, all of this, but you see, I have to be back with my men. They're such fine fellows, and it is rather difficult out there." He said it so nonchalantly—"rather difficult." As if it was merely a lopsided game of cricket.

But I knew it was not; I knew because of his nightmares, of which none of us spoke. He'd had them only once or twice, but they were terrible; loud, anguished cries—I would run to his room, closely followed by Regi, pale and wild-haired in his nightshirt; even as we hurried to our son I reflected that when he was a child, I had never run to him in this way. Nightmares, then, were the province of Nanny.

But as a man, an anguished, battle-scarred man, he was finally ours to care for. Alan's eyes would be wide open, but he could not see us; he could see only the horror of war as he cried out names we did not know; names that later I looked up. Only to find them listed in the rolls of the dead.

"There is no need to apologize," I told him. "There is never any need. You're our boy, you know. Our fine boy, and nothing you do or say can ever change that."

"Mamma." He bent down so that I could hold him; I put my arms around his shoulders, but I couldn't feel them. All I could feel was the rough wool of his uniform, thick and protective but not protective enough. I raised my head to kiss his cheek, fresh-shaven, smelling of wintergreen; the cheek of a man, not a boy.

"Alan, I was wondering—do you remember keeping an owl when you were small?" I couldn't help it; the mystery of the owl had been nagging at me ever since he'd come home.

"An owl?"

"Yes, an owl—you asked me if you could—"

"You'll miss your train if you don't leave," Regi called from the car. "Best get a move on."

"Oh! Of course, we can't have that," I said hastily, brushing an invisible piece of lint from his shoulder.

"What about the owl, Mamma?"

"Nothing—it's nonsense. You can't miss your train."

"Good-bye, Mamma."

"Good-bye, my boy." Alan swooped down and kissed me; I clung to him once more, felt his warmth, his weight against my chest, and hurried into the house before this sensation could leave me. Right at the door, I turned for one more look. Alan was standing next to Regi—who was chewing the insides of his cheeks, trying so very hard to be the gruff English gentleman—and he looked so tall and pale. But he raised his arm and smiled—the earnest, sweet smile of my brave little boy. I smiled back, then shut the door behind me, before I had to watch him drive away.

That had been in March, when the trees were still bare, the sky still gray; it was now early May. The world was in bloom again, even, one had to believe, in France.

"Is it time for the post?" Ina asked, putting aside

her knitting with an impatient sigh and reaching for her rings, which she had removed and placed on the table next to her. We were knitting balaclava helmets for the Red Cross; Ina complained that her rings snagged on the gray wool yarn.

"Soon, I would imagine." I looked up at the clock over the mantel. "It's nearly two o'clock. What time did you say that reporter was arriving?"

"Two."

"The trains haven't been very reliable, of course, so she may be delayed. Really, I don't know why I allowed you to talk me into this, Ina."

"Her mother is a friend of mine, and I happened to mention our association with Lewis Carroll, which of course intrigued the dear girl."

"*Happened* to mention?" I studied my sister, sitting so placidly, examining and admiring her many rings.

"Yes, it simply came up, and why not? Now that Mamma's gone, I think it's high time we—I mean, of course, you—came forward and let people know that Alice is quite alive. What harm can it do now?"

"What harm? Oh, Ina." I could never understand my sister; of all the people in the world, she should know why I had never wanted to speak publicly of *Alice,* of Mr. Dodgson—of all "that business," as Mr. Ruskin once so prosaically put it. "In the past, my—association—with Mr.

Dodgson has not served me well, or do you no longer recall?"

"You were very young, my dear. You seem to have things quite mixed up in your head—do you not remember the lovely times we had? The larks, the frolics, the adventures?"

"If I am quite mixed up, it's all because of you!" I shook my head and wondered at my sister, at the way she used words, mixed them up into potions that could cause your head to spin. What she said was true; what she said was always, strictly, true. Yet never was it entirely honest.

"What you do not understand, my dear Alice, is that people are not interested in Mr. Dodgson and Alice Liddell—they're interested in Lewis Carroll and Alice in Wonderland," she continued, putting her rings on her plump fingers, one by one.

"How can you be so sure?"

"Because of the times we live in, dear. Everyone longs for the simplicity of childhood, don't they?"

"I suppose so."

"So, any association with *Alice in Wonderland,* now, will only be a happy one, don't you see?"

"No, I'm not at all sure I see." That the book was cherished and beloved by millions, I knew. Of course I knew—I was not ignorant of its success, and perhaps I even felt a glow of pride at my part in it, finally. Particularly now that Mr. Dodgson was dead—as were Pricks, Mr. Ruskin, my mother; so many demons buried, while I, and the book, remained. Maybe Ina was correct. Maybe it would be only a happy association from now on.

Still, there were questions unanswered, questions that nagged at me more and more lately with all the time on my hands, and Ina was the only one left to ask. Yet I did not trust her memories any more than I trusted my own.

"Do you remember that day on the train?" My index finger was red and tender from the tip of my needle; I wrapped the yarn around my work—I had gotten only as far as the wide pattern on the neck—and placed it in my knitting basket.

"I'm not sure. Which day? As you know, we took the train often." Ina's gray eyes narrowed.

"The day we took the train home with Mr. Dodgson, instead of boating back with Mamma and Papa and those dreadful students."

"No, not really. Although I do recall that sometimes Mr. Dodgson was very bold in his actions, if that's what you're remembering. Very bold."

"No." I shook my head. "No, that is not the man I remember—not a man of action, not at all. He spoke—he lived—in dreams."

"Alice, you were young. You did not understand—" She was interrupted by the entrance of one of the Mary Anns, bringing in the post on a silver tray. Abruptly, any questions concerning the past were completely obliterated by the hope of word from one of the boys. I had to restrain myself from running over and snatching the tray from the slow girl.

With a tight smile, my hands clenched in my lap, I waited until she placed it upon the table next to me and bobbed—again, no proper curtsy!—before I grabbed the small pile of envelopes, searching for a tattered and dirty postcard, even a preprinted one, postmarked from France.

"Nothing today." I sagged in my chair. "No, nothing today," I repeated, looking up, knowing that Regi was standing in the doorway, hope in his eyes.

"Didn't think there would be," he said gruffly, as he said every day after the hope drained away. "Was wondering if that bill for my club came through, that's all."

"I'm sure there'll be something tomorrow," I tried to assure him—as I did every day. He nodded, I smiled at him, and he shuffled off toward the library in his baggy tweed suit, rumpled and tobacco-stained; he had such little regard for clothing lately. He used to be so very dashing, but now he would have worn the same suit every day, had I not protested.

He spent every afternoon in the library these days, brooding over maps of the front cut out from the newspapers when he wasn't going over accounts, or cleaning his guns, or polishing his cricket trophies. He rarely ventured out of the house, not even to haunt his old cricket club as he used to.

"He's so sad," Ina said softly.

I stiffened; I did not appreciate the tone of her voice, for there was pity in it. "He's simply concerned, as am I."

"I think men take these things much harder than women. Remember Papa, how much he cried when those little babies died?"

"Yes. Mamma didn't, though. Not a tear."

"No, well—Papa cried for the boys. Mamma cried for Edith."

I glanced at my sister, surprised; she hadn't forgotten quite as much as she said she had. "Papa didn't cry very much for Edith, that's true. Not at all like he did for the baby boys. How odd."

"How typical. Boys always are valued more. Lucky you—you should have married royalty, since all you've done is have sons—oh, I mean, rather—I'm sorry, Alice." For once, I believed my sister; she bit her lip, frowned, and could not look at me.

I didn't reply. How often had I thought the same thing! How often had I looked at the boys and wished—oh, God help me, I did wish it!—that they were Leo's boys, not Regi's? For all my activity, my determination to keep my life full and busy, I had not been able to prevent those thoughts from occurring, particularly when the boys were younger. It was wicked, wicked of me. I told myself, so many times, that one could not predict the outcome; had I married Leo, my life would have been so very different. My boys were the product of Regi and me, and I loved them, despite all my doubts when I first married Regi and started in on producing a family. I did, truly, love them all.

Still, sometimes I had wondered about the children Leo and I would have had. I had wondered if they would have been like him or like me. I had wondered if they would be slight, with soft blond hair, those gentle blue eyes.

I could not have loved my sons more, that I knew. What I would never know is if my capacity to love might have been greater had I married my true heart's desire.

"Oh dear, I do wish that reporter would hurry up!" I rose and paced in front of the fireplace; I needed to do something, stretch my muscles, tax my heart in some way. Idleness was my enemy these days; I required physical activity to chase these wicked, unproductive thoughts from my mind. Abruptly, I turned around and headed out through the open French windows. "I'm going outdoors. Do come with me."

"What?" Ina sputtered, pushing herself off the sofa. "What are you doing, Alice?"

I picked up a pair of garden shears that I kept on the terrace. "I'm cutting ivy."

"You're—what? Why, the gardener will do

that!" Ina had followed me outside but immediately sat down upon a wicker settee, as if those few steps had taxed her entirely.

"Yes, but one can never keep up with it. I despise ivy, don't you?" Walking to the low garden wall, I attacked the clinging vines with gusto, leaving them on the ground so the gardener could clear them up. With a sly smile, I looked at my sister, who clutched her arms and was shivering, very obviously, in the warm air. "It's rather invasive, I find. It shows up and never really leaves."

"I wouldn't know," she said with a sniff, settling down among the striped cushions. "We have plenty of gardeners in Scotland, and of course in London one doesn't have to worry about nature."

"I can't help but think this is all a mistake," I said, pausing to take a breath; my arms already ached from the effort, but I embraced the sensation, for it meant I was alive, I was useful—I was in charge, not entirely at the mercy of events. I inhaled deeply, closing my eyes, feeling the wind ruffle my hair; it was good to be outside, among things that were growing, reaching toward the sky. I should get Regi out here, I thought. It would do him good—perhaps he could plant a small vegetable garden.

"What is a mistake? The ivy?" Ina asked.

"No, no—speaking with this newspaper person!

As if I was one of those horrible suffragettes! Mamma would spin in her grave!"

"Mamma would be appalled at a great many things we have to do today," Ina said complacently. "It's a blessing she died when she did."

"True. However—"

"Mrs. Hargreaves, your visitor has arrived." The footman was in the doorway, ushering a smart young woman out to the terrace. She was clad in the latest style: a green wool suit, the jacket long and belted, the skirt much shorter—nearly six inches off the ground!—and rather wider than the one I was wearing; it swung out at the hem. She wore a snug hat with a brim and carried a leather notebook.

"Mrs. Skene, how lovely to see you again— Mamma sends her love."

"Dora, my dear, you look quite grown-up!" Ina rose and accepted the kiss the young woman gave her in greeting. I set the clippers down and remained where I was. Let her come to me.

"Mrs. Hargreaves, what an honor!" She rushed forward, extending her hand in that careless, breezy way typical of the younger generation. She did not even wait for Ina to introduce us.

"Yes, I'm very happy to make your acquaintance, Miss—?"

"Dora. Dora Kimball."

"Yes, Miss Kimball. Do sit down." I indicated a chair and took my seat next to Ina, our skirts overlapping just as they had done when we were small.

"The real Alice in Wonderland! I believe you're going to be quite the sensation. The country can rediscover a national treasure! I'm not sure many people today are even aware the stories were based on a real little girl."

"Young lady, many people certainly *were*!" I knew I sounded ridiculous, an indignant old martinet, but I found her ignorance insulting. I was Alice Liddell, daughter of Dean Liddell; *the* Alice Liddell. Yet—it was a shock, to realize it—I had been Alice Hargreaves for much longer than I had been Alice Liddell, and it was only what I had wanted, after all.

Why, then, did I feel such outrage upon learning that people *had* truly forgotten?

"I'm sorry, I didn't mean to upset you," Miss Kimball said. Her face paled beneath her caked-on powder, and that's when I observed that she was quite young, scarcely twenty. How did a girl that age become a feature writer for a respectable newspaper? I supposed it was because all our men were off to war; what an unusual world we were living in these days.

"Mrs. Hargreaves's sons are at the front; she's rather worried, as you can imagine," Ina hastily explained.

"Ina!" I had a desire—its origin decades long in the making—to pull my sister's hair. (If only she had enough left; dear Ina was getting rather downy-headed.) "That's none of Miss Kimball's concern. Now, do go ahead. I'm not used to this, but I will try to answer your questions truthfully. Go on."

"Right. Well, that is—so you were great friends with Mr. Carroll, when you were small?"

"We knew him as Mr. Dodgson—you do realize Lewis Carroll was simply a pen name?" I gazed at the young woman doubtfully; she blushed and nodded. "But yes, we were friends, when my sisters Ina and Edith and I were girls."

"Oh—so you grew up in Oxford?"

"Oh, yes!" Ina interrupted before I could, once again, express my disgust at Miss Kimball's ignorance. Ina folded her plump hands prettily upon her nonexistent lap, and simpered. "Yes, dear Papa was the Dean of Christ Church, you know! We grew up in the Deanery, which was just across the garden from Mr. Dodgson's rooms. He was quite fond of us all—I know he held a special place in his heart for me—and took us out rowing, and on other excursions, all the time."

"Yet it was me for whom he wrote the story, after all," I reminded her, with just a trace of a smile. Ina glared at me and pursed her lips.

"Oh. Well, this is all very interesting!" Miss Kimball was scribbling furiously in her notebook. "And it was on one of those outings when he told you the story of Alice?"

"Yes, it was."

"Are you at all like the girl in the book, then?" The young woman smiled at me, her face glowing with perspiration; I thought wool rather a poor choice for May.

"I—well, that is—" I was shocked by the question, how soon it had been asked; cursing myself for not having anticipated it, and vowing to box Ina's ears the moment this young lady left, which wouldn't be soon enough. "I've never really considered it," I lied.

"You haven't?"

"No."

"But surely, when you read the story, you must have seen yourself in it—"

"I was the sister, you know—the sister on the bank. You may write that down," Ina said, glancing over at Miss Kimball's idle hand.

"Oh, yes, of course." With a guilty start, Miss Kimball did so.

How could I tell her that I—seemingly alone of all the literate world—had never read the entire book? How could I tell her that I had no idea whether I was truly Alice—or Alice was truly me? For as long as I had lived with her—on the other side of the looking glass, staring back at me every day—I'd never dared to ask her how much, or how little, we were alike.

Yet—some facts, some *sums,* I knew very well. I had been ten when Mr. Dodgson told me the story; the other Alice, though, was seven, the same age I had been when Mr. Dodgson had taken the photograph of me as the beggar girl. My name had been immortalized as Alice, but hadn't my soul, my heart—just awakening to its power—lived on in the wild girl in a torn dress, bare feet, a triumphant gleam in her eyes? Was that not our truest collaboration? How many times did he ask, in his letters, if I remembered how it felt to roll about on the ground while he watched?

And in both the story and the photograph I lived on—always as that child of seven, who was not a child, after all.

Once Ina had warned that I would grow too old for Mr. Dodgson, but I refused to believe her. "May we be happy," he had said that day, and I had thought he meant—

"Mrs. Hargreaves?"

"I'm sorry." I shook my head, remembering where I was, *who* I was, now. "You were saying?"

But Miss Kimball was not speaking, after all. It was Mary Ann; she was standing in front of me, face ghastly white, tears oozing from her eyes. Just as I opened my mouth to inquire if she was ill, I saw her outstretched hand—and the telegram in it.

"No." I heard myself say it, in a voice loud and terrible. I shook my head, over and over, as the rest of my body froze in place; froze in time. I refused to take the envelope. If I did not take it, if I did not open it, then I would never have to know what it said.

Dimly, I heard Ina start to call for Regi as she jumped up from the settee and ran, much faster than I would have imagined, into the drawing room.

"Please, Mrs. Hargreaves," Mary Ann pleaded. "Please, ma'am." She thrust the telegram at me—she actually grasped my hand and shoved the envelope into it—and stumbled indoors, sobbing.

I was cold. The spring warmth was gone, replaced by an icy wind that rattled my bones, shook my hand as it tried to tear open the envelope. Somehow I managed it—my fingers were too numb to feel the paper—and I had to read it, then; had to read the bold typeface, short and impersonal: *Regret to inform you your son Captain Alan Knyveton Hargreaves killed in action.*

"No," I repeated, much more quietly, resignedly.

Regi was before me; he was kneeling, grasping my hand, trying to pry the telegram from my fingers, but I could not let go. "Which one? Which one is it?" Tears were already rolling down his ruddy cheeks; he was shaking my hand, grasping my shoulder so hard that it hurt. For once, he understood immediately what had happened; there was no chance for him to prepare himself. But then I realized—he was already prepared. He had been, for months.

So had I—but that did not prevent the sudden wave of realization from washing over me, so hard and fast I could not catch my breath. Something was hitting my chest, a hard, angry fist hitting at me, pounding at my lungs so that they might remember their function—and that something was my own hand, the telegram still in it.

Papa cried for the boys. Mamma cried for Edith—the words, senseless to me, nevertheless repeated themselves, over and over, in my suddenly throbbing head.

But no—I remembered holding Alan for the last time, only I didn't know it was the last time, and my arms ached at the memory, and my tears began to fall, and even through my pain I rejoiced to know that I was not like Mamma. I could cry for my son, my son, my child—

Someone was crying; Regi was crying. Regi had my face in his hands, his great dry paws; he was calling for me, saying my name—"Alice, Alice, help me, I cannot bear it."

Somehow I saw, through my tears, this man, this husband—this father. And I knew he was speaking the truth; this was a burden he could not bear. His face, his simple, guileless face, etched with a thousand lines of grief, turned to me, needing me—

Telling me that I had to be the strong one. Just as Mamma had been.

Somehow, I knew to look up, even as Regi

sagged at my feet. There, in the French windows, stood the servants; one of the Mary Anns was crying, another shaking her head, but they were all staring. Staring at us; at Regi, who was crumbling, like an ancient statue, before their very eyes; at our grief, which no one should be allowed to see.

"Go away!" I shouted, rage tearing my throat apart. I leaped to my feet and took a step toward them, waving the telegram in my hand like a weapon. "Leave us alone!" Somehow I maneuvered Regi so that I was standing between him and the house; I put my arms about him, shielding him from their prying eyes, for I could not allow them to see him like this. "Leave us be," I whispered, as Regi wrapped his arms about my waist and sobbed.

I stood there, holding him close, patting his head as my own tears dried before they could fall. I whispered soothing sounds—not even words, only murmurs and sighs, for that was all I could give him, and I knew it would be enough. A primitive emotion surged through me, from the top of my head down to the bottom of my feet; they felt like tree roots, holding me upright and tall. I was a mighty oak, sheltering my husband from the world, giving him room to grieve. I would not fail Regi; I would protect him, I would be strong for him, I would give my son up, just as Mamma had done, just as all the mothers of England were doing. It had happened to me, just as I knew it would—hadn't I known that the odds of his surviving two wars were impossible? But I would be strong, I *must* be strong, because Regi needed me to. And because I had failed him in so many ways, I would not allow myself to fail him now.

I continued to hold my husband, who continued to sob without shame, and my back remained strong and sure. The shadows now were long and deep; an owl called mournfully in the distance, and I smiled to hear it, even as its moan pierced my heart. Ina had left, Miss Kimball was gone, the servants, I prayed to God, were hiding somewhere deep within the bowels of the house.

And Regi and I were, finally, alone; together.

Chapter 16

*A*FTER ALAN'S DEATH, REGI AND I TREATED each other differently. At times more formally, overly polite and careful; other times we were too indulgent, allowing each other to say or do things that were almost hurtful, yet we pretended not to mind.

I still thought of Leo, I still wondered at what I had missed with him, although I also found myself trying to define just what it was I had found with Regi, as well. It was a way of life, I supposed; a kind, warm, safe way of life, with a gentle man who had shrunk suddenly overnight.

A life that was all about our boys, as it always

had been; they were our common prayer. Alan was like a phantom limb—we could not quite reconcile ourselves to his absence, as it had always been the three boys; three little soldiers, all in a row. We thought of them rather as a matched set; the absence of one made the others look lost, not quite right, and I had to wonder if Mamma and Papa felt that way when Edith died.

Not that we saw Rex or Caryl, of course, except for one brief leave each; the war raged on through the rest of 1915, and as 1916 drew to a close there was no sign of the horrific battles abating. Conscription had been introduced, there was talk of coal shortages, and the German submarines had taken over the oceans so that we could not import food. Our household staff shrank to skeletal proportions as men went to war and women joined the Land Army or worked in munitions factories. We closed off many rooms, and Regi faithfully tended a small vegetable patch where the cutting garden had been, proudly showing me his bounty, bothering Cook about the proper way to put it all up.

Yet still we lived for our remaining sons; we wrote regularly, we prayed, we rejoiced in their precious leaves—Caryl in the summer of 1915, Rex in the early winter of 1916. Just as Alan had been, they were changed, although Caryl appeared the least affected. He persisted in telling us stories of pranks and larks—of football matches in the mud of the battlefields, where they had to be careful of undetected land mines; he did clench his jaw as he told of one fellow who simply disintegrated after kicking what he thought was the makeshift football—and he slept peacefully enough at night. No nightmares for my youngest, at least.

Rex, my Rex, my charming, frustrating, lovable boy, did not tell stories. He scarcely talked at all, he who used to speak his mind regardless of the consequences. There was a haunted look in those eyes that used to gleam so mischievously, and he could not seem to bear the quiet of the house; it wore so obviously upon his nerves. He would sit in the drawing room after dinner, jiggling his legs, playing the gramophone as loud as it could go—anything, it seemed, to stave off the quiet, and the questions. Naturally, Regi and I wanted to know about the war, how he felt it was going, but as it was obvious it grieved him to tell us, we learned not to ask.

Once I came upon him sitting in the library; he was staring out the window toward the cricket pitch, which was now brown and covered with weeds. I started toward him—his back was to me—but then stopped. He had a knife in his hand, a small penknife. As he sat, he pressed the point of that knife into the palm of one hand; small trickles of blood snaked down his wrist and dripped upon the carpet, and for once in my life I could not care. I could not move, could not speak—my entire body was frozen in fear for my son, who was sitting not three feet from me but in reality was so far away, so already lost, that I knew I could never reach him again.

He did not appear to notice the blood. Or the pain.

Shaking, I walked backward out of the library; once in the hall, I stood sentry outside the closed door, watching for Regi and the servants. I would not allow them in; I would not allow anyone to see. After Rex went to bed that night—walking past me where I stood, unsurprised to see me there, pausing only to kiss me absently on the cheek—I took a basin of water, tore my petticoat, for I had no idea where the Mary Anns kept the old rags, found some bleach in the scullery, and tried to get the blood out of the carpet myself. I did not quite succeed, so I rearranged the furniture over it.

A week later, Rex was gone back to the front; I never once spoke to him about the scars on his hand, although he never tried to hide them from me.

Cuffnells was no longer a grand country house; it was a fading relic with rooms echoing with the laughter, the parties, and the gaiety of the past. Just like Regi and me, I could imagine the servants whispering; sometimes I saw us through their eyes, two companionable old people living on memories, for to talk of the present brought far too much pain and worry.

I often found him sitting in Caryl's room, staring out the window toward the forest, the paths where the boys had played; he often found me in Rex's room, one of his boyhood books in my hand—*Treasure Island* or *Black Beauty*.

Neither of us spoke on these occasions. It was enough to know that each was watching out for the other.

One chilly October morning the doorbell chimed; Regi himself answered it, as he was expecting a delivery of onion bulbs and wanted to make sure the lorry took them round to the gardener's house. What summoned me was the unnatural silence; I was upstairs in the hall, seeing to the hanging of a new portrait of Papa, when I became aware of an eerie stillness. I had heard the door chime but nothing after that; no voices, no footsteps. It was as if all the air had been driven from the house.

And in that moment, I knew.

Dropping the hammer I was holding as one of our few remaining footmen penciled in the nail hole, I walked slowly to the head of the stairs. "Regi?" I asked softly.

He was standing in the open door, a small white envelope in his hand; as I watched, he slowly took a step backward and leaned against the wall, the envelope fluttering to the ground. He

381

said not a word. Then he looked up at me, with eyes that were just black holes of grief.

I flew down the stairs, already knowing what the telegram said—for had I not memorized the other?—the only question in my heart being, Which son was taken from us now? I had a momentary, ridiculous thought that it was up to me to choose; if a name appeared in my head, then that was the son that was lost. And to my everlasting shame, my everlasting agony, a name did appear, did whisper itself, but it was not the name on the telegram that I snatched from the ground: *Regret to inform you your son Leopold Reginald Hargreaves killed in action.*

I stared at it, not comprehending; no, I thought, this cannot be. Leopold is already dead; haven't I mourned him enough?

Then realization dawned: Rex. They had taken Rex. My second son—the son of my heart, I knew it now, for certain; the son I had named for my first love. I had killed him; I had doomed him by naming him this. I knew it, I knew it even as I bent over in anguish, feeling as if someone had ripped my chest open and pulled my heart out with angry hands; there was no greater pain, no greater emptiness. Holding on to Regi, as he held on to me—without the other, we each would have fallen—I gasped and swallowed and blinked my eyes, remembering that I had to be strong; I was always the one who was strong.

But this time, I could not stop the images flooding my mind: Rex lying on the battlefield, Rex in a torn uniform—hadn't I always scolded him for tearing his clothes? But not like this; not a uniform shredded, ripped apart by bullets. Rex with blood pouring out from his heart, his great, compassionate, seeking heart, Rex crying out for me, wondering why I could not come—*You don't chase after us—you never! You're much too old. Although if you did, I'd most likely let you catch me, just to be nice—*

Rex lying cold and still, his eyes open but not seeing, his mouth no longer moving. No longer able to call my name.

"Alice," Regi cried out, needing me; his arms flailed about, his hands sought my comfort. But this time I could not help him; even with the footman hanging over the banister watching, I had to run from Regi, run from his grief; I felt it chasing after me as I flew down the hall, flinging myself into the library and closing the doors behind me.

Once inside, I fell to my knees, a great sob ripping my heart apart, my tears flowing freely for him. My boy, my little boy; I remembered him creeping onto my lap that day so long ago, his sturdy, warm form snug against my chest, against my heart, and I had scarcely allowed it; I had pushed him off my lap, had refused to read him that book—that wretched book! Always coming between me and those I loved! And now it was too late, oh, it was too late! I would never hold him again—how could I live one minute more with the knowledge that I could never hold him, scold him, read to him, again?

Stifling a cry, I pushed myself up onto a footstool—was it the one I had positioned over his blood?—and fixed my gaze fiercely on the mantel clock. Through my tears I watched the second hand go around and I began to count out loud—one, three, two, four—wasn't that how Mr. Dodgson used to count? Finally I reached sixty, and I held my breath—but the pain was worse, jagged edges of glass ripping my heart apart, as the second hand continued to go around again and again; it would never stop, they would never stop coming, all the hours and days and years I would have to live without my dear boy, knowing he was in his grave, alone. Somewhere I could not be.

Suddenly there were arms about me; Regi's arms. "My dear girl," he whispered, gathering me into his lap, more tenderly than anyone had held me when I was a child. "My dear, dear girl, shhhh. I'm here."

His embrace, so dear, so complete—so unexpected, but it need not have been; sobbing harder, I understood, finally, after thirty-seven years. "Oh!" I gasped, when I could at last draw a breath, fighting my way through a fresh onslaught of tears. "Oh, forgive me, forgive me! I'm so sorry!" All the times I had looked at Regi, wanting Leo instead; all the times I had imagined Leo as the father of my children, wondered what those phantom sons would have been like.

And all the time, Regi *was* here. Regi loved his sons. Regi loved *me,* as I was—there was nothing to fear, nothing to hide from him. I knew it, I knew it always—but what I did not know until this moment, this instant—

What I did not know was that I loved him, too. That was what I had found, what had been there all the time; how stupid, how selfish I had been, not to see it.

"I'm so sorry," I said again—to Regi, to Rex, to Alan. To Caryl. "I'm so very sorry." The tears would not stop, although they came more peacefully now; as if from a deep spring within me that had simply been waiting for this moment to overflow.

Still Regi held me, and I let him, and I wondered why I had not let him be strong for me before; as our tears mingled together, finally I felt a calmness come over me, and I was able to whisper "Thank you" to Rex.

For he had given me the gift I had been unable to give him when he had asked, curled up in my lap as I was now curled up in Regi's, so long ago.

IT WAS CRUEL, TOO CRUEL, to lose two sons; everyone said so, yet no one could make it stop.

For all over England, mothers and fathers were mourning sons, as the Battle of the Somme was raging. And there was still one more son left at the front who needed our prayers, our thoughts.

The son whose name had flashed in my mind before I opened the telegram; I could never betray this, but I knew, then, that I was no better mother than my own had been. I had always vowed I would not love any of my children less than the others, as Mamma had so obviously done. Yet when the moment came—the moment when, wildly, irrationally, I felt it was within my power to choose which son I could keep with me forever—I had discovered that I was no better than she. There is always so much talk about the sins of the fathers, but it is the sins of the mothers that are the most difficult to avoid repeating.

"Surely they'll send Caryl back now, won't they?" I asked Regi, who always assured me they would, no matter how many times I asked. I found myself voicing my concern for my youngest far more than I ever had for his brothers, as if to reassure myself that I wasn't a monster, after all. Perhaps I said it often enough that someone heard it; by the end of 1916 we were able to rejoice in the knowledge that Caryl had been reassigned to England. Even if he was not under our roof, at least he was no longer in France. We could not be entirely easy of mind, though, until Armistice Day.

Peace at last—but what did it mean? There was no peace for us; on that strangely hushed, melancholy day, we went to church and prayed along with the nation. Only we sat in our pew at Lyndhurst Parish Church, beneath a memorial plaque to our two dead sons.

Alan was buried in Fleurbaix, Rex in Guillemont, each one just another grave among thousands. I never visited either but received two photographs of white crosses, presumably marking their resting places, although no one could ever know with certainty if that was where they truly lay. I took my comfort instead in visiting the plaque, and the memorial in the baptistry of the church that listed all of Lyndhurst's fallen sons.

Although I was careful to visit it only at odd hours, when I could be alone with my thoughts; I was not just another grieving mother, and my boys were not just common fallen soldiers. I was Alice in Wonderland, and they were the lords of Cuffnells. It did not seem right that their names were listed among the sons of those who had been in service to us.

AND SO THE WAR WAS OVER. I had hoped that there would be some return to normalcy, to the life we had lived, but I was disappointed. No matter who I invited to dinner, there would always be two empty places. Three, actually;

Caryl moved back to his flat in London, reluctantly coming home to Cuffnells only on odd weekends. I managed to scrape together a more sufficient staff, but barely; the housemaids were rude, bickered over their wages, and the sole footman actually smoked in the kitchen.

"What the devil are you doing?" I asked the insolent fellow, who was leaning against the stove, having just lit his cigarette from a burner.

"Havin' a smoke," he said, looking at his cigarette with some surprise.

"Excuse me?"

"Oh. I mean, havin' a smoke, madam." He shrugged and continued to puff on the horrid thing; I summoned the housekeeper, intending to dismiss him, but she informed me—while the creature simply stood there, staring at us with unconcealed, ill-mannered amusement—that he was the best we could get.

"All the good young lads are dead in France, and it's just scoundrels like 'im left, especially for the wages being offered, not that I'm complainin', madam, no, but you have to admit, times is tough."

"Indeed." I left the kitchen without acknowledging her broad hint. Christmas was coming; she'd get her extra pound.

Regi scarcely noticed my difficulties keeping the house running, although I tried desperately to involve him. As soon as the war ended, he grew old overnight, somehow older than I, although we were the same age. He was almost deaf, and prone to doddering about at his old cricket club in good weather, and simply doddering about the house in bad, following me around like a small child but never really interested in what I was doing. He harped on Caryl's extravagances—of which I also disapproved—but other than that, he simply had no interest in the house. It was up to me to pay the bills, see about repairs; the land did not bring in much income any longer, and taxes were outrageous, so I urged him to sell several parcels.

Bit by bit, Cuffnells was diminishing, and so, to my great distress, was my husband. I worried about him, scolded him into wearing warm clothes in winter, drinking cool drinks in summer, but I could not prevent his decline. It was as if he simply decided he was a clock not worth winding any longer.

In February of 1926 he came down with a bad cold—he *would* insist on throwing off the muffler I tried to keep wrapped about him morning and night—and took to his bed; he was very ill but not so ill that he did not smile at the fuss I made over him.

"What's all this?" he croaked as I sat beside him, trying to coax him into sipping a spoonful of beef broth. "Mrs. Hargreaves feeding me with her own hands?"

"Do be quiet, and eat." I frowned down at him,

trying to hide my concern; the doctor had just been, warning that Regi's lungs were weak, and this was not merely a bad cold. Pneumonia, he thought.

"Yes, madam," he said meekly, trying to salute me, but he could not lift his hand. Still, he smiled, pleased at my presence; tears sprang to my eyes to see how happy it made him just to have my attention, my concern. Why had I not offered him more of that over the years?

That was the moment I finally realized that Regi was the only person whom I had ever made completely happy; he was the only person who had not needed me to be someone else; someone *more*. Even Leo had needed me to be Alice in Wonderland, a fairy tale, a dream.

But Reginald Gervis Hargreaves, Esq., needed only me—Alice. Alice Pleasance Hargreaves; twenty-four letters now, instead of twenty-one. Sitting beside his bed, stroking his arm, I wondered who I would be without him.

I removed the soup bowl to a tray and placed my hand upon his forehead; it was clammy and cold, and his breathing was much labored. Struggling to hold him up—even though he was quite frail, he still was such a tall man; he had been so very sturdy and big-boned in his youth —I propped a few pillows behind his back so that he could breathe easier. Then I helped him back down, and in doing so, I planted a kiss upon his unshaven cheek.

"What's the occasion, Mrs. Hargreaves?" he whispered with another sweet, simple smile.

"I do not require an occasion to kiss my husband," I huffed—but my voice quavered, and he reached over and took my hand, and squeezed it.

He died two hours later; I was still sitting next to him, still holding his hand, when he smiled at me, whispered that he would tell the boys I sent them my love—and then he was gone. I sat for a very long time that way, watching the snow pile up outside his window, wishing I had been a better wife to him; hoping that in the end, the love I had been able to give him was enough.

His death notice included the mention that in 1880, he had married Alice in Wonderland. I like to think he would have been pleased at that, but the truth is he was the only one to whom this didn't matter at all.

And now, for the first time in her life, Alice was truly alone. Wonderland was well and gone; I was left with a large house and larger bills—endless bills; I could not see an end to them, although I could see, alarmingly close, an end to my income. Taxes, death duties, the frightful expense of coal—at night I lay in bed, unable to sleep, doing sums in my head, never coming up with a comforting answer.

I was also left with a very impractical son who did not appear to share my concerns. Even when Caryl did come home, I cannot say I was overjoyed to see him, nor he me; we were both uneasy sitting next to each other at the long, empty dinner table. I couldn't pretend to approve of his wastrel lifestyle—how many times did I tell him his brothers surely would have managed to do something more with their lives, had they been allowed? Yet for some reason this only spurred him to greater heights of frivolity, such as the time he stormed out, drove recklessly back toward London, and got a flat on the road; instead of simply changing the tire, he paid a farmer to tow him to Epsom, where he traded in the old car for a new—more expensive—one, and continued on.

Our arguments grew more heated with every visit, and I'm quite sure it was a topic of discussion among the servants. Knowing this made me even more angry; how dare they whisper about me! It was bad enough that I had to hide my jewelry these days instead of wearing it, for there was no trusting them. If it hadn't been so difficult to find replacements, I would have sacked the whole lot.

Yet dining with Caryl, however uncomfortably, was better than sitting there alone as I did every other night, dressed in a faded evening dress (without my jewels, which made me feel rather naked), staring at the paintings—Papa's old oils of the English countryside, quite dirty now, for I could not afford to have them cleaned—on the wall.

"It is very kind of you to allow me to remain here," I told Caryl during one such occasion, after we had exhausted polite conversation before the soup course was done. "I realize that you're the rightful heir to Cuffnells."

"No, Mamma, this is your home. I'm not sure I'd want the place, anyway." He looked about the great empty room, and for the first time I saw it through his eyes—the wallpaper was out of date, the chandelier messily wired for electricity, the ceiling plaster cracked. "Have you ever thought of taking in boarders, or renting the place out? It would pay for repairs and perhaps even give us more income. It's so frightfully expensive in London, you know."

"Boarders?" I stared at my son, who was carelessly sipping his soup. Strangers living here, where I raised my family? How could he suggest such a thing? "No, I shan't be taking in boarders," I said coldly, and pressed down upon the buzzer, summoning Mary Ann. "This soup is lukewarm; do take it away, and tell Cook I'll speak to her later."

That evening, after Caryl had returned to London—he rarely stayed even one night these days, although he did manage to apologize to me before he left—I sat in the library going over accounts, too worried about the future to allow myself the luxury of remembering the past. Once I had thought I could escape sadness simply by moving on; I remembered how I could not wait to quit Oxford, after Leo left and Edith died.

Now, although the grief was greater, I did not want to escape it; I felt as if I was hanging on to Cuffnells by my very fingernails, and there was no one—least of all Caryl; renting to boarders, indeed!—to catch me if I fell. I wished I owned something of value, something I might be able to sell, in order to keep Rex's and Alan's memories alive, for it was only here, at Cuffnells, that I felt I could remember what they looked like. It was only here that I could still see them, and Regi, too—walking the grounds, now overgrown, that meant so much to them all; hearing the echoes of their laughter from the billiard room, how often they had wagered against one another even though they knew I did not approve!

I simply could not bear to lose them all over again.

I rose, massaged my stiff fingers, and roamed the room, searching the shelves for valuable first editions, even though I knew there were none; I looked anyway, hoping that perhaps Regi might have bought something that I hadn't known about. Then I smiled, fondly; Regi had never bought a book in his life.

Finally I found myself at the window, gazing out; it was dark, and I could see nothing but my own reflection, my hair—thoroughly gray now, but still with the same fringe; my serious, watchful eyes, that decided chin, now rather crinkled with age—and I thought, "Through the looking glass, indeed." For there really was no logic to my life; I had traveled and searched and questioned and loved and tried, so very hard, yet still I ended up in this place with no answers, no solutions. There was no Wonderland; there had never been a Wonderland. There was only me, looking at myself in a mottled glass, unable to recognize the child I had been, the woman I had become, alone now with nothing to my name but a crumbling old house—

Then I looked down, at the glass-encased bookshelf. Pulling up a stool—for I could no longer sink to my knees without risking never getting up again—I opened the door. Staring at all the volumes of books, some in strange languages, but all with my name very prominently featured, I realized that I did possess something of value, after all. If only I had the courage to confront it.

Alice's Adventures in Wonderland. It was there, all the valuable first editions, even the handwritten original, all along. Family heirlooms, I had thought them. But now I had no family—except for where I could remember them, here at Cuffnells.

All these years, I had been afraid to read the book; afraid to see myself within the pages. But what had I known of fear, then? I had lost my sons to war, my husband to grief, and now I was about to lose my home. *This* was fear; this horrid, sinking feeling of not knowing where the ground was, or if my feet would ever reach it again. Of not knowing how I would hold on to the memories of those I loved, even if that love had come too late. But having found it, I could not bear to relinquish it.

Now, at this moment, I could open the pages of this book and read them, and imagine my son upon my lap once more, for it was here, in this room, where it had once been possible. Realizing that, I was no longer afraid of what I might find within the yellowed pages; I was only afraid that I had waited too long.

Taking a deep breath, I pulled out the book that Rex had asked me to read to him. I opened the cover, turned to the front page. *"Down the Rabbit Hole . . . Alice was beginning to get very tired of sitting by her sister on the bank. . . ."* My voice quiet but steady, this time I continued reading aloud, even though I knew there was no one to hear. Still, I couldn't shake the notion that perhaps Rex might be listening, after all.

When I got to the part where the White Rabbit was looking at his pocket watch—just like Papa used to; I had quite forgotten!—I began to chuckle, softly at first. As I read on, however, my laughter grew until one of the Mary Anns popped her head in the door, and I waved her away, still reading out loud, not caring what she told the others, only wanting to continue, as I was eager to see what happened next.

For finally, after all the years, the twisted paths that had brought me back, again and again, to a dark and dangerous place of memory, I could see *Alice* as others must have, and as I first experienced it that long-ago afternoon in a rowboat with my sisters: as a lovely, charming story about a very unflappable little girl caught in a maze of nonsensical, talkative creatures but not in any hurry to escape them.

I was not that little girl; I knew that now. Even when I begged Mr. Dodgson to write it down so that I could remain a child forever, he understood that was not going to happen. Already, he was missing me. It was obvious in the melancholy at the end of the story, when Alice's sister thinks of her all grown-up, forgetting her dream.

Had he known that he would be the reason why I had to grow up so soon? I think that even I suspected that he would be the catalyst. Even so, the end of my childhood came about not because of what Mr. Dodgson had *written*; it was our private story, the one with an ending still unknown, that had done that. Not the story he had given to the world.

And now I would do the same. I would give it back, for I need not fear it any longer. And it would save me. *He* would save me. Mr. Dodgson, who disliked little boys; who had

397

never been able to reconcile himself to the fact that I was grown up and married, a mother, had given me the means to save my sons' home and preserve their childhood.

All it would cost was the last tangible evidence of my own.

Chapter 17

Lot 319—THE AUTOGRAPH MANUSCRIPT OF
"ALICE'S ADVENTURES UNDER GROUND,"
BY C. L. DODGSON,
The Property of "Alice" (Mrs. A. P. Hargreaves)

ADJUSTING MY SPECTACLES, I PERUSED THE catalog in my hand; it was nicely done, sturdily bound, a nice, clean font. Sotheby's reputation was certainly deserved, and I felt I had chosen well. There had been other interested auction houses, of course, but none of the stature of Sotheby's.

"Mamma, this crowd is simply astonishing!" Caryl was almost beside himself with excitement, entirely too ridiculous for a man of his age. He was nearly forty, after all, and his hair, as well as his mustache, was turning steel gray. It was difficult to realize that this distinguished-looking middle-aged gentleman with the slight pouch around the middle was my youngest son.

But then I supposed it was difficult to realize

that this elderly woman sitting next to him on the dais, clad in a smart black suit, the very *thing,* the salesgirl told me, for 1928—although I could not quite give up my corset, as one felt so very *loose* without it—was "Alice." There had been quite a bit of interest in me once the auction was advertised, particularly in my reasons for giving up the manuscript. The crowded room—apparently, there were people who viewed these auctions as a spectator sport; didn't they have better things to do with their time?—reflected that interest; the young lady in charge had said, rather breathlessly, "We've never had such a lot simply for a book!" upon greeting me at the door.

"Well, it's not simply any book, is it?" I inquired. "It's *my* book." Then I allowed her to lead me through the throng—and as I did, I had a very curious sensation. "Curiouser and curiouser," I murmured to myself, but Caryl heard, and chuckled.

For I felt as if I were finally stepping through the looking glass, into a world where everything was backward, yet now it made sense. After so many years spent being Miss Liddell, then Mrs. Reginald Hargreaves, mother of three sons, dowager of Cuffnells, I was suddenly, once again and possibly forever—simply Alice.

That was what they called me—complete strangers; as if they actually *knew* me! "There she is, that's Alice," I heard someone whisper, and it caught on, like flame to a paper, and spread about, more and more murmurs. "That's Alice in Wonderland! The real Alice—can you believe it?" While my initial reaction was to comment upon their rudeness, for there were very few people living whom I would allow to call me by my Christian name, it then stole upon me that they were all so very happy to see me. (Although, yes, this was when I first observed the shock that I was not a little girl with yellow hair.)

For the first time, my public association with my namesake was not a complicated one. These strangers were delighted merely to meet me, to shake my hand, to ask innocent questions about my childhood and Mr. Carroll. No one spoke of him as Mr. Dodgson, and I suppose that made it easier for me to talk of him and tell them what I knew they wanted to hear: that he was a kindly man, a cherished friend, who provided me with many happy memories.

Yet that was the truth, I realized. Part of the truth, at any rate.

There were, to be sure, uncomfortable questions about why I was selling the manuscript, and I was happy to allow Caryl to speak for me on this subject, at least. (He was more than eager to speak for me on every subject, but I was no shrinking violet, to his obvious disappointment.) "My mother, upon my father's death, finds herself in the unique position of being able to plan for her future while also sharing the joy of her childhood memories with the world at large."

I had to bite my tongue the first time I heard this, but I also had to admit Caryl had a bit of his aunt's blood in him; he was so very good at rearranging the truth. Well, we all were, at that; perhaps that was the most lasting lesson I had learned from Mr. Dodgson.

"How much do you think it will fetch?" I heard Caryl ask the auctioneer as he approached the podium, and I stifled the urge to yank him by the ear and banish him from the room.

"Caryl, do be quiet," I hissed. I sat straight, dignified—my back not touching my chair; my back had not touched a chair since I was twelve —and observed the crowd. We were in a large gallery, the walls hung with various pictures. Directly in front of the dais was an odd, U-shaped table at which sat the bidders; behind them were rows of chairs, upon which a crowd of nearly three hundred—or so the breathless girl had told me—were perched, eagerly watching. I was not sure what they were watching, exactly; it did not appear to me that auctions were very interesting, unless it was your own possession being auctioned off. Yet the crowd seemed breathless with anticipation—and I realized, finally, that they were anticipating *me*. My reaction, I supposed; I wondered why it mattered to them?

"Number three nineteen," the auctioneer—a slim man in a nicely tailored suit—said, rather softly, I felt. I had assumed auctions were much louder.

"Five thousand pounds," said a gentleman at the table, raising his finger.

"Six thousand," said another.

"Seven thousand," said still another.

And so it went, the bidding rising by a thousand pounds each time, the only bidders four very distinct gentlemen (I gathered one was bidding on behalf of the British Museum), one of whom was, it was whispered rather sensationally, an American. I could not help myself; I found myself leaning forward eagerly—as eagerly as I had that afternoon, long ago, straining to hear every word Mr. Dodgson said as he spun the story out. Now I was straining just as hard to hear the sum of money that story would fetch.

Curiouser and curiouser, indeed.

The bidding reached fourteen thousand pounds, fifteen thousand—Caryl was gripping my hand so tightly, I could no longer feel my finger-tips—and two of the gentlemen dropped out. Finally the American (his accent was obvious)—who was rather square and wore an absurd pince-nez that was far too small for his face—offered fifteen thousand, four hundred pounds; and the gavel came down amid a general uproar.

The crowd was very excited, although obviously disturbed that an American had won; I rather feared for the square little man, based upon the numerous angry looks cast his way. The auctioneer was wiping his face with a handkerchief, but he stopped when the American walked over to him; the two men put their heads together for a moment in deep discussion. Caryl had jumped to his feet, about to let out a whoop of delight, before he looked down and caught my disapproving frown; he sat back down again but couldn't refrain from saying, over and over, "How about that, Mamma? How about that?"

Naturally, I was pleased; smiling for the crowd, a sense of contentment came over me as I knew, for the first time in a very long time, what I would do on the morrow. Before I could rise and talk to the young lady about the particulars, the auctioneer banged his gavel once more.

"Dr. Rosenbach"—he indicated the gentleman who had won—"would like me to announce that he is prepared to sell the book back to the nation at the price for which he just bought it."

There was a murmur, as people clustered about the gentleman from the British Museum, but no further announcements.

"Will that have an effect on when I receive the check?" I could not refrain from whispering to Caryl as he helped me out of my chair.

"I don't suppose so," he replied. "But I'll make sure."

"Excuse me, Mrs. Hargreaves, would you care to comment upon the extraordinary sum? I believe it's the largest amount ever paid for a book in Britain." A reporter was at my elbow, his notebook in hand.

"Oh, is it?" I managed to hide my pleasure with a dignified nod. "That's quite nice. Well, I am very pleased with the price. It is a large sum of money, and I do not yet know what I shall do with it. Caryl, let's go home." I rapped him on the shoulder with the end of my walking stick, and he helped me through the crowd, which parted before me as if I were Royalty. I smiled and nodded at them all, remembering how, back at Oxford, crowds had done the same for Leo.

Before we left, the young woman asked me if I wanted one last look at the manuscript. I thanked her but said no; there was nothing more I needed from it. It had given me enough.

"Mamma, I do believe there are many opportunities still to come," Caryl said once we were settled into the backseat of the car. He tucked a blanket around my lap; it was a long drive back to Cuffnells.

"I'm not sure what you mean, dear." I gazed at the crowded, dirty streets of London; so many wounded men, taken to begging or sitting on overturned fruit crates instead of finding honest work. I could not wait to get back home.

"There's such an interest in you now. I believe

404

we could make something of it. I've been jotting some ideas down, as to how we could perhaps benefit even more than we have. Would you like to hear them—I was thinking about a tearoom, for instance. The Real Alice's tearoom—you wouldn't have to do a thing other than make an appearance every afternoon." He reached inside his breast pocket and removed a small notebook.

"In a white pinafore, I suppose?" I raised an eyebrow. "No, I'm afraid I'm not interested in hearing about all that now."

Caryl frowned, his lower lip thrust out in a pout that looked ridiculous, framed by his gray mustache. "But Mamma," he began in that high, wheedling tone, which was annoying when he was six but now that he was forty nearly drove me to profanity. I tightened my grip on the handle of my walking stick; the boy simply refused to act his age! As for his infernal schemes, he always had one, and it always required money, and it never turned out the way he planned. My youngest boy, so unfocused, so—well, weak. Not at all like his brothers—

I relaxed my grip, took a deep breath, and found a way to smile at my surviving son. "You may tell me about your little plan later," I said, patting him on the arm, remembering how much he needed my approval still. "I'm rather tired, as you can imagine. I believe I'd like to sit quietly, and think about what to do first with the money—I'm quite leaning toward putting in new carpets. We can talk later."

"But the time to act is now, while you're in the news—"

"I said later." I shut my eyes, leaning back against the red cushioned upholstery, slightly moth-eaten; perhaps I should get a new car, as well. We lurched over the rough London pavement, stopping and starting with the traffic; I would be very glad once we reached the open roads of the country.

I would be very glad once we reached *home*. For it was home, now and forever; I would be able to call my boys' home my own for as long as I drew breath, and it would remain in my family. Caryl had been making feeble noises about marrying some war widow, rather long in the tooth, I gathered; while I could not pretend to approve—widows, in my opinion, should never remarry—at least he was acting like someone who intended to procreate legally, which was somewhat of a relief, if not an outright surprise.

Yawning, I felt quite drowsy from all the rocking about, but then I envisioned re-laying the cricket pitch so it would be just as it had been when the boys and Regi had played on it. I could do that now; I could do so very many things to our home.

I smiled, not burdened by anything other than a plethora of choices, all quite nice to contem-

plate. I realized, after a long moment spent trying to understand just why I could not find
something to worry about, that I was, to my great
surprise, happy.

May we be happy. Somewhere, I did hope that
Mr. Dodgson was, too.

Chapter 18

*I suppose you don't remember when Mr.
Dodgson ceased coming to the Deanery?
How old were you? I said his manner
became too affectionate toward you as you
grew older and that mother spoke to him
about it, and that offended him so that he
ceased coming to see us, as one had to give
some reason for all intercourse ceasing—*

OH, INA.

I had warned her not to talk to any of the
hordes of biographers—really, it was as if they
were dropping out of the trees, like monkeys!—
that had suddenly decided, with the centenary
celebration of Mr. Dodgson's birth approaching,
to write books about him.

I had received letter after letter, all saying the
same thing: *Dear Mrs. Hargreaves, I am writing
to request an interview, as I am researching the
papers of Charles L. Dodgson, or Lewis Carroll,
my goal to be publication of a book about his*

life. As your life was obviously so very inter-
twined with his, I'm certain you will wish to
aid me in my quest to find the real man behind
the myth. Your recollections, in particular, of
the creation of the Alice story will be most
interesting and valuable, as well as any further
insight you can provide as to the nature of your
relationship with Mr. Dodgson.

The nature of your relationship with Mr. Dodgson.

Really, the impertinence of these people! They made my whole life sound like a cheap novel. What business was it of theirs?

I did not protest being trotted out as Alice in Wonderland now and then, if it was for a good cause; usually a charitable organization or some such thing. At these events—requests for my presence at which had started up after the auction—people only wanted to look at me, pose for photographs with me—generally with a stuffed rabbit, or a man in a silly top hat, holding a teacup—and ask a few benign questions: Did he really tell you the story while out rowing? Did you pose for the illustrations? Was there really a kitten named Dinah? But that was the extent of it; they simply wanted to be assured that my life was exactly like the little girl's on the pages, and I was content to give them that. It wasn't truthful, but there was no harm in it, even if it did get to be tiresome after a while.

There are only so many things one can say about rabbits, no matter how cuddly, after all.

These biographers—I was loath to use the word; sensationalists was more like it—were quite different. They came armed with information—naming names from Oxford, citing specific incidents I had thought I had forgotten but, once prompted, remembered, not always to my pleasure. Some had even inquired, boldly, as to the origin of the break in our relations. One in particular—a Mrs. Lennon, whom Ina actually allowed into her home, and whose inquiries prompted this odd letter to me; she had been very forward in her questioning, which was why I had refused to speak with her.

Yet Ina had not been so discreet and now, in somewhat of a panic, was offering either a garbled explanation—of course, dear Ina was getting rather senile in her dotage—or was seeking some sort of reassurance or forgiveness. Or was she trying to warn me?

I had no idea, and while I attempted to answer it—*Dear Ina, I received your kind letter of Tuesday last*—I could get no further; my pen froze, as did my mind, unable to direct me one way or the other. What else had Ina told the woman? What had Ina wanted her to believe; what had Ina wanted *me* to believe all these years?

What *did* I believe, after all?

It was too exhausting, and I could not find a

reason to try to muddle through it today. So I folded the unfinished letter, opened my desk drawer, removed another stack of letters, some yellowed and faded, others stained with more recent tears, all bound with a simple black silk ribbon; I added both Ina's letter and my unfinished one to the group, slipped them back inside my drawer, and shut it. I would answer it another day.

However, the memories it stirred—memories I had quite forgotten these past few years, since the boys died—haunted me for days, weeks, and before I could make any sense of them, Ina passed on. The dear soul lived to be eighty-one; a good, long age, longer than she deserved and I'm not ashamed to say it. When I thought of all who had died so young; Edith, Leopold, Alan, Rex—but that is uncharitable of me. It is not my will be done, after all, but God's.

There are many questions I believe I'll ask Him about this, however, when my time comes.

With Ina's passing, it no longer seemed necessary to sort through my thoughts, try to piece together the scattered pieces of the past. There was simply no one left to whom any of it mattered; no one, of course, but me. The biographers had even stopped pestering me, although I suppose I shouldn't have taken this to mean they were no longer interested; I was sure they'd make up their own minds, regardless of what I had to say.

Still the letter nagged at me; I was drawn to it, time and again, taking it out, picking up my pen, and then putting it away. It seemed as if I would never rest until I answered it.

Then came the invitation to America.

I sailed with Caryl, who insisted upon having a new wardrobe made up for the occasion; I received the honorary degree—I did not think I looked very nice at all in the academic robe and mortarboard cap, although I had no say whatsoever in the matter—I spoke fondly of Mr. Dodgson, as was expected of me; I put up with the endless questions and photographs and staged tea parties.

Then, mere days before I was to leave, I met a young man who looked barely thirty; no older than Alan and Rex had been when they died. He was introduced to me by the officials at Columbia—all graying, serious professors suddenly beaming like little boys at Christmas—as Peter Llewelyn-Davies, the inspiration for Mr. Barrie's *Peter Pan*.

"Ah," I said, instantly understanding. "How very delightful! The real Peter Pan!"

"And the real Alice—I suppose they couldn't pass up the opportunity; I was in America on business when I was contacted." Peter shook my hand, and we engaged in small talk while the photographers snapped away with their awful noisy flashbulbs; photography had changed so very much since Mr. Dodgson's days.

411

There was something about Peter that arrested me—a very old look about his dark eyes, a look I instantly recognized. I wore it myself, of course; but then, I was eighty. He was a young man.

"I do get tired of being Peter Pan," he confessed, after the photographers were shooed away by the Columbia contingent, and we were left alone with Caryl in the hall—so very much like the great halls of learning from my childhood, with portraits of grim, ancient professors whom no one could name. "I wasn't, really—the family thought my brother Michael was the model. And Uncle Jim wasn't quite the person people believe him to be, either. But people like to think life is a fairy tale, and it seems that I'm quite unable to shake it. However have you managed to put up with Alice for such a long time?"

I smiled, and did not take offense at the impolite reference to my age. He looked so very curious, touchingly hopeful; hopeful that somehow, I would be able to help him with merely a word or a handshake or a kiss on the cheek.

"My dear boy, I'm sure I don't know." For to tell the truth, I was tired of being Alice in Wonderland; my bones ached for the simplicity of life at Cuffnells, where no one expected anything of me other than that I pay the bills and order dinner—and where, I vowed, I would not drink another cup of tea for a very long time.

Yet the lad looked so disappointed and lost—

412

his eyes were such a peculiarly melting shade of brown; I was quite inclined to take him home with me and install him in one of the boys' bedrooms—that I forced myself to ramble on. "I suppose, at some point, we all have to decide which memories—real or otherwise—to hold on to, and which ones to let go. I'm sure I haven't quite gotten the knack of it myself. But soon, perhaps. Perhaps, soon."

"But you're—well, you're rather—well." The poor lad blushed, but I merely laughed in sympathy.

"You mean, I'm rather old, don't you?"

"Yes, well. I do apologize, but—rather."

"Perhaps it's best to look at it this way—we may be the only two people in the world who know, absolutely, what it will say on our headstones. Here lies Alice in Wonderland. Naturally I've had a great many other things happen to me in my life—a great many. But Alice is what people will want to remember. Not all the rest." Shaking my head, I tried to hold all the suddenly surging memories at bay. "All the rest belongs to us. Only to us. Remember that—and allow the public to believe what they want. We'll know the truth, after all. I hope." I whispered this last, for remembering Ina's letter, I knew that I did not.

"I suppose." He did not look as if he was really listening; he looked as if he was trying to be polite to a doddering old lady who was spouting nonsense. I decided to forgive him anyway, and kissed him on the cheek in farewell.

"I didn't ask for this, you know," Peter suddenly blurted, grabbing my hand.

"I did." The words flew out of my mouth before I could think; surprised, I pulled my hand away. What was it about this poor young man, seemingly alone, that prompted such honest confession? "I suppose that's the difference between us, then. I most certainly did ask for this—as I did a great many things, when I was young."

"Oh. Yes, I suppose that must be the difference." He smiled politely, but his soft brown eyes—like the eyes of a doe—glistened with sadness. I worried about him, for he did not appear to have the strength of character I believed myself to possess.

"Dear boy, do you have much family?" I asked, even though I knew it was not polite. Still, he seemed so alone.

"No, not much living," he said.

"Neither do I—except, of course, for Caryl." I looked round, suddenly aware that I had not included Caryl in this conversation and ashamed of myself. "Caryl, do let me present Peter Llewelyn-Davies."

Caryl stepped forward eagerly. "So delighted to meet you. I have a marvelous idea for a business venture, Peter—you do know the airline industry is going to grow by leaps and bounds.

Who better to be a spokesman than the real Peter Pan, eh? What do you think of that?"

"Caryl, for heaven's sake, please—"

"I think it sounds rather enticing," Peter interrupted, genuine interest upon his face. "I would be happy to discuss it further—airlines, you say? I'll be in London next month."

"My card, then." Caryl gave it to him, and the two shook hands eagerly.

"I must be going. It's been a pleasure." Peter turned to me, and although he was smiling, I could not shake the feeling that he was not Peter Pan but rather one of the Lost Boys. I had the oddest impulse to embrace him, and shield him from what lay ahead; just what it was, I could not tell, other than that I feared for him.

"Take care, my lad," I said, settling for a handshake instead, as unexpected tears pricked my eyes. Goodness, I was becoming rather dotty! I blinked my eyes furiously and sniffed. "Oh dear, I must be catching a cold. Good-bye, Peter!"

"Good-bye, Alice!"

We looked at each other and laughed; it was so very theatrical. I watched him walk away, so alone; then I turned to my own son.

"So, tell me all about this airline venture." I hooked my arm through his as we walked down the corridor.

"It's the most amazing coincidence, but I talked to a chap just before we sailed. . . ." Caryl

415

beamed, his face shining just like a little boy's; he talked nonstop for a quarter of an hour, and while I did not understand most of it, I knew it made him happy to share his plans with me, and it made me happy to be able to give him that.

Days later, full of tea and pomp and circumstance, we finally left for home, for—

CUFFNELLS, 1932.

But oh my dear, I am tired of being Alice in Wonderland. Does it sound ungrateful? It is. Only I do get tired.

Only I do get tired.

So tired that I recline on my chaise longue near the fire, pulling up the old red afghan—Mamma's afghan, one of the few things I've kept of hers—over my weary, aching bones. The letters are still scattered across my desk, and words pound my brain, insisting I take notice of them. Ina's unanswered questions—*I suppose you don't remember when Mr. Dodgson ceased coming to the Deanery? How old were you?*

Words, pictures, questions, and finally—dreams; it always begins with a dream, doesn't it? Alice's dream by the river, her head in her sister's lap, dreaming of a rabbit, a white rabbit; my dream, also. My *dreams*. One of them—I remember one dream when I was small; a dream after a long walk on a summer day. A dream on a

416

train, my head against Mr. Dodgson's shoulder, as I dreamed of babies on flower stems; Papa walking along, crying; a man in a tall black hat, gray gloves, a stiff way about him. "May they be happy," he whispered to me, and I smiled. Night-time, fireworks, a couple in a darkened doorway, she arched her arm, gracefully, about his neck, bringing him closer and closer to her upturned lips.

"Alice," the man in the hat said tenderly—only it was Leo. "Alice, be happy. Be happy with me."

"Of course," I said with a contented sigh. "Of course. I'll always be happy with you, my love."

But no—the man in the hat was not Leo, he was not Regi. He was Mr. Dodgson. I opened my eyes, my girl's eyes, clear and sharp, no need for spectacles, and saw only him. His soft brown hair curling at the ends, his kind blue eyes, one higher than the other.

He had acted boldly—wasn't that what Ina had said? But no. No, he was not bold; he was shy, he was kind, he loved a seven-year-old girl. I was an eleven-year-old girl, however, and I was not shy.

I was bold. I saw what I wanted and I took it; I did not know, yet, that love was not mine to claim whenever I wanted. I did not know, so I reached for it; my arm arching gracefully about his neck, pulling his face toward me, his lips so soft, seeking an answer, asking a question—

No.

My lips sought, asked; not his. He was merely trying to wake me up, gently rocking me, kissing the top of my head. It was I who reached up, met him—and kissed him, kissed him ardently, my lips parting his, asking him to be happy—*may we be happy.* And in that moment, I will always believe—the two of us were.

But then he pushed me away, shocked; but not soon enough, for I had felt his stirring, his surprise but his pleasure; I tasted it in his lips, lips that moved beneath mine—

Until he did, finally, push me away.

I was hurt; I was confused; I sat up, rubbed my still-sleepy eyes, and looked across at my sister. Ina was watching us; she had always been watching us with those eyes, those gray, unblinking camera eyes. Her face red, eyes bright with anger, she gasped, she rose—looking out the window, she saw Pricks standing at the platform, for the train had just pulled into the station.

Ina was sobbing now, even as Mr. Dodgson was holding on to her arm, trying to explain. "Ina, wait—you're upset!" Shaking her head, pulling free, she kicked against the door until the conductor reached up to open it.

I was still seated, strangely calm, watching but not understanding. Ina ran to Pricks; I saw her tug at Pricks's arm, point back at the train—back at me, and at Mr. Dodgson standing by my side, his gloves suddenly splotched with perspiration.

I looked up at him and tried to pat his arm, to comfort him, for I sensed he was agitated. For the first time in my life, he pulled away, rejecting me—as if he was ashamed.

Pricks strode over to the train carriage; she reached up to Edith, who was standing in the doorway, and helped her down. I slid off the seat, walked to the top of the step—there was steam coming from the engine, just two carriages up—and I looked at Pricks. I met her gaze levelly; she reached her hand back and slapped me across the face, hard. Tears sprang to my eyes, but they did not prevent me from seeing the horrible grin that split her ugly brown face in two.

Without a word, she grabbed my hand, pulled me roughly off the train—I tumbled down the last step, twisting my ankle—and tugged me away, off toward the waiting carriage. Only before I would follow, I turned back; Mr. Dodgson was standing on the platform, alone. His hat was in his hands, his face was pale, his soft, sensuous mouth was open, but for once he had no words; no story, to help me make sense of it all. He simply stood, a tall, slim, suddenly lesser man.

He looked as if he had just been robbed of something precious.

I did not see him again for a very long time. Pricks and Ina filled Mamma's head with words that were true, yet not; I heard them whisper, scheme, like two harpies or witches. *When I found*

419

them, she was wearing hardly any clothes. When I saw them at the fireworks, he had her head upon his breast. She said she knew all about where babies come from. They kissed, Mamma. I saw it with my own eyes. He kissed her, like Papa kisses you. I saw it, too, madam—I saw it in his eyes.

Then Mamma ordered me to show her the letters he had sent:

Do you remember how it felt, to roll about on the grass?

With a cry, a horrible, anguished—furious—cry, Mamma tore through the nursery, tore through my things—my beautiful little box where I stored all my treasures, my drawers, my cupboards and trunks—looking for something; looking for more. She took the letters, and she threw them in the nursery hearth, stirring them up, ripping them with the poker, all the while crying and saying things I could not understand. "You wicked, wicked girl! That horrible man! You're ruined, that's what! Ruined! No one will ever have you now!"

I ran after her, pulling at her arm; this felt like a violation more than anything else. "You can't read my letters! You have no right!" Hot, angry tears rushed to my eyes as I watched the papers burn.

With only one look—one deadly, disgusted look—Mamma forbade me to cry.

She did not forbid me to speak, however; but I did not. Through it all, I spoke not a word. I sat, and I listened to them ruin Mr. Dodgson for me —for us—forever. They called him horrible names; they begged Papa to dismiss him from the college. It would only be much later, when I was a parent myself, that I would wonder why Papa never appeared to consider this.

I said nothing in Mr. Dodgson's defense. Although I knew his innocence, I was more interested in protecting my own. I hid behind my age—for they were willing to give me that, at least; telling me, telling one another, that fortunately, I was young, too young. *He* had nothing to hide behind, however; after all, he was an adult. And I suspected that outside of Wonderland, adults were supposed to behave differently. Adults were supposed to know better.

So, with my silence, I banished him from Wonderland; years later, he would do the same to me.

And this—instead of happiness—would be only what the two of us deserved, after all.

THE SHADOWS ARE LONG and deep; the fire has died down to a contented glow, the embers winking lazily at me as I open my eyes. I stir, my body stiff from lying so still upon the chaise. I must have been here for an hour, at the very least.

Sitting up, clutching the afghan about my shoulders like a shawl, I blink my watery old eyes, but I am no longer tired. I am energized, all of a sudden; my thoughts no longer muddled, no dark cloud of confusion, suspicion, hovering over my mind.

Clearly, I see; finally, my memories are my own.

My words to young Peter come back to me— *I suppose, at some point, we have to decide which memories to hold on to, and which ones to let go.*

I walk to my desk. Ina's letter is still there, still unanswered. Sitting down, putting my spectacles back on, I unbind the black ribbon around the other letters and open them up with trembling fingers, forcing myself to read them one last time:

Dearest Heart,

I am wretched with worry over you. I must maintain a detached, dignified air, outwardly expressing mild concern, for naturally, as the daughter of the Dean, I would be properly anxious to hear word of your welfare.

My letters to Leo, the ones I wrote during his illness but never sent. I had intended to show them to him one day, but one day never came.

There are other letters, too: Letters to Alan, and to Rex, written after they had died. Letters of a grieving mother to her fallen sons. Letters I never shared with Regi, although I realize now—

too late—he might have found comfort in them.

Ina's letter, as well. The letter I began to her but never finished. The letter I could not have written until today.

I will not write it, after all; it is not my place to do so.

I take these letters and walk resolutely toward the fire; pulling up a low wicker stool, I sit down and clasp the packet to my heart. It is love, after all, that is within them; it is love, after all, that is within me. I started out too boldly; I wanted love too much, and I believed that was my mistake, causing all that came after: losing Leo, Edith, marrying a man I did not know I loved until it was far too late, having three sons as a result, two of whom had to lose their lives on a battlefield. Everyone I loved died, while I lived on. Is that a tragedy?

Or is it a fantasy? A wondrous tale for children? For there is still the story of a little girl.

The other stories—memories—are mine to do with as I choose, for the world, after all, only wants to know the other. And that is how it should be; she—I—should live on as a happy, plucky little girl, for whom no conundrum is too difficult to solve with common sense and patience.

I raise the packet of letters to my lips, kiss them—for if I cannot, at eighty, indulge my emotions, when can I?—and slowly let them fall into the slumbering embers. I do not poke them or tear them. I simply watch as their edges brown, then curl, then burn.

Yet they are not gone; they are within me, all of them—Leo, Edith, Alan, Rex, Regi. I will take them all with me when I am gone, which will not be long from now; I can feel it in my tired heart, a heart that has been torn up and pieced back together too many times. The threads are fraying, as fragile as the black silk ribbon in my hand; they will soon give way.

I did not choose this, Peter had said.

I did, I had replied. And so I did; so, now, I do.

For eighty years I have been, at various times, a gypsy girl, a muse, a lover, a mother, a wife. But for one man, and for the world, I will always be a seven-year-old girl named Alice. That is the only letter that need remain; it is the memory I decide, in this moment, to hold on to, as I watch the rest disappear into cinders and ash and, finally, smoke; smoke that flies up the chimney, out into the cold air, floating down across the peaceful grounds of my home, of Cuffnells.

Alice I am, Alice I will be.

Alice I have been.

A Note from the Author

SEVERAL YEARS AGO, WHILE WANDERING THE halls of the Art Institute of Chicago, I stumbled upon an interesting exhibition: *Dreaming in Pictures: The Photography of Lewis Carroll*. I knew Lewis Carroll only by his classic story *Alice's Adventures in Wonderland*. I suppose I had always pictured him as some benign, fatherly figure—if I pictured him at all.

Imagine my surprise, then, to discover that the photography of Lewis Carroll (or the Rev. Charles Lutwidge Dodgson, his real name) consisted primarily of images of—young girls. Rather provocatively posed young girls.

Even for the Victorians, this collection of images seemed a little unsettling. And even among these fascinating images, one photograph in particular stood out. It was a picture of a child clad in scanty rags, showing just enough skin to make me uncomfortable. But it was the eyes that haunted me; dark, glittering, they were wise, worldly, almost defiant. They were the eyes of a woman.

The caption said she was actually seven-year-old Alice Liddell, the privileged daughter of Dean Liddell of Christ Church, Oxford, where Dodgson taught mathematics; she was also the little girl who inspired the classic *Alice's Adventures in Wonderland*.

I wondered what happened to her, after she grew up. I wondered what happened between the two of them to result in such a startling photograph. I thought it might make an interesting story. Then I went home and promptly forgot about it.

Four years later, my friend Nic was visiting me from Australia, and I took her to the Art Institute. As we sat having coffee, I told her about that earlier exhibit, remembering how I'd thought it might make a good story.

"Write it," she said.

"But I'm working on something else."

"No. This is what you should write. Write it."

"Well, maybe."

The next morning at breakfast, Nic was a little wild-eyed; she had stayed up all night researching Charles Dodgson and Alice Liddell, and proceeded to tell me the tale:

In 1862, Charles Dodgson told ten-year-old Alice and her two sisters the story of a little girl who fell down a rabbit hole. Unusually—for he had told the three little girls many stories—Alice begged him to write this one down.

Dodgson told the girls these stories because he had rather an odd, intense friendship with them; he lived next door to the Deanery, their home as the family of the Dean of Christ Church, Oxford. In 1863, after years of this friendship, something happened that resulted in a terminal break in their relations; at the time Alice was eleven and he thirty-one. Soon after this, her mother burned all correspondence between the two. After his death, his relatives apparently cut out the pages of his diary that would have covered this period. Neither Alice nor her family ever talked publicly about Dodgson again, except late in her life after she was forced to sell her original handwritten copy of *Alice* in order to save her beloved home. It was only then that she seemed able to embrace her role in the creation of this timeless classic.

My friend was correct. This was the story I had to write.

I'm no historian, no scholar of Lewis Carroll; there are plenty of those, and this is not his story. I'm a novelist, and this is Alice's story. As I dug for further details, I discovered that Alice Liddell's childhood had been somewhat documented (with the exception of all that missing correspondence), and even fictionalized. There had been a novel, in 2001, by Katie Roiphe called *Still She Haunts Me,* about the years leading up to the break between Dodgson and Alice; also a 1985 film, *Dreamchild,* that dealt, somewhat fantastically, with the same period of time. Also two slim biographies, one a children's book, the other long out of print. But no one told the story entirely from Alice's point of view, and her later years were always glossed over or omitted entirely.

Yet these were the years that most intrigued me; as I continued my research, I found out she may have had a broken romance with Prince Leopold of England but ended up marrying another man (while wearing a diamond brooch from the Prince on her wedding dress); as a mother, she suffered heartbreak during World War I; widowed, she almost descended into anonymous, genteel poverty; finally, she enjoyed triumph and fame just before she died.

Dodgson, meanwhile, went on to publish the *Alice* books—and, of course, photograph many little girls—but it was as if he was always searching for a replacement for his original "child friend." He was heartbreakingly unable to reconcile the adult Alice with the child he had loved when they met, once more, near the end of his life.

This was the story, then, that I had to write: Alice's adventures after she left Wonderland. And it appeared to me that it all came down to what happened between man and child one seemingly lovely summer afternoon, before this mysterious break.

It must always be remembered that this is a work of fiction, not biography. I did not alter known facts about Alice's life, with the exception of the last photograph, when she was a young woman, taken by Dodgson; in reality, this occurred when Alice was eighteen, prior to

Prince Leopold's time at Oxford. Still, I strove to capture what I felt must have been the emotional impact of that moment, whether it occurred when she was eighteen or twenty-three. I sometimes leaned on the side of documented gossip and speculation—for example, there are some who believe Prince Leopold was actually interested in Alice's sister Edith. I couldn't ignore the fact, however, that Alice really did wear the brooch he gave her on her wedding dress. And that the Prince named his first daughter Alice, while she named her second son Leopold.

Alice did, indeed, marry a man named Reginald Hargreaves, and lived the rest of her life on a country estate called Cuffnells, which, sadly, has since been torn down. Near the end of her life she did travel to Columbia University in New York, where she received an honorary doctorate and met another figure from children's literature, Peter Llewelyn-Davies, who was immortalized as *Peter Pan,* but who later in life committed suicide.

The greatest liberty I have taken is in depicting Alice Liddell's relationship with John Ruskin, the eminent art and social critic of the Victorian age. While Ruskin's circumstances are historically accurate—his scandalous marriage, his tragic relationship with a young girl, Rose La Touche—I deliberately made him a more important figure in Alice's life than he probably was. Again, there is some fact on which to base this. It's obvious he and Alice knew each other socially during his years as the Slade Professor of Art at Oxford. He gave her and her sisters art lessons. And he himself described more than one occasion when he was bewitched by the young Alice in his autobiography, *Praeterita*.

Ah, but what about that break? What really happened that summer afternoon to lead to such a permanent fracture between Dodgson and Alice?

This was my greatest gift, as a novelist. Because no one—not Alice, not Dodgson, not her mother, not her sisters—ever publicly spoke of it, except for a tantalizingly vague reference in a letter to Alice from her sister Ina, near the end of their lives. There were rumors, of course, for Oxford was a great place for gossip. But that is one major event in her life—perhaps the most important event—that remains, even today, pure speculation.

However, the most important fact that endures is a piece of fiction. A slim volume, a classic of literature still today—*Alice's Adventures in Wonderland*. That is what remains; that is, I think, what Alice herself would have hoped remained.

I hope you enjoyed her story.

Melanie Benjamin

ABOUT THE AUTHOR

MELANIE BENJAMIN is a pseudonym for Melanie Hauser, who has written two contemporary novels. *Alice I Have Been* is her first work of historical fiction and her first under this name. Benjamin lives in Chicago, where she is at work on her next historical novel.

Center Point Publishing
600 Brooks Road ● PO Box 1
Thorndike ME 04986-0001 USA

(207) 568-3717

US & Canada:
1 800 929-9108
www.centerpointlargeprint.com